ADAM J. SCHOLTE

A NEW HOME

The Ramulas Chronicles Book 4: A New Home

Paperback edition ISBN: 978-1-7638864-6-9
eBook edition ISBN: 978-1-7638864-7-6

Published by Adam J Scholte
www.adamjscholte.com

First edition: May 2025

A catalogue record for this book is available from the National Library of Australia

Editor: Jason Martin
Design and Typeset: Kristine Joy Magno
Printed in Australia.

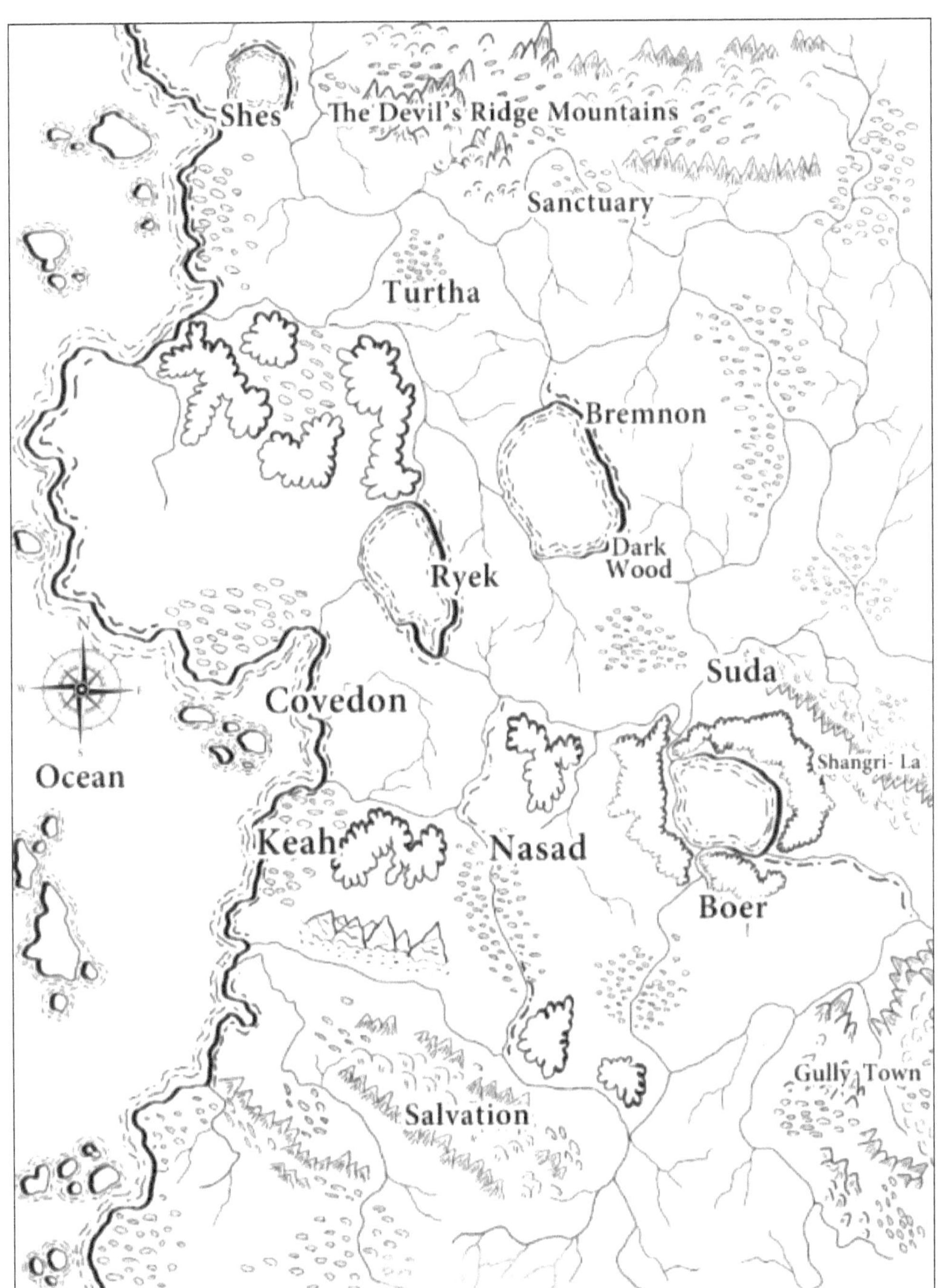

Shes
The Devil's Ridge Mountains
Sanctuary
Turtha
Bremnon
Ryek
Dark Wood
Suda
Covedon
Shangri- La
Ocean
Keah
Nasad
Boer
Gully Town
Salvation

1

'The way to a new world has been found, my queen,' the creature said eagerly.

The queen kept her body still as she loomed over the servant crawling closer to her. It was a male, and females of their species were four times larger than the males. She raised herself and tilted her head in a manner that caused the servant to shudder in fear and attempt to make itself smaller.

However, being the queen, she was twice the size of the other females and almost ten times larger than the servant cowering before her. The queen fought the almost overwhelming urge to consume this male. Using her many eyes, she scanned the pavilion they were in. Hundreds of her children crawled up and down the columns and along the ceiling and floor searching for food. For too long, they had fed on one another.

The pavilions and other buildings of this world were built eons ago by a race that had been consumed by the creatures. The land was barren and unforgiving in its lack of life. Rocky plains stretched for miles in all directions; any sign of life, plant, or food had long ago disappeared. The creatures had stumbled upon this world, ravaged it, and were now forced to feed on one another.

Her children saw her threatening gesture, and half of them changed colour to blend in with their surroundings, making them almost invisible.

Many months ago, there was a flash of light on the horizon. In this dark world, the flash called to her like a beacon. Servants were sent to investigate; they returned with news that a being of great magical power had moved in between worlds. This showed the creatures a doorway they never knew existed.

This would be their escape from this darkened existence, where they fed on one another to sate their maddening hunger, the smell of rotting husks hanging in the damp air.

The queen sent her servants to watch over the doorway. A few months ago, they returned with news of a great army moving through the passageway. The queen came to observe rows upon rows of men marching past.

Maddened by hunger, the creatures threw themselves at the doorway, but a magical ward barred their way. They did everything they could to break the seal without success. The queen stayed by the door for two months before returning to her pavilion. The servants continued to watch.

Finally, good news had arrived.

'Tell me of the doorway,' she said, standing.

The male trembled, knowing that his queen could eat him at any moment. 'There was more light, causing the seal over the doorway to shatter. We are able to go through.'

In the blink of an eye, she reached down to lift him from the floor with ease. 'Take me there,' she said, tossing him across the floor.

Her children scattered out of the way as she pounced on the male, tearing at his flesh while he struggled and shrieked. The queen tossed the half-eaten body behind her as she made her way to the gateway. Her children swarmed on the prize, hissing and screaming as they fought for the smallest piece of flesh.

A psychic wave of energy rolled past her as her children telepathically communicated this new revelation; a small number of her children were able to communicate this way and, in some cases, control others with the power of their minds.

The doorway on the horizon shone brighter than ever before. She arrived to a frenzied mass of bodies dancing in front of the light; they parted quickly as the queen came close. She felt a soft breeze as her claws probed the doorway. The queen pulled her body halfway through the doorway and found herself inside a passage. She had the choice of going left or right—either choice would take her to a new world.

She chose right.

As she crawled along the passageway of mist, the queen told her children to wait for her. She travelled to the end of the passage to find it closed with a magical ward. The queen's fangs and claws tore the ward to shreds. Once the way was clear, she saw that this world was as dark as her own.

Then she saw the stars shining in the sky.

This world's surface seemed to move with a life of its own. She quickly realised it was water when one of her legs sank into the ocean. The queen could not float on water; she would sink and drown.

But the hunters of her world could run across water. She made her way back to her world to call the hunters; they would soon find out what was on this new world.

***

'Lights to port!' the sailor called from the crow's nest.

The captain came out of his cabin, peered across the dark waters, and saw a flash of light a few miles from the ship. They had waited three miles out from the town of Shes for the tide to come in, and it would be dawn soon. He turned to see their sister ship, the *Wind Rider*, five hundred yards behind them.

Shutters quickly opened and shut on the decks of both ships, sending messages; both ships had seen the lights and would investigate together.

***

Captain Bernard Rivers looked across at the *Wind Rider* as it came closer. Despite the late hour, both crews were awake and excited by the shimmering light that seemed to dance on the surface of the waves. His ship's sails were full of wind to beat the *Wind Rider*. The light shone brighter as both ships closed in.

Lanterns on the decks swung on both ships as they raced to their target.

This was when Captain Bernard saw the first shadows jump from the water onto the deck of the *Wind Rider*. He held his breath as his eyes widened, watching the creatures swarm the deck. Then the lanterns showed their true form.

Giant spiders, some the size of a man—and others much larger—that changed colour as they moved across the ship.

Captain Bernard was transfixed observing the monstrous spiders attack the crew of the other ship and watching the sailors fighting the creatures. Some men stood their ground while others ran in terror, screaming. He was confused; the screams seemed to be getting closer, almost as if they were from his own men.

He shivered slightly as he slowly turned to see the giant spiders were, indeed, on his ship attacking his men. His mouth dropped and his eyes opened wide, his body rigid as a hunter slowly crawled towards the captain, its mandibles clicking as it closed in, its skin darkening the match the colour of the deck. Then the spider launched itself at the captain as two impossibly long fangs glistened in the moonlight before it buried him beneath its weight. Captain Bernard attempted to breathe as he struggled feebly, the fetid stench of the creature making him gag.

***

The hunters raced across the water toward the two ships while silently communicating. Every third hunter carried a small psychic spider whose smaller body shone in the moonlight. They divided their forces to attack both ships simultaneously.

Alive, alive! We need them all alive, was the call from the spiders.

The giant spiders were intelligent and cunning. They knew that the ships could take them to land, but they needed the sailors to help them achieve this goal. By the time the attack finished, every single sailor carried a hunter on their back; the spiders controlled the humans like puppets on a string.

The only thing left was the doorway of light that they came through.

Hunters ran back and forth from the ship to the light, and within a minute, hundreds of silk threads connected the doorway of light to both ships. Slowly, they made their way to Shes.

***

The harbourmaster of Shes looked out at the ocean as three fishing boats pushed away from the dock. His eyes widened as he gasped.

Two ships from the city of Keah were coming in toward the pier. 'They were supposed to wait until dawn before comin' in,' he muttered to himself.

The ships were illuminated in the pre-dawn gloom by a source of light following them.

He walked toward the end of the pier, waving his burly arms above his head, and shouted, 'Move away, there's no room.'

The crews called out to the ships in alarm as the ships closed in, some of the crews jumping into the water. The ships were fifty yards away when the harbourmaster turned to gaze at the dark shapes running across the water towards the pier. His face screwed up in puzzlement as he scratched his head, studying the forms on the water.

He clutched at his chest seeing the creatures climbing onto the fishing boats. As they attacked the crew, he slowly stepped back as his mouth opened and closed upon hearing the screams coming from the fishing boats.

The harbourmaster bumped into something large and turned to see a section of the dock transform into a giant spider and its skin lighten. The creature leapt at him, pushing the captain forward onto the wooden planks of the pier. His scream was cut short as the spider's fangs tore into his back as it began to feed.

***

The weight and size of the two ships smashed the fishing boats against the pier with the sound of splintering wood joining the screams of the dying men. The hunters swarmed off the ships onto the pier and beach. Within minutes, they had searched every area of the small beach and hills. The smaller psychic spiders told the others that more food was up the hill and directed them to follow the path.

A small group stayed on the beach while the rest ran across the water to where the doorway of light was. They pulled and pulled until it slowly moved towards the shore then into a small cave.

The queen came out of the portal followed by her children, who poured out of the doorway, then hunters, whose colour changed as they ran across the rocks and sand, larger spiders with elongated legs and large dark shiny abdomens, and then came more psychic spiders scuttling up the cliffs towards the town.

The majority guarded the entrance while others ran off, coming back with branches and other materials to cover the cave entrance.

The remaining hunters scoured nearby and soon discovered the town of Shes. Communications went back and forth that this place had dwellings with food inside them. Hunger was almost overwhelming, and many of the spiders wanted to feed, but the doorway needed to be secured first. They had waited so long that a few more hours did not matter to them.

***

The sun rose in the east, and hunters were at every road and path leading in and out of the town while hunters in the ocean concentrated on bringing the doorway to shore. If the spiders were not so hungry, they would have looked upon the rising sun in awe after spending their whole lives on their darkened world.

The queen saw the attack and spiders surrounding the town through the eyes of the psychic spiders. Even in the pre-dawn light, she could see the different contrasts of this world. There would be light not seen in generations by her kind, but the beauty of this new world was forgotten almost immediately with the thought of feeding her children.

The town of Shes came alive with the rising of the sun, no-one noticing the hidden threat that surrounded them as the hunters changed their colour to blend in with their surroundings. Several times, people walked by them without realising how close they had come to death. The psychic spiders could feel the emotions of the people as they passed by; some had family in other places like this.

Through the psychic spiders, the others relayed to the queen the different textures, smells, and sights of this new world. As the sun rose in the sky, they could feel the warmth giving them strength never felt on their world. From the soil, sand, foliage, and trees, the spiders were overloaded with sensations they could never have imagined before. The queen was almost overwhelmed with the desire to explore outside the cave, but the feeding of her children would come first.

By midday, the townspeople were going about their day as usual. A few people gave casual glances towards the docks, as the harbourmaster was long overdue; by this time, he would usually be drinking at one of the taverns. Two of his drinking friends decided to find out what was taking him so long. They both laughed as they guessed at what trouble he might have got himself into.

***

The doorway of light was safely secured in the cave and the entrance covered over as the duo came down the hill toward the docks.

Attack, came the telepathic command from the queen as she watched from within the cave.

The two friends stopped laughing as hundreds of giant spiders materialised all around them, from the docks and beach to a few yards in front of them. The two friends froze before turning and running back to town, where they collapsed to the ground upon seeing hundreds of giant spiders rushing through the streets.

2

'Emily, what are you doing here?' Ramulas gasped.

'I hid when the monsters came.'

Ramulas' face twisted in confusion as he tilted his head and said to Pip, 'Something is amiss here. I can feel fear and uncertainty coming from Emily.' He waved his hand in front of the small girl, and she was covered in a fine purple mist. Then his eyes widened.

Pip stepped forward, grabbing hold of Ramulas. He turned to her, seeing her eyes glowing purple. 'This is just a normal girl. Emily has no magic, and I don't think she has ever had any.'

Ramulas shook his head. 'I saw the same thing using my magic mixed with Oriel's powers. I do not know how this is possible, but this is the same Emily who saved Grace; at the same time, though, there is something different about her. This Emily has never been close to magic her whole life.'

He smiled as he squatted down and held out his hand. 'My name is Ramulas, and this is Pip. Come with us and we will look for your parents.'

Ramulas was reminded of when he first left his farm and met Pip. He had been unsure about his life and how the world relied on him to defeat the Legion. He saw the uncertainty in Emily's eyes and realised that this must have been how he appeared to Pip. He looked at both Pip and Emily as his daughters and would do anything to make them feel secure.

Emily hesitated for a moment before slowly taking his hand. A small spark of light flashed as they touched. Emily saw herself walking through a forest as the pair before her searched for a place called Sanctuary. Just as the memory came to her, it was gone, but Emily felt that she was safe with these two.

Ramulas and Pip glanced at each other after the flash, and he said, 'She just saw a small memory and knows we will not harm her. We should explore this place.'

As they walked to the courtyard, Pip said, 'Why did you tell her our names?'

He smiled. 'I am a father, and this little one is scared and needs comfort. We are strangers to her, and she has lost her parents.'

Pip shook her head and danced in front of Emily. 'You remember us, don't you?'

Emily looked up and studied Pip for a moment before shaking her head.

Pip pursed her lips. 'What about Grace and the dryads?'

Emily gave a blank expression.

Ramulas coughed, and Pip glanced up.

He smiled sadly. 'Leave her be. This Emily is different from the one we knew.'

Halfway through the town, Emily stopped outside of a small house and pointed. 'This is my house.'

Ramulas looked at the house, placing his chin in his cupped hand. 'I know this house. This is important, but for some reason, I can't remember why.'

The trio walked into the house and saw the table and chairs were broken and strewn across the small space. Emily made her way to a small bed in the corner. 'This is where I sleep.'

Pip smiled sadly. 'How long have you been here by yourself?'

Emily raised her head with tears filling her eyes, and her bottom lip began to tremble.

Ramulas stepped forward, taking the young girl's hand. 'Let's look in the castle to see what we can find.'

Pip waved her hand around the room. 'What about—'

Ramulas gave her a stern look, silencing her. *She is all alone and afraid,* he mouthed to her.

The former thief shrugged as they left the small building.

They walked through the courtyard to the castle, which appeared dark and foreboding; nothing could be seen through any of the windows. As they came closer, the sound of faint whispers could be heard, only to drift away.

Pip's eyes flared as throwing knives appeared in her hands, while Ramulas chanted, waving a hand through the air. After a few seconds, he smiled at Pip. 'Do not worry. The spirits of the past are trying to speak with us; we will not be harmed.'

Ramulas and Pip stopped at the entrance of the castle and peered into the gloom.

'There are no lights or torches within,' Pip said.

'With the aid of Oriel's magic, I will cover us with light,' he replied.

Pip nodded as a smile spread across her face. They walked into the castle; Ramulas waved his hands, and a purple ball of light dropped from the ceiling. The ball of light illuminated the area as it fell. Pip covered her eyes and turned away just before it hit the floor.

The ball exploded, sending a wave of light through the castle. The trio's clothes moved as the energy passed them. Ramulas and Emily did not turn from the light and were now blinking to regain their sight.

'I thought you were going to cover us in light, not drop that thing,' Pip said.

Ramulas shook his head. 'That was not me; the castle came alive when we entered.'

'Look at that.' Pip gestured down the hallway.

Dozens of purple orbs the size of oranges dotted the walls in every direction and floated an inch from the stone, making faint humming sounds. 'This is the same castle as in Sanctuary. Let's go to the throne room,' Ramulas said.

They reached the third floor and walked into the throne room, and then they saw the paintings and tapestries lining the walls.

Pip gasped. 'Look at them.'

They walked to the far wall. The images depicted a great battle of giant spiders of different shapes and sizes fighting an army of men.

The artworks told the story from when the spiders first arrived to the end of the battle.

Ramulas shook his head. 'They are different; the paintings show the army winning and the tapestries show the spiders winning.'

Pip gasped and grabbed Ramulas by the arm, pointing to the painting in front of them as it shimmered and became clearer. 'Look! That's us and the people from Sanctuary fighting the spiders.'

They watched intensely as images coalesced of Shigar casting spells alongside Iguchi and the Fallen Angels, with Grace flying overhead unleashing her own magic and Kate fighting on the ground.

'What can this mean?' she asked Ramulas. 'We have never fought giant spiders before. Why do the paintings show that we are winning and the tapestries show us losing?'

He shook his head and sighed. 'I do not know. The real question is how did these get here, and how long have they been here?'

Ramulas looked down at Emily as she squeezed his hand. 'Do you know why these are on the wall?'

She released his hand and walked to a painting, placing her hand on it. 'This is my father.'

Both Ramulas and Pip shivered as they glanced at the painting, Emily pointed to an area where Joshua and Rain fought a large group of spiders. Her finger was on Joshua.

Ramulas and Pip looked at each other with open mouths.

***

The hunters hiding along the paths and roads surrounding Shes heard the command to attack and ran into town. After years of feeding on their own species, they would feed on softer flesh.

In a synchronised manoeuvre, they attacked from all sides, not allowing any escape for the townspeople. A few people saw the danger and gave shouts of warning before mass hysteria broke out as the hunters jumped on people.

Men and soldiers rushed outside upon hearing the frantic screams of women and children. They ran back into their homes when they saw the spiders, only to be followed by the creatures. Some people were able to lock their doors with a solid beam across the inside, but the hunters, driven mad with hunger, threw their bodies at the doors and tore at the wood with their claws and fangs.

***

The pigeonmaster barred his front door and raced back to his cages, where dozens of birds waited. Each bird would have a particular destination to travel to. The pounding at the front of his store spurred him to move faster. He opened the large rear windows and picked up paper and quill.

A dark shadow filled the room.

He looked back to see a spider as big as him slowly crawl through the windows he had just opened; its large hairy legs probed the entrance while the multiple eyes focused on him. The hunter attacked, sending the men into the cages and breaking several, sending frightened birds out into the sky.

***

Soldiers stood their ground for a few moments, fighting frantically against the creatures as the spiders ran and jumped through the streets before giving way to panic and running to find shelter; however, there was nowhere to run to. Within ten minutes, the hunters had injected each of their victims with a paralysing toxin, which would give the other spiders time to wrap their prey in silk cocoons. Most of the hunters returned to the doorway.

Out of the fifteen hundred people in Shes, only thirty had escaped the attack and saw the giant spiders leave; they would wait a little longer before going to find help.

***

The remaining hunters crisscrossed the streets of the town in patterns. Those hidden could not understand what they were doing. After a few minutes, the score of remaining hunters crawled onto walls of buildings and flattened their bodies against the wood, their dark brown bodies lightening until they blended in with their surroundings to make them almost invisible.

Other spiders went to the roads and dug themselves into small holes before covering their bodies with dirt. Soon it was hard to see where the spiders were.

***

The hunters led the weavers into town. These spiders were different from the hunters; they had long, thin black legs and round colourful abdomens. They began wrapping each victim with their elongated legs covered in short spikes before attaching them to walls or surrounding trees.

The gladiator spiders came into town next. These were like the weavers, only their four front legs seemed to be longer, causing them to walk more upright.

Six hundred giant spiders gathered around the town, and another thousand were coming through the doorway. There would be enough food for all. The queen was cunning. There were hundreds of thousands of spiders on their world waiting to come here and feed. The small force in Shes was sent to investigate the defences of this world. Once it was deemed safe, the queen would bring the rest into this new world.

Two people were brought to the cave for the queen to feed. Her body shivered as she slowly moved towards them, her long spiny legs tapping at the floor and walls of the cave. The captives were held upright by the hunters, and only their eyes could move as they widened and soft moans came from them.

She attacked them in a frenzy, feeling them struggle beneath her, before throwing the husks to her children. As they fought over the leftovers, the queen knew this place would be their new home.

***

Ramulas and Pip looked at each other in silence with mouths open slightly. Pip shook her head. 'How can Joshua be Emily's father? She has been around hundreds of years before he was even born.'

'Those are the monsters that took Mother and Father,' Emily said, pointing to the paintings of the giant spiders.

Ramulas squatted down in front of her. 'When did this happen? And where did the monsters go?'

Emily shrugged, and Ramulas could see her bottom lip trembling and tears forming in her eyes. He held out his hand. 'Come with us; my daughters would love to meet you.'

Ramulas and Pip led Emily out of the castle and into the courtyard. Ramulas communicated with Rufus, who came around the corner. When they all climbed onto the warhorse, Ramulas could feel Emily shaking and her head darting from side to side.

'Don't worry, Emily,' he said. 'Soon you will be in a place surrounded by people and have plenty of children to play with.'

Ramulas took and deep breath and sent out a telepathic wave across the valley, searching for any danger. After finding no threats, he communicated for the warhorse to take them home.

Ramulas rode with a myriad of thoughts swirling through his mind. What he had seen terrified and confused him. The pictures showed Joshua and Rain fighting the spiders with their magical weapons, streams of ice shooting out at the creatures and Joshua's iron ball sending them flying in all directions.

The problem was that Nathaniel had fought them the day before, taking the magical weapons from them. After Michael took his brother home, Joshua and Rain had been healed and showed no interest in holding the weapons again.

***

The trio were silent as the warhorse walked through the passageway; they came out into Sanctuary where an expectant crowd waited. Iguchi and the Fallen Angels still held them back. Ramulas gazed across the sea of eager faces.

'Where does it lead?' someone called out.

'What's down the passage?' another called.

Ramulas smiled while holding up a hand. People gasped as they pointed to Emily sitting on the warhorse and then glanced at her statue among those of the fallen. The people knew that Ramulas and Pip had gone into the passage by themselves and had now come out with a young girl.

Emily's name swept through the crowd as people pointed to the statues of the fallen and then at Emily on Rufus.

'A moment please,' Ramulas said.

The crowd seemed not to hear Ramulas, and the talking grew louder.

'Silence for the Lord of Sanctuary!' Miles called out.

The people quietened instantly, and Ramulas raised a hand. 'I know each of you has questions. We have found something beyond the mountain. Before anyone goes through, we need to make sure it is safe for you. We have just survived a battle against the Legion, kingdom army, and Symiaks. The last thing we need is another fight on our hands. I will take the Fallen Angels with me tomorrow. If it is safe, we will all go through.'

The faces looking up at Ramulas smiled as one before they cheered and began talking to each other in excitement.

'Please go about your business and I will call for a meeting when I return with the Fallen Angels,' Ramulas said.

The crowd dispersed, and Ramulas saw Iguchi. 'Tell your Fallen Angels to rest.'

The small man nodded before vanishing into the crowd.

***

Ramulas and Pip brought Emily into the castle. 'My daughters will be very happy to see you, Emily.'

She nodded slightly before glancing up at him. 'Will you be able to find my parents?'

He sighed. 'You can stay with us until we find them.'

They walked into his quarters to find Kate and Grace playing with Makayla and Tao on the floor. Fenris barked, causing Grace and Kate to turn. They both jumped from the floor with excited smiles and ran to their father.

Grace took two steps and froze with her mouth open. Her eyes turned black and dark energy crackled around her. She blinked once and the magic vanished.

'Emily,' she cried running to her friend and embracing her.

Ramulas saw Emily shy away as Grace held her. 'Little one, Emily has been through a lot, and I think she needs some time. She does not remember us.'

Grace stepped back with wide eyes and hands held out in disbelief.

'Stay here with Emily. I need to go to the throne room.'

Ramulas quickly hugged both of his girls before leaving with Pip. As they came out into the hallway, Ramulas felt an aching void of loss growing within him. When he spoke to his girls, he could see Jacqueline's expressions in Kate. It was for the briefest moment, but he still saw it, and then he could smell his wife's perfume in the air. He shook his head, wondering how long this pain would last.

***

They walked into the throne room to find Shigar waiting for them with a wide smile. 'I have some wonderful news, my friends.'

'What news is that?' Ramulas asked.

The magician gestured to the table across the room where Joshua and his wife were seated. Joshua wore a subdued smile, and his wife offered a nervous wave.

'After all the death and sorrow, a new life will come into Sanctuary. She is pregnant.'

Joshua's wife stood, rubbing the small bump on her tummy. 'I am to have a girl.'

'What will you name her?' Pip blurted.

'We like the name Emily,' she replied.

Ramulas and Pip's jaws dropped simultaneously and they glanced at each other.

3

The sun sank into the horizon, and dusk would arrive shortly. During the day, two thousand giant spiders had gathered in Shes. They each took turns tearing open the cocoons and feeding off the people wrapped inside. The people had recovered from the paralysing toxin and screamed as the creatures fed.

Five of the townspeople ran from their hiding places, only to be caught and eaten. The remaining people hiding took this as a sign to use caution. They would wait for a better opportunity.

The sky darkened as the spiders left Shes in two columns, one down to the docks and the other south. The psychic spiders had read the thoughts of the people of Shes. Two places were mentioned that the queen knew were important: Sanctuary and the city of Keah. After the spiders explored their surroundings, they would visit these places.

The psychic spiders told the queen and the hunters that there were still people hiding in the town. The queen was happy for her children to wait and catch them when they came out of hiding.

Those in hiding held their breath, scarcely believing their luck, and then the few survivors in the cocoons began to wriggle and call out for help; the calls started softly and quickly grew in volume and urgency. When the spiders did not return, the calls were frantic as the people struggled in the cocoons.

***

Two friends hiding in a small shack saw one of the people struggling fifty yards from them. They whispered to each other, debating whether or not it would be safe to help the captives.

'No spiders have been seen in almost half an hour, and if they haven't come with all the screaming, it should be safe,' the younger man whispered.

The older man looked outside with a stern expression for a few moments before finally nodding and clapping the younger one on his shoulder. They walked to the door and the older man opened it slowly while holding his breath. They both peered out of the door before going outside.

The victims spotted the two men and called for help with more urgency. The young man walked swiftly to the cocoon, holding a small knife in his hand, with the older man trailing ten yards behind.

As the younger man reached the cocoon, everyone became silent. He stopped and glanced around.

He could see the woman's face through the lining. As he brought his knife up, her eyes widened in fear and she shook her head.

'No, it's okay. I will free you,' he explained.

'Run! Run!' she whispered while shaking her head.

He lowered the knife as he looked at her in confusion, and then he heard a thump followed by a groan behind him. As he turned, the others in hiding shouted frantically for him to run.

The older man had been pushed face-first into the ground and a hunter stood over him, its fangs glistening with poison and legs tapping the ground. The knife dropped to the ground as the spider thrust the fangs into the prone body, and the old man's scream was cut short as the spider shook him from side to side.

Other hunters that had been hiding beneath the soil or camouflaged against the walls showed themselves. He turned to flee but ran into the cocoon and was stuck. His eyes widened as he pulled frantically on the web, only to become more entangled.

Then the spiders attacked. They were cunning and knew that the hiding food would reveal itself. The people had given away their positions, and now the spiders knew where to look for them.

By midnight, the last of the people were wrapped up and ready to be taken to their queen. A small force would stay in Shes while the rest would search the lands for more food.

***

Lucas held his fist in the air, stopping the column of men and Symiaks behind him. The town of Turtha was two miles away, and the escort had ridden out to meet them.

There had been a disturbance between the Symiaks and his soldiers within Sanctuary's Forest. The royal guard left the king to quell the fighting, and a minute later Lucas heard calls that the king had been killed.

Lucas raced with the royal guard to find Zachary dead on the ground with a crossbow bolt in his mouth. For half an hour, they searched the forest for the attacker, but to no avail. The leadership of the kingdom's soldiers fell into Lucas' hands; he shook his head knowing that he would need to send word to Princess Aleesha.

The kingdom now had a new ruler.

Lucas sighed, feeling for the people of this land. Zachary had created a monster. Aleesha had no remorse or conscience, was selfish and cold-hearted, and did not care who she walked over to get what she wanted.

***

Since coming to this new world, the spiders were almost overwhelmed with the different sensations. Coming from a dark, cold world the sun alone on this world warmed them and gave them more energy. Their main objective in coming to this world was to feed and colonise, but the spiders still took time to explore their surroundings, feeling the different textures of the grass, trees, and even the ground beneath them. These were the many things that were lost on their old world.

The mayor of Turtha led ten riders to greet the remains of the kingdom army and Symiaks. Clouds of dust rose into the air behind them. He pulled his horse to a stop in front of Lucas and frowned as he saw the combined forces. 'Where are the Legion soldiers? And I thought you marched to Sanctuary with more numbers.'

Lucas sighed and shrugged. 'We lost the battle, and now we return home.'

The mayor's eyes widened. 'Where is the king?'

Lucas shook his head. 'The king was killed during the battle.'

The mayor quickly glanced at the defeated force. 'Tell your men to make camp outside the walls,' he said before gesturing to the Symiaks. 'What will you do with them?'

Lucas pinched the bridge of his nose with his thumb and forefinger. 'The Lord of Sanctuary has threatened them with dragons; they will cause no trouble.'

The mayor almost fell off his horse hearing this. 'When your men are ready, come into town and we will talk more on this.'

***

The camp sprawled out around the front of the walls as Lucas walked into Turtha with the royal guard. He saw the incredulous expressions of those on the walls; they could not take their eyes off the Symiak chieftains as they followed the royal guard.

Lucas turned and gasped, but quickly regained his composure as Slesht walked over to him. 'What are you doing? Go back with the Symiaks.'

The creature shook his head and pounded his chest. 'Slesht king of Symiaks. We come inside to talk with you.'

Lucas rolled his eyes, looked to the heavens, and held out his hands before saying, 'No Symiaks inside town. You go back out there.'

Slesht smiled. 'Your king died. Slesht is now king of Symiaks and humans.' This comment brought hooting and stomping from the other four chieftains.

Lucas looked to the camp and saw that every man and creature had watched the interaction. Just over two thousand soldiers and fifteen hundred Symiaks became tense, and Lucas knew it would not take much for them to start fighting. Then the dragons would come.

Lucas did not want to see another dragon for as long as he lived, and he sighed. 'Fine. Come into town, but no trouble.'

Slesht snarled once before pushing past Lucas and leading the chieftains into town. Lucas gestured for the royal guard to follow. He wondered what Zachary had been thinking, joining forces with the creatures they had been at war with for generations.

The people of Turtha whispered and pointed at the Symiaks as they made their way through town. Never had these people seen Symiaks this close before. The Symiaks puffed out their chests at being the focus of so much attention. After a few hundred yards, the group arrived at the mayor's quarters.

Inside the building, the mayor raised an eyebrow at Lucas and nodded to the Symiaks. Half a dozen soldiers in the room became tense.

Lucas sighed. 'It is complicated, and I will explain later, but first I must send word to Keah of the king's death.'

The mayor nodded and sent one of the men outside as he led the rest through a door leading into a large room with a rectangular table. He gestured for everyone to be seated as he took a seat at the head of the table.

The soldier returned with a quill and paper, which was handed to Lucas. He then joined the other soldiers lining the walls of the room. The mayor waited for Lucas to write the message before he spoke.

'This is a strange situation. Twice Sanctuary has been marched on, and twice *they* have won. King Zachary has died, and the Legion is gone. Tell me what happened.'

Slesht stood. 'King lost fight and run away. Symiaks follow.'

Lucas and the mayor glanced at each other in shock. The mayor forced a smile and spoke. 'Thank you, kind Symiak. Now I would like to hear the story from the royal guard.'

Lucas took a deep breath before telling his tale.

He began with the first night out of Turtha, when one hundred kingdom and Legion soldiers were killed, and then moved on to the attacks as they made their way through Sanctuary's Forest, the failed attempts to enter Sanctuary through secret passageways, and the demons attacking at night.

Then the front gate was breached, and Remus found magical portals for hundreds of the combined army to enter Sanctuary. Magical creatures attacked those who entered the maze, but the odds of winning the battle turned in their favour.

Then the Lord of Sanctuary gained the magical power sought by Remus, and scores of green dragons came from the east to fly overhead. The Lord of Sanctuary told every man and Symiak to return home and declared that any who caused trouble would be eaten by the dragons.

King Zachary was killed by a young woman with purple hair who disappeared after the murder, and all Lucas wanted was to arrive in Keah without trouble.

The mayor's mouth hung open by the time Lucas had finished talking. 'What are your plans now?'

Lucas sighed. 'We will travel to Covedon then onto Keah as fast as we can. Princess Aleesha is now a very young queen who will need advisers to help her rule.'

The mayor nodded toward the Symiaks. 'What of them?'

'When we arrive at the walls of the city, they will go back home in the mountains.'

Slesht stood quickly, causing his chair to slide across the floor as he pointed to Lucas with a snarl. 'You not tell Symiaks to go in mountains. I say where Symiaks go.'

Hands dropped to weapons as both royal guards and Symiaks stood slowly. One of the soldiers in the room called out, and a moment later, a dozen armed soldiers burst through the door, each holding a crossbow.

Slesht smiled, holding his twin stone swords.

'Hold!' Lucas called, and the whole room looked at him.

Lucas pointed to the sky while nodding at the Symiaks. 'Do you want dragons to come?'

Slesht shook his head. 'Not tell Symiaks where to go.'

Lucas inhaled sharply as his nostrils flared and his eyes widened, and then he closed his eyes, letting out a slow breath. He opened them and spoke in a calm voice. 'Then you may take the Symiaks wherever you want to, but do not harm any from the kingdom.'

'Slesht is king of Symiaks. I will take home to the mountains,' he said before leading the other chieftains out of the room.

The twelve soldiers with crossbows followed them until they were out of the gates, with the royal guard and mayor close behind. Slesht stood at the gate and yelled in his guttural language, causing the Symiaks to stomp the ground and hoot.

The mayor turned to Lucas. 'What is happening?'

The captain of the royal guard shook his head. 'I wish I knew.'

The Symiaks packed up their camp to move five hundred yards away to make a separate camp.

Slesht nodded to Lucas. 'I tell Symiaks where to move.'

Lucas and the mayor stood in stunned silence as the four chieftains walked over to the new camp.

'Come back to my quarters; we can talk more,' the mayor said to Lucas.

Lucas sighed as they walked. 'I cannot wait until they have returned home.'

***

Ramulas lay awake on his bed. He found it hard to sleep; he would wake often after vivid dreams of Jacqueline. They were so real that he always woke expecting her to be by his side.

Reality set in once he opened his eyes. The pain of loneliness grew in his chest, building a void of emptiness inside of him. With each breath, he could still smell her close to him. All he wanted to do was lie in bed and hold onto memories of his wife.

He heard Grace talking excitedly while Kate complained that it was too early for noise. He knew that they, too, missed their mother, and he needed to push aside his grief and be there for them.

The rising sun shone through the window, lighting up one side of his quarters. He knew that he and Pip would be returning to the valley with

Iguchi and the Fallen Angels. Ramulas needed to ensure the valley was safe before allowing anyone else through the passage.

He dressed in his armour and walked to his daughters, who were sitting on their beds, with Emily sitting next to Grace. Fenris barked upon seeing him.

Kate and Grace jumped off their beds and ran up to hug Ramulas. He returned the embrace before kissing them on their heads. 'I need to go out with Pip. Stay here with Jenna. I will return after midday.'

'Can I look after Emily?' Grace called out.

Ramulas nodded. 'Yes, keep her by your side.'

Screaming heralded Tao and Makayla running into the quarters, followed by Jenna and Pip. The former thief folded her arms and raised an eyebrow. 'Iguchi and the Fallen Angels wait in the throne room.'

Ramulas kissed his girls one last time before following the former thief into the hall. They entered the throne room to find Iguchi and forty-five Fallen Angels. Ramulas found it strange that he noticed Benji and Michael's absence, and then he noticed Miles' cold expression since losing his friend.

Iguchi bowed. 'Hello to you, Lord of Sanctuary.'

'Iguchi, I need you and the Fallen Angels to search the new valley with us.'

As they walked, Ramulas and Iguchi decided that, if they found the valley to be safe, they would hold a meeting with Owain, Shigar, the druids, and Rygar.

***

The group stopped at the stables for horses before going through the passage. Reaching the valley, Iguchi split his force into two groups. They would travel in opposite directions around the valley and would meet in the courtyard of the castle.

Ramulas, Pip, and Iguchi rode toward Sanctuary's twin town, the small man constantly looking all around and at the ground.

'This is very strange,' Iguchi said softly.

'What is strange?' Ramulas asked.

Iguchi swept his hand before him. 'All of this does not belong here. It is different. We are in the wrong place.'

'I don't understand,' Pip responded.

Iguchi shook his head. 'You will soon see.'

They arrived in the courtyard, and Iguchi leapt from his horse and ran up to the statues of Lodi and Jacqueline. 'These are not new, like the other ones.'

'We know,' Ramulas said.

Iguchi swept his hand to the buildings surrounding the courtyard. 'Is all of this the same as Sanctuary?'

Ramulas nodded. 'We had a quick look around before and it seems that way.'

Iguchi's foot scraped the ground, kicking up dust. 'People have not been here for months. How did the young girl survive, and where did the people go?'

Ramulas shrugged. 'We do not know.'

'There is always an answer; all one needs to do is look,' Iguchi said.

Pip's eyes widened. 'The paintings.' Iguchi turned to her and she said, 'Come with us into the throne room; there are paintings and tapestries you need to see.'

Without a word, Iguchi walked to the castle. Ramulas and Pip climbed down from Rufus before following him.

They arrived in the throne room, and Iguchi immediately walked over to the paintings and tapestries. He clucked and hummed to himself as he studied each piece of artwork. After a few moments, he walked over to Ramulas and Pip while muttering to himself.

'I will need to show my Fallen Angels these paintings. Their style and footwork is wrong.'

'What do you mean?' Ramulas asked.

The small man gestured to the artwork. 'We will fight the monsters soon.'

Ramulas and Pip's mouths dropped. 'Why do you say that?' Ramulas asked.

'The pictures tell a story and give clues to the future.'

Pip shook her head. 'How can these be of the future, when this has already happened? Emily said these were the monsters that took her parents. Are they coming back?'

Iguchi smiled and shook his head slightly. 'No, these monsters are yet to come.'

'What do you mean?' Ramulas asked.

Iguchi walked to one of the paintings. 'Come, I will show you.'

Iguchi stopped at a painting where he and the Fallen Angels fought a group of giant spiders. 'Look closely and tell me what you see.'

Pip shrugged. 'You and the Angels fighting the spiders.'

Iguchi nodded. 'Tell me, how many of my Fallen Angels do you see?'

Pip counted. "There are fifty Fallen Angels.'

Iguchi shook his head. 'Benji and three others fell in the last battle, and Michael returned home with his brother, so I only have forty-five Fallen Angels left.' He tapped his finger on the painting. 'These five are yet to join my Fallen Angels. I know now who to look for.'

Pips' eyes glowed fiercely. 'Look at the next painting; it's changed.'

The three of them went to the painting and saw the statues of the fallen standing in a protective circle around the women and children.

Ramulas gasped before he stepped forward, noticing two figures that he thought would not be seen again.

'I must go to my Angels. They need to be shown their incorrect form. There is much training to be done.'

Ramulas examined the two figures one last time before following Iguchi and Pip out of the room. The former thief grabbed Ramulas, her eyes still glowing. 'Come with me. I will find the Fallen Angels.'

She led him upstairs to the very top room, which was a circular room twenty yards in diameter with windows facing north, south, east, and west. Pip went to each window searching for the Angels.

'I found them,' she called, pointing out of the southern window. 'Twenty Angels heading west. Pip continued to search through the windows until she called out once more, 'The other twenty-five are over here, with Iguchi moving to them.'

Ramulas peered out of the window. 'How long until they return?'

After a few moments, Pip answered, 'An hour and a half.'

'Let's look around until they come,' Ramulas said.

4

Pip and Ramulas had explored most of the castle and town by the time Iguchi returned with the Fallen Angels. They had found that everything was an exact replica of Sanctuary; the only difference was the lack of walls and cliffs to protect the town.

Ramulas turned to Iguchi. 'We noticed signs of struggle in half of the houses, but none within the castle. I was wondering what that could mean.'

Iguchi smiled. 'Hello to you, Lord of Sanctuary. We will examine this later, but first there is something we must show you.'

'What is it?' Pip asked eagerly.

The small man shook a finger at Pip. 'You are nosy,' he said before turning to walk away.

They climbed onto Rufus and followed Iguchi and the Angels into the north-east of the valley.

After a few minutes, Ramulas' mind began to wander and communicate with the wildlife around him, and then it happened.

Da, I can't find Emily, Grace's voice said inside his head.

Ramulas jolted in the saddle and looked around. 'What?'

'What happened?' Pip asked.

Ramulas scanned the nearby trees. 'It's Grace. I heard her.'

'We left her back at the castle with Jenna,' Pip said.

Da, I've looked everywhere and can't find her, Grace said.

Ramulas turned in the saddle. 'There! She spoke again. Did you hear it?'

Pip shrugged.

Then Ramulas' eyes widened. He had heard Grace in the same manner that he used to hear Oriel, inside his thoughts. He focused on talking to Grace in the same way.

Grace, where are you?

I am playing in my room with Fenris. I looked away and then she was gone.

Pip poked Ramulas in the back. 'What are you doing?'

'I can hear Grace inside my head, and I am talking to her.' As soon as Ramulas spoke, he felt the softest sensation and knew the contact was gone.

Thoughts swam through his head. He never thought it possible for Grace to talk to him telepathically. When they returned, Ramulas would ask her how she did it.

'What is she saying?' Pip asked.

Ramulas sighed. 'I lost contact with her.'

They were silent for a few minutes until Iguchi and the Fallen Angels came to a stop. Their eyes widened at what was before them.

It was a golden arch fifteen feet high and ten feet wide. It appeared very out of place within the forest, but the most concerning thing was that Emily stood beside the arch. Ramulas could feel foreign energies flowing from the arch.

'Emily, what are you doing here?' Ramulas asked, climbing down from the warhorse.

She touched the arch. 'This is where the monsters came from.'

'What?' Pip said in shock as the Fallen Angels fanned out around them with weapons drawn.

Ramulas stepped forward, waving his hands through the air while chanting. Thin trails of purple mist flowed from his hands like serpents swimming through the air to the arch. After a moment, he stopped and turned to Emily.

'This archway is closed. Nothing has been through here for weeks. I will place a magical ward over it. I will know the next time it is activated.'

Ramulas held out his hand and opened his fingers like the petals of a flower. A beam of white light shot out and hit the arch, which hummed. The beam vanished and the arch was surrounded with minute white dancing lights.

Ramulas knelt next to Emily. 'I need to take you back to Sanctuary. It is not safe here. Then we will talk about how you came into the valley.'

He took Emily's hand, and his whole body went rigid for a moment as purple energies flashed in between him and Emily. He released her hand and smiled at Pip. 'The village in this valley is called Journey's End. I need you to take Emily back to my girls. I just had a vision. There is something I need to do.'

***

Hunters, weavers, and gladiators had found an ample supply of food in the farms surrounding Shes. The farmers were quickly caught and eaten while the livestock was wrapped in cocoons to be consumed later. Miles of paddocks were covered in sheets of white silk. If it had been winter, people would think it was snow.

Hundreds of sheep and cattle were taken to the doorway to feed the others on their world. The queen ordered them to wait before searching for more food. They did not know what they might be facing and needed to use their cunning to survive.

They explored the land, which was different from their world in so many ways. They were still getting used to the brightness and warmth of the sun after decades of living in a cold, dark world.

The spiders in and around Shes had enough food to last them weeks. After so many years of feeding off each other, they had found a world with food. Soon they would leave Shes and search for other towns for food. If the rest of this land was like Shes, there would be no opposition, and then the queen would bring the rest of the spiders into this world to feed.

***

Ramulas raised both hands and rose into the air as he was covered in purple flames. He stopped after a mile and surveyed the valley below. Iguchi and the Fallen Angels walked towards Sanctuary with Pip holding Emily's hand. When Ramulas had touched Emily's hand, his world had turned white and fragments of information about the valley had flooded his thoughts.

The name of the town came to him, as well as a sense that the valley itself was foreign and did not belong there. He could not understand this, but he was compelled to fly. As he floated, Ramulas felt more of Oriel's power and memories of her teachings combining with his magical ability.

Although this was powerful, he could feel its limitations. He would not be able to stay here for long, but there was something he needed to see. Looking east past the passageway, he expected to see a mile of mountain range that opened up to the forests of Sanctuary. However, all he saw were mountains in every direction. Some of them were so tall that they touched the clouds.

Ramulas flew toward the passageway to fly over it. As he passed over the passageway, Ramulas felt a faint tingle, and he saw the passageway vanish.

Ramulas held out both hands and stared below with his mouth hanging open. He shook his head and continued his flight across the mountain range.

After five minutes, Ramulas stopped and saw he was in a sea of mountains. He should have come out over Sanctuary by now. What was happening? He turned back the way he had come but could not see the valley, and his breathing began to quicken. He turned in every direction, searching the mountains, before flying up until he met the clouds.

He looked back and smiled as he saw the valley he had come from. He turned to see the opening in the mountain range. He flew that way until coming to a large valley that opened out before him. It was three miles wide, and he was unable to see the end of it; beyond the valley were other mountains.

Ramulas lowered himself in the valley while searching the surrounding forest. 'Oh no,' he said before quickly lowering to the ground.

Ramulas held out to his stomach and grunted. 'Damn, I did not think that would take so much from me. I need to learn the limits of my new powers.'

He spent a few minutes walking around the valley, excited at the prospect of what he had found before nodding to himself and flying into the air once more. This time, he flew to the valley at a much faster rate and landed as soon as the passageway became clear.

Ramulas sighed. 'I'm lucky to have made it this far. I guess I will walk home from here.'

***

Ramulas' mind swirled with thoughts of the valley. It was not part of the Devil's Ridge Mountains, but that was impossible. His flight over the mountain range only brought more questions. He needed answers, not more questions. Ramulas would send Shigar and the druids into the valley to see what they could make of it.

***

Ramulas walked into Sanctuary and a few people greeted him. He felt that his magical power had returned during the short walk. As he walked out of the passage, Ramulas felt a slight sensation in the pit of his stomach as the air shimmered before him. He waved to those around him.

He could feel Oriel's powers returning and wanted to see what they could do. A warm sensation exploded in his stomach and spread through him. His body was covered in purple flames. He leapt into the air with purple flames trailing behind, and the people cheered.

Ramulas stopped a mile above the town and turned toward where the valley was. He flew west across the Devil's Ridge Mountains toward the valley. He travelled for over three miles and knew that by now he should be able to see the valley. However, he was still in the Devil's Ridge Mountain range.

Somehow, the valley was not part of these lands, but how could this be possible?

He returned to Sanctuary, landing in the courtyard, knowing that he needed to solve the mystery of the valley, and more importantly, he needed to find out where it was. Ramulas knew that he was unable to do this alone. He would send for Iguchi, Shigar, and the druids. Together they would find the answers.

***

Joshua walked past the tunnel Oriel had come out of. He appeared more like the older version of himself. Gone was the snarling mouth, the blue eyes filled with rage, and the long blond locks of hair. He let out a deep sigh as his body sagged. He shook his head and held his hands up before him, inspecting them closely. A part of him was happy to have returned to normal, but he missed the power of the gauntlet.

'What are you doing, my friend?' Rain asked, coming up beside him.

Joshua turned to Rain with eyes of sadness. 'I was thinking about the weapons we had and how we lost them. I still have some of the gauntlet's power, but I miss it. I want it back.'

Rain clapped him on the arm and smiled. 'You should be happy, my friend. Your wife is pregnant, and you have a new life.'

Joshua grunted and turned from Rain. 'Leave me.'

'Where are you going?' Rain asked merrily.

'Nowhere.'

'This path to nowhere will take us to the place where Lord Ramulas defeated Nathaniel. Did you know that his weapons are still there, and no-one has touched them?'

Joshua winced and kept walking. He knew they were there; he walked past them every day and saw the expressions of concern from the people when they saw him there.

Rain continued talking as they made their way to the maze. 'Do you not see that the good people of Sanctuary are more accepting of us without our weapons, but it was those very weapons that helped defeat the enemy.'

Joshua tried to bite back a bitter laugh and failed. 'Those weapons connected us in some way, and that is all we have left—the connection.'

They stopped where the crystal sword and gauntlet lay by the maze. They had lost their glow and seemed dull and devoid of any magical power.

'I remember the first time the sword called to me,' Rain said in a soft voice. 'It was as if my life found purpose, but these things before us represent another life, my friend—a life we must let go.'

Joshua's body shook; an internal battle ensued as he stared at the weapons intently. Finally, he grunted and turned to leave when a small flash of light came from the sword.

'Wait,' he said, grabbing Rain by the arm. 'I saw something. Come closer to them.'

Rain grabbed Joshua's hand and shook his head. 'No, we must—'

Then they both heard the weapons calling for them. They looked at each other with open mouths as the weapons glowed softly while lifting off the ground. They smiled at each other and quickly stepped forward.

The duo stepped closer, and a bright flash exploded from the magical weapons, sending a wave of energy washing over them. The sword and gauntlet floated to them. Joshua's jaw dropped as his left hand raised and the magical weapon moulded around his hand and forearm. His body transformed as the magic of the gauntlet flowed through him once more. His eyes squeezed shut as his hair grew while transforming to blond. Then he opened his shining blue eyes, which radiated with power.

Rain's hand shot out as the smile grew on his face waiting for the sword to come to him. When he touched it, the ground beneath his feet turned to ice. He closed his eyes and grunted as his body convulsed, only to open them again to show crystal blue eyes.

Rain turned to Joshua, holding the crystal sword with mist cascading from the blade. 'We are made whole once more, my friend.'

Joshua crouched on the ground and growled in response, opening and closing the hand with the gauntlet.

***

Pip left Rufus in the stables and brought Emily back to the stables.

Grace squealed with delight upon seeing her friend. She ran up and embraced the young girl. 'Where did you go? I was worried.'

Emily's head dropped as she whispered, 'Back to my home. I was trying to find my parents.'

Pip's eyes widened. 'Joshua,' she said.

Grace held Emily's hand. 'Da says you have to stay with me.'

Then Pip remembered how Grace spoke to her father when they were in the valley. 'Grace, how did you talk to your father when he was with me?'

Grace shrugged. 'I was upset that I couldn't find Emily and just wanted to talk to him.'

Pip turned to Emily. 'Stay with Grace, Ramulas will help you find your parents when he returns.'

Emily's head snapped up. 'Does he know where they are?'

Pip nodded. 'I think he does.'

Emily nodded, and Pip walked out into the courtyard to wait for Ramulas. She had thought that after the battle with the Legion and Symiaks was finished, things would return to normal. After finding Emily and the valley, things were far from normal. Then Pip realised that after everything that had happened, nothing could return to what she knew as normal.

Pip jumped as Ramulas floated down to land in front of her. 'Did you fly here from the valley?'

He smiled and shook his head. 'No, Pip, that would be impossible.'

Pip appeared confused. 'But you came from that direction.'

'I did fly over the passageway, but from the valley, it does not bring you here; it takes you to another place. I tried to reach the valley by flying from here, but it cannot be found.'

Pip's head tilted to the side. 'What do you mean? The valley is only a short way through the passage.'

'The valley and Journey's End is not part of the kingdom; it is another place, with trees, plants, and animals I have never seen or heard of before.'

Pip's mouth dropped. 'How can this be?'

Ramulas shook his head. 'I do not know. I need to send Shigar and the druids into the valley; they will be able to tell me more. Find them and ask them to meet us in the throne room.'

Pip shook her head and looked at the entrance to the passageway before running off to search for Shigar and the druids.

***

Pip led them into the throne room and found Ramulas waiting for them.

'Hello, my friend,' Shigar said, smiling. 'Pip has told us wonderful things about this valley.'

'I need the advice of you and the druids. There are things I do not yet understand. I believe this valley is in a place far from here, even though it is only a short way through the passage.'

Shigar raised an eyebrow. 'What do you mean?'

Ramulas explained how he was unable to find the other place by flying over the mountains from both Sanctuary and the valley, and that the only way was through the passage.

Shigar's smile grew. 'That sounds exciting. When do we leave?'

'As soon as you pack provisions for a few days. It's a large valley and it will take some time to explore. You will want to stay in the castle.'

'What castle?'

It was Ramulas' turn to smile. 'In the middle of this valley is a town and castle exactly like Sanctuary.'

Shigar stepped forward, eagerness written on his face. 'Are you sure?'

Ramulas nodded. 'It even has statues of Jacqueline and Lodi.'

'This is wonderful,' the magician said before leading the druids out of the throne room.

Ramulas turned to Pip. 'While Shigar and the druids search the valley, we will discuss things with Iguchi and Rygar.'

5

Rygar wandered through Sanctuary with his head down, seemingly not knowing where he was going, but as always, he ended up standing before Lodi and Jacqueline's statues. After the battle was won and the enemies sent away, Rygar felt very much out of place. While he trained the people of Sanctuary, he'd had a purpose, but now it was too painful to be around people—hearing the talking and laughter.

He glanced toward the mountain he and Lodi had called home. The dwarf wanted to leave this place but could not go there; nor could he return to his clan. He was surrounded by so many people, but he had never felt so alone in his whole life. He felt like a burden to the people of Sanctuary and knew in his heart that he needed to find another place to call home.

'These statues are like a double-edged sword,' Ramulas said coming up beside him.

Rygar turned to see Ramulas wearing a sad smile and covered in a soft purple nimbus of light. 'It's hard for me to sleep at night or even go into my quarters and hear my girls playing. I can still smell her, hear her laughing, see her in my girls, and I still wait for her to walk into a room at any moment. But I know she's gone, and that's hard.' Ramulas nodded. 'I know you mourn for your son, but your home will always be Sanctuary. The people here are your family. I found something through the passageway, and I need you to look for me.'

Rygar's face became serious. 'Have yer Legion come back?'

Ramulas shook his head. 'No. If what I saw comes to pass, this will be a lot worse than the Legion.'

Rygar inhaled, straightened, and pulled back his shoulders with a sparkle in his eyes. 'What might this be?'

'The druids and Shigar are gathering supplies for a few days in the valley. I would like you to join them. Look for the throne room in the castle when you are in the valley; there you will find your answers.'

Ramulas smiled as the dwarf's sad expression melted away, and he turned and ran to his warehouse.

A few Khilli women waved to him as they walked by. He needed to talk to K'ayden. His people would be leaving soon.

***

Ramulas found K'ayden and his family in the upper levels of the castle. He greeted Ramulas with a warm smile. 'Hello, my friend. My people are eternally grateful that we are free at last. We will sing songs of your bravery and courage.'

Ramulas blushed. 'I am happy that your people are free.'

A sad smile grew on the Khilli warrior's face. 'This is a happy time for us, but also sad.'

'What do you mean?' Ramulas asked.

'My people will return to their homeland in the plains between the towns of Turtha and Covedon. We have been away from our land for generations and our ancestors are calling us home.'

'When will the Khilli leave?'

'In three days' time we will march for our home,' K'ayden said, swelling with pride.

Ramulas placed a hand on K'ayden's shoulder. 'I and the people of Sanctuary will miss the Khilli very much. We will hold a celebration the night before you leave. We can supply horses and wagons for your travels.'

K'ayden nodded. 'We will only need a few for the elderly and infants. The rest will walk, as has always been our way.'

K'ayden's wife walked over to embrace Ramulas. 'You have a very kind heart, and we feel your loss deeply.'

Ramulas stepped back and nodded while fighting the tears. 'Thank you. I have other matters to attend to; we will talk again soon.'

Ramulas walked down the hall, and Khilli couples greeted him with warm smiles as they showed signs of open affection to each other. Ramulas' breath began to quicken, and he shook his head while walking faster.

He walked into his quarters to find Grace playing with Emily on her bed. Then, he took a step back, his eyes widened, his mouth dropped, and his hand went to his heart. Jacqueline had come into the room holding the hands of Makayla and Tao.

Kate saw her father's reaction and let go of the children's hands. 'I'm sorry, Father, I just wanted to try on one of Mother's dresses.'

Ramulas' expression showed the internal battle within—a mix of pain, anger, and sorrow. Finally, he took a deep breath and calmed himself. He opened his arms and smiled as she came in to hug him.

'I miss your mother very much and wish for her to return to us. I thought that came true when I saw you. I know that you and your sister miss her too. Try not to tear your mother's dress.'

He kissed her on the forehead, and she returned to her quarters. He watched his daughter walk away as the feeling of loss and emptiness almost overwhelmed him. Ramulas no longer wanted to lead his people; all he wanted was to be alone with his family.

'Have you found my parents?' Emily asked, breaking him out of his thoughts.

Ramulas smiled as he turned to her. 'We are still searching for them. Trust me, you will be with them soon.'

A soft cough caused Ramulas to turn and find Pip leaning against the wall. 'I think now is a good time to bring Emily to Joshua and his wife, but how do we explain her to them?'

'I do not know; all I know is that she needs her parents.'

Pip sighed while glancing at Emily before nodding and leading Ramulas out of the room.

***

She stood outside his door. 'What will they say?' she whispered to Ramulas, who just shrugged.

Ramulas knocked on the door, and Joshua's wife opened the door.

Pip's eyes widened as she looked to Ramulas for help. He smiled and shook his head. She sighed. 'Is Joshua home?'

His wife shook her head. 'He is out and will return soon. Can I help you?'

Pip forced a smile. 'I did not get your name.'

'I am Juliette.'

'Lord Ramulas would like to show something to the both of you.'

Juliette's eyes widened as she gasped and shook her head stepping back and looking past Pip. 'Please, no!'

Pip turned to see Joshua with Rain. He was wearing the gauntlet, sporting a feral smile, and swinging his iron ball with ease. Rain held his crystal sword with mist flowing from the blade. He had blond, flowing locks and crystal-blue eyes.

'Oh no. When did they get their weapons back?'

'Why are you at my home?' Joshua growled.

Pip shook her head, stepping back as her hands dropped to the many throwing knives on her vest, thinking that the last time she saw them they had lost their weapons. 'The paintings said that they would have their weapons back,' she whispered.

Ramulas placed a hand on her shoulder and gently pulled her behind him as he nodded to Joshua. 'I have something to show you and your wife in the throne room.'

Joshua growled and stepped forward opening and closing his hands. 'What is it?'

Pip pointed to Juliette's stomach. 'It has something to do with your baby.'

Rain smiled, clapping Joshua on the shoulder. 'This seems interesting, my friend, let us see what our lord has to show us.'

Joshua nodded and walked with Rain towards the castle. Juliette stood with her mouth open until Pip took her hand, and they joined Ramulas in following the pair.

As the small group walked to the castle, the eyes of the townspeople widened, and they pointed to Rain and Joshua holding their weapons. The whispering sounded like a swarm of angry bees.

The group entered the throne room, and Pip stepped to one side. 'Wait here and I will bring you something.'

Joshua, Rain, and Juliette looked at Ramulas, but all he did was shrug.

Pip returned a moment later with Emily, holding her hand. Emily's head shot up at the trio. 'Mother,' she whispered.

Emily released Pip's hand and raced toward Juliette, who wore a confused expression. Then Emily reached Juliette, hugging her tightly. A flash of purple light exploded from Juliette's stomach, and she gasped as the energy filled the room.

Juliette's mannerisms changed in the blink of an eye. No longer was she unsure of Emily; she held her like a protective mother would a child.

Juliette turned to Joshua. 'This is our Emily.'

Joshua's scowl faded, and he stepped forward hesitantly as Emily stepped away from Juliette. Faint strands of purple energy flowed from Emily to Juliette's stomach and Joshua. As he came closer, the energy strands grew brighter and hummed softly. Joshua reached out to touch Emily, and the air popped as the energy vanished.

Joshua pulled Juliette and Emily in close for an embrace as he turned to Ramulas. 'How?'

Ramulas shook his head, holding his hands out wide.

Juliette smiled as she picked up Emily. 'Come, child, you are coming home with us.' She took Joshua's hand and walked past Ramulas and Pip as if they were not there.

Rain smiled. 'This will prove to be interesting.'

***

Pip's emerald eyes glowed as she watched Emily run to Juliette. She could see the baby in the womb move. As Emily hugged her mother, strands of white energy flowed from her to the baby. It was at that moment that Pip saw that Emily and the baby were one and the same.

When Joshua came up to hug Emily, Pip saw something that made her realise what Emily was and where she came from. She glanced at Ramulas, knowing that he would not like what she had to say.

***

'My, this is very interesting.' Rain said, smiling at Joshua.

Joshua turned to his friend. The presence of a monster just beneath the surface about to explode at any moment had diminished; in its place was a man who had found a sense of peace. However, Rain could still see the rage that was pushed deep inside Joshua and knew his friend could call on the inner rage to summon his strength at will. Somehow, he had more control over his powers.

Juliette watched her husband with a mix of relief and disbelief. She had become used to being wary around Joshua when he wore the gauntlet.

'What happened?' Joshua asked without the growl in his voice.

Rain's smile widened. 'You have mastered control of your power, my friend.'

Joshua tilted his head as he turned to Ramulas. 'How can this be? My wife is pregnant with a child, and I know that this Emily before us is our child. Is she the same? And if so, how is this possible?'

Ramulas nodded. 'She is the same person as the baby within your wife's stomach. It will take time to work out how this came to pass. When I am certain of how it happened, I will let you know first.'

Emily! Grace shouted.

Ramulas turned but could not see his daughter, and Pip gave him a confused expression.

'Did you hear Grace call out?'

As Pip shook her head, Grace came running into the throne room with Fenris close behind. 'There are two Emilys,' she said with a smile.

'How do you know?' Pip asked.

Grace's eyes became dark and ancient energies crackled around her. 'I felt it.'

Juliette stepped forward taking Emily's hand. 'She is coming home with us,' she said in a tone that implied she would not take no for an answer.

Ramulas nodded as Joshua and Juliette walked out with Emily. Grace tapped Ramulas on his shoulder. 'Can I go play with Emily?'

Ramulas smiled and shook his head. 'Not now, little one. I think they need some time alone.'

Grace sighed and dropped her head.

Ramulas tousled her hair. 'Why don't you take Kate and walk around town? The people would love to see the lady and princess of Sanctuary and talk to them. You are both very important here now.'

Grace squealed and ran from the throne room.

Ramulas turned to Pip. 'I think the passageway that leads us to Journey's End takes us to another world that is somehow tied to ours.'

Pip nodded as her eyes glowed. 'I can see parts of Emily that are not from this world and yet very similar. How can this be?'

'I have no idea, but I will wait for Iguchi, Shigar, Rygar, and the druids to return. Then we can speak to them and decide what to do next.'

'What does that mean for the people of Sanctuary?' Pip asked.

Ramulas sighed. 'I do not know. That is why I cannot allow the people to enter the valley until we know it is safe.'

***

Iguchi studied one of the paintings with intensity, tutting to himself every now and then and slightly shaking his head. Then he turned, opening his arms wide. 'Oh, woe is me. I give my Angels knowledge, and how quickly they cast my teachings away.'

He motioned for Miles to stand before him. 'Look at these paintings,' he instructed. 'Your elbow is slightly bent with this move. This is laziness. This is not of my teachings. You bring much sorrow into my heart.'

Miles sharply inhaled, pointing to the painting before regaining his composure and returning to his previous position.

Iguchi waved him away from the wall. 'Come, show me the stance within the painting.'

Without comment or hesitation, Miles' body flowed into the position. He leaned forward, thrusting his sword with his right hand. His left held the shield above him with his arm slightly bent. Iguchi moved in a blur, grabbing the edge of the shield and pulling down.

Miles fell forward to his knees, and Iguchi's sword was on his neck before he was able to recover. 'If your elbow was straight, you would still be standing,' Iguchi said before turning to the rest of the Fallen Angels. 'Each of you will study the art of the walls to learn the flaws of your technique. If we are to fight these giant spiders, we will need to train hard.'

***

Iguchi and the Fallen Angels worked on the moves and techniques over and over until Iguchi was pleased with their movements. Then, they were told to search the valley in small groups on their way to Sanctuary, where they would begin new training.

Iguchi walked into the courtyard to be greeted by Shigar, the druids, and Rygar. He gave a slight bow. 'Hello to you, and welcome to Journey's End.'

Rygar was the first to break away from the group. He approached the statues of Lodi and Jacqueline, studying the statue of his son with tears brimming in his eyes.

'This cannot be,' Shigar said, climbing down from his horse. 'This looks exactly the same as Sanctuary.'

The magician walked over to the statues and waved his hands while murmuring, then he clapped his hands together and both statues shimmered.

Shigar gasped. 'Oh my, these are the exact statues as Sanctuary, but they are years old.' He turned to the druids. 'Come with me. There is much to discover here.'

The group walked into the castle with Rygar in tow.

***

Shigar and the druids had spent the day and half the night exploring the castle. They had been intrigued by the tapestries and paintings and attempted to decipher their meaning. Now they were close to mental exhaustion. They needed to rest so they could search the town and valley the following day.

The magician smiled standing on the balcony of the throne room with his head tilted up at the sky. There were so many groups of stars he had never seen before, and with this, he knew Ramulas to be right: this place was a very long way from Sanctuary.

The two moons told him that they were on another world.

***

Lucas saw the town of Covedon nestled on the coast. He had stopped the column five miles from the town; they would reach it by sunset. It had taken three days from Turtha, and each night, the Symiaks camped five hundred yards away, hooting and singing in their guttural language.

Lucas sighed and waved the men forward once more.

***

Lucas stopped three hundred yards from the wall, giving orders for camp to be set out while the escort from the town rode out to greet the party. The mayor was followed by a score of soldiers who stopped before Lucas and quickly scanned the kingdom soldiers and then the Symiaks.

He held out several silver tubes. 'We have messages for you and accommodation for one hundred of your men. Please follow me where we can talk.'

Lucas nodded and gave orders for twenty of the royal guard to follow him while the rest were to organise camp. Lucas and his men were shown into the mayor's quarters, where servants stood by a long table. The mayor waited until they were seated before sitting at the head of the table.

Lucas opened one of the silver tubes, read it, and sighed while shaking his head. He looked up at the mayor who shrugged.

Lucas read it out for all to hear. '*Captain, you will return to Sanctuary and kill everyone in the town. My father's death will be avenged. Do not return until this is done. Queen Aleesha.*'

Lucas opened the other messages, which were the same. He dropped them on the table and seemed to collapse as he looked to the heavens for help. Then he turned to the mayor. 'When did these arrive?'

'They came yesterday with pigeons from Shes.'

Lucas appeared puzzled. 'What messages came from the town of Shes?'

The mayor shrugged, holding out his hands. 'The towns of Turtha, Nasad, and Boer have reported the same thing: pigeons from Shes holding no messages.'

Lucas appeared puzzled. 'What could this mean? Several towns receiving pigeons without messages.'

The mayor shrugged. 'I do not know. I have heard of the occasional bird escaping, but never this many.'

Lucas shook his head. 'This will need to be investigated, but for now, more pressing matters lay in the city of Keah. I need every seaworthy vessel to take as many of my men as they can to Keah tomorrow morning.'

The mayor paled. 'I have only five fishing boats. They might be able to take one hundred soldiers.'

Lucas put his hand to his chin and thought for a moment. 'I will go with the men by boat, and the rest will make their way over land. You will have no trouble from the Symiaks; they just want to return home to their mountains.'

Lucas thought about arriving in Keah after reading the messages from Aleesha. A shudder went through him thinking that she was now queen. He just hoped that he would be able to guide her in the right ways to rule over her people.

6

Men, women, and children danced in the streets of Sanctuary as the Khilli sang and danced with them. It was a day of celebration; the Khilli people were free and would be returning to their homelands the following day.

Ramulas wore a sad smile while his heart ached watching Kate and Grace dance and laugh with the other children. 'My love, why did you have to leave? It's times like these that make your loss hurt so much more,' he whispered.

He shook his head. 'No. I cannot allow this to affect me. My daughters and the people need me to be strong. I am the Lord of Sanctuary, and my girls need me to be there for them.'

'Who are you talking to?' Pip asked him.

Ramulas turned to see Pip smiling up at him. 'I was not talking.'

'Lies,' Pip replied with a bigger smile.

Ramulas sighed. 'If you must know, I was talking to Jacqueline. I miss her all the time, especially times like this.'

Pip's smile grew. She took his hand and pulled him into the crowd of dancing people until Ramulas found himself standing in front of one of Sanctuary's widows; her husband had died fighting the Legion.

Ramulas and the widow stood a few feet apart, staring at each other awkwardly.

'This is Rachael; she is in need of a dancing partner.'

'But it's too soon,' Ramulas stammered, stepping away.

Pip scowled and slapped his arm. 'You are a fool. Life is too short.'

She took Ramulas' hand, placed it in Rachael's, and shook her finger at him before disappearing into the crowd.

Ramulas turned to Rachael, forcing a smile and stepping back with one foot as if ready to leave. Then he saw the loss and heartache in her eyes as she fought to hold back the tears. He stopped thinking about his own pain and gave her a genuine smile. 'I think dancing will do us both good.'

The people of Sanctuary danced until the early hours of the morning, and Ramulas laughed with Rachael as they talked. Then people broke away in small groups to their homes. Ramulas thanked Rachael for her company and walked his two tired girls into the castle.

Ramulas sat on the edge of his bed, not wanting to sleep, knowing that it would bring more dreams of Jacqueline and that the pain of loneliness would return when he woke. He felt so lost without his wife and did not know what he was supposed to do with his daughters or the people of Sanctuary.

****

The sun shone in the late morning as the people gathered to bid the Khilli farewell. Women and children hugged one last time. K'ayden stood before Ramulas and his family with a broad smile.

'My friend, you have given my people the gift of freedom. We will sing many songs of you and the people of Sanctuary.'

Ramulas smiled. 'You showed me much kindness in the tombs. Freeing your people was the least I could do. Please know that you and your people will always be welcome here.'

'Do not worry, my friend; we will return soon.'

K'ayden slapped Ramulas on the shoulder before leading his people out of Sanctuary.

Ramulas stood in the courtyard with his girls for five minutes after the last Khilli had left. Kate and Grace stared up at the stature of their mother, and Ramulas was lost in his own thoughts.

A shout of alarm brought Ramulas back to the present moment, and then more shouts came from the direction of Oriel's tunnel.

He turned to his girls. 'Wait here until I return.'

Ramulas ran while communicating for his hell hounds to stay with his girls. He passed several streets and houses before stopping at the entrance of the tunnel, and his mouth dropped at the sight before him.

Royce and Shayn, the earth elementals, stood at the entrance of the tunnel.

'Are me eyes playin' tricks on me?' Edwin said next to him.

Ramulas shook his head as the two elementals walked toward them. 'What happened to you two? We thought you dead.'

Shayn hiked a thumb over his shoulder. 'In the tunnel.'

The dwarf shook his head. 'I searched the tunnel; there was no sign o' yer both.'

Royce smiled. 'We were knocked into the chasm. It was very deep, and it took us a long time to climb up the wall.'

'What are your plans now?' Ramulas asked.

The duo looked around at the people, the wall, and the castle, and then Royce spoke. 'Where is Oriel? I cannot feel her.'

Ramulas smiled. 'You missed a big battle, and so much more. Oriel is now inside of me.' He opened his arms and purple flames danced along his arm, and the elementals were covered in a soft glow.

Ramulas' eyes widened and he turned to the dwarf. 'Take these two into the cavern where Oriel was and dig into the rear wall. There are many surprises within.'

Ramulas walked away, leaving them confused.

***

Ramulas sat in his quarters watching his girls play with Makayla and Tao. Grace used her magical ability to help Tao build with his blocks. She saw him and smiled. *Look at what I'm doing, Da.*

Ramulas smiled. 'I know, little one. You are doing a very good job.'

Kate tilted her head and looked at him. 'Grace did not talk, Father.'

His jaw dropped as Grace smiled at him.

What's wrong, Da? Grace asked telepathically.

Ramulas frowned and silently communicated with her. *It's rude to talk to me like this when there are other people around, little one.*

Grace sighed as her shoulders sagged and her head dropped slightly. Then she raised her head as the whites of her eyes became black, and the blocks in front of Tao floated in the air. Tao laughed while clapping. Ramulas and Kate were too stunned to move. The blocks dropped around the small boy, forming a little house.

Grace blinked, and her eyes returned to normal.

The house of blocks collapsed, and Pip coughed next to Ramulas, who spun around.

'Everyone has returned from the valley, and they're waiting for you in the throne room. Owain is there as well.'

Ramulas told his girls to wait and followed Pip out of the room.

An excited Shigar walked up to Ramulas when he entered the throne room. 'My friend, do you have any idea what you have found in the valley?'

Ramulas and Pip shook their heads.

'The valley is on another world completely. It has two moons, and I have never seen the patterns of the stars in the sky before, but there are many similar elements that connect both our worlds.'

Ramulas and Pip's eyes widened as Shigar continued, 'I do not know how the passageway works, but it was strange that I felt no magic as I passed through. You will need to come and stay the night there, and you will understand when you look at the sky.'

'Hello to you, Lord of Sanctuary,' Iguchi said, walking over to him. 'The user of magic is correct. You will learn much by spending the night there.'

'But what is the valley? Will it be safe enough for the people? '

'My Fallen Angels have looked through the valley and found no enemies. There are several paths leading out of the valley that have not been used in years, so yes, Lord of Sanctuary, the valley is safe,' Iguchi said.

One of the druids stepped forward. 'We have studied the animal and plant life in the valley. It is very similar to ours in this forest but with small differences. You will need to come see for yourself.'

'When do you want me to spend time in the valley?' Ramulas asked.

'Tonight,' Shigar said.

He turned to Pip. 'Watch my daughters until I return.'

The former thief shook her head. 'I'm coming with you.'

'Then who will look after Kate and Grace?'

Shigar shrugged. 'Bring them with you. They will be safe.'

***

Lucas stood on the bow of the lead fishing boat. There were twenty soldiers on each of the five vessels making their way to the harbour of Keah. It was midafternoon, and chaos reigned on the docks.

Boats and ships navigated the waterways. Yelling and curses could be heard as vessels narrowly missed each other. Lucas guided the five fishing boats into the dock, and the harbourmaster waved for them to move back and wait. Lucas glanced at the captain of his boat and gestured for him to dock.

The harbourmaster became furious, screaming at the fishing boats until he recognised the captain of the royal guard. His body language changed as he quickly waved other boats and people on the docks away to make room for the fishing boats.

Lucas nodded to the harbourmaster as he led the soldiers into the city of Keah. His eyes widened, watching the fishing boats move back out into the harbour and the speed at which the soldiers made their way to the castle.

Lucas led the way with rapid, marching steps. The footsteps of the following soldiers echoed around him as he thought, *The last time we were in this city, Legion soldiers filled the streets. What was King Zachary thinking?*

None of that was important. He needed to talk with Aleesha.

***

The guards at the castle gate showed signs of relief and smiled seeing Lucas and the soldiers. The sergeant of the gate walked up to meet them.

'Thank the gods you have arrived. Aleesha has been a terror since hearing the news of the king's death. She has ordered the death of any who oppose her every whim.'

Lucas sighed. 'With King Zachary dead, this makes Aleesha the queen. Now tell me, how many have been put to death?'

The sergeant shook his head. 'No-one yet, sir, but there is a score of servants in the dungeon awaiting execution.'

Lucas gasped and took a step back. 'What did they do to deserve this?'

'Nothing, sir. The queen is very cruel; she has been searching for anyone to take her anger out on. If you do not do what pleases her at that very moment, she punishes you and sends you away.'

'Who helps Aleesha put them in the dungeon?'

'She has ten of the king's old agents and a handful of handpicked soldiers who are loyal to her and enjoy her sadistic ways.'

Lucas nodded once and led the soldiers away wearing an expression of grim determination. He quickly found her in Zachary's old chambers. She sat on the throne sneering down at a servant who was curled into a ball below her.

Aleesha laughed, not noticing Lucas with ten of his royal guard standing twenty yards from her. 'You will learn. I am queen and should not have to wait for my food. Next time you will run to the kitchen.'

The servant lifted her head, showing the cuts and bruises mixed with tears on her face.

'Enough,' Lucas roared, moving forward as Aleesha and the agents all jumped.

Then Aleesha quickly composed herself and glared at Lucas with contempt. 'Who are you to enter the queen's chambers without my leave? Have you done as ordered and killed those in Sanctuary?'

Lucas flinched as if he had been slapped. He closed his eyes, taking a deep breath before replying, 'It was best for us to return.'

One of the agents closest to Aleesha leaned in and whispered something to her, causing the queen to smile without emotion. 'You will address me as "Queen Aleesha" or "my queen" when to speak to me.'

Lucas' hands raised, and he made signals with his hands. The royal guard fanned out on either side of him.

'Well, my queen,' Lucas said in a bored tone. 'You are yet to see your sixteenth summer, am I correct?'

Aleesha appeared confused but nodded.

'In the event of your father's death, I am to help guide you in ruling these lands until you are eighteen years of age. Ruling over the people does not mean you treat them like this.'

Aleesha's face turned crimson as she began to shake and point at him. 'You dare speak to your queen this way? To the dungeon with you!'

She turned her head from left to right, making eye contact with the two agents on either side of her, and became confused when they did not move. 'Take him away now.'

Lucas sighed. 'The agents face eleven of the royal guard, and one would be enough to keep them at bay. One hundred soldiers came to the city with me and will answer only to me. Since the death of your father, I have shown leadership, and all the kingdom soldiers are loyal to me and will follow my orders over yours.'

Aleesha jumped to a standing position, holding the armrests of the throne. 'This is treason!' she shouted.

Lucas shook his head with a sad smile. 'My queen, this is not treason, I am here to guide you in ruling the people until you come of age. I understand your sorrow and pain at your father's passing, but you are not to abuse people at your whim. This is the fastest way to lose your kingdom. I will ask you to release those you placed in the dungeons.'

'And if I do not?' she replied.

Lucas shrugged. 'Then I will send my men to do it. This will appear better coming from you, my queen.'

She glared at Lucas for a few moments before turning to the agents. 'Release them now.'

After the agents left, she regarded Lucas with cold eyes. 'Tell me what happened to my father.'

Lucas gave her a brief summary of their march to Sanctuary and how the battle went, telling her how, after the Lord of Sanctuary gained Oriel's magical power, he opened a portal sending the Legion back home and then, under the threat of dragons, he sent the kingdom soldiers and Symiaks to their homes. He concluded by relaying that, in the forests of Sanctuary, her father was shot with a crossbow by a young lady with purple hair, the soldiers reporting her to be a former thief from Keah.

When he finished, Aleesha asked, 'Where are the gems from Oriel's cave?'

Lucas' eyes widened and his mouth fell open. 'What?'

'Remus told my father that if we helped him there would be lots of gems as a reward from Oriel's cavern.'

Lucas shook his head and thought, *I have just told the queen how her father died, and all she seems to care about is the treasure. Aleesha has a long road to travel if she is to become queen of these lands.*

Lucas sighed. 'There were never any gems. Your father was lied to by the Legion, just as they lied to the Symiaks.'

'Then who will pay for my father's death?'

Lucas shook his head and pinched the bridge of his nose with a finger and thumb. 'At this time, we are lucky that the Lord of Sanctuary allowed us to live.'

'Father said that the people of Sanctuary were to be punished for leaving the towns without his permission. When will you go back and punish them?'

Lucas held his tongue, knowing that this would be a difficult task with the queen.

***

Ramulas told his girls to pack for the night, saying that they were going somewhere special. As they gathered their things, he asked Pip and the Fallen Angels to pass on word about what they had found in the valley but to say it was not quite safe to travel there yet. When Ramulas returned the next day, he would talk to the people.

The small group had packed and was ready to leave with a large crowd eager to see them off. Ramulas rode his warhorse over to Rygar. 'I will need someone to stay behind and watch the entrance of the passage so no curious people follow us.'

The dwarf puffed out his chest. 'Then why is yerself lookin' at me?'

'Because, good dwarf, I need someone that I can rely on. Pick out a few of Sanctuary's soldiers to help you.'

The dwarf nodded. 'Then why didn't ye say so in the first place?'

Ramulas smiled as he watched Rygar walk off calling out orders. He nodded to Pip, and they led the group into the passageway with his girls close behind. The hell hound hounds ran ahead sniffing the ground, Shigar and the druids followed his girls, and Iguchi and the Fallen Angels made up the rearguard.

Miles was now the unofficial leader of the Fallen Angels, with Iguchi stepping back allowing this to happen. They had not trained since the battle with the Legion, but they were still a close-knit group and moved as one.

'Once we return to Sanctuary, I will look for the five who become our new Angels,' Iguchi said.

Miles turned to Iguchi with a sad smile. 'No-one will ever replace Benji."

Iguchi smiled and touched Miles on his breastplate. 'Benji is with us always. You carry him here within you.'

***

Kate and Grace gasped as they entered the valley. After asking their father and Pip countless times where they were going, they had finally arrived. Ramulas pointed to Journey's End and told them that was where they would be sleeping that night.

Grace's eyes turned black as dark energies crackled around her. She stared at the distant town for a moment before the energy around her receded and Grace returned to normal.

She turned to Ramulas. 'Da, that's—'

He quickly shook his head and pointed to Kate. 'No, little one, that would spoil things for your sister. If you like, the both of you could ride ahead and meet us in the town.'

Kate and Grace looked at each other before spurring their horses into a quick trot. Ramulas communicated with the animals to keep them from getting too far ahead and for the hell hounds to stay close.

He smiled seeing two black shapes sprinting out of nearby trees, heading for his girls.

***

Kate and Grace were awestruck as they stood in the middle of the courtyard. Ramulas smiled down at them from Rufus. 'You both are free to explore the castle and town, but you will each have an escort of ten Fallen Angels and druids with you.'

The excitement in the girls faded slightly, and then Garce jumped up, waving her arms. 'Can I do magic, Da?'

Ramulas shook his head. 'No. That is why Shigar will go with you. You now have Emily's magic inside, and this is very dangerous. You girls be back here by dusk.'

The girls looked at each other before dashing into the castle, followed by the hell hounds and their escorts, leaving Ramulas and Pip, who winked at him. 'Let's have another look around.'

***

Everyone gathered in the throne room and waited. Shigar had instructed all the windows to be covered and, when asked what was happening, would only smile and say that the impatient Ramulas would have to wait.

An hour later, Shigar led Ramulas, his daughters, and Pip onto the balcony. He smiled as they gasped looking up into the night sky. Both Pip's and Grace's eyes glowed fiercely as they studied the stars.

Ramulas turned to Shigar with wide eyes. 'There are two moons.'

The magician nodded. 'Yes, there are, my friend, and look how different the stars in the sky are compared to Sanctuary. I would say that we are standing on a world far away from home.'

Ramulas was transfixed by the sky. He was lost for words.

7

Ramulas and his girls woke a few hours after dawn. Together with Pip, they had stayed awake until the early hours of the morning. They had discussed how strange things were in the castle and town; everything was the same as Sanctuary, down to the furniture and bedding.

Ramulas was lost in his thoughts. *Another world? How could this be possible?* Then he remembered that Oriel and he had travelled to this world. He could feel something very familiar about this place.

Using Oriel's magic, Ramulas levitated just above the height of the castle and began to chant while waving his hands through the air. Streams of purple energy flowed from his body like large lazy serpents. After a few moments, Ramulas brought his hands together.

A thunderclap rolled across the valley, sending his magic away from the town in an expanding circle. He waited for a few minutes, and then his energies came rushing back to him. The sense of this world being familiar and important came to him, but Ramulas could not understand why.

But the valley itself was safe, and he would allow his people to come to it the following day after the meeting.

***

Everyone in the party sat on their horses and started off toward home. Ramulas led the way with Pip and his girls. His thoughts constantly drifted to the possibilities of what discovering this new world could mean.

He came back to the present moment and found they were halfway through the passageway and Grace was telepathically talking to him. *Da, can I tell Emily that we saw her home?*

Ramulas sighed and communicated back to her, *Emily has been through a lot, and her parents need to understand the idea of having two Emilys.*

A wave of disappointment washed over Ramulas from his daughter. *Little one, you can see her, but only for a short while.*

Grace squealed and startled everyone in the group except her father. Ramulas shook his head and gave her a stern look, which did not diminish her smile.

Little one, we have to be careful talking like this around people.

'Sorry, Da,' Grace said out loud.

Ramulas rolled his eyes.

***

Ramulas asked Pip and the Fallen Angels to spread the word of a meeting that afternoon, where the people would be told of the valley and Journey's End, and then he would lead them into a new world. Only time would tell if they would visit or settle there.

Edwin ran up to Ramulas as he was about to enter the castle. 'Me lord, ye be needin' to come with me into the tunnel.'

The dwarf turned and walked off with Ramulas close behind. Just before reaching the tunnel, Ramulas flinched and turned to his side as if something was about to attack him. He took a deep breath and saw the reason for the sensation; a pigeon sat on a nearby roof sending out waves of fear. Ramulas communicated with the animal.

He soon found that this was a carrier pigeon from Shes used to carry messages. Something large and dark had attacked its home. He searched the bird's mind deeper to see if he could gain a clearer picture.

He saw the inside of the aviary, with all the birds in small wooden cages. He saw through the bird's eyes as the human rushed into the room and frantically opened the windows. A dark shadow fell across the room. A pain flashed behind Ramulas' eyes as the pigeon's heart stopped after reliving the terror.

Before Ramulas could think of what this could mean, Edwin called him from within the tunnel. Ramulas would send someone down to Shes to see what had happened.

***

The duo walked deeper into the tunnel to where the elementals had built the stone bridge. Ramulas stood at the edge of the chasm, looking down into the darkness; using his magical ability, he could see a mile deep into the chasm and was unable to see the bottom. However, he could see handholds moulded into the stone that allowed the elementals to climb out.

'Come across 'ere, me lord,' Edwin said as he crossed the stone bridge.

Ramulas followed the dwarf across and through the doorway that led to the cavern that held Oriel and found that the rear wall had been dug out. Shadows danced along the walls as the torches flickered.

A faint whispering could be heard calling him into the newest section of the cavern, and Ramulas walked there as if in a trance. His jaw dropped as he entered.

He found himself in a cavern twice the size of his throne room; it was filled with piles of gems, crystals, and gold coins. The piles were of varying sizes and littered the whole floor. 'What Remus said about the gifts was true. How did he know?' Ramulas whispered.

Ramulas' body twitched one way then the other, wanting to inspect every pile all at the same time; then a smile grew on his face. *Pip would think this place a miracle.* He turned to Edwin and the earth elementals, who were smiling.

'Ye were right about lots o' surprises in 'ere. How did ye know?'

Ramulas shrugged. 'After casting the spell on these two, the dust that covered them told me that there would be things that glitter in here, but I did not expect this.'

Edwin walked over to the nearest pile, picked up a handful of gems, and let out a low whistle. 'If me clan, or any other, found out about this, they would want to stake a claim.'

'What do you mean?' Ramulas asked.

Edwin waved his arm in a tight arc. 'Dwarves claim all that is found in the mountains across the lands. If any other finds anything in the mountains, the closest clan will come stake a claim. And with this lot,' Edwin said, waving his free hand at the piles of treasure, 'there won't be anything left.'

Ramulas tilted his head. 'But you dug the tunnel; you could stake the claim for Sanctuary.'

The dwarf shook his head. 'The elementals were helpin' meself. Now the closest clan can claim this; it's the dwarven law.'

Ramulas held his chin in a cupped hand, wondering what he could do, and then the solution came to him. 'Rygar. He lived in the mountains a few miles from here.'

Ramulas walked out of the cavern and knew Rygar would be happy with this find. The dwarf had lost the spark in his eyes the day Lodi died. The treasure and training of the people would give Rygar a new sense of purpose.

The paintings and tapestries in Journey's End still played on his mind. How would the people of Sanctuary cope with fighting giant spiders?

***

Ramulas found Rygar walking through the training grounds with a few people. 'Hello, good dwarf. I need you to look at something and give me your opinion.'

Rygar raised his head and stroked his beard. What stood out the most was the loss in Rygar's eyes, which Ramulas felt as a father.

'What are ye wantin' me to look at?'

Ramulas smiled. 'Just come with me into the tunnel.'

He led the way and was happy that Rygar followed without any questions. As they went deeper into the tunnel, the dwarf asked rhetorical questions to himself as to what they would find, making Ramulas smile at the distraction this mystery had given the dwarf.

Rygar was fidgeting by the time they crossed the stone bridge, his eyes wide, and then he stood like a statue at the entrance of the treasure cavern, his mouth hanging open and, for a moment, he was unable to speak.

Ramulas waved his hand. 'Edwin told me about this cavern and the right to claim. My understanding is that, with your old home close to Sanctuary, this is yours to claim. I would be happy if you shared this with the people of Sanctuary.'

Rygar could only nod.

***

Ramulas stood on the balcony of the throne room, watching as the people gathered below in the courtyard. He was flanked by Pip and his daughters. He turned to search for Jacqueline a moment before realising that she was no longer there, and the sense of loss grew within him.

The people's faces were full of anticipation as they spoke to one another. Ramulas held up his hands while chanting, and a faint mist covered the people.

Ramulas let out deep sigh as he lowered his hands. 'People of Sanctuary, we have been through much hardship,' he said in an amplified voice. 'We have fought and won two major battles.'

A hush fell over the crowd, and Ramulas stayed silent for a moment. 'However, we have suffered too many losses. I promised you a better life if you fought for your freedom. We have found something truly wonderful through the passageway.

'There is a valley, and in that valley is a town called Journey's End. This town is exactly like Sanctuary, from the castle to the houses and other buildings.'

The people below erupted into questions, and murmuring swept through the people like a wave. Ramulas tapped into Oriel's magic and was surrounded by a purple nimbus. He could hear each individual question and statement by his people; each one of them was excited and wanted to go into the valley and look for themselves.

Ramulas raised his hands and waited for the people to silence. 'There is one small detail I have not said; this valley and town are on another world.'

The crowd below exploded with excitement and questions shouted up to Ramulas and the people around them. He smiled, allowing them their time.

Then Ramulas' head tilted to the east as a serious expression came over him. 'Something is coming that will quieten the people,' he whispered to Pip and his girls.

***

A large shape appeared in the sky flying towards Sanctuary.

It was a green dragon.

A few people called out in alarm as they saw the mythical creature coming closer, then everyone pointed to the sky, seeing it come closer.

Ramulas smiled as some of the people panicked. He waved his hands through the air, sending out shimmering waves of energy, and called down to those below, 'Do not worry; the dragon will not harm anyone.'

The dragon beat its wings to slow its decent and landed on the wall of the maze opposite the courtyard. People nearby moved away.

Greetings, spirit of the dragon. The dragon communicated telepathically with Ramulas. *I have returned because we felt a call from out ancient homeland.*

Homeland? What do you mean?

Dragons are not of this world. Our ancestors came here a millennia ago, then the way home was lost to them. Now we felt the way open once more.

Tell me, where did you feel the opening to your homeland?

The dragon's head swivelled towards the passageway. *Our homeland is through the passage, I will go in search of our home.*

Ramulas nodded and turned to Pip. 'Run to the passageway and watch over it.'

Without a word, she disappeared. The dragon lifted itself from the wall with powerful beats of its wings, which pulled at the people's hair and clothing in the courtyard, then the creature flew over the castle.

The crowd below followed the dragon with wide eyes and open mouths, and Ramulas called down to them, 'I have just spoken with the dragon. It told me that the valley we are going to used to be a home for them. Once the dragon returns, we will go into the valley.'

The thought of dragons coming from the valley gave Ramulas more questions to think about.

*****

Pip sprinted through the halls of the castle, vaulted over the railing of the balcony, landed on a nearby roof, and skipped across a few more before the dragon's shadow fell over her. It landed near the entrance of the passageway, crouched down with wings folded, and prepared to crawl in.

Pip called out to it from one hundred yards away. 'Wait!' The creature's head shot up and it looked at the former thief. 'Take me with you. I want to see what you see!' she called, running closer.

The mythical creature studied Pip for a few moments before lowering its head to the ground.

Pip skidded to a stop near the dragon, not quite understanding what this meant. Then it hit her, and she climbed onto the dragon. She sat at the base of its neck holding two large scales. The dragon crawled through the passageway. Pip felt a change within the dragon as they came out into the valley.

The dragon shot into the air so fast that Pip almost lost her grip as they flew over the mountains.

Pip punched the air and screamed in joy.

***

Over the past few days, on separate occasions, two men riding in a cart pulled by horse came into the town of Shes. The hunters, which formed a protective and invisible perimeter around the town, watched them as they entered. However, if either of the men had stopped and wondered why all the surrounding fields were covered in silk, making it appear like snow, they might have stayed away.

The hunters communicated with the others that food was coming into town. Both times, the men pulled up one hundred yards from the town, seeing all the buildings covered in silk and bodies in cocoons hanging from several places.

They would turn away from the town only to find scores of giant spiders had followed them, and there was no escape. Man and horse were wrapped in cocoons and sent to the queen on their world with messages that the spider would be travelling south and east very soon in search more food.

When they found more towns, word would be sent back to the queen, then tens of thousands more of their kind would come into this world to feed.

***

Two agents ran along the docks, chasing a younger member of the Shadows, no older than fifteen. His dirty blond hair flowed in the wind as he ran, discarding his vest, leaving him with only a loose pair of leggings. A store owner had seen the boy steal a loaf of bread and called out the alarm.

The boy smiled as he turned, seeing the agent falling further behind, then he ran into a group of four soldiers coming the other way. One of them lashed out at the boy's face; his blond hair whipped around as his head snapped back and he fell to the ground, unconscious. His limp body was picked up and carried to the edge of the poor section.

His body was dumped at the base of the gallows that had been erected two weeks earlier. A bucket of water was thrown on the boy, who spluttered and tried to stand but was held down by two soldiers.

One of the agents stepped forward on the gallows and spoke in a clear and loud voice. 'Good people of Keah and the kingdom. By order of queen Aleesha, the punishment for theft is death. The punishment for being a member of the Shadows is death. Associating with any member of the Shadows will mean Gullytown.'

The agent nodded to the four soldiers, who picked the boy up as he began to frantically struggle, his wild eyes searching for any means of escape. 'No, please! I won't do it again. Please let me go. Someone call the Master of Shadows.'

Ten agents stood behind the crowd and saw several people quietly leave the crowd as the boy pleaded. The agents knew these to be Shadows and followed them; this way, they would find even more of the Thieves' Guild.

The young boy was dragged over to the noose, screaming as it was placed over his head and tightened around his neck. The agent smiled at those watching from below. 'Queen Aleesha cares deeply for the people of this city, but there must be rules. Let this be an example of her ruling.'

The agent waved his hand, and the trapdoor opened. The boy's scream was cut short as the rope tightened at the end of the drop. His feet kicked a few times before the body went still.

The agent waved to the body. 'The boy is to remain here.'

The message was clear. Queen Aleesha had declared war on the Shadows.

***

Lucas jumped up from his chair so fast that it skidded across the floor and slammed his fist on his desk, his eyes wide with fury. 'Are you certain?' he asked the soldier who informed him of the hanging.

The soldier nodded, and Lucas followed him out of his chambers while sending word for his royal guard. By the time he had left the castle, Lucas had twenty of the royal guard with him. Within minutes, they stood before the gallows, watching the young boy's body swing gently in the breeze. Lucas and the royal guard appeared if they were going to be sick at this sight.

'She has gone too far,' he said as he turned to the nearest royal guard. 'Cut him down and give him a proper burial.'

A man stepped out of the crowd with a concerned expression. 'But he was to stay up there by order of the queen, sir.'

Lucas began to shake as he saw the people nodding. He needed a way out of this without appearing to go against the queen's orders; then a miracle came in the form of a soldier riding up to him.

'The kingdom army is coming.'

Lucas nodded. 'Take the boy down. I will talk to the queen after seeing to the army.'

He stood on the northern wall watching the army approaching. Five hundred yards behind were the Symiaks. Rumours of the loss at Sanctuary had spread like wildfire through the city, and the soldiers on the wall were nervous about the Symiaks coming so close to the walls. Lucas sighed and made his way down to the gate with ten of the royal guard.

Lucas rode out to meet the rest of the kingdom army five hundred yards from the wall, knowing that every available soldier in Keah was watching on the wall.

He nodded to the Symiaks, who stopped a few hundred yards behind the soldiers. 'Were there any troubles?'

The sergeant shook his head. 'The have stayed away from us; they made a bit of noise, but no trouble.'

Lucas nodded. 'Take the men inside, and I will join you shortly. Queen Aleesha is being difficult. Inform them they are only to take orders from me.'

The sergeant nodded, and Lucas waited until they had left before riding with his royal guard to the Symiaks.

The Symiaks fanned out as they approached, all appearing eager for a fight, fists clenching. Slesht walk forward, puffing out his chest. 'Slesht is king now. You leave Symiaks alone.'

The creature turned to yell out in his guttural language and the Symiaks began stomping and hooting. The sound rolled across the plain like thunder. Lucas shook his head and sighed.

Then the Symiaks gradually became quiet and Slesht pointed to the sky. 'Not attack Symiaks. Dragons will eat you.'

Without waiting for a response, he called out again and the Symiaks marched to the eastern road, which would take them to their home in the mountains.

Lucas sent one of the royal guards into the city with instructions for the soldiers on the wall to watch the Symiaks but not to attack. He took the remaining royal guard and followed from a few hundred yards away.

***

Pip held onto the scales tightly as the dragon flew across mountain ranges and valleys, her hair whipping in the wind and her eyes watering. The dragon circled the valley several times before returning to the entrance of the passageway.

Pip held a hand to her chest, fighting for breath, thinking, *I actually rode on a dragon. I never thought such a thing could happen.*

The dragon crawled out into Sanctuary and lowered its head for Pip to climb down. As soon as Pip's feet touched the ground, the dragon took flight once more.

8

Ramulas stood on the balcony, watching the people below, when he felt the dragon's presence return. People soon pointed to the sky in excitement, and the dragon landed on the wall opposite the courtyard. The people were not as afraid this time and gathered closer to the dragon.

Ramulas communicated with the dragon. 'What did you find in the valley?'

'Spirit of the dragon, I have found our homeland.'

Ramulas smiled. 'I share your joy. What will you and the other dragons do now?'

'I will tell the others, then we will come here and return to our home. It has been too long.'

'There is a town within the valley. My people would like to visit there.'

The dragon's head snaked down towards the people in the courtyard, who backed away a few feet. 'Spirit of the dragon, you and you people are welcome into the valley once the dragons have returned to our homeland.'

Ramulas nodded.

The dragon shot into the air, flying east along the mountain range. Ramulas watched until it was a small speck in the distance before turning to the people.

'Through the passageway is the old homeland of the dragons. They will come here soon to return to their home; once they do, we are free to walk through the passageway. The dragons will welcome us there.'

The people below shouted and cheered.

'Prepare supplies for a few days. The dragons will return soon.'

People walked away in small groups, talking to each other in excited tones about the dragons being in the valley with them. Then Ramulas felt a tug on his sleeve and saw Grace and Kate smiling up at him.

'Da, can we play with the dragons?'

Ramulas smiled and shook his head. 'I don't think they would like that, little one. The dragons have not seen their home in a very long time, and you two girls have a lot to pack before we leave for the valley.' Both sets of eyes widened as the realisation set in. 'And Kate is the lady of Sanctuary. She will help organise which families enter the valley first.'

Kate gasped and took a step back at the words her father said. 'Father, how do I know which ones to let through first?'

Ramulas shrugged. 'Ask others to help you.'

Kate's expression changed, and she reminded Ramulas of Jacqueline. The hole inside his chest grew bigger; he pushed away the feelings and turned to Grace. 'Now, little one, I want you to find Shigar. He will help you with your new magical powers.'

Grace squealed and ran from the balcony.

Pip smiled as she walked over to Ramulas as he gazed into the maze.

'What made you so happy?' he asked her.

'I rode on the back of the dragon as it went into the valley,' Pip said, excitedly flourishing her arms as she told the tale.

Ramulas tilted his head, waiting for Pip to reveal she was joking; when she didn't, he began laughing. 'Pip, you are one special person.'

Ramulas laughed harder when she punched him in the arm.

***

Ramulas felt an ancient magic probe the edges of his mind and heard the faintest of whispers. At first, he was unsure what it was, and he searched the areas close to him. Then Oriel's magic told him that the mountains were trying to communicate with him.

The mountains spoke to Ramulas in a foreign language that was hard to understand; then he closed his eyes and concentrated on Oriel's magical powers to communicate with them. An image of Oriel's cavern flashed before him, and Ramulas quickly made his way to the tunnel.

Walking into the tunnel, Ramulas began to understand the language of the mountains as they spoke. By the time he reached Oriel's cavern, he understood it clearly. The mountains told him of the passageway in the cliffs that led to the dragon's true homeland.

However, when people stepped into the passageway, the mountains could no longer see them. Only the people of Sanctuary would be able to see the entrance of the passage; outsiders will only see a cliff face.

Ramulas felt a shift in the ancient magic before it drifted away.

'What ye doin'?' Edwin asked, coming into the cavern.

Ramulas noticed the dwarf smiling up at him.

'Believe or not, the mountains were talking to me.'

Edwin shrugged. 'The mountains talk to Shayn and Royce all the time; why shouldn't the mountains talk to yerself?'

Royce and Shayn walked out of the treasure cavern. Ramulas sighed. 'You two will need to come into the valley with the people. There are things you will want to see.'

Both elementals appeared confused, and Royce asked, 'What things do we need to see?'

Rygar came out of the cavern with a determined expression. 'Monsters are comin', and yerselves will be fightin' 'em.'

'What about you?' Ramulas asked Rygar.

The dwarf's determined expression deepened. 'The people will be seein' a lot more trainin'.'

***

Grace sat on the floor of the throne room in front of Shigar and six druids. Her hands fidgeted in excitement; this would be the first time she practiced magic since the battle.

The magician smiled as he watched her. His fingers danced lightly across the surface of a leather-bound book on his lap. 'Now, Grace, the druids will send some bubbles and wasps your way. Do not allow them to touch you.'

Shigar nodded, and the druids produced their wands. Grace's eyes shone with excitement as the first bubbles drifted down towards her. She reached out with her hands, wiggling her chubby fingers. The bubbles began to swim through the air in patterns above her. More and more bubbles joined the swirling pattern as she waved her hands.

Grace gazed at the wands held by the druids, and the bubbles quickly stuck to the wands as they appeared. The druids quickly gave up and put the wands in their robes. They threw handfuls of stones into the air, which transformed into stone wasps.

Grace squealed with delight and clapped her hands as the wasps buzzed angrily above her head. She jumped into a standing position and touched as many as she could. A succession of rapid white flashes of light exploded as the wasps transformed into normal creatures with yellow and black stripes.

Out of the corner of her eye, Grace saw something large creeping toward her.

It was a giant spider three feet high; it was dark brown and covered in short, thick hairs. Its eight large black eyes seemed to look right through Grace as it slowly crawled towards her, its fangs glistening with poison as it came closer.

Her eyes became black as dark energies crackled around her. She saw the giant spider and heard the wasps buzzing above her. A memory came to Grace of when she was at the farm with her father. He had called her over to a small bush, and what she saw both surprised and excited her: a wasp with black and yellow stripes dancing on the ground, tapping its feet.

A spider had rushed out from a hole in the ground. As soon as the spider came out, the wasp had pounced on it. Both creatures had rolled around on the ground, Ramulas explaining that the wasp would lay its eggs in the spider if it won the battle and then the babies would eat the spider alive. After a few moments, the wasp stung the spider and the fight was over.

Grace returned to the present moment and searched for the wasps overhead. She waved her hands in patterns while chanting. The buzzing increased in volume as the wasps grew to four times their size.

Grace waved her hands, and the wasps attacked the giant spider as one. The spider was six feet from Grace when it realised the threat. It reared up on its back legs and swiped at the wasps with its front legs. The wasps avoided the legs and attacked the body. The spider jumped and rolled around the floor, trying to dislodge the wasps.

It was stung several times as Shigar and the druids moved away from the scene. Grace motioned for the bubbles above; they slowly descended and, with several pops, the spider and wasps were covered in sticky green goo.

The energy crackling around Grace ceased and her eyes returned to normal before they rolled back in her head and she collapsed.

***

The dragon returned to Shangri-La, telling its family that the way to their homeland was once again open and the spirit of the dragon had given permission for them to return home.

The dragons were overcome with joy at this. They shot into the air, sending streams of fire over the forests of Shangri-La.

The people from the nearby village stared at the sky in wonder. The dragons had lived with them and been their security for decades, but they had never witnessed such a sight. After a while, the dragons landed in and around the village of Shangri-La. The people gathered around, eagerness written on their faces.

'People of Shangri-La, we have lived in these forests for many years and have welcomed your company,' one of the dragons said, 'but the way to our homeland has opened and we must return to our rightful home.'

The people called out in dismay, and the leader of the council pushed his way through the crowd. 'But what of the kingdom army? The dragons have been our only hope against the king's revenge. You cannot leave us.'

The dragon shook its head. 'Our time in these forests has always been temporary; now we must leave.'

With beats of their powerful wings, the dragons lifted into the air. The people shielded their faces as the wind pulled at their clothing and hair. The dragons flew to the north-east and were gone in moments.

People panicked and wailed in fear. The head of the council held up his hands and called for silence. 'The dragons were the only thing that kept us safe from the outside world for years. If people know the dragons have left, we will be in trouble. We need to think of other ways to protect Shangri-La.'

***

The dragons arrived at Sanctuary and flew above the castle in circles, calling out for Ramulas.

By the time he came out onto the balcony, everyone in the town gathered in and around the courtyard. He watched as the dragons dropped onto the wall of the maze opposite him one by one.

Greetings, spirit of the dragon. We have come to return home, one of the dragons communicated to him.

Ramulas replied, *Return home. We will wait a couple of days before we come into the valley.*

We are thankful, spirit of the dragon, the dragon said before it shot into the air with strong beats of its wings. The other dragons followed. The people below gasped and talked excitedly as the dragons flew over the castle towards the passageway.

Ramulas looked down at the courtyard. 'I have spoken with the dragons, and we will go into the valley soon. Prepare for entering a new world.'

***

Pip walked into the throne room with Rachael, Grace, and Kate following wearing mischievous smiles. 'Rachael has come to thank you for the dance,' Pip said as she gave Rachael a gentle push.

Ramulas' mouth fell open, and he had the expression of a trapped animal as she walked towards him. She appeared more beautiful to him than the night of the dance. Then Ramulas realised that she wore a new dress made from blue silk, and her hair had been arranged to highlight her face. He could tell a lot of effort had been put into her appearance.

She stopped a few feet from him with a nervous smile. Ramulas looked around the throne room, fidgeting with his hands and searching for a distraction.

Rachael smiled at him. 'Thank you for the dance,' she said softly.

Ramulas nodded awkwardly. 'You are welcome.'

They both stood there in silence waiting for the other to make the next move. Pip sighed, slapping her forehead, and walked up to them. She took Ramulas' hand and placed it in Rachael's, turned her head to Ramulas, and whispered, 'Talk to her.'

Kate and Grace giggled as Ramulas looked as if he wanted to run from the room.

'It was a nice dance the other night,' he blurted and winched regretfully.

His daughters exploded into fits of laughter as Rachael squeezed his hand gently and smiled up at him.

Ramulas had never felt this trapped before. All he wanted to do was run away.

Then Tilly came flying through the window of the balcony, and Ramulas sighed in relief as if a prayer had been answered, and he released Rachael's hand.

The sprite stopped six feet from Ramulas, floating in the air with her wings buzzing. 'You must come to the forest. The dryads are waiting for you.'

Tilly flew outside, and Ramulas turned to Rachael with an apologetic smile. 'I am truly sorry; I must go. We will talk again soon.'

Rachael forced a smile and nodded.

Pip followed Ramulas out into the hall and punched him in the arm with all her strength, and he jumped in shock when he saw her anger.

'How dare you act like that! If lady puts so much effort into looking her best for you, you don't run off the way you did.'

Ramulas held out his hands. 'But the dryads need me outside.'

He was rewarded with another punch from Pip before she pointed to the throne room. 'You go back in there and ask her to wait and tell her you will come back after you speak to the dryads. Can you not see that she likes you?'

Ramulas shook his head. 'It's too early. I still mourn the loss of my wife. I cannot.'

A stern expression came across Pip's face as she shook her finger at him. 'Your girls need a woman around, and they love being with Rachael. This is not just about you.'

Ramulas sighed as he walked into the throne room, and Rachael looked at him expectantly. 'Please stay here with Kate and Grace until I return.'

His daughters jumped around excitedly while Rachael smiled.

***

Ramulas walked out into the courtyard to find the sprite hovering ten feet above a crowd of people. As soon as Tilly saw him, she shot through the passage into the clearing. When he arrived, Ramulas found five dryads waiting for him.

Eady stepped forward, concern on her face. 'We saw dragons and thought another battle was occurring.'

Ramulas smiled and shook his head. 'No, there is no battle. The dragons have found a way to a new world where their homeland is; they have gone home.'

Then Ramulas realised that he had not seen the dryads since the previous battle. 'How many losses did you suffer during the fight?'

Eady seemed to collapse within herself. 'We have lost many, but the injured are healing well. We saw the evil in the enemy when they entered our forest home. We would have lost more if we did not join the fight.'

'What do you mean?'

'If Sanctuary had fallen, the enemy would have hunted us down through the forest for sport.'

Ramulas tilted his head. 'How could you know such things?'

'When we pulled the Legion soldiers into the trees and they died, we saw into their souls and saw how evil they were.'

Ramulas' heart broke thinking about those losses of the dryads. This was another burden he would have to carry.

'I am truly sorry for your loss,' he said.

Eady touched his arm. 'Do not be sorry. We have moved on from our sorrow. I would like to see this new world you have found.'

'Follow me, and I will show you,' Ramulas said, walking back to Sanctuary.

Ramulas smiled when he saw the shocked expressions of the people, and he knew the dryads were following; they had all heard of the dryads, but only a few had seen them before. A growing crowd of excited people followed Ramulas and the dryads to the entrance of the passageway.

Ramulas arrived at the entrance and waved his hand in triumph. 'Here it is.'

Eady and the dryads seemed confused. 'We can see nothing.'

Ramulas appeared stunned and waved his hand at the passageway one more time. 'It is here.'

This time, his hand went deeper into the passage, causing that section of the cliff to shimmer. Eady walked up to where Ramulas' hand went through the cliff and attempted to do the same. Ramulas' mouth fell open when Eady's hand slapped on the face of the cliff.

***

K'ayden had led his people to their homeland over the past few days. Each day, their excitement and anticipation built as they approached

Khilli lands. By mid-afternoon, they had reached the edge of their homeland twenty miles from Turtha.

Tears came to K'ayden as he saw what his ancestors had seen for generations, and childhood memories came flooding back. His people spoke excitedly as the children ran forward. Long grass blanketed the old Khilli village, coming up to his knees. The forty mud houses were covered in thick vines but stood strong in the sea of grass.

It would take time to restore the village, but K'ayden did not mind. His people had returned home.

He would gather some of the men who could track down the herds that would crop the grass and supply them with food.

A group of hunters had grown restless in the town of Shes and wanted to search for more food. Without asking permission or informing the others, they had marched south-east.

After a while, the rest of the spiders noticed the twenty that had gone. The queen was informed, and she sent a party of three hundred to follow the smaller group and bring them back.

The smaller group were headed directly towards the Khilli village.

9

Old John stood impassively watching the agent standing on the gallows calling out to the gathered crowd. Beside him was younger member of the Shadows on his knees, who looked at out the crowd with wide eyes searching for a way to escape. The boy was about to be hanged for stealing a loaf of bread.

The agent told of the boy's crime and how the new laws must be carried out; the boy was hauled to his feet by two soldiers as he screamed out for mercy. Old John wanted to reassure the boy, but the agents in the crowd were watching everyone.

A few of the Shadows in the crowd left and were followed by agents, Old John gave the call of a wren, which was three short whistles. This call echoed through the crowd from other Shadows, showing that they understood.

Old John followed an agent who, in turn, followed a female member of the Shadows. He watched as she made subtle hand gestures as she walked through certain parts of the city. Other Shadow members gave their own gestures, saying that they would help.

Old John saw where she was headed and walked to the front of a building that would give him the best vantage point. The agent was twenty yards behind the woman and closing in when he lost sight of her. Two fully loaded carts were pushed onto the road as she walked past; as the carts were pulled away, she was nowhere to be seen.

The agent stood for a moment searching the area before running to where he last saw her. Then he heard a woman cough; he turned and, to his surprise, saw her fearfully glance around before running through a doorway.

The door slammed shut behind her as the agent started to run. He reached the door to find it locked. He slammed both fists on the wooden door, demanding it to be opened by order of Queen Aleesha. A window opened above the door; the agent raised his head in time to see a bucket of rancid water being poured down on him.

The agent coughed and gagged, spitting out the water in his mouth as he backed away from the doorway. Several younger Shadows ran up to him, throwing small sacks of flour over him and running off.

By the time the agent had recovered, everyone in the street was laughing at him. The flour stuck to him like glue and the smell of the rancid water made him gag. His eyes promised death to those in this area.

'You will all pay for this when I return,' he promised.

This made the people laugh harder. This was the first time the agent had not seen fear in the eyes of the people.

***

Old John stood before the Master of Shadows in the basement of a derelict house. He had just finished telling of the young Shadow who was hanged for stealing a loaf of bread.

The Master clicked his tongue a few times while nodding and staring into space. After a few moments, he looked at John with eyes devoid of emotion. 'A member of the Shadows was hanged for stealing. This crime warrants no more than a few days in the dungeon.'

The Master began to pace in front of old John. The four enforcers in the room became alert as tension became evident in his body language. 'Theft and being a Member of the Shadows warrants death. Anyone who talks to the Shadows will be sent to Gullytown.'

The Master stopped suddenly, and his black silk shirt seemed to move around his large frame. A cold smile spread on his face as he held up a finger. 'This Queen Aleesha needs to learn who really controls the streets of Keah. Her father was harsh, but power has gone to her head. An example must be made. Go find one of the soldiers who helped hang our young shadow. I want him brought to me.'

Old John nodded and left the room. There was much work to be done.

***

An hour before midnight, the soldier was found drunk in one of the local inns. This made it easy for one of the whores to lure him out into a laneway where Shadows were waiting. He was beaten unconscious and brought to the Master of Shadows.

When the soldier woke, he found the Master of Shadows standing over him. He recoiled and scuttled back, running into the legs of an enforcer. He saw five others in the dim room.

Two pairs of strong hands roughly brought him to his feet. He struggled to free himself from the iron grips but quickly accepted his fate.

The Master of Shadows walked over to the soldier, holding a loaf of bread. 'Do you know what this is?'

The soldier's eyes widened as he scanned the room and then focused on the loaf. 'What? I don't understand.'

The Master glided closer to the man and shook the bread in front of his face. 'Tell me what this is.'

'It's a loaf of bread,' the soldier replied.

The Master laughed softly while shaking his head and holding up the loaf. 'This is your death sentence. I have witnesses who saw you steal the bread. As Queen Aleesha orders, theft is punishable by death.'

As a noose was thrown over the soldier's head, his eyes bulged and he screamed in protest; that scream was cut short when the noose tightened.

***

Early the next morning, the soldier was found hanging from the gallows in the poor section with a loaf of bread tied to his neck. The message was clear. The Shadows had declared war on Queen Aleesha.

***

Iguchi stood in front of the five new Fallen Angels. They wore new uniforms and fresh face paint. Each of the men were calm, but Iguchi could see the underlying nerves.

'You will train with the other Angels until you are worthy.'

Each one of the new members was placed with a group of nine of the original Fallen Angels. This would hasten their training and development. Miles and the others would guide them.

'We have won two battles,' Iguchi said, shaking a finger, 'but if the paintings of the spiders are true, we will fight monsters who move in ways we have not seen before. We will study the paintings so we may study how to kill without being killed.'

Iguchi nodded before leading the Fallen Angels running out into the forest. This would be a day of baptism for the new recruits.

***

Owain led the archers to a different part of the forest. He had lost fifteen archers in the last battle, and they had not been replaced. Ramulas and Pip had described to him in detail the tapestries and paintings in which the people of Sanctuary fought an army of giant spiders.

Because there was a probability that this may come to pass, Owain devised new ways of training for the archers. He had spoken with Rygar and a few others about what he needed to be built. This had taken a couple of days but was now ready.

Multiple targets had been hidden throughout the forest. People waited near the targets for the archers to come past before pulling a lever that would activate the target. Owain instructed the archers that, when the targets appeared, they needed to shoot the red dot in the centre, which would show a kill. The targets with blue dots were to be untouched.

The red targets represented the giant spiders, and the blue represented the people of Sanctuary. The blue targets were constructed of denser wood, allowing Owain to hear the difference. Many of the red and blue dot targets were clustered together, making the training harder for the archers.

Owain turned to the archers, who each had twenty arrows in their quivers. He smiled, knowing that there were forty red targets to hit.

'You will go through the course in pairs, and you will need to work as a team,' Owain said, sweeping his arm to the right. 'Each of you has walked the path without knowing where the targets are. Once you have hit all the red targets, you will wait for the other teams to finish. Remember, the blue targets are the people of Sanctuary and must not be hit.'

Owain clicked his tongue a few times. Once he knew his archers were ready and each had a partner, he nodded, and the first pair ran into the trees.

Owain rapidly clicked his tongue to follow their progress. They both had arrows nocked as they passed the first tree. They moved slowly, scanning the area as they walked, sweeping loaded bows from left to right.

With a click, the first target slid out from behind a bush. Both archers turned and released an arrow, hitting the target close to the red dot. They reloaded their bows and continued.

More targets came out from behind bushes and trees, with the archers quickly responding to each out. Then two targets came out together, one red and one blue. An arrow hit each target, followed the archers cursing before they moved on.

They came near the end of the course each with one arrow remaining. Four targets shot out in front of them; only two were hit. The archers looked at each other with confused expressions, gesturing at the remaining targets. Then a person stepped out from behind a tree and beckoned them forward. They walked ten yards before two more targets came out on the path. Both sighed, shaking their heads, and walked to the finish point.

Arrows were removed from all the targets before the next pair came down the path. Soon enough, all the archers had finished the course and not one was smiling.

Owain stepped forward. 'Each pair that came through hit at least one blue target, and each pair ran out of arrows before finishing. The enemy still lives.'

'But we were short of arrows,' one of the archers said.

Owain shook his head. 'You were short on communication. You will talk to your partner more.'

***

Over the past few days, rumours had been spreading about Joshua and Rain retrieving their magical weapons; however, few people had seen them lately.

A group of fifty soldiers stood in the training grounds with Rygar. It was going to be their first training session since the last battle. 'Now, yer had ye rest, so it's time to begin yer trainin'. All ye must do is pass those two wooden crates over there, touch the fence, and return.'

Rygar nodded, and the group ran towards the crates. Both crates exploded when they were ten feet away. Joshua and Rain emerged from the wreckage with their weapons swinging. Before the group could recover, ten of them had been struck and were sent flying through the air.

Joshua and Rain waded into the rest of the group, who frantically held up their shields and made wild swings with their swords. By the time the group was organised, there were only fifteen remaining—too few to stop the onslaught of the duo.

Rygar stormed forward, his face a mask of fury. 'What do ye call that? One little surprise and ye fall apart. The enemy we face will have lots o' surprises for ye. On yer feet and we will start again.'

Members of the group stood and watched Joshua with confused expressions. They were used to the snarling beast of a man, but now Joshua stood before them swinging his iron ball with ease and wearing a calm smile.

'Fight!' Rygar called.

The group jumped back in shock as Joshua transformed into the monster in the blink of an eye and charged them. They had time to gasp before Joshua and Rain were amongst them again.

Time after time, Joshua and Rain trained with different groups, each one telling the same story—they were unused to the pair's different fighting styles. Rygar knew they would understand once they saw the artwork in Journey's End.

***

Ramulas sat on his warhorse near the passageway entrance with Pip, Kate, and Grace, all wearing smiles. This would be the day when everyone could see the valley. The air buzzed with excitement, with people talking about what they might find in the valley. They watched their lord expectantly.

He smiled and raised his hands, and the crowd became quiet. 'People of Sanctuary, I will delay no longer. Follow me into Journey's End.'

He turned his warhorse and led the way with Pip and his daughters. The excited chatter grew louder as they went deeper into the passageway. Ramulas winced and held his chest as thoughts of Jacqueline came to him. She would have loved to see the valley. He shook his head, pushing the thoughts away.

'Stop it,' Pip said, punching him in the back. 'I can see regret in you. Stop punishing yourself.'

He turned to Pip and saw Grace holding a large bag with a guilty expression. She tried to move it behind her.

'What's in the bag, little one?' he asked.

She quickly shook her head holding the bag on the other side of her horse. 'Nothing, Da.'

Pip was on the other side, and her eyes glowed fiercely before she gasped and pointed to the bag. 'Tilly is in there.'

Ramulas sighed. 'I know. Tilly will be safe to come out now, little one.'

Grace opened the bag, and the sprite flew out, causing the people to call out in surprise. The sprite looked around before shooting off towards the valley.

'How did you know Grace had Tilly?' Pip asked.

'Grace was very quiet, and I knew she was hiding something, and I saw something move as she held the bag.'

***

Ramulas stopped at the entrance of the valley and held up a hand. He turned to see everyone's eyes wide with excitement. 'In the middle of this valley lies a town called Journey's End. My daughter will lead you to this place.'

Ramulas and Pip moved aside as Kate and Grace held their heads proudly, walking their horses and leading the people into the valley. Ramulas communicated with the hell hounds, telling them to stay close to his daughters.

Pip and Ramulas watched as the people slowly came out of the passageway into the valley, then he turned in surprise to see Rachael patting Rufus. Pip gave Ramulas a wink and climbed down.

'You should take Rachael into Journey's End and show her around,' the former thief said.

'But you—' Ramulas started before Pip gave a quick wave and melted into the crowd.

He looked down at Rachael, offering an awkward smile. She responded with a shy smile and waited expectantly.

It was one of the few moments in his recent life that Ramulas did not know what to do. He had recently lost Jacqueline and was still mourning her, and he could see that Rachael was also suffering. However, they enjoyed each other's company, and his girls seemed to like her. He made up his mind and reached down to pull her up onto Rufus behind him.

***

Iguchi and the Fallen Angels followed the last of the people into the valley. Ramulas walked forward with the people, talking with them, using this as an excuse not to talk with Rachael. For the first time in years, Ramulas was at a loss for words when it came to talking to a woman. Then he remembered the time he first met Jacqueline, and the void inside opened again.

***

Neither of them spoke as they rode towards Journey's End. By the time they reached the town, it was a hive of excited activity, countless people coming up and asking Ramulas questions. It was almost overwhelming, with too many people talking at once.

He smiled politely while scanning the crowd for his daughters, whom he could not find. Ramulas raised his hands and waited until the crowd quietened down. 'Please look through the town and castle and we will talk soon.'

As the crowd dispersed, Ramulas felt a familiar presence probe his mind coming from the valley. He turned to Rachael. 'I am sorry; I have to go into the valley. Please wait for me to return.'

He helped lower her to the ground before guiding Rufus through the people while communicating with Grace. He smiled when she told him that she and Kate were showing people around the town.

Two hundred yards from the town, Ramulas saw a dark shape fly over the mountains. He climbed down from the warhorse to wait for the dragon.

A minute later, the dragon landed in front of Ramulas and lowered its body to the ground as the crowd behind gasped in amazement.

'Show me your homeland,' Ramulas said as he climbed onto the creature's back.

As you wish, spirit of the dragon.

With a few powerful beats of its wings, the dragon lifted, and they were on their way to the mountain range. *Everything you see before you is our homeland. Where do you wish to go?*

Ramulas thought of the mountains east of the valley where he had flown before. The dragon turned its body as soon as Ramulas' thought coalesced in his mind. They reached the valley in under a minute, and Ramulas felt another presence calling to him.

He communicated with the dragon, and it dropped down to land on one of the mountains. Ramulas placed both hands on the side of his head as he communicated with the mountains of this world. They told him the history of Journey's End and the people who lived there.

As the mountain spoke, a cold chill ran through Ramulas, causing him to shiver. It was virtually the same as the history of Sanctuary that Oriel had told him. An enemy came into the valley, but the people of Journey's End were able to erect a magical barrier that surrounded the town.

Most of the enemy died during the battle. They withdrew, leaving a small wooden box covered in intricate patterns amongst the dead bodies. When this box was taken inside the magical barrier, the spirits of the dead emerged in the form of giant spiders.

The mountains ceased their communication, and Ramulas could feel a sense of confusion. Then a moment later, they said something that shocked Ramulas.

Another race had now entered the valley with the people of Sanctuary and were within the forests near the town of Journey's End.

With a thought, Ramulas told the dragon to take flight, and they flew west as fast as the dragon could.

***

Pip walked through Journey's End, mingling with the people as they walked through the town. Everyone repeated the same joy of this place being the same as Sanctuary. Certain groups were debating whether Journey's End or Sanctuary was the better place.

Then Pip's eyes glowed fiercely. She saw a glowing line just beneath the surface of the ground; it was twenty yards away from the town and seemed to encircle the town itself.

She followed it for one hundred yards until she saw Grace standing next to it, focusing on the ground at her feet. Dark energy crackled around Grace as she waved her hands in small circles.

'This cannot be good,' Pip mumbled as she ran towards Grace.

Ten feet away from Grace, Pip felt the ground under her feet shake slightly before the vibrations increased, causing people to panic and start screaming. Kate stood near her sister, not knowing what to do.

The glowing line began pushing its way through the earth. Pip realised quickly that this was a wall two feet thick as it appeared out of the ground. She did not want the people trapped in there.

Pip grabbed Grace by her shoulders and shook her. 'Grace, you stop this right now.'

Grace looked at Pip as her eyes returned to normal and the dark energies evaporated around her body.

The ground trembled again as the wall sunk back into its original position and disappeared. In a few moments, the soil covered the wall, leaving no trace that anything had happened.

'Grace, what were you doing?' Pip asked.

'I saw the wall under the ground, and I wanted to look at it,' Grace said, shrugging.

Pip shook her finger at the young girl. 'You can't do things like this. People will be hurt. We'll wait for your father to come back. I need to show him something in the castle.'

Then Pip saw movement out of the corner of her eye. Something was happening near the courtyard; people began running towards it. Both Pip's and Grace's eyes glowed. In a few seconds, both saw what had come out of the nearby forests.

Using Grace's magical ability, they pushed their way to the front of the growing crowd to see the creatures slowly coming towards the town.

10

K'ayden led the warriors on what was to be their first hunt since returning to their homeland. They had travelled ten miles from the village, K'ayden following the fresh tracks of a few deer. The warriors moved slowly through the grass and bracken, making almost no noise. They spotted the deer within a small grove of trees a few hundred yards away.

They moved towards the deer in a slow crouch, and K'ayden smiled to himself. The teachings of the elders that had been passed down had not been in vain. He made hand gestures, and the warriors fanned out on either side of him, ready to attack.

They kept this formation as they closed in on the grove of trees, occasionally pausing when one of the deer glanced in their direction. When they were one hundred yards away, K'ayden gave the signal to attack.

Several deer lifted their heads from grazing. They searched the area, ears flicking to and fro in search of danger. The warriors ducked back under the cover of the foliage; only K'ayden remained standing to see what had frightened the animals.

Several large dark shapes dropped from the trees onto the deer, sending the rest running towards the hidden warriors. K'ayden saw that his warriors were ready. They waited until the frightened animals were almost upon them before jumping up and attacking with knives, spears, and throwing disks. Four deer fell at the feet of the Khilli.

K'ayden turned back to the grove, wondering what had attacked the other deer, then the dark shapes came out into the open. He had time to call out in alarm before twenty giant spiders were amongst them.

***

Ramulas held on tightly as the dragon raced for Journey's End, his mind full of conflicting thoughts. He had checked the valley several times with Shigar, the druids, and Iguchi, and there were no dangers. What could be in the valley?

His mind was screaming at him that the giant spiders from the artwork had somehow come into the valley.

Coming closer to Journey's End, Ramulas could see people moving towards the forests. They seemed to be moving towards trees that had not been there previously. The dragon landed one hundred yards from the people, and Ramulas hit the ground running.

He stopped ten feet from the trees as his mouth fell open. Before him stood Eady and five other dryads. The only difference was that they had silver leaves covering them instead of green. Eady turned to smile at Ramulas.

'How did you come here? We are on another world,' he said in shock.

Eady smiled. 'Tilly was brought here and showed us the way when she returned through the trees.'

Ramulas shook his head slowly. 'But you could not walk through the passage. I don't know how this is happening; and why are your leaves silver?'

She looked down at her body before glancing up at Ramulas. 'Our travel through into this world did feel different in a way I cannot explain.'

Ramulas waved his hands while tapping into Oriel's power. Soon the dryads were covered in purple aura; then his eyes widened as he dropped his hands. 'This world is slowly killing you; you must return to the forests of Sanctuary.'

Eady studied Ramulas for a moment before walking into the tree; she was followed by the others. Ramulas was still in shock with the appearance of the dryads on this world and the effect it had on them. How would this world affect his people?

Ramulas waved his hands through the air and chanted, sending sheets of fine mist over the people of Sanctuary. He grunted with effort of the spell. Within a minute, everyone was bathed in faint light, and Ramulas breathed a sigh of relief knowing that his people were not affected like the dryads and were safe there.

Then he was swamped with people asking him of the dragons, dryads, and a myriad of other subjects in this new world. It was almost overwhelming for him; then he saw Shigar.

Ramulas pointed to the magician. 'All questions will be answered by Shigar.'

Shigar sighed as the people gathered around him, and Ramulas gave a small wave before he saw Pip with Grace and Kate. Pip came up to him. 'You need to look at the paintings and tapestries; they have changed.'

Ramulas gasped and gestured for Pip to lead the way into the castle.

***

The duo stood before the paintings, both wearing concerned expressions.

'Last time we were here,' Ramulas said, 'the tapestries showed the giant spiders winning the battle, and the paintings showed we were winning. How are both the paintings and tapestries showing that we lose?'

Pip shrugged. 'I just saw this before.'

Ramulas turned to the noise of people outside. 'We have to bring them back to Sanctuary. I need to keep them safe.'

'But they just arrived.'

Ramulas sighed. 'In a few hours, we will take them back. Find my daughters and keep them close.'

'Grace found a magical wall that protects this town.'

Ramulas turned in surprise. 'Show me.'

Pip shrugged. 'It's a few inches under the ground. Grace pulled it out, and I made her put it back where she found it.' Pip went on to explain the events of what happened, and Ramulas was shocked.

Ramulas walked to the door of the throne room. 'When we find my girls, I will ask everyone to look at the artwork before they leave, then we go home.'

***

Ramulas stood on the balcony of the throne room. He could see the valley and mountains in the distance. His people were gathered below in the courtyard and surrounding streets.

'By now, you have all seen the artwork in the castle, with all of us fighting the giant spiders. These pictures have changed from depicting us having a chance to win to showing us losing. I am not sure what this means, but I think it would be safer for us to return to Sanctuary for now. Once I am sure we are safe, we will come back here.'

The people cheered before slowly making their way towards the passageway.

***

K'ayden jumped back as one of the hunters jumped at him. Instinct saved his life as he lifted his spear and thrust the tip towards the creature. The spider impaled itself on the spear. He almost gagged with the stench of the creature being so close to him. K'ayden released the spear and rolled away from the thrashing spider.

K'ayden saw that his warriors battled the giant spiders on both sides of him. He saw a young warrior ten yards to his right facing off against a hunter. The creature waved its front legs in the air while tapping the ground with its rear legs, confusing the young warrior. He held a spear out before him, jabbing out now and again to keep the spider away. It began to move to the side, searching for a way around the spear.

K'ayden threw his Khilli throwing disk at the creature, severing two of its front lags and causing it to rear up and hiss, turning to face K'ayden. He called for the young warrior to attack the distracted creature; he threw his spear, and it entered one of the spider's many black eyes. It shuddered while changing colours for a second before shuddering once and collapsing.

K'ayden ran up to the dead spider, pulled out the spear, and tossed it back to the young warrior. Then he retrieved his throwing disk before telling the warrior to move to the next spider and attack it from behind as it fought another Khilli. They both raced at the spider that was fighting other Khilli, spear and throwing disk cutting into its rear legs and abdomen.

The spider hissed loudly and clicked its mandibles. It raised its abdomen and sprayed a fine sheet of web into the air, hitting a nearby warrior who shouted in alarm as his right arm and weapon was now stuck to his body.

Within seconds, the four Khilli had killed the creature. K'ayden quickly sent them to help other warriors fight the spiders. The air was filled with warriors grunting and calling out to each other, spiders hissing and clicking their mandibles, and the foul odour that came from the creatures.

K'ayden and the young warrior ran, and K'ayden threw his disk, hitting a spider in the side of its body twenty yards away, causing enough distraction for the other warriors to kill it.

K'ayden gathered more warriors to help repel the creatures. Time had no meaning for the Khilli as they fought; they just knew that the giant spiders did not belong in their homeland.

Finally, the battle had come to an end, and K'ayden called his warriors close to him. They all fought for breath as they came in together. All were covered in cuts, abrasions, and sticky gore from the slain spiders, which made them gag.

K'ayden scanned the warriors, and then his eyes widened when he realised five were missing. He quickly called out for his warriors to search for the missing.

In under a minute, they were found; three had suffered broken bones and the remaining two had been bitten by the spiders, leaving ragged wounds in their bodies that had caused them to die from blood loss. All the warriors seemed to collapse at the sight of their dead brothers.

K'ayden said that a ceremony would be held for them at their homeland and the injured would be attended to.

'We need to search the area to see what we can find before any more of those creatures come,' K'ayden said before sending a few warriors back home with the news of the attack.

Over the next few hours, the Khilli searched through the grove of trees and surrounding grasslands for traces of more giant spiders. By the time they had finished, one hundred more warriors had arrived, ready for battle. They had brought horses and carts to transport the dead and injured.

Once the dead were on the carts, the warriors gathered around the bodies of the slain spiders, which had been piled into a mound. The Khilli warriors took their time closely inspecting the bodies of the creatures, noticing the hard outer shells of their bodies covered in thick hairs that felt like thorns. Their many eyes seemed to follow their every move, and their fangs were like daggers.

K'ayden shook his head. 'This is not a good sign. In all my years, I have never heard of such things. We must meet with the elders to see if they can help us with this problem, then I will travel to Sanctuary and talk with Ramulas.'

K'ayden cut one of the legs off and held it before him. It was as thick as his arm. He would talk to the elders that night and leave for Sanctuary the following day. Ramulas would know what to do.

***

The hunter climbed down from the tree as its colour changed to its darker shade. It had stayed in the tree watching the other spiders fight. The queen would want to know about these warriors, who were very different from the people of Shes.

It changed the texture and colour of its skin to blend in with the surface of the tree as the warriors searched below. It fought back the urge several times to attack them. It had seen how they fought. The spider would return with many more to face these warriors.

The queen of spiders had taught them well. It knew to return and tell the other of the Khilli fighting technique. The spiders would be victorious next time they faced these warriors.

***

K'ayden led the way back to the village, where they were met by mourning women and children; they had been told of the attack. The injured were taken away and preparations were made to celebrate the fallen warriors with the deer they had killed.

The two warriors were wrapped from head to toe in thick white cloth and placed into a hole at the base of a large elm tree at the edge of the village. The warrior's spears, knives, and throwing disks were placed into the hole with them so that they could fight in the afterlife.

Men, women, and children passed the hole, throwing handfuls of dirt into it until the hole was filled. As the Khilli moved away from the tree, K'ayden saw two ravens drop from the sky to land in the branches of the elm tree. He called out to his people to look upon the good omen the ravens had brought to them.

In the eyes of the Khilli, ravens were spirits of their ancestors returned to watch over them.

***

It was just before dawn, and Rygar made last-minute checks on the horses and wagons. Three wagons would be travelling to Shes, each pulled by a single horse. Two other drivers would be following the dwarf's wagon. Ramulas had asked Rygar to travel to Shes for supplies.

Rygar grunted in approval before climbing down next to an excited Grace.

Ramulas walked in and smiled. 'Are you ready to leave, good dwarf?'

Rygar nodded. 'Best to leave early.'

Ramulas walked over to Grace and kissed her on the top of her head. 'Remember, little one, to be on your best behaviour with Rygar, and I do not want you using any magic.'

Grace sighed for a moment before she looked at the wagons and her excitement returned. She climbed onto the front of the cart next to Rygar, and Ramulas waved as they left.

Ramulas sighed as Pip walked up to him. 'Don't worry about Grace; she will be fine. She is with Rygar, and the dryads will watch over her as they travel through the forest.'

Ramulas shrugged. 'I know, but as a father, it is my duty to worry about my daughters.'

The pair stood and watched as the last wagon disappeared. Rygar had told him that if they left early, they would reach Shes by the following afternoon, the supplies loaded overnight, and then it would take two days to return.

Ramulas sighed, knowing that he could not always be there to watch over his daughter's every move. Nothing could happen to Grace on a simple trip to Shes, he thought.

***

Ramulas sat on his throne as Pip spoke about the paintings and tapestries in Journey's End. They were trying to understand why the artwork had changed.

Da, we're in the forest, and I can see the dryads, Grace communicated to Ramulas, causing him to smile.

Pip tilted her head. 'What happened?'

Ramulas tapped the side of his head. 'Grace just spoke to me.'

Pip smiled. 'Tell her I said hello.'

Ramulas concentrated and then sighed when he felt the connection disappear. 'She is gone.'

***

Grace tugged on Rygar's arm and pointed to the trees. 'I can see the dryads following us.'

He turned to her. 'Can ye really, girly?'

She nodded and smiled. 'They are on both sides of the road.'

The dwarf nodded. 'That's nice. As long as they don't slow us down, they can follow as long as they like.'

A faint humming sound came from the trees and grew louder. Grace's eyes glowed a fierce emerald a moment before Tilly burst from the trees and hovered above their cart. Grace squealed in delight and clapped her hands.

The sprite pulled out her short sword. 'I am here to escort you to the edge of our forest.'

Grace's tongue poked out the side of her mouth as she waved her hands in front of her. Rygar felt the hairs on the back of his neck stand on end. He turned to Grace. 'Yer da said no magic.'

Grace dropped her hands and sighed. 'That's not fair. I just wanted to play with Tilly.'

The dwarf shrugged. 'If yer like, I can turn the cart around and drop yerself of at yer castle.'

Grace quickly shook her head. 'No, I won't do any more magic. I want to go to Shes.'

Rygar smiled to himself as they continued through the forest.

***

By mid-afternoon the next day, they had emerged from the forest near Shes, which was ten miles away. Rygar was happy with the time they had made; they would arrive in Shes an hour early. Grace hummed softly to herself as they travelled along the road to town, and Rygar wondered why it was so quiet.

He scanned the surrounding fields and trees; not a single animal could be seen or heard.

They came closer to the town of Shes and the dwarf saw farms on either side of the road near Shes. Some farms were for crops and others for livestock, but he could still see no sign of animals.

Then he noticed something out of place.

Some of the paddocks were covered in large white sheets that moved in the light breeze. Rygar did not know what to make of it.

***

The hunters had seen the three wagons come out from the forest and move towards the town. They sent word to the other spiders that food was coming, but not to attack until they reached the town.

For half an hour, the hunters followed the three wagons unseen as they changed colours to blend in with their surroundings. The other spiders remained hidden alongside the road. They would only move once the wagons had passed, each of the spiders fighting the urge to attack and feed.

The spiders were cunning; they knew how to wait.

Passing another farm, Rygar noticed dark bulging shapes beneath the silken sheets covering the farms. This confused him until they came past the farmhouse on the road. Two bodies hung in silken cocoons.

Then Rygar flinched as his eyes widened. 'This cannot be,' he whispered. 'This is the work o' spiders, but how big could these spiders be?'

Rygar pulled his wagon to a stop and saw Grace smiling up at him. He quickly stood and turned around to look back at the other two wagons.

He gasped and paled seeing several large dark shapes scuttling away from the last wagon.

Rygar pulled out his axe and shield and called, 'Danger! Turn back as fast as you can!'

Grace screamed, causing the dwarf to turn as a hunter leapt over the horse onto the front of the wagon. Its fangs bounced off Rygar's shield as he fell back under the creature's weight. He turned to see Grace's eyes darken.

***

Ramulas stood at the end of the long table in the throne room with Pip and Shigar. They studied a hologram of a map of the valley Journey's End was in. They were discussing how the dryads were able to cross over into this other world.

Goosebumps covered Ramulas' arms as he looked up and smiled and tilted his head. 'Grace is trying to talk to me.'

His eyes widened in surprise before he was lifted off the ground and thrown back ten feet to slide across the floor. He lay there covering his ears with his hands, his face a mask of agony.

Pip ran over and knelt next to Ramulas. 'What happened?'

Ramulas' mouth opened and closed as he shook his head, but no words came out; then the throne room was filled with the sound of rushing wind. Shigar searched the room with wide eyes.

The magician's expression changed to horror. 'Beware, something is coming.'

A burst of bright light appeared twenty yards from them for a split second before vanishing, and in its place was Grace and Rygar sitting on the seat of the wagon with the front half of a giant spider.

Green fluids flowed from the dissected abdomen. Its fangs quivered as the creature's legs pulled it closer to Grace and the dwarf; its multiple dark eyes shone in the light. Pip jumped away from Ramulas and pumped her hands. Four throwing knives appeared in the eyes of the spider. It shuddered once before dying.

Pip shook her head, slowly pointing at the spider's body. 'What is this? I thought you two were supposed to be in Shes?'

11

The Shadows had been playing a dangerous game of cat-and-mouse over the last few days with the soldiers. After the Master of Shadows ordered the death of a soldier in retaliation for the hanging of a young boy, Aleesha had sent her army out to destroy all the Shadows.

Shops in the poor section had all been destroyed, numerous houses raided, and the dungeons were overcrowded; this had driven the moral in the city to an all-time low. Random people were being punished for the presumption of guilt, when in fact they had done nothing wrong and knew nothing of the Shadows.

The people of Keah were reminded of the time King Zachary had locked them down when searching for the escaped prisoner who they now knew as the Lord of Sanctuary. Queen Aleesha was worse than her father.

At least King Zachary knew when to stop before the people rebelled against him. Queen Aleesha did not care; she just wanted to punish as many as she could.

Lucas walked through the hallways of the castle to the queen's chambers. He was not happy with the way Aleesha had been conducting herself and how the people of Keah were being treated.

However, things had taken a dramatic turn—one of his soldiers had been killed. It did not matter that he had been cruel and sadistic; he was still a soldier. Two of the royal guard stood to attention by the doors of her chambers as he entered.

Lucas let out a long sigh as he entered, seeing two secret agents talking with Aleesha. She raised her head, giving him an annoyed expression.

'Yes? Can I help you?' she sneered.

Lucas bit back a retort as he walked over to Aleesha sitting on the throne, forcing a smile on his face. He stopped ten feet from her and gave a slight nod, and each agent took a step away from the queen.

Lucas smiled to himself and thought that he needed to find a way to guide Aleesha to being a proper queen to her people, then he sighed and spoke. 'This has gone on long enough, my queen. We need to stop this.'

Aleesha's sneer turned into an expression of rage as she stood and jabbed a finger at Lucas. 'This will come to an end when every thief in Keah has been caught and killed.'

The smile melted from Lucas' face when both agents stepped in and whispered in Aleesha's ear. The young queen smiled and stood with renewed power.

Lucas sighed. 'Many of the people you have punished have nothing to do with the Shadows. This is causing resentment towards you by your own people.'

Aleesha sneered and barked a bitter laugh. 'I do not care what the people think of me. I am their queen, and they are beneath me.'

Lucas recoiled as if slapped, and the two agents nodded and murmured their approval.

'Enough!' Lucas shouted, clapping his hands once loudly.

Aleesha and the two agents jumped as the doors of the chambers flew open and a dozen royal guards ran into the room.

Lucas nodded to the two agents. 'Take those two to the dungeons.'

The royal guard fanned out, blocking any escape by the agents, who frantically searched for a way out.

'You dare,' Aleesha said, stepping forward and shaking in rage.

Lucas pointed to Aleesha and shouted, 'Sit on your throne now.' Startled, Aleesha stepped back and sat down; then Lucas continued, in a softer tone, 'Please remain seated, my queen.'

Aleesha sat on the throne watching as her agents were taken away by four of the royal guard. Once they were gone, Lucas walked to within six feet of the throne.

'After one of my soldiers was murdered, the Shadows have completely vanished from the streets. The people you are punishing could not help you if they wanted to. Tell me, my queen, why you need to punish so many people.'

Aleesha glanced at the door the agents had been taken out of before turning back to Lucas with an expression of uncertainty. It was at that moment Lucas knew that the agents had been using Aleesha.

Lucas opened his arms, offering a warm smile. 'This is not the way to rule, my queen. When people refuse to listen to you, you then stop being a queen.'

She gripped the armrests of the throne and leaned forward. 'One of my soldiers was killed.'

Lucas shook his head and sighed. 'No, it was one of *my* soldiers. He hanged a young thief for stealing a loaf of bread.' Lucas shook his head. 'What were you thinking when you handed out a death sentence for theft?'

Aleesha looked at the door once more, which spoke volumes. 'A former thief killed my father.'

Lucas glanced to the heavens while opening his arms before slowly bringing his gaze back to Aleesha. 'The person who killed your father is in Sanctuary.'

As soon as he mentioned Sanctuary, a flicker of anger showed in her eyes. 'The people of Sanctuary have defied the laws of our land. I want the Lord of Sanctuary and all his people punished.'

Lucas shook his head, rubbing his temples with the palms of his hands while taking slow breaths. He dropped his hands and spoke. 'We have marched on Sanctuary twice—the last time with the Legion and Symiaks—and twice we have been defeated. The Lord of Sanctuary controls dragons and could have killed all of us, but chose to show us mercy. Next time, no-one will return.'

Aleesha opened her mouth to protest, and he shook his head. 'My queen, another fight will come to your door if it is not stopped. The people of Keah are close to revolting against my soldiers, and there will be many deaths. My soldiers have just returned from a second defeat and do not need this. How many soldiers will fight against those they swore to protect?'

Aleesha's expression of defiance was slowly melting away.

'We need to repair the damage that has been caused,' Lucas continued. 'People from the dungeon need to be released and their damaged property repaired with money from the royal chest.'

Aleesha leaned forward and opened her mouth to speak, but Lucas held up his hand. 'Their property was damaged on your orders, and innocent people were punished for things they did not do. You must atone for this or lose the city of Keah.'

'But what of the Shadows?' she asked. 'They must be punished for their crimes.'

Lucas sighed. 'They will, but they will be punished fairly, as when your father ruled.' Aleesha winced, and he continued, 'Your way has turned the people against you. Some of them secretly hope the Shadows throw you from your throne.'

Aleesha's eyes widened in anger. 'Then punish them.'

Lucas slowly shook his head, wishing Shigar were still there to help him reason with the queen. He could not understand why the magician had left Keah.

***

Grace and Rygar jumped from the driver's seat of the wagon in opposite directions. The legs of the giant spider still twitched as the pair backed away, scratching at the floor. Rygar still held his axe and shield, never taking his eyes of the creature.

Grace was on the verge of crying as tears filled her eyes. She scanned the throne room until she saw Ramulas kneeling on the floor, cradling his head. She ran over to him and embraced her father tightly.

Shigar snapped out his shock and hurried over to Rygar while waving patterns in the air, causing streams of energy to float down on the spider's body and pinning it to the ground. 'Good dwarf, tell what has happened.'

Rygar slowly shook his head pointing to the creatures just yards away. 'The town of Shes is gone. I still dunno how she did it, but little Grace saved us.' The dwarf shuddered, took a short breath, and continued. 'Farms and fields outside of the town are covered in silk. Livestock and people are wrapped up in cocoons, an' there are so many the size o' this one,' he finished, nodding to the spider.

Shigar took a step back, holding his chest, while Pip stepped forward. 'Shes cannot be gone. Are you sure there are more like this? And did you see the town?' she asked.

Rygar nodded. 'I was a mile from town and could see that the whole town was covered in silk, an' there were beasts everywhere crawling around.'

A moan of pain brought everyone's attention to Ramulas who slowly stood and took a few slow steps forward while holding Grace's hand. He stood, still murmuring a magical phrase, before his body was covered in a purple nimbus.

After a moment, the light subsided, and Remulas' strength returned; he smiled down at Grace. 'You are getting stronger, little one.'

She grinned sheepishly at her father. 'I'm sorry, Da.'

Ramulas shook his head. 'Do not be sorry, little one. You saved Rygar from that giant spider.'

Grace puffed out her chest, smiling proudly at the dwarf.

'Now, little one, we need to find out more about this giant spider. I need you to watch over Kate, Makayla, and Tao. Make sure they stay away from the throne room.'

As Grace rushed through the door, Ramulas turned to the dwarf with a serious expression. 'Tell me everything.'

The dwarf went into detail about their travel through the forest near Shes until when they were attacked.

When he was finished, Ramulas asked one question. 'How many of these giant spiders do you think are out there?'

Rygar held out his hands. 'By what me own eyes have seen with the amount of silk everywhere, there'd be hundreds o' the beasts.'

Ramulas turned to Shigar and Pip. 'We need a council of war. Find Owain, Iguchi, and the druids; we need to warn the people.'

They nodded and left Ramulas alone with his thoughts. He waved his hands as he walked forward, and the creature's body began to glow and show him what it really was.

His mouth dropped as he realised what these spiders really were.

They had come from a cold, dark world where they had been feeding off one another for years. Their queen had been searching for a place for her children to feed, and now they were in Shes with plenty of food for the spiders. They would make this land their new home.

He thought fighting the Symiaks, kingdom army, and the Legion was hard; that would be nothing compared to many these giant spiders. Rygar had said there were hundreds, and he saw that some were different than the one before him. The giant spider had one thing in its nature, and that was to kill and feed.

Sanctuary would be able to fight a few hundred, but if the dwarf was mistaken and there were thousands, they would be in a lot of trouble. The leg and front half of its body was thick and stronger than hardened leather. It reminded Ramulas of the crabs that scaled the wall when the Legion had attacked them. From what Rygar had told him and what he had seen in the paintings, the giant spiders were very agile; that, combined with the thickness of their outer shell, would make it hard for them to be killed.

Ramulas needed to find out if all the people in Shes had been killed. If any lived, they would need help. Then Ramulas remembered the pigeon he had found from Shes; something large and dark had attacked its aviary. He would speak about Shes at the council of war.

Ramulas just hoped the dwarf was wrong about the number of giant spiders. If a few hundred came to Sanctuary, they would be in trouble.

***

Lucas woke to a world of pain and confusion. He could not move or use his limbs; then it occurred to him he was sitting upright tied to a chair and his head was covered in some dark material. The bonds were tight and threatened to cut the supply of blood to his hands and feet.

Lucas fought back the almost overwhelming urge to panic and focused on what he knew. With a few calming breaths, the captain assessed his body. He had suffered a beating; his jaw hurt when it moved. His whole face felt swollen, and his chest hurt every time he breathed.

Try as hard as he might, Lucas could not remember the beating and who dealt it. The last thing he could recall was explaining to Aleesha that she had done was wrong. The prisoners had been released from the dungeon, and plans were made to repair the damaged stores.

The only people in the dungeon were the handful of agents who had used Alicia as a pawn to gain power. The captain knew they were not happy and would have the people sympathetic to their cause, but he did not think they would be so foolish as to attack him.

Lucas heard a foot scrape the ground to his right, and he turned his head to toward the noise.

'This one is awake,' a deep, unfamiliar voice said. 'Send word.'

He heard a chair scrape along the floor, followed by a door opening and closing. The captain could hear someone slowly pace back and forth in front of him.

'Where am I?' the captain croaked through his dry throat.

Lucas was answered by a brutal blow to the stomach. The air was forced from his lungs as the chair tipped back. A second later, the captain's head hit the floor and stars filled his eyes. He gasped as a pair of rough hands gripped his shoulders and brought the chair upright once more.

'Only talk when you are told,' the voice said. 'Talking again will be bad for you.'

He gave a short nod to say that he understood. Lucas waited while he sat and listened. Two thoughts came to mind—the first was that if his captors wanted to kill him, he would already be dead; secondly, he would soon find out who gave him the beating and why.

***

The measurement of time was foreign to Lucas. He could not tell how long he had been waiting. Anxiety began to creep into his thoughts. He could hear soft sounds from different parts of the room. By this stage, he was not sure if they were real or if his mind was playing tricks on him.

Then the material was pulled from his head. Lucas blinked a few times, adjusting to the sudden brightness, and a soft moan escaped his lips as the piercing light seem to send daggers deep into his brain.

A moment later, Lucas' eyes had adjusted to the light. The first thing he saw was a large man in a black silk shirt. He was tanned with white spiky hair. In his massive right hand he held the dark material that had covered Lucas's head.

The large man stood at ease, but Lucas could see underlying power and authority in his eyes. He was in a small room bare of any furniture except for a few chairs. Four large men in vests stood near the rear wall, which could only mean the large man in front of him was the Master of Shadows.

The Master of Shadows said in a soft voice, 'The Shadows are being hunted like stray dogs to be put down. A lot of these are not yet adults, and I look upon them as my children; why do you wish harm upon my children?'

'A soldier was hanged on the gallows—'

A backhand swipe sent Lucas across the room until he slid into a wall. Before he could recover, the Master of Shadows had one of his huge hands around the captain's neck; he lifted Lucas off the floor as if he weighed no more than a kitten.

With his arms and legs still tied to the chair, he was helpless. He could not fight back. The Master of Shadows produced a short sword, and Lucas prepared himself for the killing blow.

The short sword swept through the air, cutting away at the ropes. The chair fell to the ground as the circulation return to Lucas' outer limbs. Small explosions of pains travelled to his hands and feet as the Master dropped him to the floor.

'The soldier you mourn killed a young boy for stealing a loaf of bread,' the Master said in a calm voice. 'The people of this city are very unhappy with the new laws. The laws are too harsh and need to be changed. We can do this the hard way, or the easy way; the choice is yours.'

Lucas turned to the Master. 'What?'

The Master smiled without humour. 'The hard way will see you tied to an anchor and thrown into the harbour.'

Lucas knew he was in a lot of trouble.

***

The hunters and weavers were shocked when Grace teleported herself and the dwarf away; however, they recovered quickly, attacking the other two wagon drivers and their horses. When the food was wrapped in silk cocoons, it was carried back to the town of Shes.

Word would be passed to the queen that one of her children had been killed with magic, and this was the first time they had encountered magic on this world. The queen was cunning; she would know of a way to deal with the magic user.

Two groups came into the town of Shes from different directions; the first from the plains to the south, where three hundred came with the only survivor from the Khilli encounter. The hunter had told the group of the warriors' fearlessness in battle and how they were stronger than those of Shes. The surviving hunter left after seeing more warriors coming to where the battle took place.

The second group joined the first. They needed to inform the queen. She would know what to do.

***

The surviving hunter from the Khilli battle and small group of spiders that witnessed Grace's magic entered the portal. They would bring news of the resistance and gifts wrapped in cocoons.

The spider queen waited for them in the cave, which in some ways reminded her of their dark dying world. They communicated what had transpired to the south and east of Shes; the other towns would not fall as easily as this one.

Her response was instantaneous. With a thought, ten thousand spiders were ordered to come through to Shes. The queen wanted to see if the people of this new world would attack the spiders in Shes. If the people did not come within a few days, she would send her children to the south and east to feast.

After the ten thousand began their march east and south, the queen would send tens of thousands into this new world. Her children would feast like never before.

12

Ramulas stood next to the body of the giant spider with Iguchi and the Fallen Angels, the druids, Eady, Shigar, Pip, Rygar, and Owain, who constantly clicked his tongue.

The Lord of Sanctuary saw that every person wore a grim expression watching the body of the creature. Ramulas had told everyone what had happened outside of Shes.

'The question we need to ask ourselves, is what do we do now?' Ramulas said. 'Do we wait here in Sanctuary or travel down to Shes and see for ourselves?'

Rygar snorted. 'Bah! We cannot go there so soon after what happened. People of the kingdom will see the army of Sanctuary an' think we're startin' another fight.'

Shigar nodded. 'My friend, after beating the kingdom soldiers twice, we do not know how the people will see us.'

'But we need to help the people of Shes,' Ramulas said.

Shigar opened his arms. 'Most people are unable to think for themselves. They wait for someone in authority to tell them what to think.'

Ramulas shook his head and sighed, frustration visible in his features. 'But we have been trading with the towns of Turtha, Bremnon, and Shes.'

Rygar chuckled. 'Meself is thinkin that they are happy to trade because we pay double the cost an' only deal with the shady types.'

Ramulas shook his head. 'I cannot just wait for the spiders to come to Sanctuary.' He turned to Eady. 'We need the forests near Shes watched. If the spiders come through, we need to know and prepare.'

The dryad nodded. 'I will pass word, and we will watch.'

Ramulas turned to the remaining people. 'We need to show the people of Sanctuary this creature, so they know what might be coming. Seeing this will help them understand what we might face.'

'What is this strange creature?' Rain asked, walking into the throne room with Joshua.

Everyone in the throne room watched as the pair walked over and examined the severed body.

'We thought something was happening when the Fallen Angels and a dryad came into the castle,' Rain said as he ran a hand along one of the spider's legs. 'We thought we would invite ourselves to the fun.'

Rain turned and smiled at Ramulas, raising an eyebrow. 'You were going to tell us about this?'

Ramulas smiled apologetically. 'This situation is strange to us, and you were going to be called. I am trying to work out things as I go.'

'Nice fangs,' Joshua said as he broke one of them off with an audible snap to examine it closer.' Does anyone know where this came from?'

Ramulas sighed and told them about Shes and everything he knew about the giant spiders and Shes.

When he was finished, the duo smiled. 'This looks like a bit of fun,' Rain said. 'You will need people like us. Joshua and the elementals have hardened skin, which would protect them from the fangs.'

Ramulas' eyes widened. 'The statues of the fallen could help in the fight as well, if they could leave Sanctuary. I will send them to Shes to see if there are any survivors.' Then Ramulas smiled. 'The dragons—I could ask the dragons to help us with the giant spiders.'

There was much to do. Ramulas organised with the council for the people of Sanctuary to look at the spider's body. He needed to speak with the dragons.

***

Lucas sat on a hard wooden chair while a plain-looking woman leaned over him. His head was tilted back as she dabbed his face with a wet cloth. He tried not to wince every time alcohol seeped into his wounds, and the strong smell filled the small space.

'Oh, you are a clumsy boy,' she said, pouring more wine onto the cloth. 'You need to be more careful, or you will fall from your horse again.'

The Master of Shadows and Lucas had discussed the story of where his injuries had come from, which was believable under any scrutiny. He had come to an agreement with the Master of Shadows, and they had formed an uneasy alliance.

Lucas would persuade Aleesha to change the new laws, bringing back her father's old laws.

The captain of the royal guard was not used to being told what to do; however, he saw the reasoning in what the Master of Shadows was saying. He had seen tensions rise in the city since the death of the young Shadow after stealing bread.

'There we go,' the woman said, stepping back and admiring her work. 'You're as good as new.'

As she stepped away, the Master of Shadows came into view. He stood in front of Lucas and smiled. 'The Shadows will be a part of the city streets once more. They will return to doing what they do best, and your soldiers will try their best to catch them. The people of Keah will rejoice at their lives returning to normal. The young queen wanted change, as we all do, but change must come slowly. Change too quickly and even the most loyal will turn on you.'

Lucas stood. 'What now?'

'You will return to the castle and wait outside the queen's chambers.'

Lucas cocked his head. 'What do you mean?'

The Master smiled. 'It is two hours until dawn. The Shadows have paid a visit to your young queen.' The Master smiled, holding up a hand as he saw anger on Lucas' face. 'I assure you she has not been harmed in any way. In fact, I doubt she knew anyone was in her chambers. We just wanted to send a message that the Shadows can walk through walls and touch anyone.'

The captain of the royal guard scanned the room once before facing the Master of Shadows. 'I know what you look like; after leaving here, I will know how to find you. I can bring enough soldiers to arrest everyone here.'

The Master sighed and nodded. 'And why do you think the Shadows have lasted so long? I am not the Master by being foolish. You have never seen me before, and you will never see me again if I do not want you to.'

Lucas opened his mouth to answer when a sack was thrown over his head.

The Master spoke. 'My men will lead you to the castle. They have instructions to kill you if you attempt to escape. If you come searching for us, I will be the last thing you see before you die.'

***

For what seemed like hours, Lucas was led through the streets, listening to the people and noises around him. Strong but gentle hands guided him around in circles until the sack was roughly pulled from his head. After blinking a few times, Lucas saw that he was in front of the castle, and the morning sun was rising.

He turned to see two large enforcers, each holding a dagger, and they gestured for him to go into the castle.

Lucas sighed and knew that his priority lay with Aleesha. He ran past the startled guards at the gate and into the castle. He waved away questions as he made his way through the halls. People moved away after seeing the determined expression on his face.

Dawn was just breaking as he entered the queen's chambers. Two of the royal guard lay by the door snoring loudly. Lucas kicked one of them in the leg, rousing the man before rushing into the room.

'My queen,' he called across the dim room.

Lucas focused on the large four-post bed twenty yards from him. Something moved under the covers, and then Aleesha screamed in alarm and began to struggle as Lucas ran to her side.

With a few quick strides, he reached her bed, pulled off the covers, and stepped back with wide eyes. Aleesha's hands and feet were tied to the bed posts.

'Get them off me!' she screamed as she struggled against the bonds.

Lucas reached for the sword by his side that was no longer there then ran out into the hall to retrieve a sword from one of guards outside the door. He quickly returned and cut the bonds.

Aleesha rubbed her wrists, attempting to appear annoyed. 'Who would do this to me? How did they get past the guards?'

At that moment she saw the groggy guards trying to stand by the door, holding the frame to support them.

'I'll have those two whipped,' she screamed, pointing a finger at them.

Lucas blocked her view. 'My queen, we need to talk.'

She shook her head. 'I could have been killed. Those two must be punished.'

Lucas shook his head. 'You were in no danger. Someone wanted to send a message. This is why I need to talk to you.'

Her eyes widened as she faced him. 'Do you know who did this? Then her mouth fell open when she saw his face. 'What happened to you?'

'I fell from my horse.'

'What horse can do this much damage?'

Lucas sighed. 'The same horse that tied you to your bed.'

A flicker of fear showed in her eyes, and Lucas explained why the new laws against the Shadows and the people needed to change.

***

Ramulas had spent the past two days going into the valley in search of the dragons. He could feel their presence, but they would not answer his calls. He could not understand why they did not respond. Ramulas wanted to fly east to where he knew they were; however, he did not have enough magic to make it there and back.

He stood before the statues of the fallen. Using Oriel's magical power, he could see the souls of the fallen lying dormant inside the statues. He remembered the statues coming to life when the Legion attacked the women and children.

He had tried to wake the statues several times without success and was losing faith that the dragons and statues would answer him. Ramulas needed some certainty in how he was going to deal with the giant spiders.

'Ramulas,' Pip called. Ramulas turned to see her on the balcony of the throne room. 'Come quick; K'ayden has returned.'

Ramulas took a step back. 'What?'

Pip nodded. 'Giant spiders have attacked the Khilli.'

Ramulas looked down at his arms to see his skin covered in goosebumps. He quickly made his way into the castle, thinking about the Khilli. Their homeland was sixty miles from the town of Shes and halfway between Turtha and Covedon. He needed to find out what he could from K'ayden.

He did not expect them to have travelled so far.

***

Everyone in Sanctuary was talking about the giant spiders and what it might mean for them after seeing the creature in the throne room. They did not need to be told that more training was coming their way; they needed to do whatever it took to protect themselves.

Ramulas reached the throne room, and he had heard people talking about the spiders in the Khilli homeland. A few had heard Pip calling down to Ramulas, and the word had spread like wildfire.

He walked in to find K'ayden studying the half body of the spider. He held a severed leg of one of the spiders that had attacked his people. Then Ramulas noticed Shigar, Pip, and the druids in the room as well. The body of the half spider still glowed a soft white after Shigar had cast a spell on it to hold it still and preserve it.

Ramulas walked over to K'ayden as the warrior looked up. 'My friend, I am sorry that bad news has brought you back here to us. Please, tell me what happened.'

K'ayden dropped the spider's leg and told of his people returning to their homeland and going on their first hunt.

Ramulas' expression saddened as K'ayden spoke about the warriors dying during the battle, then K'ayden explained that he came to Sanctuary seeking help; he was worried for the women and children if more of the spiders found their village. He could not go to Turtha or Covedon for help after everything that had happened. The Khilli people had just been freed after Sanctuary defeated the kingdom army twice.

'Where are your people?' Ramulas asked.

K'ayden shrugged. 'Still at our homeland. It was quicker for me to come alone for help.'

'What?' Ramulas and Pip said simultaneously.

K'ayden seemed confused at their response.

Ramulas held up his hand. 'How many spiders did your warriors kill?'

'Nineteen,' the Khilli replied.

Ramulas pointed to the half body of the spider on the floor. 'This one attacked Grace and Rygar outside of Shes. Luckily, Grace's magic saved them. From what Rygar could see with the silk, there could be hundreds of them in that town. He also saw some were following the wagons as they came into town, and it seemed like they were intelligent.'

Pip cocked her head. 'If there are spiders in Shes and the Khilli homeland…'

'This means that the spiders are moving,' Ramulas finished for her.

Ramulas opened his hands and turned to the large table. A glowing map of the kingdom appeared on the wooden surface. Everyone gathered around to take a closer look. Ramulas ran his finger from Sanctuary to the town of Shes, tapping his finger just outside of the town.

'This is where Grace and Rygar were attacked,' he said before running his finger and leaving a trail to the Khilli homeland, 'and here is where they attacked the Khilli. Where could they go now?'

Pip leaned over, tapping three places on the map. Ramulas gasped and took a step back. Pip had tapped the towns of Turtha, Covedon, and Rylek.

'Where are the Fallen Angels?' Ramulas asked. 'We need them to run and warn the Khilli of the danger. I have used my magic to try to contact the dragons without any luck, otherwise I could fly there.'

Pip shrugged. 'It will be too late. It could be too late already. It took K'ayden two days to ride here; who knows what has happened?'

Pip's lack of emotion shocked Ramulas, however, he knew she was right; it had been too long, and any help may come too late.

K'ayden walked over to Ramulas and patted him on the shoulder. 'Do not worry, my friend. The spiders surprised us once, but we are ready, and they will have a fight on their hands.'

'What will your people do if the spiders attack them again?' Pip asked.

'Pip!' Ramulas exclaimed. 'You should not say such things.'

K'ayden smiled. 'Do not worry. My people will fight. The spiders were wary last time they saw us fight.'

Then Ramulas' eyes widened. 'I know who can help us.'

'Who?' Shigar asked.

'I will ask the mayors of Turtha and Covedon to help us. They will want to help after seeing what we have here.'

Pip shook her head. 'It will take you too long to get there, and I do not think they will welcome you with open arms. You could ask the dryads to help get you closer.'

Ramulas shook his head. 'I have a better idea, but does anyone know where Iguchi has taken the Fallen Angels?'

Shigar stepped forward, a worried expression forming on his face. 'Iguchi has taken them to the outskirts of Shes. He wishes to study the spiders.'

'Damn,' Ramulas swore. 'I cannot worry about the Angels *and* the Khilli people. Things are going too quick for me.'

Pip spoke. 'What will you do?'

Ramulas pointed to the spider's body. 'I will send an astral image of myself and our new friend to the mayor of Turtha.'

Ramulas took a few slow breaths, channelling Oriel's magical power, before waving his hands in front of him, leaving faint strands of purple energy hanging in the air. Then he and the body of the giant spider began to glow.

***

Iguchi ran alongside Miles as they led the Fallen Angels through the forest. They had been travelling with minimal rest for two days and one night; the five newest recruits had kept up for as long as they could, but Iguchi had left them the day before, telling them to make camp and wait until the Fallen Angels returned.

Iguchi nodded to himself. They had made good time and would reach the edge of the forest within the hour. He glanced at his Angels, seeing that they were close to exhaustion, but he knew they could be pushed for few more hours before rest.

The trees began to thin as they reached the outer edges of the forest. Iguchi could feel his Fallen Angels morale lifting, then he saw the sunlight sparkle from a line running across the ground between two trees. It was the combination of the sun's position and Iguchi constantly scanning the forest that helped him see it.

Instantly, he knew what it was; his Fallen Angels were in grave danger.

Iguchi stopped and put an arm out to stop Miles from stepping on the shimmering line on the ground. Miles was unable to stop in time and was knocked to the ground after running into Iguchi's arm. The other Fallen Angels stopped, thinking this was another of Iguchi's training exercises.

As Miles stood, Iguchi could see the shining thread stuck to his foot. 'Do not move. We are all in danger.'

Miles opened his mouth to answer when he saw movement from above Iguchi in the trees. A gladiator spider dropped from the foliage directly above Iguchi. It held a web netting in its four front legs, stretching it as it came closer.

Miles' eyes widened as he pointed above Iguchi. 'Look out!'

The giant spider dropped down; Iguchi was caught in its net and was pulled back up into the treetops. Iguchi struggled in the net, which only entangled him more, restricting his movements. Then the hunters, who had remained hidden around the Fallen Angels on the tree trunks and on the ground, came out of their hiding places and attacked.

The forest filled with hissing, clicking, and the Fallen Angels shouting.

***

Ramulas focused and found himself floating above Sanctuary. He lifted himself until he was a mile above the town. Using Oriel's magical ability, he saw shafts of white light shooting into the sky, each one representing a town of the kingdom. He turned towards the town of Turtha.

Da, why are you glowing? Grace communicated with him.

Ramulas smiled. *Because I am using magic. I need to talk to someone. What are you doing?*

He could feel her excitement. *I am with Emily. Her mother said we could play together.*

Ramulas nodded. *Play with her until I return, and then Shigar can teach you more magic.*

He focused and began moving towards Turtha. Ramulas wondered how he would be received by the mayor, and if the town would be willing to help the Khilli people. This was a time that Sanctuary would need to fight alongside the towns of Covedon and Turtha if they were to survive. He just hoped they would look past recent events.

***

Ramulas came to a stop at Turtha's gate. No-one was able to see him as he floated through the town. He saw the mayor with his red-crested vest walking the streets and followed him into his chambers. As he followed the mayor, Ramulas thought of him more as a soldier than mayor, given the way he held himself around people. He waited for the mayor to sit before willing himself to be visible. The mayor jumped out of his seat, pulling his sword from his hip in one swift movement.

Ramulas smiled and held out both of his hands. 'Hello. I mean you no harm.'

'How did you get in here, traitor?' the mayor said as he shuffled around his desk and delivered a backhanded swipe through Ramulas' image, wearing a mask of rage.

Ramulas stood calmly as the mayor stepped back after the sword passed through the image. The mayor shook his head. 'You're a ghost.'

Ramulas shook his head. 'Not a ghost. I am using magic to send my image to you.'

The mayor snarled. 'You are the enemy of the kingdom and must be killed on sight. One of your people killed the king. The queen wants everyone in Sanctuary to suffer for this.'

Ramulas sighed and slowly shook his head. 'It is a long story about why the people of Sanctuary came to be there and why we resisted the king's rule, and the person who killed the king acted out of vengeance for the death of her parents, who were unjustly sent to Gullytown.'

The mayor shook with rage and pointed his sword at Ramulas. 'The king was a fine man and would never do anything unjust.'

Ramulas shrugged. 'I will let Pip talk to you another time about why she killed the king, but we face a greater danger than the Legion.'

The mayor wore a confused expression. 'The Legion was only a danger to the people of Sanctuary. They came to help king Zachary.'

A bitter laugh escaped Ramulas. 'The Legion had come for Oriel, who was under our protection. She fled from their world in fear of her life. They were after her magical powers, and if they had have got them, the Legion would have killed and enslaved everyone in the kingdom.'

Ramulas waved his hands through the air, and an image of the Legion appeared in front of the mayor. They were in the town of Bremnon. Smoke rose in the air as buildings burned and lines of people in chains slowly walked through the streets with Legion soldiers walking alongside them.

The mayor's jaw dropped. 'This cannot be true. What is this?'

Ramulas sighed and gave the mayor a sad smile. 'This is what I was shown by Oriel; this would have happened if we did not stop the Legion. At the time I was shown this, I did not want to believe it either. Oriel told me that I was the only one to stop the Legion. I was just a simple farmer and a father.'

The mayor looked at Ramulas. 'Why did Oriel say that you were the only one to stop the Legion?'

'Did you meet Remus when the Legion was here?' Ramulas asked.

The mayor nodded before his eyes widened in shock. 'You look just like him, except for the scar on your face.'

Ramulas nodded. 'Remus is my twin. I came from the same world many years ago and could not recall any of my memories. When Oriel first came to me, I told her that I did not want to train an army to fight the Legion, I just wanted to be a farmer, but she told me that if I did not, I would lose all that I hold dear.'

The mayor's expression softened as he stroked his chin. 'Can you really control dragons? I thought they were just myth until the king returned from his first battle and spoke of them.'

Ramulas quickly shook his head, 'I do not control them, I simply talk to them.'

'Are they the mythical dragons from Shangri-La?'

Ramulas nodded. 'Yes, that is where I met them.'

Ramulas inwardly sighed. The conversation was not going as he planned. 'I have come to warn you of danger.'

'What danger?'

Ramulas waved his hands through the air in patterns. The image of the Legion vanished, replaced with the image of the giant spider, which appeared a few feet from the mayor. He screamed and jumped back while swinging his sword frantically at the image.

'What in the name of the gods is that?'

'This is an image of a creature killed outside of the town of Shes,' Ramulas said, walking over to the creature. 'There are hundreds more, perhaps even thousands. The town of Shes has fallen, and the surrounding farms have as well.'

The mayor nodded slowly. 'Two pigeons arrived from Shes a few days ago without messages. Word from Covedon says they have pigeons as well. How many people from Shes have survived?'

Ramulas shook his head. 'We do not think any have survived.'

The mayor paled, and Ramulas continued. 'There is more. You know of the Khilli people coming to Sanctuary?'

The mayor nodded. 'The king told me after his first defeat.'

'They have returned to their homeland in between here and Covedon. They were attacked by the giant spiders two days ago. We think that the spiders are moving away from Shes. Your town and Covedon are in danger. We need to work together and ask the city of Keah for help.'

The mayor hesitated, unsure what he should do, before turning to Ramulas. 'Why didn't you come here in person? How do I know this is not some trick?'

Ramulas fought back the growing frustration and took a deep breath. 'What? After all I have shown you? If we do not act now, it will be too late.'

The mayor smiled at Ramulas. His years in the kingdom army had taught him many things. Before him he saw a man who was frustrated and did not know what to do. This was not some trick.

'I will help you, but I do not know about Covedon and Keah.'

'I will talk to the mayor of Covedon.'

'I do not think the queen will listen to you, but I will send her a message.'

Ramulas nodded. 'After you send her a message, I will bring you with me to Covedon to convince that mayor to send a message as well. The more who plead for help the better.'

The mayor nodded. 'I will tell of the spiders coming up from Shes into the Khilli homeland, but I do not think the queen will be happy. The Khilli people served the royal family for generations, and now they have left.'

A sad smile spread on Ramulas' face. 'There is more to the Khilli story. Hopefully soon you will know their story and support them being free.'

Ramulas told the mayor of when he was imprisoned in the tombs and learned the Khilli story of how they were tricked and enslaved. After K'ayden helped him, Ramulas had sworn to help his people if he could. By the time he had finished, the mayor wore an expression of disbelief.

'This cannot be true; the king would never do such a thing.'

Ramulas shrugged. 'You can judge for yourself when you meet the Khilli.'

'Why would I want to meet the Khilli? Orders are to kill or bring any Khilli back to the castle to be tried for treason by the queen.'

Ramulas' expression grew stern. 'There are women, children, and families out there with those spiders. Your job is to protect all families of the kingdom.'

Ramulas inwardly smiled as he saw that he had hit the mayor's weak spot.

The mayor nodded. 'I will help, but first we send messages.'

13

Grace took Emily by the hand and led her out of the throne room. 'We have to find Shigar. Da said I could learn more magic.'

After a few minutes of walking through the castle with Fenris trailing behind them, they had come no closer to finding the magician.

Grace stopped, her eyes becoming dark, and ancient energies crackled around her. Then she smiled, knowing where Shigar could be found. Her eyes returned to normal, and the energy around her faded. 'Come with me, Emily. I know where he is.'

As the energies crackled around Grace, fragments of memories came to Emily about holding the same power. As soon as these came to her, they vanished, and she wondered what they meant.

The two girls and Fenris found themselves in the chamber where Nathaniel's weapons were found. Shigar stood with Edwin and the two earth elementals. The magician held open a large leather book in his hands while murmuring a spell. An image of the weapons appeared in front of the dwarf.

'Did you see that, Emily?' Grace said with excitement. 'I can do magic like that.'

Shigar spun around and saw the two girls. Edwin and the elementals were in shock; no-one had heard them come into the cavern.

Shigar smiled. 'Hello. What are you two doing in here?'

Grace smiled proudly. 'Da said that you can teach me more magic. I want to show Emily.'

The magician looked at both girls, thinking how strange it was for Grace to have Emily's magical power and Emily simply be a normal girl from another world.

'Where is your da now?' he asked.

'He is flying.'

Shigar nodded, knowing Ramulas had sent his astral image to the mayor of Turtha. 'I will teach you magic only after your father returns, and I don't think it would be safe for you to learn with Emily around.'

Grace pouted and crossed her arms, and then Royce stepped towards Grace. 'I have not seen your magic. I will watch while Shigar teaches you.'

Emily stepped back, unsure of the walking statue. Grace smiled at her friend. 'Don't worry, they won't hurt you. Look—I'll show you.'

Energies crackled around Grace as her eyes turned dark. Shigar's eyes widened. 'Grace, no!'

But it was too late. Grace waved her hands in front of her while speaking in an ancient tongue. White mist flowed from her hands into the floor three feet in front of her, which glowed and rippled like the surface of a lake. The two elementals glanced at each other before stepping back.

They could not believe what the mountain was telling them.

Something rose out of the glowing cavern floor; a molten form began to take shape before their eyes. Shigar and Edwin gasped in shock.

Before them was a glowing statue of Grace. The statue changed from red to grey as it quickly cooled, then something happened that caused Shigar to gasp and hold his chest.

The statue opened its eyes, smiled, and walked forward.

***

Miles ran two steps before jumping in the air towards Iguchi. He slashed one of the spider's front legs. The creature hissed and dropped Iguchi before pulling itself up into the trees.

He saw Iguchi hit the ground and saw the surrounding forest explode with movement as the giant spiders came out of their hiding places.

'Monsters behind you!' he shouted, holding out his sword and shield.

Miles winced, seeing that his warning had come too late. Ten of the hunters leapt from the trees, and the Angel's reactions were too slow. Then his eyes widened, seeing movement in the tree trunks as five dryads stepped out into the fray. They held out their fists, sending streams of darts at the spiders.

Half the darts had missed; however, green fluid exploded from the bodies of the spiders that were hit. These creatures hissed loudly and leapt away, leaving trails of blood behind.

This was a welcome distraction that forced the spiders to scuttle away. The Fallen Angels took full advantage of this, running towards the creatures and hacking away at them. Miles stood guard over Iguchi as he cut his way out of the sticky netting. By the time he was free, the spiders were cut to pieces. The Fallen Angels and Iguchi were covered in gore.

Iguchi rose in a fluid movement, picking himself free of the web. He scanned the surrounding forest and pointed to a fleeing shadow to his right. 'Quickly, my Angels, there is one more we must kill.'

The Fallen Angels followed Iguchi as he ran through the trees, chasing the hunter into the open fields. After two hundred yards, Iguchi held up his hand and the Fallen Angels stopped. The hunter ceased running and turned to face them from one hundred feet away.

The spider could have run much faster if it wanted to, but it needed to keep the humans close enough to follow. But Iguchi had seen the unnatural mounds in the soil ahead. He unshouldered his bow and let fly with an arrow. He watched it sail through the air and hit one of the mounds. A hunter scrambled out of the earth with the arrow in its front leg. Five other spiders emerged as well.

The Fallen Angels gasped as the six spiders ran one hundred yards away before stopping and turning to face them. Iguchi watched the creatures, knowing they were intelligent. 'My Angels, run twenty paces to the spiders and stop.'

The spiders moved with the Fallen Angels, running from them and stopping when they stopped, and again the spiders sat and watched the Fallen Angels.

'Quickly, my Angels—run for the trees. These creatures are cunning. They wish to lead us into a trap,' Iguchi said.

Iguchi stood watching the spiders for a few moments before racing after the Fallen Angels into the cover of the trees. He stopped and turned to find the spiders had not moved. Eady walked over to him with five other dryads.

Iguchi said, 'I thank you for your help. We must now return to Sanctuary.'

***

Grace squealed in delight, clapping her hands as her statue smiled and walked forward. Emily took a step back with a worried expression.

Grace smiled at her friend. 'Don't be scared. It will not hurt you. I will show you.'

Grace leaned into Emily until their foreheads touched and dark energies flowed between the two girls. More memories of Emily holding magical abilities flooded through her, as well as memories of when she lived in Sanctuary. Shigar and Edwin gasped as Emily's head jolted back and she almost lost balance, but Grace reached out to hold her arms. Emily's head tilted up to the ceiling and her eyes were closed.

Then Emily opened her eyes and turned towards Shigar; the magician's mouth opened at the sight of both girls' eyes being filled with dark energy. Grace had given Emily some of her power.

Dark energies crackled around Emily as Grace clapped and laughed. Shigar and Edwin felt the hairs on their arms rise. Emily waved her hands through the air and the same area of the cavern floor glowed red. The magician panicked when another shape rose out of the ground.

Shigar's heart almost burst from his chest as he watched Grace help Emily pull the shape from the cavern floor. He opened his thick book and quickly flicked through the pages, saying, 'Girls, you stop that right now.'

Grace and Emily ignored him as a glowing form of Emily began to cool in front of them. Finally, Shigar found the spell he was looking for and cast it. The two statues walked into one another, melding into one. The floor below the statues glowed as they sank down. With the sound of rushing air, the dark energies around the two girls vanished, leaving them disappointed.

'That's not fair,' Grace said before losing consciousness.

***

Ramulas finished speaking with the mayors of Turtha and Covedon. They had both sent messages to the queen telling her of the giant spiders and what they had done to the town of Shes, asking for her help.

Ramulas sent his astral image flying across the plains towards the Khilli homeland, and he soon came to the Khilli village and saw that everyone was safe. He then flew to the place where K'ayden said they had battled the giant spiders; he saw the dead spiders but no other danger nearby. He made his way back to Sanctuary, where he would tell K'ayden that his people were safe.

***

Ramulas flew over Sanctuary's Forest and saw a woman riding a black stallion towards Sanctuary. He was surprised to see her riding confidently, and he knew he had not seen her before.

He sent his image down to the tree tops and saw several dryads following the stranger, then he felt his magic waning and quickly returned to the throne room.

***

Ramulas opened his eyes in the throne room and was rewarded with waves of dizziness. He quickly steadied himself and saw that twelve druids had formed a tight circle around him. He felt gentle hands take his arms and guide him to the throne.

The room seemed to sway with every step as he fought back the urge to vomit. Once he sat on the throne, the head druid smiled at him. 'You were gone a long time. Your body and mind need to get used to this. Close your eyes and allow yourself to heal.'

Ramulas was too tired to argue and closed his eyes and focused only on his breathing. Slowly, the dizzy sensation left him. He felt his energy and magical powers returning.

A polite cough caused Ramulas to open his eyes. He saw Shigar standing with Grace and Emily, who both had their heads bowed.

Ramulas sighed. 'Tell me what happened.'

Shigar explained how he had been in the tunnel with the elementals and Edwin when Grace and Emily had come into the cavern and created life-sized statues of themselves after Grace gave Emily some of her powers.

Ramulas sighed while holding out his hands. 'Grace, I said that Shigar would teach you magic when I return. Your magic can hurt people if you are not careful. You need to listen to people.'

Grace appeared dejected as Ramulas talked to her. Then he turned to Shigar. 'What exactly happened to Emily?'

Emily raised her head to look at Ramulas, and his jaw dropped seeing the dark energies in her eyes. 'By the gods,' he whispered.

'How did Emily get her power back?' Pip said walking in the room with her emerald eyes blazing.

Ramulas shook his head as he turned to Pip. 'This Emily never had any magical powers.'

'Then how did this happen?' she asked.

Ramulas waved his hands through the air as he chanted. Soon Emily and Grace were covered in a fine glowing mist, and then Ramulas knew the answer.

He tilted his head at Grace. 'Grace gave some of her magical energy to Emily. Little one, you need to be careful. That could have hurt Emily.'

Grace had tears forming in her eyes, and Ramulas knew she was sorry; however, he needed a way for her to control her growing magical abilities.

Pip stepped forward. 'Does Emily know how to use her magic?'

Ramulas shook his head. 'No, she does not, and I cannot remove it either. What are we going to tell Joshua and Juliette?'

Ramulas sent the girls into Grace's chamber to play while he thought of something.

***

Tilly flew into the throne room through the balcony window and hovered in front of Ramulas. 'Someone comes through the forest on a horse. They will be at the gates soon.'

Ramulas smiled. 'Thank you, Tilly. I will go and meet them.'

He turned to Pip. 'Let's go meet this person.'

Grace came running into the throne room with her green eyes blazing. 'Where is Tilly?'

Ramulas laughed. 'After what happened today, I need you to stay in your room and think about what might have happened with Emily.'

Grace sighed while her body slumped, and Ramulas said, 'You have Makayla and Tao to play with ...'

The rest of the words were caught in his throat as Jacqueline walked out and put her hand on Grace's shoulder. 'I'll take her.'

He took a step forward with a hand reaching out, and Pip softly punched him in the back. 'We need to meet someone outside.'

He pointed to where Grace had just been. 'But Jacqueline was just there. Didn't you see her?'

Pip shook her head with a sad smile. 'There was no-one there, only Grace.'

He looked at Pip with a mix of desperation and hope. 'I saw her. Didn't you see her take Grace out of the throne room?'

She shook her head once more. 'I know that you saw her, but you are the only one because she is still inside your heart. She will always be there, just like my parents. Now we need to see who is coming to Sanctuary.'

Ramulas saw the briefest glimpse of Pip's vulnerable side before she led him out of the throne room.

*****

Ramulas and Pip met Owain on top of the wall and watched the clearing. He clicked his tongue a few times before smiling and walking over to greet them. 'Welcome. What brings the two of you up here?'

Ramulas pointed to the forest. 'Someone is riding a horse here and will arrive soon. We wanted to meet them.'

Ramulas and Pip watched the archers shoot at targets in the clearing below.

Pip's eyes glowed. 'I will see how far this person is.'

The leaves in the trees seemed to disappear for Pip. This was followed by the bracken and small bushes. She saw countless birds and animals going about their daily routine safely hidden in the foliage.

Pip's eyes followed the path leading away from Sanctuary until she found the woman on the horse a mile away.

Her eyes stopped glowing as she turned to Ramulas. 'She will be here soon.'

'Owain,' Ramulas said.

The blind archer nodded while calling out instructions; the archers stopped their practice and came up to the top of the wall while they waited.

The woman rode out of the forest as if she belonged in Sanctuary. She stopped her horse to gaze up at the archers on the wall and focused on Owain, Pip, and Ramulas, who stood in the middle of the wall.

Pip felt an involuntary shiver as the woman studied her. She could feel that this was no ordinary traveller. There was something dark about her—the way she casually brushed her long black hair away from her pale face and blue vest. She moved with the essence of a snake.

'Hello!' Ramulas called down. 'What brings you to Sanctuary?'

The woman smiled, guiding her horse closer to the wall. 'I have come searching for my father.'

Ramulas took a step back. 'Who is your father?'

'Iguchi,' she answered.

'What?' Ramulas and Pip said in disbelief.

The woman nodded. 'My father is Iguchi, and he sent for me.'

Ramulas quickly recovered from his shock and waved to her. 'Come through the gate. We will see you in the courtyard.'

Pip turned to Ramulas. 'Did you know Iguchi had a daughter? And when did he call for her?'

Ramulas shrugged.

***

The woman rode her horse into the courtyard and slowly turned her head, scanning her surroundings.

'Welcome to Sanctuary,' Ramulas said. 'Come into the castle. I will have someone bring your things and look after your horse.'

With a nod, the woman dismounted and landed with the agility of a cat in front of Pip. She smiled as the former thief studied the two swords on her hip. Ramulas led the way into the castle.

As they walked into the throne room, Ramulas said, 'We have known Iguchi for a while, and he has never told us that he had a daughter. I am Ramulas, and this is Pip. What is your name?'

The woman shrugged, and Pip noticed the corded muscles on her arms. 'My father is a man of mystery. My name is Berenice. Do you know where my father is?'

'He is out training the Fallen Angels, a small group of soldiers that have been helpful in our battles.'

As Berenice nodded, Ramulas asked, 'How did you come here? There is much danger to the west of here.'

'I travelled by ship to the city of Keah, then by horse through the kingdom to here. Father knows that I will not travel by ship if I can ride.'

'Why did your father call you here?' Pip asked.

'I have come to finish my training as a warrior to represent our clan. I will be the first warrior woman of our family.' She said proudly, 'Father comes from a long line of warriors whose skills have been passed down through the generations.'

Ramulas and Pip glanced at each other in disbelief.

'Iguchi never told us about this,' Ramulas said.

Berenice nodded. 'He is a man of many secrets,' she said, turning to Pip. 'You wear throwing knives; are you good with them? Are you fast?'

Pip smiled. 'That's why I wear them.'

Berenice nodded. 'Do you think you are able to draw one before I can take out one of my blades?'

Pip accepted the challenge with a tight nod. 'That would be easy.'

Berenice winked. 'Then we will move when Ramulas calls.'

Pip nodded while Ramulas appeared confused.

'Just wait a few seconds and then call,' Pip said.

Ramulas nodded and took a step back. Berenice smiled and folded her arms while Pip let her hands hang at her sides.

'Go!' Ramulas called.

Both moved quickly; however, by the time Pip had one of her knives halfway out of its sheath, Berenice had the blade of her sword resting on the side of the former thief's neck. Pip froze with eyes as wide as saucers.

Ramulas held his breath until Berenice stepped back and sheathed her weapon in the blink of an eye.

'You are very fast, but I am faster,' Berenice said.

'How did you do that? I did not see you move.'

Berenice shrugged. 'It is easy once you know how. I might teach you some day. Now you can show me to my quarters.'

'Your quarters?' Pip asked.

'Yes. I will be staying here for a while.'

Ramulas and pip looked at each other, unsure what to make of Berenice.

14

Aleesha waited as the agent came towards her throne where she was seated. He was one of the few that had been released from the dungeon after promising to conform with Lucas' new rule. He stopped ten feet from the young queen and bowed.

'My gracious queen, two messages have arrived from the towns of Turtha and Covedon.' He walked to her, handing over the slim silver tubes. As with king Zachary, this agent made sure he read all messages coming or going from the city.

Aleesha opened the tubes and read both messages. After a moment, a cruel smile spread on her face. 'These messages mean that my problem with the people of Sanctuary will be solved. I do not care for the town of Shes. These spiders have been sent to avenge my father. They will head for Sanctuary and kill everyone inside.'

She turned to the agent. 'Dear agent, does anyone else know of these messages?'

He gave a slight bow. 'No, my queen, only you have seen them.'

'Not even the captain of the guard?' she asked, tilting her head.

He shook his head. 'Only you, my queen.'

Elation flooded through Aleesha, knowing that Lucas would rush to help the towns of Turtha and Covedon, and therefore Sanctuary. Both mayors had said that they had spoken to the Lord of Sanctuary. They knew him to be the enemy of the kingdom and they had not arrested him; in her eyes, these towns had taken the side of Sanctuary over the kingdom.

She smiled at the agent. 'If the towns of Turtha and Covedon want to help Sanctuary, then let them face the spiders without our help. I will send a reply saying that the kingdom army will not help.'

The agent smiled, holding out a quill and paper.

***

The Master of Shadows smiled as old John delivered tribute. The word from the city street was that things were returning to the way they had been; the Shadows had been stealing, extorting, and sending whores out to work again.

Of course, there were the few rumblings of people who were not happy, but they were quickly silenced. Most of the people understood the balance of the way of life in Keah relied on the Shadows and the soldiers.

The game of cat-and-mouse was a daily thing in the city. The soldiers had their job, and so too did the Shadows. If thieves were caught, they faced punishment, but it was a game worth playing.

The people of Keah felt a sense of freedom returning; however, this had a price that needed to be paid to the Master of Shadows, who was more than happy to collect. He knew that time would tell if the truce between he and Lucas would hold. He did not need to worry.

Several servants who worked with the Shadows brought themselves closer to the young queen, and a member of the royal guard now worked for the Shadows. The Master smiled, knowing everyone had their price. The Master was happy with the turmoil caused by the queen. She had allowed the Shadows to have more power than they had ever had before.

The Master had learned long ago to use his enemies as puppets. Lucas and Aleesha were fine examples of this. They had the appearance of being in control and even the sense of it, but they both did what the Master wanted.

Never before had circumstances opened up opportunities like this for the Master. If he played his cards right and allowed the captain of the guard to focus on the young queen, then he could take control of Keah.

***

The queen of the spiders sat in the cave near Shes, listening to reports of resistance in the new world. There were warriors from the plains that fought and killed without any signs of fear.

Three wagons had been intercepted outside of Shes, where one of the hunters was killed with magic as the lead wagon disappeared. The hunters and gladiator spiders followed the trail of the wagons into the great forest, where they waited to ambush any more who would follow.

When this group came through the trees into the ambush, they had attacked with fury and been assisted by creatures who walked in and out of the trees, but they were smart and did not follow the spiders into another awaiting trap.

The queen knew it was time to invade this new world. Her children had feasted on the soft flesh and hungered for more. She gave orders for two waves of attacking groups—one to go through the great forest and the other to head towards the plains where they had encountered the warriors; from there they would track them.

But this time, the queen would send thousands of her children to feed on the humans, and then the spiders would make this world their new home.

***

Ramulas and Pip helped Berenice bring her belongings into Iguchi's quarters and came back to the throne room to find Tilly waiting for them. 'You must come to the clearing,' the sprite said. 'Something has happened.'

She flew out the window, and Pip turned to Ramulas. 'What was that about?'

He shook his head. 'I am not sure, but I think we will find out soon enough.'

Ramulas led Pip out of the castle and into the clearing, where they found Eady and four other dryads waiting for them by the trees.

Eady stepped forward with a serious expression. 'There has been some trouble in the forest near Shes. Creatures have attacked Iguchi and the Fallen Angels.'

Ramulas' eyes widened as he stepped forward. 'Tell me what happened.'

'The creatures lay in hiding along the border of the forest, waiting for the Angels to pass. They were ambushed and fought back with the help of the dryads. None of the Fallen Angels were seriously hurt. They return with news of the battle.'

Ramulas let out a sigh of relief. 'My thanks to you and the dryads. Could you watch over the Angels until they return home?'

Eady nodded; the dryads melted into the trees, and Ramulas turned for the gate.

'Where are you going?' Pip asked.

'We need to make plans for battle. I think the spiders will be here soon. I need to contact the mayors of Covedon and Turtha to see if any word has come from the queen.'

'What will we tell Berenice about Iguchi?'

Ramulas shook his head. 'For now, we say nothing. He can tell her when he returns.'

***

Ramulas stood at the end of the long table in the throne room with Pip, Rygar, Shigar, and the druids. A magical hologram of the kingdom glowed on the table. Ramulas tapped his finger on the town of Shes and the border of the forest, making both shine.

'The wagons were attacked two miles from Shes. This was where the webs were in the fields and farms. Iguchi and the Fallen Angels were attacked at the edge of the forest, which is fifteen miles closer. That means fifteen miles closer to Sanctuary.'

'The towns of Turtha and Covedon?' Shigar asked.

Ramulas sighed. 'I believe that the spiders are somewhere in the plains. Both towns and the Khilli could be in danger. We need to find a way to work together.'

The magician smiled. 'I believe that the druids may have an answer to your problem.'

Ramulas raised an eyebrow. 'What is that?'

One of the druids stepped away from the table to where the body of the giant spider lay hidden. He waved his arm, and it reappeared. He removed his wand from his robes and pointed it at the creature. Small black bubbles floated down to the spider's body and started to pop and sizzle when they touched the legs.

Pip ran to inspect the damage, clearly excited. 'What magic is this?'

The druid held up his wand, showing the black residue on its tip. 'We have been studying the body of the spider and discovered a way for the bubbles to become stronger. These bubbles do not form webs; they eat through any surface they touch.'

Ramulas nodded with a smile. 'This is good news. We will need all the help we can get if the spiders come to Sanctuary.'

The druid nodded. 'We cannot make as many as the green bubbles. These stronger ones take longer to make.'

Ramulas' smile disappeared as his hopes were dashed. On one hand, they had something that could hurt the spiders, and on the other, they could not affect as many as he would like.

'There were no black bubbles on the paintings or tapestries,' Pip said, 'but they have already changed once; they might change again.'

'We will go into the valley after Iguchi returns. I want to hear his story of the spiders. I will communicate with the mayor of Turtha to see if any help is coming from Keah.'

***

Using his astral form, Ramulas travelled to Turtha. He floated above the people and stayed invisible until coming to the mayor's quarters. He entered to find the mayor sorting paperwork on his desk.

With a thought, Ramulas made himself visible. 'Please do not be alarmed.'

145

The mayor jumped out of his seat and reached for the sword on his hip. Then he stopped and smiled. 'I should have you ring a bell or something to tell of your arrival.'

Ramulas smiled for a moment before clicking his fingers; a soft tone echoed in the room, causing the smile on the mayor's face to grow. 'That is better.'

Ramulas stepped forward. 'I have come to ask you to inform me when word comes from Keah. Click your fingers while sitting at your desk, and I will hear the same tone in my castle.'

'Have you heard any more about the giant spiders?' the mayor asked.

Ramulas nodded slightly. 'A group of our soldiers were attacked in the forests near the town of Shes. We think the spiders are moving and have grave concerns for the people of the kingdom if something is not done. I must return home; there is much for us to do.'

As Ramulas' image faded, the mayor's doubts about the people of Sanctuary increased. From the time people began disappearing across the kingdom, he had been told that they were the enemy, but after these visits from the Lord of Sanctuary, he was not sure that he had been told the whole story.

The mayor recalled what Lucas had said to him about the last battle of Sanctuary and the Legion being sent home—Ramulas had the power to destroy everyone but chose to allow them to leave.

This went with the sincerity shown by Ramulas for the welfare not only of his people but of everyone in the kingdom. The mayor was also curious to see the Khilli people living in the plains. He had been told that they were to be killed or brought in to the queen, but he wanted to know their side of the story.

***

Rygar stood in the training grounds with two guilty looking half-giants. He shook a finger at them. 'Where have ye been all o' this time? Ye do not just run away after a fight.'

Deep inside, the dwarf knew that these two had formed a close bond with Lodi and were deeply affected by his death. With the help of the dryads, Rygar had found them living in the Devil's Ridge Mountains where Rygar and Lodi had lived.

But the dwarf was happy to have them back. In some way they helped fill a small part of the void left by Lodi. News of the giant spiders moving was troubling for him, and Sanctuary would need all the help they could get if the creatures attacked.

Rygar smiled as the giant-kin avoided him with their eyes. They both towered over him, holding broadswords that could cut him in two, but they still feared him.

He stomped him font. 'Now, get ye back to trainin'.'

Both half-giants jumped when a blast of ice exploded at their feet. They turned to see Joshua and Rain behind them with weapons ready.

The giants roared in rage, running at the pair as people flocked to the fences. They did not want to miss this.

***

The queen of spiders sat in the cave as six thousand spiders made their way into the new world. With the spiders already in Shes, they would number just over seven thousand. Some would remain in the town while the rest would head out towards the forest and the plains in search of food.

The spiders had been shown how the warriors of this world fought, and they would be ready for them this time.

***

Ramulas and Pip stood on the wall, watching the archers shooting targets. Every now and then, Pip's eyes blazed with emerald fire as she searched the forest for Iguchi and the Fallen Angels. Then she smiled as she finally saw them coming through the trees.

Pip pointed out into the trees. 'They're coming.'

Ramulas watched the forest and waited for them to appear. 'How long until they arrive?'

Pip shrugged. 'A few moments.'

'We need to talk with Iguchi about his fight with the spiders when he comes,' Ramulas said before turning to Owain. 'Tell your archers to make the Angels dance as they cross the clearing.'

The blind archer raised an eyebrow before smiling and called out orders.

'Father has returned,' Berenice said as she walked between them.

Both Ramulas and Pip jumped. They had not heard her come close to them or even known she was there.

'Where did you come from?' Ramulas asked. 'I did not know you were here.'

Berenice shrugged. 'I did not want you to know,' she said as she walked along the wall behind the archers.

Pip called out, saying that the Fallen Angels had arrived, and Owain raised his hand before quickly dropping it and calling, 'Now!'

The archers quickly fired their arrows down onto the Fallen Angels, who moved as the first wave came down around them. They twisted their bodies at impossible angles and turned away from the missiles, then Ramulas called out, 'Enough!'

The archers stopped and leaned their bows against the inner section of the wall, and Iguchi waved up to Ramulas. 'Hello to you, Lord of Sanctuary. You thought to catch my Angels sleeping.'

Ramulas shrugged. 'I wanted to know if you were training them hard enough. Come into the throne room, and we will talk about the giant spiders.'

Iguchi nodded and led the Fallen Angels to the gate. Out of the corner of his eye, Ramulas saw Berenice pick up a bow, aiming an arrow at Iguchi. Before he could react, she shot at her father.

Pip gasped as the arrow flew towards the small man. She grabbed Ramulas' arm and called, 'Look out!'

Iguchi smiled up at them, waving as the arrow was a few feet from him. At the last possible moment, he twisted his body and plucked the arrow out of the air. He examined it, and his smile grew.

'My daughter has arrived. This is good.'

Iguchi led the Fallen Angels inside while Ramulas and Pip looked at each other.

'What just happened?' Ramulas asked Pip.

She slowly shook her head. 'I don't know.'

Berenice walked past them and down the stairs after her father.

***

Ramulas and Pip walked into the throne room in time to see Iguchi and Berenice separate from an embrace.

'Oh, I almost forgot,' Ramulas said as he walked over to Berenice and waved his hand in front of her. Berenice was soon covered in a light purple nimbus. Ramulas' eyes widened as he stepped back with what he discovered about Berenice. Then he heard Pip gasp and turned to see her eyes glowing.

Ramulas wondered if Pip saw the same thing that he did—that Berenice was not Iguchi's daughter.

Pip pointed to Berenice and turned to Iguchi. 'I thought she was—'

Iguchi seemed to float to the former thief and poke her in the ribs, cutting her off. 'You are very nosy. I will tell you about things at a later time. We are here to talk about spiders.'

Iguchi glided away to talk to Ramulas about the Fallen Angels' encounter with the giant spiders. When he was finished, Ramulas said that the dryads had told him what had happened.

A low tone sounded in the throne room. Everyone except for Ramulas looked around in surprise. He smiled, holding up his hand. 'That tone means that the mayor of Turtha wishes to see me. Rest your Angels, Iguchi. I will return soon.'

Ramulas turned to Pip. 'Ask Shigar to visit Emily and her parents. I would like to know how her new magic is affecting her.'

Pip nodded and raced out of the throne room. Iguchi and Berenice gave identical bows before leading the Fallen Angels out.

***

Ramulas' astral form stood before the mayor's desk, watching him hold a small scroll in his fingers. The man muttered to himself softly while slowly shaking his head.

Ramulas sounded the tone before allowing himself to appear before the mayor. The mayor sighed in relief and smiled at Ramulas.

'What has happened?' Ramulas asked.

The mayor leaned over his desk, handing Ramulas the note. 'You will need to read this for yourself.'

Ramulas took the message and unrolled it.

There will be no help from Keah.
The people of Sanctuary are enemies of the kingdom.
Working with them is treason.
You are ordered to kill the Lord of Sanctuary.
Queen Aleesha.

Ramulas looked up to see the mayor shaking his head. 'The queen does not care what happened to the town of Shes or the danger we could all be in.'

Ramulas let out a slow breath. 'Shigar told me that this might happen.'

'Who is Shigar?'

'He used to be King Zachary's magician. He left to join Sanctuary after he saw that I was fighting for a noble cause. He said that Aleesha was a very spoilt child. I can see now that she is not fit to rule over the kingdom.'

The mayor shrugged. 'What do we do?'

'We need to work together to fight the spiders if they come this way.'

The mayor's eyes widened. 'You want us to work with the people of Sanctuary after the queen said it is treason? I do not know what to believe.'

'All I ask is that you do what you know to be right. The people of Sanctuary, Turtha, and Covedon will need to work together with the help of the Khilli if we want to survive. No-one is coming to help us.'

15

After Ramulas told K'ayden that his people were safe and help would be coming, the Khilli warrior had left to return to his people.

Ten miles out of Turtha, K'ayden encountered a dozen soldiers on horseback from Turtha. He slowed his horse as they approached. His animal had travelled non-stop from Sanctuary, and K'ayden knew that he could not outrun the soldiers.

He would need to either talk or fight his way out of this to return home.

The patrol came close, and the sergeant held up a hand, stopping them ten feet from K'ayden. He smiled at the warrior without warmth. 'We have heard much about your people. What are you doing out here?'

K'ayden tilted his head to his right. 'I am returning to my people in our homeland.'

All the soldiers turned towards the plains before the sergeant turned back to K'ayden. 'We have heard that the Khilli left the king and now fight with Sanctuary against the kingdom.'

K'ayden sat straight and pulled his shoulders back. 'The Khilli people had been held against our will for a very long time. The Lord of Sanctuary saw this and allowed us to return to our homeland.'

The sergeant tilted his head as he thought. The mayor had said similar things. 'You will come with us back to Turtha. The mayor would like a word with you.'

K'ayden stiffened as thoughts of his people being trapped resurfaced. 'My people are in danger. We have been attacked by dark creatures. I must return to them.'

The sergeant's eyes widened at this response. No-one had ever responded to him like this. He noticed that his soldiers slowly fanned out on either side of him. The Khilli's eyes scanned them as his hand dropped to his Khilli throwing disk.

The sergeant shook his head. 'I am ordering you to come with us back to Turtha.'

In the blink of an eye, the throwing disk was in K'ayden's hand. He looped a thong of leather through it and swung it in lazy circles by his side. The soldiers pulled back their horses, knowing that the disk could cut through their chainmail. They glanced at the sergeant, waiting for orders.

'Two of my warriors have fallen to these creatures, and my people need me. How many of you are willing to die to bring me to Turtha? I am ready for a warrior's death,' K'ayden said while scanning the soldiers.

The sergeant saw the expression on the warrior's face; he knew that many of his soldiers would die attempting to capture him, and he could see the soldiers tense, waiting for orders. He shook his head. 'The mayor wanted you alive. Return to your people. I want none of my men harmed today.'

The sergeant waved his hand, and the patrol turned away from K'ayden as he thought of something Iguchi had once told him—*Most battles are won without weapons being drawn.*

***

K'ayden arrived at the village, and the Khilli rejoiced at has safe return. His heart soared to see them safe as well. The village would prepare a celebratory feast that evening.

K'ayden told them of his meeting with the Lord of Sanctuary, what had happened in Shes, and the Fallen Angels fighting them as well; however, he did not tell them of his meeting with the patrol outside of Turtha. His people had enough to worry about, and he needed them to concentrate on the spiders.

K'ayden was told that warriors had searched the area where they had been attacked by the spiders and that there was no trace of them.

*****

A group of eighty hunters and gladiators ran along the edge of the forests near Shes. They were the scouting party for the spiders that would go into the plains. They would not be caught unawares again, and they would soon feast on more victims.

As the creatures entered the forest, they could not help but touch the trees, leaves, and foliage as they passed. Coming from their dying world where all life had been stripped made this world fascinating to them. A call came from the queen through the psychic spiders to stop exploring the world and hurry to their destination. The spiders knew that after defeating every obstacle, they could take their time to explore this new world.

*****

Lucas stared at the young serving girl who had told him the message. His mouth hung open, and he blinked rapidly. 'What did you just say?'

'The town of Shes has fallen. Everyone is dead. The Master of Shadows wants to see you. You must come with me.'

Lucas fought to control his breathing as he scanned the room. There were so many questions to ask. What had happened at Shes? Why did he not hear about it? How did the Master of Shadows know? And did Sanctuary play a part in this?

She took his hand. 'You need to come with me now.'

It was then that Lucas saw she wore a kitchen worker's uniform. 'How long have you been with the Shadows? How many others from the Shadows work in the castle?'

The young girl just smiled as she pulled him through the hallways. He found himself in a daze as he walked, not able to focus on where they were going. They left the castle and walked through several alleys and backstreets of the city for minutes, and soon Lucas had lost all sense of direction.

They stopped outside of an inn in the poor section of the city, and she pointed to the door. 'You need to go in there.'

The street was busy as the sun shone directly overhead, but the sailors, rogues, and beggars gave him a wide berth and would not make eye contact.

Lucas walked into the inn and had to blink a few times to adjust his eyes to the dim setting after being bathed in the bright sun. Strong hands grabbed him by the arms, and Lucas saw two solid men guide him to a table in the corner.

Lucas was shown to the seat opposite the Master and sat on his chair. The Master of Shadows' face held no expression; he sat as still as a statue as a candle flickered on the table, sending shadows dancing on the wall behind him.

Lucas sighed. 'I thought the next time I saw you, I was to be killed. Is this where I die?'

The Master laid both hands on the table. 'Things have changed. The town of Shes is no more. I have heard whispers that everyone was killed by monsters. These monsters have been seen in the plains near Turtha. The mayor of Turtha has asked the queen for help. She has refused; there will be no help from the kingdom army.'

Lucas studied the Master as he spoke and then searched the surrounding area before turning back to the Master. 'How do I know if this is true? Am I to trust the Master of the thieves' guild?'

The Master tapped his fingertips on the table lightly as he tilted his head up and sighed. Then he looked at Lucas with a sad smile. 'The Shadows have spies everywhere. One of my most trusted spies told me this information.'

Lucas leaned forward in his chair. 'Who is this spy?'

The Master shrugged. 'To expose this person would cause them to be arrested and maybe even sent to Gullytown. If this happens, the rest of my spies would not work for me again.'

Lucas let out a slow breath and glared at the Master. 'No action will be taken. I just need to know.'

The Master smiled. 'It is the aviary master who sends out and collects the pigeons with the messages. He reads everything coming in and going out of the castle. When I learned of Shes, I sent word out for you to come to me.'

'Why did you send for me? What do you gain from this?'

'If Shes has truly gone, the Shadows have lost business. If these monsters are real, we could lose Covedon, Turtha, and Rylek. Then what becomes of Keah?'

Lucas stood suddenly, fists clenched by his side, and quickly shrugged off the hands trying to grab at him. The Master waved his hand, and the enforcers backed away, and then Lucas turned and walked towards the door of the inn.

'Where are you going?' the Master asked.

'To have a little chat with our young queen.'

***

Shigar stood outside Joshua's house, not knowing what to say. He had come to see how Emily's new-found magic was affecting her. The magician jumped when the door suddenly opened.

Grace smiled at him. 'Don't just stand there, silly; come inside.'

Shigar entered and noticed Grace's eyes glowing emerald green, which was part of the dryad magic she had within her. He saw Emily and Juliette and waved to them.

'Hello. I have come to look at Emily after a small incident in the tunnel. Would you mind if I examine her?' he asked Juliette.

Juliette smiled. 'The girls told me that they made a statue.'

He raised an eyebrow. 'And that's the only thing that happened?'

Both girls nodded, and Shigar smiled at the lie. Grace had forgotten to mention that Emily now had some of her magic. 'I just wanted to ensure that Emily was not affected when they made the statue.'

Juliette nodded, and Shigar pulled out a leather-bound book from his robes and motioned for Emily to come closer.

The magician flicked through the pages until he found the passage he was searching for; he chanted while waving his free hand in front of Emily. The girl's hair stood on end as the energy built up around her. He quickly discovered that Grace's magical energy was inside of Emily, but it was hidden deep inside where Emily could not feel its presence.

Shigar smiled, stopped chanting, and closed the book, knowing that the magic was in a place where it would not cause any harm. It would take something catastrophic to release this magical energy; and if that happened, he did not want to be anywhere near her.

***

Lucas stormed into Aleesha's chambers, followed by ten of the royal guard, each of them wearing stern expressions. The two agents speaking with the queen stepped back in shock.

Aleesha sneered as she stood in her throne. 'You dare walk in here unannounced.'

Lucas walked to within ten feet of her. 'Sit down, my queen.'

Aleesha sat down, her sneer replaced with a shocked expression.

Lucas held up a finger. 'We need to talk about the town of Shes and why you have ignored pleas for help from the town of Turtha.'

Aleesha had the appearance of a child caught stealing and fought to regain her composure. 'The mayor of Turtha has spoken with the Lord of Sanctuary, who has made up these stories. People of Sanctuary are enemies of the kingdom and so are those who help them.'

Lucas stepped back as his mouth fell open. 'What of the town of Shes? What enquiries have you made?'

Aleesha folded her arms. 'I do not believe the lies from Sanctuary.'

Lucas shook his head. 'If you had have made enquiries of Shes, you would have known that two ships were due here today from there. They have not arrived. There have been no messages from Shes for days.'

Aleesha seemed to sink into her throne as the agents shrank away. 'But the Lord of Sanctuary—'

'The Lord of Sanctuary has fought the kingdom army twice and won. He is a magician and controls dragons. If Shes has fallen, we will need to help Turtha.'

She shook her head. 'I will not help Sanctuary.'

Lucas stepped forward holding out his hands. 'This is not about Sanctuary; this is about the people of the kingdom—the people under *your* protection.'

Aleesha glanced at one of the agents. 'Who told you about Shes and Turtha?'

Lucas shook his head. 'It doesn't matter. Something needs to be done about this situation. I have sent a ship with one hundred soldiers; they will send word when they arrive.'

Aleesha slapped the armrest of her throne. 'You do not send soldiers anywhere without my permission. I am the queen.'

Lucas let out a slow breath, thinking, *No, you are a spoilt brat who will soon lose her throne.*

Then he sighed. 'My queen, anger has no place for those in power. I will leave one of the royal guards to oversee your duties until I return.' Lucas waved his hand, and a guard stepped forward. 'He will be with you to advise on certain matters in the court, my queen, and will know when to call for me.'

'But I have my agents,' Aleesha protested.

Lucas smiled, shaking his head. 'They can still advise you, but the royal guard I leave with you will have the final word.'

Lucas gave a short bow before walking out of the chambers with the rest of his guards. The remaining guard smiled to himself, knowing that he would report everything not only to Lucas, but also to the Master of Shadows, his new employer.

***

Lucas walked into the aviary, and the pigeonmaster greeted him with a warm smile. The captain of the royal guard patted the man on his shoulder. 'I have come to praise you for the fine work that you have been doing.' He watched the pigeonmaster swell with pride. 'And to think, if you did not tell the Master of Shadows about the events in Shes, Turtha, and Sanctuary, I would not be here.'

The man's smile faded as he moved away from Lucas with the expression of a trapped animal, turning his head searching for an escape.

Lucas forced a smile. 'Do not worry. I promised the Master of Shadows that you would not be arrested.' Lucas shook a finger at the man while tilting his head. 'I am not happy that you have been working with the thieves' guild. Continue what you are doing, but relay all messages to the royal guard with the queen and no-one else. Just know that one day I will come to ask a favour, and you will honour that for me.'

Lucas walked out of the building, surprised at how he had controlled himself, as he thought that being on the right side of the law had only got him so far. He had seen people like the Shadows take what they wanted for many years.

'I think it's time for me to start walking on the darker side in order to help the kingdom. Rules need to be broken and new ones made,' he whispered to himself.

***

Lucas walked into the royal vault, stood before Zachary's tomb, and sighed while shaking his head. He truly believed that he was doing the right thing and guiding Aleesha in the way that King Zachary would have approved of. But this seemed almost impossible with the young queen acting the way she did.

He was torn between helping to guide her to be the people's queen and locking her away, stripping her of her powers, and ruling in her name until she came of age. The latter option would be the easier road to take, but Lucas needed to honour his former king. Then he decided to try to show Aleesha reason.

***

Ramulas and Pip rode the warhorse through the passageway into the valley, followed by Kate, Grace, and the hell hounds; behind them rode Iguchi and the Fallen Angels, Shigar, the earth elementals, the druids, the giant-kin, and Berenice.

They had come to learn whether anything had changed with the paintings and tapestries.

Berenice, the half-giants, and the elementals scanned the valley with eyes full of wonder. Ramulas attempted to contact the dragons once more, but he felt them way off beyond the mountains.

When they arrived at Journey's End, Ramulas spoke to his daughters. 'Explore with the hell hounds. We will be in the castle.'

Both girls ran off, excited, and Ramulas led the group into the castle and up to the throne room. As they entered, Ramulas noticed that the paintings and tapestries had changed once more.

'The artwork has become much darker, 'Pip said as Ramulas saw that her eyes were glowing.

Iguchi quickly made his way to the far wall, and as the others caught up, they could hear him muttering to himself. They talked to each other about their concerns while pointing to the artwork.

The paintings and the tapestries showed more spiders.

Thousands and thousands of them.

The battle scenes had changed as well. The druids used their black bubbles, and Joshua and Rain fought alongside the elementals. Then Ramulas gasped and stepped back when he saw the depiction of Grace and Emily; he was happy that his daughters could not see it.

Ramulas turned to everyone. 'I have a very bad feeling about this. Everyone study these closely, because when we are finished, we will go home to train.'

He focused on his magical ability to communicate with Grace, telling her and Kate to stay near the castle and that they would be leaving soon. Her could feel her disappointment, but he had a grave feeling about the spiders.

***

The sergeant stood before the mayor of Turtha; he had just told him of their encounter with K'ayden. The mayor was more curious about what the warrior had to say about the creatures. After speaking with the Lord of Sanctuary twice, the mayor wanted to hear the Khilli side of the story.

The mayor stood up. 'Gather one hundred and fifty men. We will go and talk with the Khilli ourselves. Are you sure of the direction he headed in?'

The sergeant nodded, and the mayor continued, 'Have the men ready by dawn.'

The sergeant nodded and left the building.

***

Everyone had gathered in the courtyard of Journey's End and were ready to leave.

'Da, look,' Grace said, pointing to the valley.

Eady stepped out of a silver-leafed oak tree and smiled as she walked towards them. She stopped a few feet from them. 'Greetings. I have come with news of the spiders in the forests near Shes.'

'What has happened?' Ramulas asked.

'They are massing near its border; more than we saw last time.'

'How many?' Pip blurted.

Eady shrugged. 'There are many, but we are unable to tell the grass from the bodies of the spiders as they swarm along the border.'

Ramulas nodded and noticed one of the silver leaves falling from Eady's body. He walked to her, chanting and waving a hand through the air. The dryad was covered in a light mist, and Ramulas gasped. He had been mistaken when he thought that the dryads were dying when they came to the valley; they were reverting to their human form.

'I need to speak with the dryads in the sacred grove when we return after we deal with the spiders,' he said.

***

K'ayden smiled as he walked around the village. It was two hours after dawn, and the people were going about their daily duties as if they had always lived here. The women weaved baskets from long blades of grass while the children chased each other around the mud huts, and the warriors were preparing for another hunt.

One of the ravens in the tree called out. K'ayden turned with a smile to two birds sitting in the top of the elm tree. They had appeared after two of the warriors died in battle, and the Khilli saw them as a good omen.

Now both birds called out urgently while flapping their wings and looking out to the plains. K'ayden shivered slightly, turned to glance at his people who had stopped what they were doing, and then ran for the elm tree. The wind had changed direction, and a familiar foul odour caused K'ayden to wrinkle his nose.

He quickly climbed, and his body slumped as he saw a large group of giant spiders heading toward the village. The creatures were two miles away and would arrive soon. He saw that his people had no idea of the danger they were in.

'Run! The spiders are coming; many more than last time,' he shouted, waving an arm above his head. The Khilli seemed frozen to the spot and no-one moved. K'ayden shouted again, and they all ran. The women gathered the children, while the warriors grabbed their weapons and formed lines in front of the women and children.

The women and children ran from the village towards Turtha as the warriors began to chant and hold a defensive line to hold the spiders at bay. K'ayden thought of the last time they fought the spiders; they lost two warriors. Even though they had more warriors, there were so many spiders.

K'ayden and the warriors waited, watching the grassland beyond the elm tree. Then everything became quiet; all the birds and other animals were silent.

'The longer we keep the spiders here, the further away our families will be from danger,' K'ayden said.

K'ayden froze as long, spiked legs probed out of the grass near the elm tree, then dark shapes slowly pushed their way through the long grass. He heard gasps from his warriors and turned to see that spiders were coming in from the sides of the village as well.

The tall grass exploded as hundreds of giant spiders attacked.

16

The mayor of Turtha rode alongside the sergeant who had encountered K'ayden. They led one hundred and fifty soldiers in full battle gear, each with sword and shield. The mayor wanted to talk with the Khilli to understand their side of the story and get to the bottom of what was going on.

A scout came racing over the rise, sending a cloud of dust behind him. He waved a hand above his head and shouted. He pulled his horse up in front of the column; the horse was lathered in sweat and foaming at the mouth. The scout's eyes were wide as he fought for breath.

'Mayor, the Khilli are coming. We have to hurry.'

The mayor looked at the rise, expecting the Khilli to appear. 'Are they coming to attack us?'

The scout shook his head. 'No, they are in trouble. Follow me,' he said before turning his horse and racing off the way he had come.

The mayor nodded to the sergeant, who shouted orders, and they raced over the rise, where they saw a group of Khilli women and children a mile away hurrying towards them. They quickened their pace until they met the group.

The mayor saw that the women and children had been crying, were covered in dust, and all kept glancing behind them with eyes wide with fear.

A woman holding an infant on her hip came up to the mayor's horse. 'Please, you must help us. Giant spiders have come out of the plains and are attacking our village.' She turned, pointing the way they had come.

The mayor had been a soldier in the king's army for twenty years, and his soldier instincts never left him. His main concern was his men, followed by the people of the kingdom, but the Khilli had left the king and were now enemies of the kingdom by decree of the queen.

He knew that the enemies of the kingdom were not to be helped. Under the rule of King Zachary, the mayor had been very loyal; he would have taken the women and children back to Turtha and let the spiders deal with the Khilli warriors.

Before him stood women and children begging for help. A cold sensation spread through his body as he made up his mind and turned to his soldiers. 'Ready your weapons. We have monsters to kill.'

He raised a fist and raced ahead with his horse; his soldiers followed as the women and children parted for them.

***

K'ayden swung his throwing disk in tight arcs around his body with the leather strap attached to his hand. With a quick glance, he saw that the other warriors had their knives and disks ready as the creatures closed in.

Small groups of hunters charged out of the grass and attacked the Khilli warriors. His warriors fought with a fury K'ayden had never seen before. The giant spiders had attacked them in their own home and threatened their families.

Shouts of rage and grunts of pain mixed in with the high-pitched screaming of the creatures, and both races fought to the death. The hunters changed their tactics, jumping onto the mud huts then onto groups of warriors, knocking one down before jumping away again.

Three of the giant spiders ran straight for K'ayden. He heard shouts of warning from his warriors and knew that he would not be facing them alone. He ran forward a few steps, spinning his throwing disk at the lead spider. The creature raised its body, waving its front legs at the warrior, and poison glistened on its dagger-sized fangs.

K'ayden rushed in and took off one of the spider's legs with a swing of the disk. The spider hissed, raising its body higher, spraying green fluid from the wound. K'ayden took this opportunity to thrust his spear into the spider's abdomen. Green fluid gushed out, covering K'ayden, and the spear was violently pulled from his grip as the spider convulsed in death spasms.

He turned to see his warriors had killed the other two spiders.

He turned to assess the situation and saw that his warriors were holding the spiders back; several spider's bodies lay before them and the Khilli numbers were slightly higher than the spiders. He called out for the warriors who were free to help the others hold the line.

In the long grass surrounding the village lay the gladiator spiders, who silently watched while communicating with each other. They had been waiting for a moment like this.

The leader of the enemy had shown himself.

It was time for them to join the fight.

The gladiators rushed out of the grass, their front legs spread wide holding sticky nets. Calls of alarm and surprise spread among the warriors as they became entangled in the nets. The more they struggled, the more entangled they became and could not move.

The tide was quickly turning in favour of the spiders.

K'ayden had seen what these spiders were capable of and was wary when one ran towards him holding a net. He ran to it, pulling out a throwing knife and throwing it low at the creature. He smiled as the knife entered the spider's eye. The creature stumbled and rolled on the ground, getting caught in its own net.

He did not see the second gladiator as it crept up behind him. K'ayden realised his mistake as the sticky net fell over him. He twisted, and both his arms were pinned to his sides. He was hit from behind and the air was forced from his body as the spider landed on top of him. He breathed through his mouth as the stench of the creature washed over him. He turned to see the fangs dripping with poison slowly lowering.

The nearest warriors were fighting for their lives, and none could help him.

K'ayden prepared himself for death.

***

Ramulas walked out into the clearing with Pip, Kate, and Grace. Five dryads stepped out of the trees to greet them, Eady smiling when she saw Grace.

'Hello, child,' Eady said, stroking Grace's face. 'We have not seen you in a long time. You must come to the sacred grove and bring your sister.'

Both girl's eyes lit up as they looked to Ramulas, who nodded. 'You can go with the hell hounds, but come back when I call.'

Both girls ran into the forest with the hell hounds as a buzzing sound came through the trees, and Grace squealed with delight.

Ramulas turned to Eady. 'Tell me of the spiders.'

Eady sighed. 'They gather along the border of the forest near Shes. The spiders cover every inch of ground and crawl over each other. They have yet to enter the forest. We think they wait for something.'

'How long have they been there?'

'They arrived yesterday, and now they wait.'

Ramulas knew that it took a person on horseback two days to travel from Shes to Sanctuary. If he was notified when the spiders entered the forest, it would give them two days to prepare. 'When the spiders enter the forest, please let me know. We need to prepare.'

Eady nodded, and Ramulas noticed the faint tinge of silver in the leaves on their bodies. They were returning to their normal form. 'When dryads go into the valley, you do not die as I first thought, but if you stay in the valley too long you will return to your former human bodies. This is why the leaves are turning silver.'

Eady smiled sadly. 'For a dryad, this is worse than death.'

'I need to plan for the coming of the spiders. Please stay away from the valley,' Ramulas said as he led Pip back into Sanctuary.

'Do you think Iguchi will listen to you?' Pip asked.

Ramulas nodded. 'He will want to stay close with the threat of the spiders coming here.'

***

They reached the throne room, and Ramulas communicated with Grace, making sure his daughters were safe. He broke contact after he realised they were with the dryad children and having fun.

Ramulas sat on his throne and began deep breathing while casting a spell to send an astral form to speak with the mayor of Turtha. He soon found himself floating above Sanctuary and sent his form to Turtha.

He was confused as to why the town was so quiet, and he could not see any of the soldiers in the streets or on the walls. He entered the mayor's quarters and found it empty. He floated through the streets and could see no sign of the mayor or any soldiers. Ramulas wondered where they could be.

Without knowing where to search, Ramulas knew that it would be pointless to waste his time. He returned to the throne room to find Pip standing in front of him with Rachael by her side.

He jolted in shock before forcing a smile and stepping down to greet Rachael. 'I did not know you were here.'

Rachael looked to the ground and smiled. 'Pip said that you wanted to see me.'

Ramulas saw Pip shrug behind Rachael. 'One moment please, Rachael. I wish to thank Pip.'

He walked to the former thief, who wore an innocent expression. He took her out of earshot. 'I don't have the time for this.'

Pip smiled at him. 'Your girls are with the dryads, and you will be told when the spiders are coming.'

'I must be ready,' he protested.

'Things that other people are already doing. You need to stop avoiding her; I know that if you had your way, you would avoid her forever and make excuses. She's good for you.'

Pip pushed Ramulas towards Rachael before leaving. They stood facing each other, neither wanting to make the first move.

***

Iguchi stood in front of the Fallen Angels with his daughter by his side. They were in a clearing two miles from Sanctuary to train for the battle with the spiders.

When they had last encountered the spiders, the Fallen Angels made mistakes and were saved by the dryads coming from the trees. Some of the Angels would have died, and when Iguchi was caught in the net, not all the Angels saw it happen. A few should have rushed in to help while the others made a protective circle.

'This is my daughter Berenice,' Iguchi said, sweeping his hand to her. 'My poor, defenceless daughter; the swords she wears are only to frighten thieves. She has never learnt how to use them. Ten Angels will try to stop her from reaching that oak tree,' he said, pointing to a tree one hundred yards away with a red ribbon tied to a branch.

Iguchi picked Miles and nine other Fallen Angels, who quickly made a line between Berenice and the oak tree.

'You will need your swords and shields to stop this frail woman.'

The Fallen Angels glanced at Iguchi with questioning expressions. He nodded, and they readied themselves. Berenice seemed to shrink as she turned her head from side to side as if searching for an escape.

She turned to Iguchi and spoke in a soft trembling voice. 'Father, please do not make me do this. I will be hurt.'

Iguchi grunted and pushed his daughter, who lost her footing and stumbled the first few steps before meekly walking up to the Angels. She stopped four feet from them before turning to Iguchi.

He waved to Miles and the other Fallen Angels. 'Do not allow her to reach the tree.'

Berenice lifted her head to look at Miles with tears filling her eyes. 'Can you please allow me to pass?'

Miles was confused. There was something wrong here, but he could not work it out. Since Iguchi's daughter had arrived, she had not shown any fighting skills, and yet something about the way she moved sent alarm bells through him.

'You will not pass,' Miles said, standing his ground.

Berenice moved with such speed that her arms blurred in from of Miles. Before he knew it, she held both swords in her hands. Her expression of fear faded as she leapt into the air. Her swords pushed Miles' sword and shield out wide, then she kicked him in his breastplate. Miles flew, and the other Fallen Angels reacted.

But it was too late; Berenice was already in motion.

She spun, kicking an Angel to her left. He was sent crashing back into the Angels behind him. Then she turned with her swords spinning in front of her to face five Fallen Angels on the other side.

Swords and shields were battered out of the way. Fallen Angels were thrown through the air, had their legs swept from underneath them, and were knocked to the ground. Within seconds, six Fallen Angels were out of the fight, and the remaining four charged toward her.

'Berenice, go to the tree,' Iguchi called.

She shot him a quick sideways glance before sprinting to the tree. The change of the fight confused the Angels. They hesitated before giving chase, but they knew it was too late when she touched the tree.

Miles stood holding his chest, wincing every time he breathed. He looked around in disbelief at what just happened.

'Woe is me; my Fallen Angels have become lazy,' Iguchi said, shaking his head. 'A weak woman walks up to them, and they fall over themselves in fear. You will need more training.'

Miles shook his head and whispered, 'If she is a weak woman, then I am the Lord of Sanctuary.'

Miles had never been hit so hard in his life. There was a lot more to Iguchi's daughter than there appeared, but Iguchi would not say anything to his Angels.

***

169

K'ayden watched as the large fangs came closer. He struggled fiercely but could not move. Then the sound of thunder filled his ears as horses came into the village. A horse knocked the spider off him, and K'ayden turned to see soldiers on horses battling the spiders next to his warriors as dust rose from the ground.

The Khilli cheered as the soldiers hacked away at the spiders from horseback. The creatures were surprised by this new development but quickly recovered, and a few leapt through the air, taking soldiers from their horses.

The mayor saw this and called out orders; the soldiers quickly moved to fight side by side with the Khilli. K'ayden and other warrior were cut free of the nets and joined the fight. By this time, over half the spiders had been killed. Both soldiers and Khilli were covered in gore, and the spiders still attacked fiercely, some running and others jumping at the humans.

K'ayden called out and led his warriors in a charge that forced the spiders back, then before the spiders could recover, the soldiers charged passed their lines, cutting through them with their swords and trampling them with their horses.

As the tide turned in favour of the humans, eight hunters ran back the way they had come, changing colour as they entered the long grass. K'ayden saw this as the last spider was killed, and he called out. The sergeant quickly issued orders and ten soldiers rode after them; however, the long grass slowed the horses down, and the spiders leapt in and out of the grass quickly, distancing themselves from the soldiers. The sergeant swore and called his men back.

Soldiers and Khilli warriors walked around the village, checking each spider to make sure it had been killed. Then they counted their own losses—a handful of Khilli and soldiers were injured, and three Khilli, eight soldiers, and five horses were killed in the battle.

K'ayden stood before the three warriors with grief written on his face. 'These men died protecting our families,' K'ayden said before turning to the mayor. 'And we thank you for coming to our aid.'

The mayor stood twenty feet away near the bodies of his soldiers, his face an emotionless mask. He nodded once to K'ayden. With the danger of the spiders now in the past, the soldiers and Khilli stood in separate groups. They studied each other, not knowing what to do.

The kingdom soldiers had always known the Khilli to work for the king—until recently—and they were the best fighters of the land, but things had taken a dramatic change—the Khilli had left the king's service to live in Sanctuary, which made them enemies of the queen.

For the Khilli warriors, the kingdom soldiers represented their time as prisoners in the city of Keah, with their women and children held captive to ensure they followed orders.

Now that the greater enemy was gone, tensions between the two groups grew. Each person still held their weapons.

The mayor walked towards his men and shouted, 'Stand down! Put your weapons away. The fighting has finished.'

Without a word, the soldiers stepped back and sheathed their swords, but they still warily watched the Khilli. The sergeant came over to the mayor and they stood between the two groups. The sergeant whispered to the mayor and pointed to K'ayden.

The mayor nodded and walked to K'ayden. 'My men saw you outside of Turtha yesterday.' The Khilli warriors began to talk and move to K'ayden, but he waved them away. 'It is strange to see the Khilli people in these parts after many years, and after the stories of the battles at Sanctuary, you told my soldiers of large creatures and that is why you could not come to talk with me.'

K'ayden's eyes scanned the ground looking at the bodies of slain spiders before turning back to the mayor.

'The Lord of Sanctuary has come to me using magic and told me of the danger these spiders hold for everyone in the kingdom. I wanted to hear the story from you. This is why I came here. Imagine my surprise when we saw the Khilli women and children begging for our help.'

K'ayden and the rest of the warriors stiffened at the mention of their families. The mayor noticed this and turned to the way they had come. 'Your families are heading towards Turtha and were well when we left them.'

'They may still be in danger. Some of the spiders may have moved past us.'

K'ayden turned and shouted in Khilli, and twenty warriors raced off toward Turtha.

'Where are they going?' the mayor asked.

'Our women and children may be in danger.'

The mayor looked back down the road. 'They are a few miles down the road. Horses will get there faster.'

The mayor spoke to the sergeant, who shouted orders, and twenty soldiers dismounted from their horses and brought them to the Khilli. K'ayden stood still, not knowing what to do.

The mayor smiled. 'Take the horses. You will reach your families faster.'

K'ayden shook his head as the memories of his people being tricked came flooding back to him, but the kingdom soldiers had come to their rescue.

The mayor saw the Khilli's internal conflict. 'Twenty of my soldiers will come with you to help your families.'

K'ayden knew that time was wasting and gave the order for his warriors to go on horseback with the soldiers. When the forty had left, the mayor turned to him. 'After what we have seen, I don't think it would be wise for your people to stay out in the plains for now. Your people can stay in Turtha.'

A wave of anger washed over K'ayden. 'My people will not be tricked by the kingdom soldiers again.'

The Khilli warriors fanned out behind K'ayden, and the kingdom soldiers readied their weapons as tensions rose again.

The mayor turned. 'Put your weapons away! The next man who holds a weapon without my saying so will watch while I eat his heart.'

As the weapons were sheathed, the mayor smiled at K'ayden. 'The Lord of Sanctuary told some of your story, of how your women and children were kept prisoner. I want to hear it from you.'

K'ayden stood silently studying the mayor. The man seemed genuine in what he was saying and was interested in the Khilli. K'ayden told the mayor of the Khilli's people history before the king came to them offering gifts, and how they had then been tricked, separated, and forced into service, and that from that day on, the warriors were forced to do what was asked or their families would suffer.

Then K'ayden spoke of meeting the Lord of Sanctuary in the dungeon, how he showed the heart of a true warrior and repaid the debt to the Khilli by freeing them. As K'ayden spoke, the mayor saw the pain and anguish on the faces of the warriors as they relived this dark part of their lives.

The mayor knew that everything he was being told was the truth, and the sadness from the warriors was contagious. He truly felt for these warriors and could not understand how he had not seen the signs before. He had been fiercely loyal to King Zachary for so many years, but knowing the story about the Khilli would change the way he viewed the king.

When K'ayden had finished, the mayor sighed and shook his head. 'Please come to Turtha as equals. Your people may come and go as you please, but first, talk with the Lord of Sanctuary in my quarters.'

'Tell me why we should trust you,' K'ayden said.

The mayor told him of Ramulas coming with warning of the giant spiders, sending a message to Keah for help, and the queen replying that help would not come and that he should kill the Lord of Sanctuary. He concluded by saying the Lord of Sanctuary had insisted that working together was their only chance against the creatures.

K'ayden stepped back and quickly spoke with his warriors before coming back to the mayor. 'We will come after burying our dead.'

The mayor smiled with relief and called for his men to ready the horses; they were returning home.

17

'Town of Shes ahead!' the sailor called from the crow's nest.

The deck below became busy with sailors running around preparing to dock into port. Once they completed their duties, the one hundred soldiers stood on the deck in the mid-afternoon sun, seeming not to notice the spray of water as the waves hit the ship. They had been told something had happened in Shes and wondered what they might find.

As the ship came closer to land, the captain took out his spyglass and extended the tube, which allowed him to see great distances. After a few moments, he turned to the sergeant. 'There is trouble on the docks.'

The sergeant took the spyglass to look at the dock himself; it was just over two miles away. He saw two fishing boats tied to the docks and two ships that had broken their moorings and were leaning against the rocks near the cliffs one hundred yards from the dock.

The fishing boats seemed to be covered in silk sheets. He turned to the captain. 'Take us in a little closer. I want to see more.'

***

The hunter sat on a rocky outcrop above the docks bathing in the sun. It had seen the ship approaching and called out to the other spiders in Shes.

The news quickly spread, and hundreds of spiders came down to cover the docks and surrounding shore. Among these creatures were the psychic spiders, which were half the size of the hunters. The psychic spiders could retain the short-term memories of their victims and control them. The queen knew that the ships had come from somewhere and wanted to find this place. The psychics would read the sailors' minds and bring the ship back to where it came from.

***

Sails were lowered as the ship came closer to the docks. It was three hundred yards out, and everyone noticed the docks, boats, and ships covered in silk, which moved as the slight breeze blew in from the ocean. At two hundred yards out, the sailor in the crow's nest saw movement along the rocks of the shore.

The sailor blinked a few times before realising what he had seen, and he pointed to the shore. 'Monsters on the shore! Pull away. Turn back to sea.'

The others on board had seen movement as well, and the ship slowly turned about as the helmsman turned the wheel as fast as he could. Shouts of alarm travelled around the deck as the men witnessed the number of spiders.

The sergeant stepped back, his mouth open in shock upon seeing the dock covered in so many creatures that it seemed to be a living thing.

Scores of hunters had lightened the colour of their bodies to blend in with the silk covering the docks. They waited for the ship to come closer, but now it began to move away, and they would need to chase it.

They reverted to their normal colour as they raced along the dock and jumped into the water. Sailors called out in terror as the spiders skipped across the water. Sails were raised to increase speed, but the spiders were closing the distance fast.

One of the side cannons boomed. People on board watched as the cannonball sailed out to hit the dock. Cheers went up as the front of the dock exploded, throwing spiders and shards of wood into the air; however, the celebrations were short-lived.

The hunters and psychics began flowing over the sides of the ship. The psychics attacked the sailors while the hunters chose the sailors. The battle was hard and fierce, the soldiers forming a defensive circle in the middle of the deck, holding swords and shields. The sailors grabbed makeshift weapons and fought back.

But there were too many creatures, and fear spread quickly when fellow soldiers and sailors were eaten on the deck, the captain and twenty sailors were killed by the psychic spiders, and hunters began jumping from the masts onto the soldiers as they fought.

A few sailors and soldiers panicked and jumped overboard, thinking it was safer in the ocean, but they were quickly eaten by the hunters surrounding the ship.

When the last person had been killed, a message had been sent to their queen. She would tell them when to go to the place where the ship came from.

***

Ramulas stood on the balcony of the throne room with Rachael by his side. He struggled with the conflict of emotions he was experiencing. Jacqueline's death was still with him; he found it hard to enter his quarters without seeing a part of her there, and now Pip had been bringing Rachael into his life.

His emotional state was in turmoil. He enjoyed Rachael's company, and she was a lovely person, but he wanted to mourn his loss and did not know how long he needed before moving on with his life—if he even wanted to move on.

Rachael brushed against him as she pointed to an eagle flying over the mountains. The touch sent goosebumps through Ramulas, and he instantly felt guilty about enjoying the touch of another woman. He took a small step away, hoping for a way out of this situation without hurting her feelings, and he could hear Pip saying that he would make excuses not to see anyone else until he died.

He turned to talk to Rachael, then shook his head and turned as she smiled at him. He looked down at his hands, unsure what he should do next, and was angry at himself for feeling so awkward.

Then he saw Kate and Grace come into the courtyard with the hell hounds. He had communicated with Grace to come back. The girls both smiled and waved at the pair on the balcony.

A few moments later, they were coming into the throne room. Kate and Grace ran up to Rachael, each grabbing one of her hands. This brought back another thing Pip had said: that his daughters needed a woman in their lives. He watched as his girls talked excitedly with Rachael; things had not gone as he had planned.

Then a low tone sounded in the throne room. He turned to Rachael. 'I am sorry. Duty calls. I have enjoyed our time and will call on you soon.'

'I can show her my room, Da,' Grace said excitedly.

Kate nodded her head as they pulled Rachael towards the door. Rachael twisted free and walked over to Ramulas, kissing him on the cheek before walking out with his daughters. Ramulas stood like an animal caught in a trap. The tone sounded again, and he knew the mayor of Turtha was calling him.

****

K'ayden walked alongside his wife, leading his people heading towards Turtha. It had taken some time to conquer the fear that they were being tricked again and would be held captive.

The soldiers and Khilli walked and rode together. The mayor had taken care to ensure that the soldiers did not act like escorts; everyone needed to be seen as equals.

When they reached the town, the mayor raised his hand, and the column stopped. The Khilli women and children talked excitedly. They were one hundred yards from the open gate. They could see the towns people and spoke about what life would be in the town.

The mayor turned to K'ayden and smiled. 'Let your people stay here. Come inside with me and talk with the Lord of Sanctuary. After this, you can decide what is best for your people.'

K'ayden turned and spoke to his people in Khilli, and they nodded before he followed the mayor inside with the soldiers. Once inside,

K'ayden was happy to see two things—first, all the soldiers had come inside the walls, and second, the gate was left open.

The mayor led K'ayden into his quarters and sounded the tone; at first, nothing happened, and K'ayden watched the mayor closely. A few moments later, another tone sounded and an image of Ramulas appeared before them.

Ramulas' eyes widened as he smiled. 'K'ayden, my friend, what are you doing there? And why are your people outside the gate?'

K'ayden sighed. 'Our village was attacked by the giant spiders. The soldiers of Turtha came to our aid,' he said, nodding to the mayor.

Ramulas' jaw dropped, and then he listened to accounts from K'ayden and the mayor. By the time they had finished, an involuntary shiver ran through Ramulas. 'I need to travel to your village and see for myself. It sounds like there were more spiders than last time. I want to see if there are any more where they came from.'

K'ayden turned from the mayor to Ramulas. 'He has welcomed my people to stay here. Is it a good idea?'

Ramulas' eyes widened as he opened his arms. 'Yes, my friend, he is a good man, and your people will be safe here.'

Ramulas turned to the mayor. 'I need you to send another message to Keah to tell them what you witnessed and ask for them to send urgent help.'

Ramulas' image faded, and K'ayden turned to leave the mayor's quarters.

'Where are you going?' the mayor called.

'To bring my people inside.'

***

Ramulas flew across the plains toward the Khilli village, following the tracks left by the Khilli and soldiers. When he arrived, Ramulas saw the bodies of giant spiders covering the ground. He shook his head, thinking that they were lucky there were not more casualties from the Khilli and kingdom forces—there were so many spiders. He knew that

179

if the soldiers had not come, the Khilli warriors would have lost many warriors.

Ramulas lifted his astral image higher and saw the trails left by the giant spiders coming towards the village. He decided to follow the tracks and see where they led. He shook his head a few times as he became dizzy, and his magical energies began to falter. Ramulas knew that he would have to return home soon.

That is when he saw movement a few miles away. A determined expression came over Ramulas, and he pushed himself forward. He stopped and shook his head at the sight before him: there were hundreds, perhaps thousands of the giant spiders. Then his eyes widened as he realised there were thousands and thousands of the creatures.

Ramulas floated above the sea of spiders that slowly moved towards the Khilli village. He thought that if the Khilli and Turtha's soldiers had trouble with one hundred giant spiders, they would not stand a chance facing this many.

Ramulas tapped into his ability to communicate with animals and touched one of the spider's minds. He wanted to know why they were here, where they had come from, and how to stop them.

The spider's language was strange, and it was hard to comprehend its thoughts, but what he did understand frightened him as he saw through the creature's eyes.

The spiders had come from a dark and dying world to the kingdom for the purpose of finding a new home and food. The surviving spiders from the Khilli encounter were now with this group. The spiders had studied the fighting style of the Khilli and knew ways to defeat them and planned to kill all in their path.

Da, the dryads are here, Grace communicated with him.

Ramulas felt his magical reserves almost depleted and flew as fast as he could for Sanctuary.

He opened his eyes to find himself sitting on the floor of the throne room. He winced as he opened his eyes and fell to his side with a moan.

Pip raced over to him. 'You pushed yourself too far this time. Why did you do it?'

Ramulas took a few short breaths before pushing himself back up into a seated position on the floor. 'What happened while I was gone?'

'The dryads have come into the courtyard. They caused a little trouble with the people, so now they wait in the clearing.'

Ramulas squeezed his eyes shut and took a few deep breaths before standing and gesturing for Pip to lead the way.

Coming out into the courtyard, Ramulas saw a large group of people staring down the passageway into the clearing where he could see several dryads.

Pip pulled him by the arm. 'This is what happens when dryads come into Sanctuary, so I had them wait outside until you returned from your astral journey.'

Ramulas raised an eyebrow as Pip cleared the way through the people leading him out into the clearing. Once there, they found Kate and Grace talking with Eady.

Eady turned to Ramulas. 'The giant spiders at the edge of the forests near Shes have now entered.'

Ramulas' eyes widened. 'Do they come for Sanctuary?'

The dryad shook her head. 'No, they head for the plains.'

He shook his head. 'They are heading for Turtha. I think they will join with the group I saw earlier; this cannot be good. There is much work to be done.'

'Do you need the help of the dryads?' Eady asked.

Ramulas shook his head. 'For now, just watch them, and let me know if they come back into the forest.'

Eady nodded and the dryads melted into the trees. Ramulas turned to his girls. 'Kate, Grace, I want you both inside. It might not be safe out here.'

Grace's eyes turned black as dark energies crackled around her. 'Da, I can help.'

Ramulas smiled. 'You can help later, little one, but for now, I want you and Kate inside.'

As they walked through the passage, he turned to Pip. 'Spread the word—no-one is to leave Sanctuary. We all need to stay inside and train.'

Pip smiled. 'I don't think Iguchi will listen to me.'

'He will if you say there will be a battle soon. I will need to train as well. Since losing Jacqueline, I have not touched my weapons. I have a feeling that I might need them soon.'

***

Ramulas walked into the training room and smiled at the four strawmen. Seeing them brought back a lot of memories. It felt like a lifetime ago when Oriel had come into his life and everything changed. Since that day, so much had happened. Ramulas had become stronger than he could have ever dreamed.

Then he realised that he had been given no other choice but to be who he was now.

His smile grew as the strawmen transformed into four Legion soldiers, watching Ramulas with eyes full of hate. He knew they would kill him if they had the chance.

Ramulas would not have it any other way.

Ramulas stepped into the middle of the four and activated them. The four Legion soldiers exploded into motion as Ramulas spun his weapons. He parried, dodged, and blocked strikes before delivering his own devastating attacks.

When the four soldiers lay broken at his feet, Ramulas stepped away and could feel some of his magical reserve returning. He knew the Legion soldiers were made of magic and would soon repair themselves.

In a few moments, they stood strong once more, watching Ramulas with pure rage in their eyes and ready to fight again. Ramulas smiled and gave them what they wanted. Time and time again he fought and beat the Legion soldiers.

He heard soft clapping behind him, and he turned to see Pip leaning on the wall, smiling at him. 'You are happy when you fight them. I can see it in your eyes.'

Ramulas looked at Pip with a knowing smile. 'This might sound strange, but I feel free fighting them.'

'Have you finished?' she asked.

Ramulas nodded. 'Thousands of giant spiders are marching toward Turtha. They have attacked the Khilli village. Now they return with greater numbers.'

Pip's eyes widened. 'What happened to the Khilli?'

'Two died, and the rest are now in Turtha where it is safer for them. I need to talk with the mayor. We can help them.'

Pip crossed her arms and scowled. 'Why should we help them? They helped the king twice when he attacked us.'

Ramulas shook his head and sighed. 'Pip, things have changed. The town of Shes is no more, King Zachary is dead, and his daughter refuses to help her own people.'

Pip shrugged. 'So?'

'If we do not come together and fight the spiders as one, the people of Sanctuary will have to fight them after they have gone through the other towns. Have you not seen the artwork in Journey's End? I want to face these creatures on my terms.'

Pip walked over and poked a finger at Ramulas' breastplate. 'I will help, but that does not mean I am happy about it.'

***

Ramulas sat on the floor of the throne room, preparing for astral travel. He sent Pip to gather the elementals, Rain and Joshua, the giant-kin, Iguchi, and the Fallen Angels, Shigar, the druids, and Rygar. He would tell them of his plans for Turtha. He was not sure if they would agree, but in his mind, this was the only way.

Ramulas flew across the land until he came to the town of Turtha. He smiled seeing the Khilli people moving around and mingling with the people of the town.

Ramulas sounded the tone in the mayor's quarters before making himself visible. The mayor and K'ayden walked over to the image to greet him.

Ramulas sighed. 'I have returned with grave news. Thousands of the giant spiders have left Shes and are coming this way.'

The mayor took a step back, sucking in a quick gasp. 'What? Are you sure? How far away are they?'

'The spiders will arrive within the next two days.'

The mayor glanced around the room quickly. 'We need to get the people out of here to somewhere safe. We cannot fight that many spiders.'

Ramulas shook his head. 'Women, children, supplies, and the elderly will slow you down, and the spiders will be able to track you and hunt you outside of the walls. Everyone needs to stay here and fight. That is our only chance. I will bring the army of Sanctuary.

'I will send the image of both of us to the mayor of Covedon. Did you receive a reply from Keah for the help you asked for?'

The mayor shook his head.

'Then let us go to Covedon and see what the mayor says when he hears what has been happening.'

The mayor of Turtha nodded, and Ramulas waved his hands through the air while chanting.

***

The aviarymaster looked up as a pigeon flew in through the window with a silver tube tied to its leg. He opened the tube and gasped as he read the message. He needed to speak with the Master of Shadows after he handed it to the royal guard watching over the queen.

He quickly made his way through the castle to the queen's chambers, eyes cast down every time he passed someone, subconsciously brushing away at his dirty clothing. He nodded to the two guards at the door, who let him in.

The agent who usually took the messages shook his head slightly and tried to gesture to the aviarymaster to leave the room, but the royal guard smiled and walked over to him.

'Thank you. I will take that,' the royal guard said, taking the tube.

The agent in the corner froze as Aleesha jumped off her throne with her hand outstretched. 'Give that to me. It belongs to me.'

He ignored her while unrolling the tube as the aviarymaster walked away. Then his jaw dropped as he read the message.

One hundred giant spiders have attacked Khilli village near Turtha.
Soldiers of Turtha helped them.
Khilli inside Turtha.
Send help now.
More spiders coming.

He took a deep breath and handed the message to Aleesha, stepped back, and waited for her reaction. He gasped and stepped back when a cruel smile spread on her face reading the note.

Aleesha motioned for the agent to come closer. 'The Khilli belong to me. Send a message for the mayor of Turtha to put them in chains and bring them to me. I will see them all punished for taking the side of Sanctuary, and I want the Lord of Sanctuary brought to me as well.'

The agent smiled, patting her on the forearm before disappearing out the door. The royal guard shook his head as he walked towards the queen. 'My queen, what of the giant spiders? Should we not help kill them?'

Aleesha shook her head and sneered. 'The giant spiders have been sent by my father's vengeful spirit to punish those in Sanctuary and everyone that helped them.'

He held out his arms. 'But the town of Shes and its people?'

Aleesha waved her hand dismissively. 'That was a warning to the other towns to obey my rule.'

The royal guard stood shaking his head slowly. After a few moments, he gave a short bow and left the chambers. He would talk to the Master of Shadows and then to the captain of the royal guard.

18

The royal guard quickly changed out of his uniform and, within a few minutes, walked through the poor section near the docks. He stopped outside a store that appeared abandoned, with a broken window that had been boarded up.

He walked over and knocked a pattern on the door—two-three-two—and waited. He stood with his back to the street with his head down. The royal guard did not want to be recognised.

The door opened, and a strong pair of hands pulled him in and the door shut again. If someone was watching and blinked, they would have missed it.

He was pulled into a dim room, the only light coming from the cracks in the walls. He tried to make sense of the outlines of the shapes around him in the gloom. A pile of crates and barrels filled one corner, and three large figures stood before him.

'My husband has gone fishing,' a female voice said from behind him.

The royal guard nodded. 'And he has forgotten his net.'

The three large figures backed away, and a thin figure walked into his vision. 'Tell me why you are here,' she said.

'I have news about the queen for the Master of Shadows.'

She came closer, and he was able to see her long dark hair and pale face. 'Tell me, and I will pass the word.'

The royal guard told of the message from Turtha and the queen's rection to it. When he had finished, she nodded. 'Thank you. You will be shown the way out.'

Two pairs of hands held his arms and guided him the rear of the store. If it were lighter, the royal guard would have seen the aviarymaster standing quite still by the barrels and crates.

This was the way of the Shadows: many informers telling and always kept apart, the left hand never knew what the right hand was doing.

Except for the Master of Shadows. He he controlled everything.

***

Lucas raised his head as the royal guard approached wearing a worried expression. It was the one he had appointed to watch over the queen.

He raised a hand, stopping the guard. 'Tell me what has happened.'

Lucas sat in stunned silence as the guard retold the story of the message from Turtha and the queen. When he had finished, Lucas was on his feet and walking out of the door. 'Come with me. We need to talk to the queen.'

They walked into the queen's chambers to see her laughing at something one of her agents had said. She turned to Lucas with a sneer before turning back to the agent and smiling.

'My queen,' Lucas said in a stern voice. 'I hear there have been more reports of giant spiders. What are your intentions?'

Aleesha shrugged. 'I will do nothing. They have been sent to destroy Sanctuary and those who support them.'

Lucas flinched and took a step back. Aleesha had allowed the death of her father to cloud her judgements. These were not the actions of a queen but of a spoilt child.

Lucas composed himself. 'I will ready the armies and march for Turtha at dawn. I will wait for the ship to return with news from Shes; if it is grave, we will march with all haste.'

Aleesha stood from her throne, shaking with rage as her face turned red, and pointed to Lucas. 'I am queen. I will say when and where my army goes.'

The agent closest to her clapped and turned to her. 'My queen, as always, you are correct.'

Five other agents stepped out from behind curtains drawing swords and made a semicircle around Lucas and the royal guard.

Lucas ignored them and turned to Aleesha. 'My queen, please listen to reason. I am here to guide you in ruling. This is not the way.'

Aleesha stamped her foot. 'I am queen, and no-one tells me what to do. Get rid of the two of them.'

The agents closed in, smiling and waving their swords. Lucas turned to the door and whistled loudly. The door burst open, and twenty royal guards poured into the room. The six agents froze mid-step, dropping their weapons.

'No!' Aleesha screamed. 'I will not let you get away with this.'

Lucas smiled at her as the agents were bound and escorted from her chambers. 'From this moment, you are no longer queen. The royal guard will rule the kingdom until such time as you are able to show you are worthy to be a queen to the people. You will be permitted to stay here in your quarters and be present when decisions are made, but you will have no say in these matters.'

Aleesha shook her fist at Lucas. 'You cannot do this! This is treason, and I will have you hanged.'

Lucas sighed and nodded. 'I *can* do this. You are no longer queen and have no power.'

He nodded to the six agents who knelt on the floor with their hands tied behind their backs. 'Your agents have caused too much trouble. Their advice has turned you against your people. This is not how a queen acts.'

As the agents were led away, Aleesha sat on the throne and cried.

***

The queen of spiders was told that a ship had been taken. The memories of those on board now belonged to the spiders. This ship had come from a place much larger than Shes, with many, many more humans to feed from. The spiders knew how to sail this ship. The queen ordered three hundred of her children to travel to this place.

The ship sailed away with gladiators, hunters, and psychic spiders crawling up the masts and over the deck of the vessel.

The queen thought of the two large groups of spiders she had sent into the kingdom; the psychic spiders would communicate when their battle was successful.

Soon the queen would bring hundreds of thousands of her children to this new world to feed.

***

Ramulas sighed as he stood with Pip in the throne room. He was about to make another choice that he knew meant people would die, but if they did not help Turtha, many more would die, including the Khilli.

He sighed. 'We need to bring the people of Sanctuary to help those in Turtha from the giant spiders.'

Pip shook her head. 'They fought alongside the king twice when he marched on Sanctuary; why would we help those who attacked us?'

'Things change. King Zachary is dead, and the queen refuses to help them. If we do not help, a lot of people will die.'

'We need to crush our enemies, not help them,' Pip said, crossing her arms.

'They were not our enemy by choice. They were led astray by an evil king. I have spoken to the mayor of Turtha, and he understands his mistakes. We need to show unity when we talk of helping Turtha. The people cannot see us divided; can you ask the people into the courtyard?'

Pip scowled. 'We should let the spiders take them. They followed a king who killed my parents. The new queen does not care about them; why should we?'

Ramulas sighed. 'We need to show unity. I know you are hurting from the king's actions, as are as many others, but this is different. If we do not work together, we could lose this battle.'

Pip shook her head. 'I will do as you ask, but I am not happy about it.'

Ramulas prayed that she would see reason over her anger towards the royal family.

***

Ramulas stood on the balcony and saw the people filling the courtyard and surrounding streets. Pip, Iguchi, and Shigar were there with him.

The people below murmured with excitement, pointing up to those on the balcony. Rumours of the giant spiders have been spreading for days, and now people were talking about the spiders coming to Sanctuary. Why else would the Lord of Sanctuary hold this meeting?

Ramulas raised both hands and waited for the people to stop. 'I have news of the spiders. They attacked the Khilli village.' Ramulas paused while people shouted in outrage, asking what happened.

Ramulas held his hands up once more. 'The Khilli received help from the soldiers of Turtha, and the Khilli are now there for their safety.'

This brought even more questions from the people below. They could not understand why a town of the kingdom would help the Khilli. Ramulas waved his hands through the air while casting a spell. In a few moments, an image of the Khilli village appeared on the wall of the castle.

This had the desired effect, as the people gasped at the ground covered with the bodies of the dead spiders throughout the village.

'Two Khilli died on this day, and it would have been many more if the soldiers from Turtha had not turned up when they did. The Khilli are all inside Turtha.'

More people from the crowd called out, with the main question being why the Khilli didn't come back to Sanctuary.

Again, he raised his hands. 'The reason the Khilli went to Turtha is because they might not have made it this far.'

Ramulas waved his hands through the air, casting another spell. This time, an image of thousands of spiders marching toward Turtha could be seen. The people below gasped as they saw the sheer number of creatures.

'These are the spiders from Shes. They will kill everything in their path on their way to Turtha. I know the people of Sanctuary have doubts about helping those in Turtha, but we need to unite to stop this threat from spreading throughout the kingdom.'

Ramulas paused for a moment before continuing. 'When I first found out about the giant spiders and what happened at Shes, I contacted the mayor of Turtha. He sent a message to the queen in Keah asking for help. She replied that she would not send help and Turtha would need to fend for themselves.

'Then the mayor saw the lies that King Zachary had told him all these years. They need our help to fight a greater enemy, and I could not refuse, because if the spiders kill everyone in Turtha, we could be next. If you are with me, we leave at dawn tomorrow.'

The crowd erupted into a frenzy with people shouting and fists punching the air.

***

Ramulas stood in the throne room at the head of the table. With him were Pip, Shigar, the druids, Iguchi and the Fallen Angels, Joshua and Rain, the giant-kin, the elementals, Owain, and Rygar. A hologram map of the kingdom floated on the table. Sanctuary and Turtha glowed brightly.

'We need to move everyone from Sanctuary through the forest and across the plains to Turtha. This will take us two days. We need to arrive before the giant spiders.'

Rygar shook his head. 'Then you'll be tired before the fightin' begins.'

Ramulas shrugged. 'But we cannot get there faster.'

Shigar smiled. 'I know a way. When we fought the Legion, I teleported some of the enemy from the clearing to a place closer to Turtha. I could reactivate the spell, and we all could be in Turtha by tomorrow afternoon.'

'Will it harm the people?' Ramulas asked.

Shigar shook his head. 'Apart from feeling a little dizzy, they will be fine if they move away from the spot as soon as they arrive to allow space for others to come. But the only problem with this spell is that it is one way; we will all be walking home.'

Ramulas sighed with relief before waving his hands over the table. The image of the kingdom faded and was replaced with the town of Turtha. The town was surrounded by a twelve-foot wall with gates facing north, east, south, and west.

'The spiders will be able to climb the walls,' Iguchi said.

Shigar nodded. 'And the people will be trapped inside.'

Ramulas shook his head. 'I don't like this, but we need to find a way of hurting the spiders before they reach the walls.'

'This will be difficult,' Iguchi said.

'I know.'

'It will be very difficult, Lord of Sanctuary, but I have faith in you.'

***

Battle plans and tactics were discussed for hours until they had covered every foreseeable situation. Then came time to prepare for their journey. Ramulas watched those around him gather what they needed. He thought about the dragons. They would make a big difference in the battle. He had attempted to contact them several times, but they were too far away from Journey's End.

Ramulas communicated with Rufus to wait for him. He leapt into the air and tapped into Oriel's magical ability. Great wings of purple energy grew from his back, and he flew out of the window and through the passageway into the valley.

Ramulas took one last look at the valley before flying east as fast as he could. Mountains raced passed him in a blur, and he soon came to a valley he had been to before. A few miles past this valley, Ramulas became dizzy and needed to rest.

Ramulas stood on a mountain and faced east, where he saw that the mountain ranges gave way to rolling grasslands. He tried once more to contact the dragons. After a few moments, one of the dragons responded.

Hello, spirit of the dragon.

Ramulas smiled, sighing in relief. *There is an evil force in the kingdom. We need the help of the dragons before it comes to Sanctuary.*

We cannot leave this place. There is danger to the east. Dark magic is at play. We wait to see where this leads.

Ramulas' smile disappeared as his jaw dropped, and he blinked a few times. *What danger is there? Tell me of the dark magic.*

We cannot say. All we know is that this magic is old and very powerful; it could be strong enough to destroy us. This is why we must study this magic.

Ramulas shook his head. *Without your help Sanctuary could be no more. I would not ask if it were not so dire.*

I will consult the others about your plight.

***

Lucas had instructed the royal guard to remain within the castle. During the transfer of power from the queen, many things could go wrong. Most of the secret agents who used Aleesha as a pawn had been rounded up and imprisoned; however, a few agents had gone into hiding.

These agents could cause a lot of trouble.

It was when Lucas was searching for them that he saw a figure duck into a doorway one hundred yards from him. He quickly followed, and it soon became clear that he was following the royal guard who was to watch over Aleesha. But he was not in uniform. He had come out of the servant's entrance of the castle. Lucas decided to follow him.

Lucas waited for the royal guard to walk out of the gate before he went to the guardhouse. The soldiers became instantly alert and saluted. Lucas removed his black guardsman cloak and handed it to a soldier, pointing to a worn grey cloak hanging on the wall.

'Give me that cloak and watch mine until I return.'

Lucas walked into the city, following his royal guard from one hundred yards away on the other side of the street. In no time, they had reached the docks, and the guardsman stopped at an abandoned store and knocked on the door before turning to glance into the street behind him. Lucas ducked behind a pile of crates, only to come out a second later and find the man had vanished.

Lucas waited and searched the area for a few minutes before returning to the castle. Thoughts swam through his head. The Master of Shadows had told him that he had people in the castle working for him, and then he was told of the aviarymaster. He did not want to believe that a member of the royal guard would be working for the Shadows. Not at a time like this.

Lucas found himself in the aviary and walked up to the master, who was feeding the pigeons. 'I want answers.'

The man's eyes widened as he held up his hands. 'I cannot tell you anything. The Shadows will kill me.'

'If I do not have the answers I want, *I* will kill you,' Lucas said, dropping his body slightly and swinging a left hook into the man's side. The aviarymaster gasped as one of his ribs broke, and he dropped to his knees, holding his side.

Lucas walked over, kicking the man in the face. 'I want answers.'

The aviarymaster held up his hands and shook his head. Lucas beat the man for a few moments as a satisfying smile spread on his face.

***

Lucas walked through the streets of Keah, dragging a bruised and battered aviarymaster. People on the street quickly moved aside when the duo came close.

They stopped at the abandoned building that Lucas had seen the royal guard go into. Lucas pushed the aviarymaster to stand in front of the door while he pressed his back against the front of the building.

The aviarymaster glanced at Lucas with pleading eyes. 'Please do not make me do this.'

Lucas sneered. 'Knock on the door, or I will eat your heart in front of you while you die.'

His body seemed to collapse on itself as the aviarymaster sighed, giving the secret knock on the door. The door opened, and Lucas pushed the aviarymaster into the building and followed him into the dim room.

The aviarymaster fell to the floor as the door was slammed shut. Lucas covered his eyes and pulled out his sword as shutters of the lamps were raised and flooded the room with light. He saw four large men, each holding a club and rushing toward him.

Lucas shook his head, lowering the tip of the sword, danced sideways, and ducked a swinging club. He stabbed the Shadow in the forearm, causing the man to drop his weapon with a grunt. Lucas stood and turned before charging ahead with a flurry of slashes from his sword.

Two more Shadows dropped their weapons, holding onto bloodied hands.

A whistle sounded, and the room was bathed in darkness. Lucas froze for a moment, holding both hands out before him. There was no sound except for his own breathing. Lucas turned in slow circles, using his sword to probe the darkness.

Once again, there was brightness, forcing Lucas to turn away while covering his eyes.

Standing before Lucas was an enraged Master of Shadows.

Lucas never saw the blow that lifted him from his feet. He landed on the floor with a grunt of pain, and the Master was on top of him. Lucas reached out for his dropped sword a few feet away, but the Master grabbed his hand and squeezed. 'You should not have come here.'

The Master thrust the tip of his dagger into Lucas' chest.

19

Ramulas waited as he looked out to the east, wondering what this dark magic could be. Then a small speck appeared on the horizon; it grew bigger and began to take shape as it came closer. In a few moments, he could see a dragon coming to him.

When it landed, Ramulas saw that it was the smallest of the dragons. This was the dragon that protected his daughters after Jacqueline had died.

Greetings spirit of the dragon, it communicated, landing in front of him.

The people of Sanctuary need the dragons' help. A great evil in coming. That is why I have come.

Ramulas studied the dragon's twenty-foot length. The other dragons were at least twice its size. He was unsure how much this dragon could help.

Are the other dragons coming?

The dragon shook its head. *They study the dark magic. I am the only dragon to come. There will be no other.*

Ramulas could feel that this dragon was young, vain, and full of pride. He needed to choose his words properly so not to offend the creature.

Ramulas bowed. *I am humbled by your presence and thankful that you are able to help us.*

He smiled as the young dragon swelled with pride. An idea came to Ramulas of how the dragon could help during the battle with the spiders.

He spoke with the dragon of what it needed to do and when to do these things. By the end of the conversation Ramulas was satisfied.

Take me back to Sanctuary so we can prepare for battle, Ramulas said.

The young dragon lowered itself so that Ramulas could climb onto its back. With a thought from Ramulas, the dragon shot into the air and sped towards Journey's End.

***

Ramulas stood in the throne room with his daughters in front of him, Grace visibly upset. 'I want to come, Da.'

Ramulas smiled, shaking his head. 'Little one, you cannot come. The people of Sanctuary are going to help the town of Turtha against the giant spiders, and I want to two of you to be safe here.'

Grace shivered as her eyes turned black and dark energies crackled around her.

Kate gasped as both her and Grace floated a foot off the ground.

Ramulas' expression grew stern. 'Grace, stop this right now and put your sister down.'

Both girls floated down, and the dark energies dissipated as Pip walked into the room holding Emily by the hand. Emily let go of Pip and ran to Grace. When the two young girls embraced, dark energies crackled around them.

Ramulas and Pip could see that both girl's eye went dark for a moment. Pip turned to Ramulas. 'Emily's powers are growing.'

Ramulas saw that the former thief's eyes glowed emerald, which meant she saw things missed by others. Ramulas waved his hands in front of the girls while chanting; they were soon covered in a white nimbus of light.

Ramulas gasped as he dropped his arms. 'Emily's power is growing, but it is growing through feeding off Grace's magical power, and as Grace feeds Emily, her power is growing as well. Kate and Grace, you will stay here with Jenna, Makayla, Tao, and Rachael until we return.'

The girl's eyes lit up at the mention of Rachael, and Ramulas knew that his daughters really liked her. This brought feelings of guilt, because he had feelings for her as well, but he still mourned the loss of Jacqueline.

He turned to Pip. 'We have a lot to do. We need to talk with the dryads.'

Pip nodded and followed him out of the throne room.

***

Ramulas and Pip stood at the edge of the clearing.

'I can see three of the dryads in the trees,' Pip said as her emerald eyes glowed.

Eady and two other dryads smiled as they stepped out the trees in front of the pair. 'Hello, Lord of Sanctuary,' Eady said.

'Is there any more movement from the spiders near the Forest of Shes?' Ramulas asked.

'All of the giant spiders have left the forest and moved to the plains.'

Ramulas sighed. 'Tomorrow, we leave for the town of Turtha. We will help them fight the giant spiders. I just hope the spiders don't come to Sanctuary while we are gone. I will ask you tomorrow morning if the spiders have changed course.'

The dryads nodded before melting back into the trees.

***

Lucas almost fainted from the pain as the sword twisted in his side. The Master of Shadows stood above him with the tip of his sword in Lucas' flesh just below the ribs. The Master was an expert of gathering information through pain.

The tip of the sword had passed through the skin and a layer of muscle but had not damaged any internal organs or arteries. The pain Lucas was experiencing would cause most men to give up their mothers.

But not Lucas, who grunted through the pain. 'Damn you.'

'My, you have been busy,' the Master said. 'You were watched as you followed your royal guard here. We were not surprised to see you return. What did you hope to find here?'

Lucas screamed once more as the sword twisted in his side and pushed further into the muscle. The Master smiled as Lucas twisted his body and delivered a weak kick to him.

The Master laughed. 'This one does have spirit. Tell me why you are here.'

Lucas grimaced. 'To protect the kingdom.'

The Master shook his head. 'The Shadows are no threat to the kingdom, or even this city. Tell me why you are here.'

'The queen,' he gasped.

'Yes, we know that the queen is no longer in power. You and the royal guard rule the kingdom in her place, and now the person who rules the kingdom lies at my feet. What do you offer me for your life?'

Lucas shot the Master an expression of pure rage. 'You will get nothing from me. I will not beg or give you one copper coin. If you kill me, my spirit will come to haunt you.'

This was said with such certainty that the Master smiled and stepped back, pulling out his sword. He gave a slight nod, and a woman ran in from the side to kneel at Lucas' side, holding a flask.

'I like you,' the Master said as he paced the room, watching as liquid from the flask was poured onto Lucas' wound. 'If I did not like you, you would have died a long time ago.'

Lucas tried to push the woman away as she pulled out a needle and thread.

The Master shook his head. 'Allow her to seal the wound, or it will become infected, and you will die painfully.'

Lucas sighed as he dropped his hands, and the woman went to work.

'The people of Keah and of the kingdom must not be told the queen has been dethroned. It would be too much change for them, bringing unrest,' the Master said.

'But she is unfit to rule,' Lucas said. 'She does not care for her people.'

The Master nodded. 'I know this, and you know this, but the people need to be led and told what to do. This has always been a part of their life. Take away a leader or replace a leader too quickly, and chaos will rule.'

Lucas frowned. 'What are you saying?'

The Master sighed. 'The people of Keah were not happy with King Zachary months before his death. Now Aleesha is queen, her actions are making the people wish her father was alive. Now if you remove her from power, the people will think the worst. I know things need to change, but it must be done slowly.'

'What of Aleesha?'

The Master waved a dismissive hand. 'She is nothing but a puppet on a string, and you will control the string.'

'What of her actions? The people have not forgotten.'

'Her agents are to be sent to Gullytown. They will be paraded through the streets as scapegoats. Let the people think that once the agents are gone, their lives will become better. Then the queen will be forgiven.'

Lucas cocked his head. 'Are you sure this will work?'

The Master raised an eyebrow. 'Do you know how many innocent people were sent to Gullytown and into the dungeons for crimes they have not committed? All it takes is one or two people to point fingers, telling small lies of what they saw, and the rest will blindly follow.'

Lucas gasped as he looked into the Master's eyes. 'I don't want to think how many people have gone through this. What happens now between the two of us?'

The Master smiled, opening his arms. 'I like you, and we have much in common.'

Lucas shook his head. 'I have nothing in common with you.'

The Master burst into laughter, clapping his hands before sighing. 'You interest me, my captain; that is why my Shadows have been watching your every move.'

The Master shrugged when Lucas shot him an expression of disbelief. 'You are not married and live alone near the castle. If a lady shows you affection, you always politely decline. You are a man who is married to his role as the captain of the royal guard, and nothing will take your attention away from your tasks. There will be no time for another in your life.'

Lucas lay still as the last stitch was tied off in his side, his face a mask of concentration and puzzlement. 'Tell me what we have in common.'

The Master spread his arms. 'We both love the city of Keah and will do anything to protect it.'

'What are you telling me?' Lucas asked.

The Master smiled. 'I am saying that we should work together and make decisions about how this fine city is ruled.'

***

Ramulas and Pip had been awake since an hour before dawn. There was much to do in such a short amount of time.

They stood on the balcony of the throne room, looking down at Sanctuary's army. The courtyard and surrounding streets were filled with people, horses, carts, and supplies.

'It seemed I worried for nothing,' Ramulas said to Pip.

She smiled up at him. 'It is better to worry than to not be ready.'

The people were now ready, and Shigar had reactivated the teleportation sections. Ramulas was told by the dryads that there was no spider movement towards Sanctuary, and the hell hounds would be staying in the castle with his girls.

'Time to go,' Pip said.

They walked to their quarters to say farewell to their families, and Ramulas saw Rachael standing with his daughters. She smiled at him, and butterflies danced inside of him. He hugged both of his girls, and Rachael walked over to him.

She gently held his shoulders and leaned in to kiss him on the cheek. Ramulas started to sway as the butterflies in his stomach grew. So many conflicting emotions ran through his head.

'I want you to come back safe to us,' Rachael said.

Kate and Grace giggled as she walked back to them. For a moment, he saw Jacqueline standing with his girls; then Rachael smiled before leading them away.

Pip punched him in the arm. 'I told you that life is too short. Kate and Grace really like her, and so do you, but now we have a battle to fight.'

***

Ramulas stood with Shigar and the druids in the middle of the clearing. The teleporting sections glowed brightly, as if the ground beneath was on fire.

'Everything is ready,' Shigar said. 'I have spoken to the people, and they will walk through in groups, knowing that when they come out on the other side they need to walk away.'

Ramulas saw that the people were lined up behind him and were ready to move. 'We will lead the way.'

He communicated with his warhorse. When Rufus came, he and Pip climbed on and moved to one of the sections. Their world grew bright for a moment before fading, and they found themselves in the plains near Turtha, which could be seen a few miles away.

They moved away just as Iguchi and the Fallen Angels appeared. They stayed to assist Ramulas and Pip move every group as they came out of the glowing light. By the time Shigar and the druids came through, the army of Sanctuary was lined up in columns across the grassland.

Ramulas turned to inspect his army one last time before turning to the town of Turtha. 'We will reach the town by midday.'

Pip winked at him. 'We'd better move, then.'

Ramulas nodded and led the way.

***

The harbourmaster of Keah watched the ships coming in and leaving the port. Three of the docks were full. Dock workers ran around unloading and loading ships. The fourth dock was kept free for fishing boats or rich merchants willing to pay inflated prices.

Shielding his eyes against the midday sun, he saw what most people would call chaos. There were ships scattered in the harbour in no apparent order. Some ships would come and others would leave while others stayed out for days. But he knew the order of what vessels came in and when. He had his assistants out in small boats passing out instructions.

Then he saw something out of place.

A ship sailed into the harbour and had not dropped its sails. All ships were to drop sail as they came into the harbour and wait for instructions. As the vessel came closer, he recognised it as the one sent by the royal guard to investigate Shes.

The harbourmaster waved his hands above his head, trying to alert his assistants to intercept the ship, but they were on the other side of the harbour.

The harbourmaster shook his head as the ship came to within two hundred yards. He searched for the captain or anyone else to signal to, but strangely, there was no-one on deck.

Then calls of alarm sounded as the ship passed other vessels. Dark shapes could be seen moving along the masts and the deck. The ship was one hundred yards away and heading for the empty dock. The harbourmaster called for people to move away.

He watched in horror as the ship ploughed into the empty dock. The sound of wood groaning and splintering echoed above the sound of the gulls and shouting of nearby people. Shards of the dock and ship flew into the air as the ship came to a stop.

By this time, everyone in the harbour and on the docks had seen this. Workers on the docks raced to the fourth dock. The harbourmaster waved his arms, calling out warnings, trying to tell people to stay away from the ship.

Then the giant spiders swarmed out onto the docks.

Those closest to the ship did not stand a chance as three hundred hungry spiders attacked.

Screams of terror quickly spread from the docks into the streets. Sailors on the ships called out to the people on the docks to run for their lives. They thought themselves lucky because they were on the water and therefore safe. Their thoughts quickly changed as the hunters skipped across the water to attack those on nearby ships.

***

The queen of spiders sat in the town of Shes, communicating with the four psychic spiders aboard the ship as it came into Keah's harbour. She was able to see, hear, and feel what the psychic spiders could.

The city of Keah was much larger than Shes, with many more ships on the water and buildings on land, which meant more food for her children.

She told her children to attack, to bring more food and ships back to Shes. The queen would need these ships to send thousands more spiders to this city.

Soldiers on the dock were the first to respond to the attack.

Four soldiers watching over the vendor carts ran for the docks when they first heard the screams. They fought against the sea of people running from the docks in panic. Once they broke through, they gasped and stepped back. The spiders came pouring off the docks, and a score of people fell under the wave of spiders.

The sergeant turned, hearing a whimper next to him, and saw a young private who had only been in the army for a week. Tears filled his eyes as he slowly shook his head, mouthing 'No' over and over.

The sergeant slapped the private across the face. The boy blinked before snapping to attention. The sergeant grabbed him by the shoulders. 'Run to the castle and bring back the army.'

He pushed the private away before leading the other two soldiers towards the giant spiders. They pulled out their swords as they ran. The sergeant knew they would not survive but wanted to take as many of the spiders with him as he could.

The hunters saw the threat and leapt through the air at the coming soldiers. The sergeant grunted, hacking off a spider's leg before he was buried under its weight and fell to the ground. The last thing he saw was the young private disappearing into the crowd.

***

By the time Lucas led the royal guard to the docks on horseback, they saw several groups of soldiers battling the giant spiders. 'The messages from Turtha were true,' he whispered, touching his side where the Master had stabbed him. The wound still throbbed and needed time to heal, but that would have to wait.

The docks and surrounding area still held hundreds of people. They ran screaming without any direction, often running straight into the path of one of the giant spiders.

A group of spiders broke away and headed towards the market.

'Follow me,' Lucas shouted as he led the charge.

Coming closer, he pulled out his sword and saw movement out of the corner of his eye. He turned and smiled, seeing scores of soldiers running to the docks with weapons drawn. Lucas wore a grim smile as he pushed his horse faster.

The front line of spiders turned and reared their front legs as the royal guard closed in. A few jumped over Lucas as he slashed at his first spider. Lucas found himself surrounded by spiders and hacked away at creatures on both sides. Soldiers and the royal guard joined the fray. Men grunted and swore as they fought the spiders.

Lucas' horse became spooked as a spider climbed on its rear, and Lucas had to hold on with both hands as it jumped and kicked out. He had just settled his horse when a hunter jumped onto Lucas, knocking him to the ground. He screamed, holding onto his injured side, and saw the sea of men and creatures battling around him.

Lucas got to his hands and knees with his sword in hand, searching for the spider that knocked him from his horse. He was hit from the side, and a pair of dark fangs caught his sword arm. Lucas turned and recoiled, seeing his own image in the creature's many eyes.

With a jerk, Lucas was pulled to the ground and dragged through the mass of bodies. He kicked at the creature and attempted to break free. He soon found himself away from the other royal guard and soldiers. All were busy fighting for their lives.

The spider released its grip on Lucas, and he flipped onto his side as the spider jumped onto him. Lucas kicked out as the fangs came closer to his face. The creature pushed down, and Lucas grunted with the effort of holding the weight of the spider as it flailed its legs at him.

The spider continued to push down while striking out with its front legs. His strength was leaving him as he deflected the blows, and he did not know how long he could hold it back.

A dark shadow knocked the creature off him. Lucas turned to see two large men attack the spider with spears. In a few moments, it lay dead.

'It looked like you needed some help,' a familiar voice said as a pair of strong hands lifted him to his feet.

Lucas found himself facing the Master of Shadows, and behind him were scores of people of all ages—street rats, beggars, rogues, sailors, and enforcers—each one carrying a weapon. The Shadows had come to the party. All of them wore angry expressions.

'Attack!' the Master shouted.

With a roar, the Shadows ran forward, waving their weapons. They hit the wall of spiders at the same time as hundreds of soldiers who had rushed from the barracks. The Master and his enforcers stayed close to Lucas. The tide had turned, and the surviving spiders began to break away from the main group.

Lucas collapsed to the ground holding his side. His wound had torn open, and he tried to stem the blood. He sat watching the Master and his four enforcers protect him from any spiders that came too close.

Slowly, the sounds of battle started to shift. People began to cheer as the spiders were killed or ran from the fight. Within a few moments, a final cheer rang out as the last of the spiders on the dock were killed.

Lucas was lifted to see bodies of giant spiders and people scattered along the docks and surrounding streets; many people were dead while the injured began to call out for help.

Then Lucas saw that the soldiers and royal guard had surrounded the Shadows. The thieves' guild had played their hand and, in doing so, had exposed themselves. They were outnumbered by more than ten to one.

Soldiers who had hunted the Shadows smiled; this would be the end of the thieves' guild.

20

Ramulas held up his hand, and the people of Sanctuary stopped five hundred yards from Turtha. A welcoming party rode out to meet them. He heard Pip counting the horses till she reached one hundred, then she said, 'I didn't expect to see that.'

Ramulas noticed that half of the riders from Turtha wore the kingdom uniform and the other half were Khilli warriors who smiled and nodded at the people from Sanctuary. The mayor pulled his horse to stop fifteen yards from Ramulas, and his soldiers fanned out behind him. The Khilli rode past the mayor to mingle with the people of Sanctuary.

K'ayden smiled as he came up to Ramulas. 'Hello, my friend. I am happy to see you once more.'

Ramulas sighed and smiled sadly. 'I am sorry for the loss of your people, but happy you have found shelter. Where can we set up camp?'

Pip jumped down from the back of Rufus as Ramulas turned to the mayor. 'The people of Sanctuary have come to help you fight a common enemy, I have word that a great number are travelling across the plains. We have much planning to do before they arrive.'

The mayor's eyes were locked on Pip as she walked around with her hair flowing in the breeze. 'To fight a common enemy, we are willing to forget the past for now. The queen will not be sending help. We welcome for you to fight alongside us and the soldiers from Covedon.'

Ramulas raised an eyebrow. 'How many are coming from Covedon?'

The mayor shrugged. 'We don't know. They are a two days' ride from here. I just hope they arrive in time.'

Ramulas noticed that the mayor had focused on Pip the whole time they had been talking. Pip had also noticed, stopped, and gave him a defiant glare.

Ramulas nodded to the former thief. 'Is there a problem here?'

The mayor nodded. 'King Zachary was killed by a young woman with purple hair. Would you be that person?'

The soldiers of Turtha tensed at what was said.

Pip smiled, opening her cloak to reveal her throwing knives, and raised her chin. 'He deserved to die, but he went too quickly. I wish he had suffered more.'

Several of the soldiers pulled out their swords upon hearing this.

'Hold!' the mayor shouted, holding up his hand. 'I want to hear the reason behind this.'

Pip looked at Ramulas who nodded.

Pip took a deep breath and told the story of how her parents had been unjustly sent to Gullytown and their family home burnt to the ground. Pip and her sister had been forced to fend for themselves before being taken in by the Shadows, and then she had found out, while living in Sanctuary, that both her parents had been killed in Gullytown, and she blamed the king for this.

Royce and Shayn stepped from the crowd, each placing a hand on her shoulder. The mayor and soldiers of Turtha were shocked to see the earth elementals. They told of their accounts of what life was like living in Gullytown and that most of the people that died there did not deserve to be there.

The mayor frowned and shook his head slightly; after hearing what King Zachary had done to the Khilli people, he had doubts about his loyalty to the crown. Now this pushed him even further into questioning where to place his loyalty.

The mayor nodded. 'For now, we need to work together. The past will be forgotten. Many lives will be lost if we don't act as one.'

Ramulas sighed with relief. 'We need to do a lot of planning before the spiders come.'

The mayor waved his hand. 'Bring your people inside,' he said before turning his horse and leading the way into the town.

***

Ramulas, Pip, Rygar, Iguchi, Owain, Shigar, and the druids stood with the mayor in his chambers. Berenice was the only one who sat in a chair. Pip watched as Iguchi's daughter tilted her chair back until it was balancing on the rear two legs. The former thief gasped as Berenice lifted both feet from the floor and the chair remained tilted. Pip's eyes glowed as she saw that the warrior woman's balance was perfect.

Pip smiled, knowing that it would only take the smallest shift in weight for the chair to come back down. She pulled out three of her throwing knives and threw them at Berenice. Without looking Pip's way, Berenice caught the knives in midair and began to juggle them.

Pip gasped before growling and shaking her head and threw more knives at her.

Ramulas elbowed Pip and whispered, 'Pip, stop that.'

Pip's eyes widened, and she pointed at Iguchi's daughter. 'It's not just me.'

Berenice winked at the former thief and continued to juggle the knives while keeping perfect balance.

'We received word from the queen,' the mayor said. 'She claims ownership of the Khilli people and demands we send them back to Keah. There was no word of any help to deal with our spider problem.'

Ramulas sighed. 'Then we must do everything we can with what we have.'

The mayor nodded to the druids, who stood to one side. 'What of them? Word has spread of them being here, and some people here fear the druids more than the giant spiders.'

Ramulas smiled while nodding. 'The people of Sanctuary were the same when the druids showed up there, but they quickly saw them as no threat and accepted them. But time is one thing that we do not have.

Tell your people that the druids will play a major role in protecting them from the spiders.'

Ramulas turned towards the door and thought of all of the people inside the walls of Turtha. There weren't many, and the archers lined the walls, with Owain making sure his archers were scattered throughout.

The most important thing was that no-one except for the Fallen Angels were outside the walls. Miles had taken the Fallen Angels out in search of the giant spiders.

'I need to see where the spiders are so we can be ready for when they come,' Ramulas said as he sat on the floor. Everyone backed away as he began to glow.

Ramulas' astral image rose above the town, taking in the combined people organising for the upcoming battle. Then he sent his image across the grasslands in search of the giant spiders.

He found them ten miles east of the Khilli village. The army of giant spiders covered the surrounding area for miles in every direction, appearing like a moving mass of brown earth rolling and moving as the spiders crawled over one another.

Ramulas used his ability to communicate with animals on the spiders. He connected with one and could tell that the spiders were tired and needed rest. They would move again during the night.

He tried to persuade the creatures to turn back but was rewarded with a wave of hostility and rage.

Ramulas opened his eyes to see expectant faces peering at him. He shook his head. 'The spiders are near the Khilli village. They will be here soon.'

***

'Check all of the spiders,' Lucas ordered. 'I want to know that every one of them is dead. Then check for the dead and injured of our people.'

The sergeant held his sword to the Master of Shadows' neck and smiled. 'But what do we do with the Shadows?'

Shouts of alarm from the harbour stole everyone's attention. Lucas saw that two ships controlled by spiders were slowly headed out of the harbour.

'Bring the harbourmaster to me now,' Lucas shouted. 'I want archers out on the water. Kill any of the creatures on the ships and then burn them.'

Soldiers ran off in different directions calling out orders.

'What of the Shadows, captain?' the sergeant asked again.

Lucas watched the soldiers running towards the harbourmaster while archers ran for the docks. He scanned the nearby area, seeing the dead and wounded Shadows and soldiers.

One still form caught his attention; a young boy no older than twelve and dressed in rags lay dead on the ground clutching his makeshift spear. Two ragged holes were torn into his chest, and an expression of terror was frozen on his face.

Lucas nodded at the small form. 'Look over there—that small boy all by himself.'

The sergeant nodded when he saw the boy, and Lucas continued, 'That boy came to fight when the city needed him the most. He had no training, armour, or even a proper weapon, and he died a terrible death so that we live. He was one of the Shadows. The Shadows saved my life and many more.

'Today is not the day where soldiers and Shadows are enemies. We will gather our dead and injured, and all Shadows who took part in defending our city will be pardoned for all past crimes.'

Lucas smiled grimly at the shocked expressions of both soldiers and Shadows at hearing this. Then a strong hand grasped his shoulder; he turned to see the Master of Shadows.

'Thank you, my friend. You have changed many lives.'

Lucas shook his head. 'You saved my life. You could have let me die.'

The Master laughed softly. 'Then who would help me run the kingdom?'

***

Priests and healers moved through the docks, praying over the dead and helping the injured.

Lucas sniffed the air and wrinkled his nose before looking across the harbour to see one of the ships taken by the spiders alight with smoke pouring from the sails. Sailors from nearby ships shot flaming arrows at the ship while others shot at the spiders that jumped into the water.

Behind him, Lucas saw something that brought a smile to his face— Shadows were helping injured soldiers and soldiers helping Shadows, and the people combined to push the dead spiders into the ocean.

Lucas turned to the Master and smiled. 'And tomorrow they will be enemies once more.'

The Master nodded. 'New beginnings.'

***

Lucas walked into Aleesha's quarters to find her cowering behind two soldiers.

He turned to the hallway. 'Bring it in,' he called out.

Four royal guards dragged in the body of a giant spider, which was half as high as Lucas. The queen screamed and grabbed one of the soldiers in front of her.

Lucas sighed and waved to the body. 'Hundreds of these creatures attacked our city. They came via the ship that was sent to Shes. These would be the same creatures that attacked the Khilli village as well, and we have received reports that they are on their way to Turtha. If you had told me of these creatures sooner, we could have saved more people.'

Lucas shook his head while sighing and then waved the soldiers and royal guard out of the room and followed them out.

'Wait,' Aleesha shrieked. 'Where are you going? You have to take that thing away.'

Lucas stopped in the doorway but did not turn to face her. 'I am needed to help repair the damage made by the spider attack. The giant spider will stay here to remind you of the terror that your people faced because you did not care about them.'

Lucas walked from the room while Aleesha pushed herself into the corner as much as she could while never taking her eyes of the spider's body. A shiver ran through her, and then she began to quietly sob. After her father was killed, she had become queen of the kingdom. Her agents had been there to give her advice and guidance. Most had been placed in Gullytown or the dungeon, but a small number had escaped.

Now Lucas had taken all her power away, and she was miserable. She closed her eyes and hung her head. 'It is not fair. It is just not fair. I want to be queen again.'

A comforting hand was placed on her shoulder and gently squeezed, and a familiar voice spoke. 'Do not worry, my queen. Very soon your power will be restored.'

Aleesha raised her head to see the two agents that had gone into hiding kneeling in front of her.

Aleesha sniffled and wiped tears from her face. 'I want the captain of the royal guard to pay.'

Both agents smiled and gave each other a knowing look.

The same agent spoke. 'Do not worry, my queen. He will pay dearly for his deeds.'

Aleesha could not contain her smile.

***

Miles and the Fallen Angels returned to Turtha an hour before dawn, saying that the force from Covedon would arrive soon. One hundred and fifty cavalry came into the gates at dawn with word that three hundred soldiers were on their way. The cavalry had raced through the night, and introductions were made before the mayor and sheriff of Covedon were invited to discuss tactics.

Ramulas, Shigar, the mayor and sheriff of Covedon, and Rygar stood in the mayor's quarters.

Ramulas shook his head and sighed. 'The soldiers from Covedon may not arrive in time. If they are too late, we will need to send them away. They will be out in the open with the spiders.'

The mayor and sheriff of Covedon turned to Ramulas with open mouths, and the sheriff spoke. 'Who does he think he is? Why does he give orders in your town?'

Shigar smiled and raised a finger. 'This is a man who truly cares about the people. If you want your men to live, it would be best to listen to this man.'

Ramulas nodded to the sheriff. 'If your men are caught outside with thousands of giant spiders, they will not stand a chance. We all need to face them as one.'

The sheriff saw that everyone in the room was nodding in agreement.

'I will search for the spiders,' Ramulas said as he sat on the floor.

***

Ramulas' image flew across the plains in search of the horde of giant spiders. He soon found them at the Khilli village, where they were slowly moving towards Turtha.

Ramulas opened his eyes and found everyone staring down at him. He stood and said, 'The spiders have just left the Khilli village and will be here in a few hours. We need to prepare.'

Everyone raced out of the room, except for the sheriff of Covedon, who walked up to Ramulas. 'Why should my soldiers listen to you?'

Ramulas shrugged. 'Fighting alongside us gives your men a better chance of living. If the spiders are not stopped here, they could move onto Covedon.'

Ramulas walked outside without waiting for an answer. There was much to do in little time. Pip ran up to him. 'Shigar said that the spiders will be here soon.'

Ramulas nodded. 'Where are the Fallen Angels?'

'Outside the west gate. They are putting rocks in the grasslands.'

He gave her a puzzled expression.

She shrugged. 'Something to do with Shigar.'

'Spread the word for everyone to be ready.'

Ramulas heard Pip shouting as he walked out of the west gate and saw the Fallen Angels scattered out in the long grass two hundred yards from him. They had formed a semicircle, and each of the Angels held a large rock above their heads. Iguchi and Berenice stood in front of the Fallen Angels.

Ramulas walked up to the duo. 'The spiders will arrive in a few hours.'

Iguchi clapped his hands, and the Fallen Angels dropped the rocks and ran to the gate. Ramulas asked, 'Are the Fallen Angels ready?'

Iguchi and Berenice bowed, and Iguchi said, 'Hello to you, Lord of Sanctuary. My Angels are ready. My daughter and I will fight alongside them.'

Ramulas looked at Iguchi's daughter and realised that he knew nothing about her. 'I never knew you had a daughter. Why did you not say anything before she came?'

The small man smiled. 'Before was not the right time. Now is the right time, but I will tell you more about her when the time is right.'

Ramulas shook his head appearing confused. 'When will I know more about her?'

Iguchi raised a slender finger. 'Another time. But now, we ready for battle.'

Ramulas turned towards Turtha and froze when he saw the wall. Over half of the surface on the outside had been covered in black and green bubbles of varying sizes. Ramulas smiled to himself, knowing the spiders would have a hard time climbing the walls.

He saw that there were one hundred archers from Sanctuary on the walls, and mixed in amongst them were the archers of Turtha. The mayor of Turtha stood with Owain and Rygar, talking directly above the gate. The druids had broken into two groups, one on either side of the wall.

Just inside the gate stood Joshua, Rain, the elementals, and the two half-giants. This group would be the welcoming party to greet the spiders when they came. Joshua and the elementals had stone-like skin, and Ramulas knew that gave them an edge in the battle. Rain had his crystal blade, which controlled ice and could do a lot of damage to the creatures, and the half-giants had their broadswords as big as a man.

Rygar was busy lining up horses in groups of fifty while shouting out orders for soldiers of Covedon and Turtha to join with Sanctuary's forces.

Iguchi and Berenice spoke with the Angels, and Pip came up to Ramulas. 'We did not see this in the paintings or tapestries. What does this mean?'

Ramulas shook his head. 'I do not know. We will visit Journey's End after the battle.'

'You seem confident that we will win this battle,' she said.

Ramulas sighed. 'We *need* to win this battle.'

They walked through the town, checking every strategic point and battle plan. One small mistake could mean disaster. Then Ramulas knew they were as ready as they would be for the giant spiders.

21

Ramulas brought the sheriff of Covedon into the mayor of Turtha's quarters. 'I need your help. The giant spiders will be here in half an hour, and your three hundred soldiers are an hour away. They will be caught outside the gates and slaughtered.'

The sheriff glanced at the mayor before turning to Ramulas. 'What do I do?'

Ramulas sighed. 'I need them to stay where they are. They will arrive in time.'

The sheriff's expression grew grim as he waved his hand behind him. 'But we need every man we can get to defend this town.'

Ramulas held up his hand. 'There are almost two and a half thousand people in Turtha. That will be enough for now, but I have a plan, and with your help, it might work.'

Ramulas placed his hand on the sheriff's shoulder. 'Do not be alarmed.'

The sheriff froze as he and Ramulas' astral images floated through the ceiling and into the sky. The grasslands sped beneath them as they raced towards the Khilli village for a few miles before seeing the army of giant spiders.

The sheriff gasped as Ramulas said, 'This is what we will be facing, and now I will show you something else.'

They headed back to Turtha before passing the town to where the three hundred soldiers marched alongside supply wagons.

'They won't make it in time,' the sheriff whispered.

'We need to talk to them,' Ramulas said as the pair began to descend towards them. When they touched the ground one hundred yards away, Ramulas made them visible to the soldiers.

The sergeant leading the column jumped back as his eyes widened. He then shouted orders, and four soldiers on horseback accompanied the sergeant and raced to the pair. They stopped a few yards away and formed a circle around them.

The sergeant nodded to the sheriff and said, 'What news do you bring?'

'You will arrive too late and be in danger. The Lord of Sanctuary has a plan where you can still help,' he said, tilting his head to Ramulas.

Ramulas smiled. 'I have a role for your men to play, but timing is everything. For this to work, we must make our move at the right time.'

***

Two scouts raced to the west gate of Turtha, shouting and waving their arms. 'They are coming!'

Ramulas stood with Pip on the wall, and her eyes glowed fiercely. 'There are so many of them,' she whispered.

The gate was closed as the scouts came in. Ramulas wanted to agree with Pip, but he took one more look around the town. Shigar and the druids were on the wall with the archers. The people within the walls were in their groups and ready to fight.

Footsteps pounding up the stairs behind Ramulas caused him to turn, and he saw Rain at the top of the stairs with his sword out, mist cascading from the blue crystal blade.

'Are you ready?' Ramulas asked.

Rain nodded, pointed his blade over the top of the wall, and unleased a blast of ice that hit the ground fifty yards away. Turtha's archers jumped in shock and turned to Rain, awestruck by what they had seen. Rain continued to blast the grass outside the wall, covering the ground in ice.

When Rain was finished, he walked back down to Joshua at the bottom of the stairs.

The dark mass of spiders on the horizon began to take shape as the creatures came closer. Everyone on the wall took a small step back and became tense.

'We need to make the first move,' Ramulas said as he communicated with the young dragon hiding in Sanctuary's Forest. Then he turned to the people in the town behind him. 'The battle is about to begin.'

He could feel the young dragon's joy as it came closer. He saw Shigar murmuring spells with his eyes closed, and everyone waited for the spider to come into range.

***

The rolling horde of giant spiders stopped five hundred yards from the town. People on the wall began to fidget as they openly wondered what was happening.

Then, as one, the giant spiders rushed towards the wall. The archers raised their bows and shouted in defiance. The spiders passed the rocks dropped by the Fallen Angels.

People on the wall raised their weapons and shouted in defiance as the spiders lost their footing on the thin layer of ice. Ramulas turned to the people manning the catapult and made a chopping motion with his hand.

The machine released its load, sending barrels of lamp oil sailing through the air. They seemed to move in slow motion until they exploded in front of the first line of creatures, spilling the contents on the ice.

'It would have been better to light the barrels before throwing the oil at the spiders,' Pip said.

Ramulas winked at the former thief. 'Don't worry; fire is coming.'

People on the wall called out in alarm as the young dragon came into view as it dropped from the sky. It dropped down closer to the spiders, unleashing streams of flame. The lamp oil quickly caught, sending up a wall of flame. Giant spiders screamed as they burned while others scurried away from the flames.

The first six rows of giant spiders were separated from the main force by the wall of flame.

'Shigar!' Ramulas called.

He turned to see the magician reading from a thick leather-bound book while waving his free hand in front of him. The large rocks dropped by the Fallen Angels rose ten feet into the air and transformed into giant stone wasps.

Archers on the wall cheered as fifty stone wasps attacked the giant spiders. The wasps picked up the spiders, repeatedly stung them, and tore away body parts with their stone mandibles.

After a few moments of spiders being slaughtered, they changed their behaviour. As the stone wasps dropped onto a spider, the creatures surrounding it would attempt to jump onto it and bring it to the ground, and then they would pile on top of it to weigh it down.

Ramulas turned to Pip. 'It looks like they learn from their mistakes.'

He communicated with the young dragon to help the stone wasps, and it dived from the sky, spraying fire onto the creatures holding down the wasps.

Ramulas' eyes widened as spiders began jumping through the wall of flames only to hit the ground covered in fire and race toward the walls. Then the spiders rushed around the edges of the fire wall.

Ramulas knew it was too soon and needed to slow them down. 'Shigar, fence them in.'

The magician waved his hands through the air while chanting, and the stone wasps flew to meet the outer edges of the spider army. They would dive in and harass the spiders, pushing them closer to the middle. When the spiders jumped onto one wasp, the others would tear it apart.

Ramulas communicated with the young dragon, asking it to help keep the spiders in one group. He would have liked the dragon to cover the creatures in fire, but knew it had its limitations.

The horde of spiders pushed through the gap in the flames and moved towards the wall. They lost their footing when they stepped onto the ice and began to slide on the surface, losing all control.

'Owain!' Ramulas called.

The blind archer clicked his tongue rapidly for a few moments before raising his hand. The archers nocked their bows and waited.

Owain dropped his hand, and the first wave of arrows hammered into the spiders, followed by a second and third wave. Owain smiled to hear the bows sing. He had told the Turtha archers not to panic when the spiders came but to simply follow the archers of Sanctuary. So far, no-one had lost control to fear or panic.

Wave after wave of arrows peppered the creatures as they jumped over one another to get to the wall. It did not seem to matter how many died, more and more kept coming. The spiders soon adapted to the ice; scores of hunters would lie flat on the ice and link their legs, forming a makeshift surface that other spiders could run across.

Ramulas called out another command, and the north and south gates opened. Twenty archers on horseback came out of each gate. They came to the edges of the ice and fired arrows into the mass of giant spiders. After three waves of arrows, the spiders reacted and surged towards them. Iguchi had told them that when this happened, they should fall back one hundred yards and fire again.

The spiders became infuriated and attempted to attack the archers with renewed fury. They rushed towards the archers, and then the first green bubbles exploded.

Earlier that day, the druids had taken the archers out and shown them where they had hidden green bubbles amongst the grass and instructed them to lure the spiders into these areas without activating the bubbles themselves.

The archers cheered as bubbles exploded along the lines. Spiders were covered in green sticky goo, and any spider that tried to climb over them became stuck as well. The archers fired into the central mass until they were out of arrows and then returned behind the wall.

As the gates closed, the first of the black bubbles began to float down.

***

Ramulas, Rygar, Pip, and Shigar stood on the wall with the mayor of Turtha. They watched as the stone wasps and young dragon kept the army of giant spiders boxed in. The archers on horseback had just returned after leading the spiders into the mass of hidden green bubbles. Other spiders were now leaping over the sticky green mass of trapped spiders.

Small black bubbles drifted down to land on the spiders, popping and sizzling. The spiders screamed as the bubbles ate through their hardened skin. The direction of the wind changed, and the smell of the burning spiders drifted to those on the wall. Ramulas and Rygar winkled their noses, and Pip smiled at Ramulas.

'Why are you smiling?'

She shrugged. 'Smells like chicken.'

Ramulas rolled his eyes and turned away as Shigar shouted, 'Here they come.'

Ramulas saw a wave of giant spiders rushing for the wall.

Streams of green bubbles shot out from the wall towards the oncoming horde, followed by a wave of arrows hitting the bubbles ten feet above the spiders, causing a chain reaction of exploding bubbles. Hundreds of giant spiders were caught under the blanket of sticky goo. They thrashed and fought against the trap but only became more entangled.

Ramulas waved his hands through the air while chanting, and the mass of spiders caught in the sticky trap rose in the air. People on the wall gasped as the spiders rose higher and higher.

Ramulas started to shake as sweat formed on his face.

Ramulas turned to Shigar. 'Now.'

As the mass of spiders rose to fifty feet, the magician sent a blue bolt of energy at them. A plume of blue flame rose into the air as the ball of spiders exploded.

***

Three hundred soldiers from Covedon looked to the north, waiting for the signal. When they saw the blue flame flash in the sky, they knew their time had come. They began to make their way to Turtha.

***

The dragon swooped down over two lines of spiders stuck in the web, spewing streams of flame before rising into the air once more. The spiders had learned to try to jump on the dragon as it came down.

As the spiders burst into flame, the dragon communicated with Ramulas. *Spirit of the dragon, I have no more fire, and I am growing tired.*

Ramulas nodded. *You are still able to take part in the battle.*

The dragon shot towards the sky, and Ramulas turned to Shigar. 'Release the wasps.'

Shigar waved his hand, and the wasps stopped their attack on the spiders and followed the dragon into the sky.

'Here they come again,' Pip said.

Another group of spiders rushed the wall. Wave after wave of arrows rained down on them. No matter how many of the creatures died, more and more came.

Ramulas turned back, searching through the groups within Turtha until he found who he was looking for. He called out, 'Joshua, Rain, when the gate opens, your group goes out first.'

Rain pulled out his crystal blade and shot blasts of ice into the air. Joshua unleashed a primal scream and beat his iron ball onto the ground. Not to be outdone, the two half-giants screamed while swinging their broadswords. Royce and Shayn smiled at each other while their hands lengthened to form short swords.

The mayor of Turtha shook his head as the small group walked to the gate and said to Ramulas, 'You can't send only the six out with so many spiders. It will be slaughter.'

'I know,' Pip said. 'The spiders are in for a surprise.'

The spiders were fifty yards from the wall when Ramulas felt a small explosion in the pit of his stomach and was covered in purple flames. He pushed that sensation through his body. People close to him backed away as the as the flame around him intensified.

A series of pops sounded, letting those on the wall know that the spiders had hit the bubbles on the wall. Then the spiders screamed as the black bubbles were set off and burnt them. The main body of spiders hesitated as the rest were stuck to the wall and being burnt.

Ramulas sent arcs of purple energy into the spiders. Scores of spiders were thrown into the air, their bodies twitching as they were cooked from the energy.

Ramulas unleashed one more stream of energy and shouted, 'Now!'

Two things happened simultaneously—the young dragon and the stone wasps dropped from the sky, attacking the spiders, and the gate opened, allowing the group of six out amongst the spiders.

The group charged out screaming and decimated the spiders near the wall. Bodies of giant spiders were thrown around like leaves in a storm. Rain blasted ice at spiders that moved away from the group.

Ramulas was about to send Iguchi and the Fallen Angels out, but he saw something out of the corner of his eye; as the group of six moved deeper into the mass of creatures, the spiders closed in around them. It was as if the creatures thought with one mind.

He turned to the catapult, which was loaded with the last three barrels of lamp oil. 'Release the catapult,' Ramulas called.

He watched as the barrels shattered amongst the spiders one hundred and fifty yards away,

'Shigar, fireball.'

The magician waved his hand, sending a small fireball into the oil, which erupted into flames, scattering the creatures, and their previous organisation faltered.

'Iguchi, bring your Angels out now.'

Iguchi and Berenice led the Fallen Angels out of the gate; Owain whistled, and the archers on the wall stopped firing.

Ramulas watched in fascination as the Fallen Angels split into five groups of ten, each group forming a tight circle. These circles slowly turned as they moved forward with swords and shields facing outwards. Iguchi and Berenice stood in the middle of the five circles back to back, with their swords waving intricate patterns through the air.

Any of the giant spiders near the Fallen Angels were cut to pieces. Even the few creatures that attempted to jump into the middle of the circles were cut down.

Iguchi noticed the spiders keeping their distance and ordered the circles to break away, leaving him and Berenice alone and unprotected.

The creatures avoided the Fallen Angels and rushed towards the father-and-daughter team.

Ramulas held his breath as he saw waves of spiders rushing the duo.

Iguchi and Berenice stood like statues, allowing the creatures closer; then, at the last moment, they exploded into motion, their spinning blades cutting through the giant spiders as they slowly turned back to back.

***

Ramulas watched as the mass of giant spiders broke apart. The combination of the young dragon and wasps attacking from the air, Joshua's group, and the Fallen Angels was having an effect.

The spiders began heading towards the northern and southern walls of the town. Ramulas turned and saw that the next phase of the battle was ready. He opened his arms and floated above Turtha. People from Turtha and Covedon watched in awe as the Lord of Sanctuary rose into the air covered in purple flame.

Ramulas waited until the spiders had come to the southern and northern walls, with a few climbing the walls and setting of green bubbles.

'Eyes!' Ramulas called out in an amplified voice.

Everyone had been warned about this and turned away as Ramulas set off the spell. The light around Ramulas seemed to be drawn into the purple light surrounding him, then it exploded beneath him ten times brighter than the midday sun.

The spiders surrounding Turtha rolled around on the ground screaming in a pitch so high that the people behind the walls dropped to their knees holding their ears. Then the spiders ran in every direction, bumping into each other and setting off the bubbles on the wall.

Ramulas waved his hands through the air, casting another spell. A circle of white light spread from his body and dropped to the ground. The only areas it avoided was the Fallen Angels and Joshua's group. Every giant spider in the affected areas was covered in a faint white light, and their movements were slow and jerky.

'Open the gates,' Ramulas called out.

The north and south gates opened, and the cavalry poured out in a spearhead formation that easily cut through the slow-moving spiders. Then came the soldiers from within Turtha.

The soldiers came out in tight formations of fifty that ploughed into different areas of the creatures. Ramulas smiled to see those on horseback slamming into the rearguard of the spiders, using lances and spears to cut down their prey. A small group of soldiers stood guard at both gates while the archers sent wave after wave of arrows into the mass of creatures as they attempted to defend against the multi-sided attack.

Ramulas lowered himself back down to the wall. Pip held two of her throwing knives out to a druid who covered the handles in small green bubbles. She flipped the knives to catch them by the handles, and the bubbles exploded, covering her hands with goo.

'Why did you do that?' Ramulas asked.

Pip shrugged, holding up her hands. 'There will be a lot of killing soon, which means a lot of spider blood. I don't want my knives to slip out of my hands,' she said before diving off the wall.

Ramulas' jaw dropped as he watched Pip land in the middle of a group of giant spiders. She was in her element, slashing and stabbing at everything close to her. A roar caused Ramulas to turn and see Rygar running towards him.

The dwarf winked, pulling out his axe. 'I can't let the girl steal all o' me fun,' he said before jumping off to join her.

Ramulas shook his head and muttered, 'That was not part of the plan.'

'Ramulas, the wasps,' Shigar called.

Ramulas turned to see the stone wasps start to crumble and fall apart and be covered by the mass of giant spiders.

The magician shrugged. 'The spell was temporary.'

Ramulas nodded as he watched the young dragon swoop over the spiders, attacking them. Over half of the creatures lay dead, which brought a smile to his face.

A chime sounded in the distance, and Ramulas sighed. The spells of slowness and blinding had worn off. The creatures turned as one, rushing for the walls of Turtha. They ignored Joshua's group and the Fallen Angels.

Continuous popping sounded as the spiders set off the bubbles on the walls. Ramulas looked down to see that they were just throwing themselves at the wall with abandon, sacrificing themselves so that other spiders could climb over them. Shouting from both gates told Ramulas that the defenders were trying to keep the spiders out of the town.

Then the first of the spiders climbed over the wall.

'Archers!' Ramulas called out.

The archers held their bows to their bodies and took a step back from the metal railing above the wall. Ramulas cast a spell and held his hands above the metal, sending streams of white arcs of energy along the railing.

Creatures screamed and caught fire before falling.

Combining his own magical ability with Oriel's, Ramulas dived from the wall and stopped himself six feet off the ground. He flew above the spiders, covered in purple flames, with arcs of white energy dancing along his body. As he did this, the arcs of white energy would reach out and touch nearby spiders, causing them to explode. People fighting spiders saw this and cheered as their morale was boosted.

Ramulas had killed hundreds of the creatures before the flames and energy around him began to falter. He flew one last time across the battlefield before his flame went out, and he landed unsteadily near a large group of spiders. Without hesitation, they swarmed, only to be met with his spinning weapons. He slowly turned as he spun the weapons.

The spiders could not find any holes in his defence. When Ramulas had killed half of the creatures, he saw groups of Fallen Angels fighting their way towards him. Miles' group arrived first, followed by others.

Owain called down from the wall. 'We have won! The spiders are retreating.'

A stern expression crossed Ramulas' face. He could not allow them to get away so easily. Some of his magical ability had returned. He leapt into the air and saw that only a few hundred spiders had survived and were running.

Ramulas waved his hands through the air, casting another spell and causing the ground beneath the spiders to shift, trapping the creature's feet and immobilising them.

'Iguchi, I need one alive,' Ramulas called down as his magic died and he fell fifteen feet to the ground. The air was forced out of his lungs, and Ramulas lay moaning on the ground. Miles and other Fallen Angels quickly formed a circle around him as he fell unconscious.

22

Ramulas opened his eyes and saw that he was still on the battlefield. Pip and Rygar had joined the Angels in standing by him. 'What happened to the spiders?' he asked.

'Hello to you, Lord of Sanctuary,' Iguchi said with a bow. 'All of the creatures have been killed except one.'

Ramulas struggled to sit up. 'Take me to it.'

Iguchi and Miles reached down to help him stand. They led him through hundreds of dead spiders and dead and injured soldiers. One hundred yards away was a large spider with a shiny black abdomen. It struggled as he came closer, but its feet remained buried in the ground.

Ramulas stopped ten feet from the creature and communicated with it. He stumbled back, holding his head as dizzy spells almost caused him to fall. The spider was full of rage and wanted nothing more than to kill everyone nearby.

Ramulas shook his head and pushed deeper into the spider's mind. After a few seconds, he turned to Iguchi. 'Kill it.'

Iguchi stabbed the spider in between its eyes. It shuddered once before dying.

'What did you see?' Pip asked.

Ramulas shook his head as he scanned the battlefield. 'This is nothing. These spiders come from a dark world where their numbers are beyond counting. They have found a way to our world and want to eat us. We are like cattle to them.' Ramulas paused, watching everyone's shocked expressions. 'The spiders have a queen, and she is in Shes watching over the doorway that the spiders come through. There are about one hundred spiders in Shes. We need to go there, kill the queen, and destroy the doorway.'

Rygar shook his head. 'Ye don't look like yer ready for more fightin''

Ramulas sighed as he scanned the faces around him. 'None of us are ready for a fight. We will count our losses, recover, and then we march for Shes.'

Ramulas looked up and saw the young dragon circling above. *Can you see any more spiders?*

Spirit of the dragon, they are all dead.

Ramulas told the dragon to hunt and rest. He knew it would return when he called.

For now, there was work to be done in Turtha.

***

The queen of spiders sat in the middle of Shes. She had been communicating with the psychic spiders who were with the three hundred that attacked Keah. All her children had been killed, even the hunters who tried to sail ships out of the harbour.

However, she was not concerned with a few hundred dying; there were hundreds of thousands to replace them. The queen was happy to now know the defences of the city and how to counter them.

The people killed by the psychic spiders had their thoughts and memories sent to the queen. This told her everything she needed to know about invading the city without using the harbour. She would send her children across by land, and they would feed along the way.

After the attack on Keah, the queen communicated with the group that attacked Turtha. She had sent thousands of her children there, and there were fewer humans, but they had still lost. She learned that powerful magic had played a part in that battle.

The queen went over every detail of the battle of Turtha, and the people killed by the psychic spiders had their thoughts and memories sent to the queen. All these people told her that the Lord of Sanctuary was the key.

She saw him in her mind's eye flying above the battlefield bathed in flame, shooting arcs of energy at her children. His presence brought joy and hope to the humans, The queen of spiders knew this Lord of Sanctuary was dangerous, and now with the memories of the humans, she knew where to find Sanctuary. This man had united enemies to fight her children.

In that instant, the queen knew that she needed to kill the Lord of Sanctuary and everyone else within Sanctuary. Only then could her children roam freely across this new world. But the queen wanted to gather more information before going to Sanctuary, because this time, she would join her children.

***

Lucas scanned the docks and smiled. The dead and injured of Keah had been taken away, no traces of the giant spiders could be seen, and life on the docks was slowly returning to normal. Vendors were calling out, and the harbourmaster was busy bringing vessels in and sending them out to sea.

The royal guard, the soldiers, and Shadows had worked hand-in-hand to repair the damage done to Keah. It had taken days, but it was done. Now that the work was complete, everyone stood in uneasy silence, glancing at one another.

Lucas clapped once and shouted, 'Royal guard, to the castle; soldiers, return to your duties and patrols.'

A few of the soldiers gave sideway glances at nearby Shadows, and Lucas shook his head. 'The Shadows have all been pardoned for joining our fight with the spiders. Today, everyone walks away free.'

One by one, the Shadows melted away into the crowds, and the Master of Shadows gave a slight nod of his head before turning away.

Lucas needed to talk to Aleesha. There was much work to be done.

***

The first thing Lucas noticed when he walked into the queen's chambers was that the body of the giant spider was gone. Aleesha sat on her throne with a defiant expression.

'Where has the spider gone?' he asked.

'It has been taken away,' she replied before turning away from him.

'Taken by who?'

Aleesha shrugged without turning back to face him.

Lucas sighed and shook his head as he walked closer to her. 'I know you did not like the spider being here, but you needed to know what your people faced. When the people of your kingdom ask for your help, it is your duty to help them.'

Aleesha turned with a scowl. 'The mayor of Turtha helped the Lord of Sanctuary. The people of Sanctuary are enemies of the kingdom.'

Lucas shook his head and held his arms out. 'They were warning us about the giant spiders and asking for help; now that town could be under attack at any time. But after the attack on the docks, I will not send any soldiers from the city. There could be another attack.'

Aleesha shrugged. 'The people of Turtha are being punished for helping those who killed my father.'

Lucas' eyes widened as he fought to control himself. He counted to ten in his head before speaking. 'Aleesha, when you grow older, you will understand what I am trying to teach you. I hope you will be ready to be queen in two years from now.'

Aleesha forced a smile and gave a slight nod while thinking, *You will be long-gone by then.* 'Captain, I am tired after today's events, I wish to be alone and rest.'

'I will leave two of my royal guard outside if you need anything,' he said before leaving the room.

Aleesha waited until the door had closed before squealing with delight and clapping her hands. 'Just when I thought all was lost, my two missing agents returned to me.'

Tapestries on the wall moved as the agents stepped out and bowed. The trio sat and discussed how Aleesha would take back the power of the throne and be rid of the captain of the royal guard.

***

The dead were laid out in centre of Turtha. Ramulas had used his magic to help heal his people. Tapping into Oriel's power, he was able to fully heal all but the most seriously wounded.

Ramulas sighed, feeling the heavy burden weigh on his shoulders. Eleven people of Sanctuary lay dead before him and fifty from the towns of Covedon and Turtha. He replayed the battle in his head over and over, trying to think of how he could have acted differently and saved these people.

The answer was always the same: he had done everything that he could. Why, then, did he feel so guilty when he passed people with grief-stricken eyes?

Ramulas sighed slowly and shook his head as the mayor of Turtha walked over to him. 'I am truly sorry that I could not have done more.'

The mayor barked a bitter laugh. 'If you and your people had not come, everyone in this town would be dead. You have nothing to be sorry for. We offer you our thanks and gratitude.'

Ramulas nodded, accepting the praise and knowing the hard part was to come. 'At dawn tomorrow, I will take some men to Shes and kill their queen.'

Pip appeared next to Ramulas. 'Yes, let's kill more of those spiders.'

Ramulas turned to her and shook his head. 'Not this battle, Pip. I want you to return to Sanctuary.'

He saw that Pip was about to protest and turned to the mayor. 'May I use your quarters for a few moments?

The mayor nodded, and Ramulas motioned for Pip, Shigar, Rygar, Iguchi, and the druids to join him inside. Once everyone was inside, Pip exploded. 'Why do you not want me to come to Shes? I have been by your side every battle; I am coming with you.'

The former thief stood with the arms crossed and looked defiantly at everyone.

'Because our families are there, and you are the only one I trust with my daughters. I need someone they trust to be with them and protect them if danger comes.'

Pip's arms fell to her side as her chest swelled with pride while Ramulas continued. 'There is only the spider queen and a few hundred spiders in Shes. I will bring Iguchi and the Fallen Angels, Joshua, Rain, the half-giants, Shigar, the druids, and two hundred from Sanctuary. The remaining will bring the fallen and injured back home.'

Rygar coughed, and Ramulas saw the dwarf standing with his arms crossed and one foot tapping the ground. 'Don't ye be thinkin meself will be babysitting when there's spiders to be squashed.'

Ramulas smiled. 'I'm sorry, good dwarf. Of course you are coming to Shes.'

***

Da, Ramulas heard inside his mind while helping to clean up Turtha.

He stood and smiled. *Hello, little one. Have you been looking after Kate?*

Yes, Da. When are you coming home?

He sighed. *Can you bring your sister into the throne room? I have something to show you both.*

Ramulas cut the communication and walked to a nearby empty building and sat on the floor. He sent his astral image to Sanctuary and into the throne room where his daughters were waiting with Rachael. He willed his image to become visible. Grace and Kate ran to the image with broad smiles, and he laughed as they passed through him.

They stood in front of him, passing their hands through his image with awe written on their faces. Rachael stood back, smiling at the interaction between Ramulas and his daughters.

'I am using magic to send my image to you,' he said.

'Da, can I use magic to come to you?' Grace said as her eyes grew dark.

Ramulas quickly shook his head, holding out a hand. 'No, Grace. Wait until I come home. I need to travel to Shes to kill the last of them, and then I will be coming home. It will take no longer than five days.'

He noticed both girls sigh as their shoulders slumped, and he saw that Rachael looked disappointed as well.

'Pip will arrive home in two days with most of Sanctuary, and I will visit you every night like this.'

Kate, Grace, and even Rachael smiled at this news, and Rachael said, 'Stay safe.'

Ramulas swayed on his feet as he blushed and tried to stammer a response. He turned to his daughters. 'I love you and will talk to you tomorrow.'

They both replied the same to him, and Ramulas could have sworn that Rachael mouthed the words as well.

***

Turtha was busy with the army of Sanctuary leaving, with the majority heading home and the rest on to Shes led by Ramulas. He had given last-minute instructions to Pip and the druids.

The fallen from Sanctuary were wrapped in sheets of Oriel's magic to stop them from decaying until Ramulas could return and turn them into statues of the fallen.

The soldiers of Covedon headed back home with the sun rising in the horizon. Ramulas said his final farewells before heading off.

***

The queen of spiders was still sitting in the middle of Shes when a psychic spider contacted her, saying that an army was coming to Shes. Then, the communication was cut short. The queen knew it had been killed.

She was happy with the warning. Now she needed a way to deal with the Lord of Sanctuary and his people. Once they were killed and eaten, the kingdom would belong to the spiders. The queen now knew all the human's fighting tricks used in battle.

This time, they would be caught unaware.

23

Ramulas knew that time was of the essence. The sooner they arrived at Shes and killed the queen and the spiders, the sooner he would be back home with his girls. The threat of the giant spiders in the kingdom would be no more, and they could keep exploring the mysteries of the valley.

Everyone in this group rode horses, and the ride was uneventful for the first hour, until Iguchi saw movement ahead and called out a warning before leading the Fallen Angels to run down a single spider in the long grass.

Ramulas soon caught up and saw the trampled body of one of the smaller spiders. For the rest of the day, the group were vigilant for any more. The only ones they saw were the ones killed in the Khilli village. There were no more sightings that day. By late afternoon, the group set up camp while Iguchi and his daughter patrolled the area.

****

The sun had begun to drop over the Devil's Ridge Mountains. Ramulas sat and sent another astral image to his girls. He was not surprised to see that Rachael was with them. After talking with them, he wanted to talk with the mayor of Turtha.

He flew across the forest and saw Pip and the others had made camp just outside the tree line. He pushed his image and soon arrived at Turtha. Ramulas saw the mounds of fresh dirt where the dead had been buried and the scorch marks on the grass from the young dragon. Wisps of smoke spiralled up from the piles of dead spiders five hundred yards from the walls.

Ramulas flew into the town and made his image appear in the mayor's quarters to find the mayor fast asleep in his chair behind the desk. Ramulas smiled and sounded the tone. The mayor was instantly awake and jumped to his feet when he saw Ramulas.

'I did not mean to startle you,' Ramulas said.

The mayor stifled a yawn. 'We have had a busy day, and we received another message from Keah.'

Ramulas sighed. 'What did the queen say this time?'

The mayor shook his head. 'It was not from the queen; it was from the captain of the royal guard. He said that hundreds of giant spiders have come by ship and attacked the city of Keah. They cannot send us any soldiers in fear of another attack.'

Ramulas' jaw dropped as the mayor showed him the message. 'How did the spiders get there by ship? Where else will they attack?' He shook his head. 'Send a message to the captain of the royal guard. Tell him of our battle here, and of our plan to travel to Shes to kill the queen of spiders.'

The mayor nodded, and Ramulas felt dizzy. 'I need to return. I will talk to you tomorrow.'

***

Lucas sat across from Aleesha. She had sent word via one of the royal guards that she wished to see him. Once they were both seated, Aleesha picked up two goblets of wine from a nearby table. She handed one to him.

She smiled while raising her drink. 'I have asked you here so that we can discuss how I can become a proper queen.'

Lucas flinched as if he had been struck and almost dropped his wine. This was the last thing he had expected this early. He quickly recovered. 'This is good; the people need their queen.'

'Then let us drink in celebration,' she said, drinking her wine.

Lucas followed suit, and they both placed the goblets on the table. The red wine had a tart aftertaste, Lucas thought as the roof of his mouth grew numb. Something was not right with the wine; he leaned over to inspect his goblet, and his hand knocked them both from the table.

'Are you well, captain?' Aleesha asked.

Lucas turned toward the voice, which seemed faraway and distorted, to see Aleesha's image blur and fade. 'Yes, I am fine. The wine tasted funny; did you notice anything?'

She quickly shook her head as she moved away from him. 'No, there was nothing wrong with the wine.'

Lucas did not usually drink alcohol, and wondered if this was a normal reaction to wine. After a moment, the taste and sensation passed, and Lucas was relieved. They sat for a while talking about how Aleesha could be the queen her people needed, then Aleesha said she was tired and wanted rest.

Lucas left her chambers happy that she had finally come to her senses, and they agree to talk again the following day.

Lucas left, and Aleesha cursed herself for putting too much poison into his wine. The agents had told her that this was a slow-working poison and only to give small doses. If done correctly, the captain would die a painful death within a week.

Then she would be queen once more.

***

'We will be in Shes by nightfall,' Ramulas said as they passed the border of the forest.

Iguchi nodded. 'We will make camp here, then. We will meet our enemy in the morning after we have rested.'

Ramulas nodded and Iguchi continued. 'I can see you have much on your mind, Lord of Sanctuary. You are eager to reach Shes, but night-time would be dangerous for us.'

***

Once the camp was set and the Fallen Angels were on patrol, Ramulas found a quiet place to sit and send his astral image.

He appeared in the throne room to find both of his daughters, Rachael, and Pip waiting for him. Kate, Grace, and Pip all attempted to talk at once, bringing a smile to his face. He held his hands up.

'Pip, let my girls talk first.'

After a quick conversation with Kate and Grace, Ramulas turned his attention to Pip after Rachael took them from the throne room. 'Is everything well at Sanctuary?'

Pip nodded. 'There have been no sightings of the spiders, and the dryads tell us where you have set up camp.'

Ramulas sighed. 'The giant spiders have attacked Keah.'

Pip's smile vanished. 'What happened?'

'I don't know. The captain of the royal guard sent a message to Turtha, and the mayor told me.'

Ramulas knew his time was growing short, so he sent his image to Turtha. He spoke with the mayor and was told that no more word had been received from Keah. Ramulas told the mayor that they would be in Shes the following morning, and he would contact him when the spiders were all dead.

***

Ramulas walked out of his tent, restless, knowing the next day would be important and wanting to ensure everything was ready. He walked a few hundred yards into the trees, holding his weapons, and started some basic fighting drills.

'I have not seen you train before,' a female voice said from behind.

Ramulas turned to see Berenice leaning against a tree twenty yards away, her two swords held casually in her hands. 'Would you like someone to train with?'

242

Ramulas thought for a moment before nodding, then Berenice rushed at him with both arms out wide. His eyes widened as he back-pedalled while spinning his weapons. Ramulas was able to block the first five strikes until she found a gap in his defences. She thrust her sword at his unprotected hip. The tip of the blade came to within an inch before Ramulas blocked it with a magical shield.

Berenice's eyes widened as she rolled away from him and stopped in a crouching position. 'I didn't know you could do that.'

Ramulas shrugged. 'I didn't know Iguchi had a daughter. Please, tell me more about yourself.'

A cold smile spread across her face. 'Father has already told you, now is not the time.'

Before Ramulas could respond, she rushed forward, leading with a flurry of strikes and thrusts. As Ramulas blocked, dodged, parried, and countered, he saw that she was a very skilled fighter. She was a few levels above Pip, and he knew that Berenice could hurt him if she wanted.

Berenice reminded Ramulas of Iguchi in the way she moved. The weapons in her hands were like an extension of her body. They clashed for a few minutes while Ramulas thought there was something out of place with her, but he didn't know what it was.

Then it hit him.

In all her mannerisms and facial expressions, he saw no trace of Iguchi. With all the children that Ramulas had known, he could always see a part of their parents in them. He could even see traces of Joshua and Juliette in Emily.

Ramulas dropped his arms by his side and smiled at Berenice.

She stopped and tilted her head. 'What are you doing?'

Ramulas smiled. 'Iguchi said that you are his daughter, but I cannot see—'

The rest of the sentence was cut short when Berenice kicked Ramulas in the chest, sending him flying ten feet before hitting the ground and gasping for air.

Ramulas opened his eyes to see Iguchi smiling down at him. 'Hello to you, Lord of Sanctuary. You are nosy. Her story will be told when the time is right.'

As Iguchi walked away, Ramulas knew not to bring up the subject again.

***

The queen of spiders sat in the middle of Shes surrounded by two hundred of her children. She had been told of the small army that camped outside the nearby forest. They would come the following day for her and her children.

Ten thousand spiders had come out of the portal and been sent out in search of food.

The queen of spiders did not want to call them back to help fight the force that would arrive shortly or bring more through the portal. She had a plan that would destroy the people of Sanctuary. She would find out everything about their town, its magic users, and its defences, and when she did, the queen of spiders would call thousands of her children to Sanctuary.

***

Ramulas woke just before dawn and found that he was not the only one who was eager to reach Shes. By the time the sun appeared on the eastern horizon, their group was on the march.

Halfway between the forest and Shes, they noticed the first signs of the spiders, with white sheets of silk covering fields and farms. Rygar explained that this was his first warning that something had happened.

The thing that stood out the most for the group was the stillness and silence around them. There were no sounds from animals or birdlife. Nothing seemed to be alive.

Shigar pointed to large mounds under the silk sheets. 'What are those things?'

'Cattle and sheep,' Rygar answered.

Everyone in the group looked around them as if spiders could jump out at them at any given moment. They were still a few miles from the town, and nothing seemed to be alive.

As they walked, they came across horses and carts buried beneath silk. Then they saw the town of Shes. Ramulas used his magic to search the immediate area and found that his group were the only living things.

'This is where me and yer young'un were attacked,' Rygar said as they came up to the two carts and horses.

Ramulas and the group inspected the scene, and then he looked up and saw Shes in the distance.

The town appeared to be covered in snow. Every building, and some of the streets were covered in white sheets.

'I see none of the giant spiders,' Iguchi said next to Ramulas.

Ramulas nodded. 'I have a feeling they are waiting for us in Shes.'

They walked towards the town a mile away, and Ramulas had an uneasy feeling. He had tried to send his magic ahead to communicate with the spiders, but something was blocking his magic.

'They are there. I think they will be hiding and waiting to surprise us,' Ramulas said.

Iguchi nodded. 'They will attack when we are in the town—not attack from the front.'

Ramulas nodded. 'We will divide into two groups. The first will go in while the other waits for the spiders to attack.'

Iguchi shook his head. 'We need to stay as one in tight formation. This is our only way.'

The dwarf nodded and pulled out his axe. 'Let the spiders come to us.'

Ramulas nodded as everyone took out their weapons and walked forward.

***

As they passed the first buildings on the outskirts of town, Shigar read an incantation from his book, and the air around the group shimmered. 'This spell will confuse the spiders for the first attack. They will see our image two feet to the left. After this attack, we will be visible to them.'

Walking deeper into the town, Ramulas remembered when he first came to the town with Pip on their way to Sanctuary. There had been so many people, and now there was nothing.

'I see movement on the roof to the right,' Rygar whispered.

Ramulas saw the Fallen Angels breaking away from the main group. Joshua and Rain had their weapons ready, leading the rest down the street. Shigar murmured while preparing other spells, and Ramulas could see movement on the walls and roofs around them.

A warm sensation exploded within Ramulas' stomach, and he willed it to flow through his body until he was bathed in purple flame. Sanctuary's soldiers held their swords and shields ready.

The dwarf scanned the rooftops and screamed, 'What are ye waitin fer? Come out and get to fightin'!'

The spell was broken.

Dark shapes swarmed over the roofs and from the alleyways. Spiders on the walls became visible as they moved and darkened their skin. Ramulas turned to his left and right at the movement all around him. 'Look how many there are.'

Joshua unleashed a primal scream of rage as he sent his iron ball through the nearby wall of a building, sending spiders and splinters of wood into the air. Rain shot blasts from his crystal sword, freezing a few of the spiders on the roof. Rygar jumped from his horse with a roar, striking down a spider that raced at the group.

Several spiders jumped from nearby rooftops. Ramulas held his hands above his head and chanted; arcs of white energy leapt from his fingertips, killing eight spiders in midair.

The soldiers charged down the street on horseback as the spiders came out of hiding. Five were pulled from their mounts. Ramulas flinched as multi-coloured lights shot passed him. Several energy balls hit the mass of spiders attacking the fallen soldiers. The soldiers recovered to find the elementals and the two half-giants amongst them.

Shouts of warnings rang out as the second wave of spiders appeared on the rooftops and the alleyways. Ramulas saw that everyone was occupied. He leapt out of his saddle and activated his magical ability.

The Lord of Sanctuary floated ten feet above the ground, covered in bright purple flames. Ramulas reached out with both hands, sending streams of energy at the closest spiders. The energy would hit a spider, causing it to scream and jerk, before passing onto the next couple, causing the same damage.

The soldiers of Sanctuary were quick to act, rushing in and hacking away at the spiders as they fell to the ground.

Joshua's group had a similar experience, where the spiders seemed to throw themselves at the group, focusing on attacking without defence. It was messy work, but all the spiders had been killed in a few minutes.

Ramulas shook his head, searching the area around them. 'No, this is too easy after Turtha; there has to be more.'

The force from Sanctuary split into groups of twenty and spread out as they walked through the town. Ramulas lifted himself one hundred feet into the air to search the town. From that height, he could see movement on the docks. A score of hunters climbed over one of the ships by the docks.

'Shigar, Iguchi, come with me with your Angels to the docks; there are spiders down there. The rest, search every building.'

Ramulas dropped down to his warhorse and led the way to the docks. As they walked, Iguchi said that he counted just under two hundred spiders that were killed. Ramulas thought that was a small number compared to those that attacked Turtha.

Halfway down to the docks, they could see the hunters crawling over the ship that was wrecked on the rocks. The creatures jumped from the ship onto the rocks as the group came closer and ran towards the Fallen Angels.

Ramulas thrust out his hand, sending a stream of purple flame at the ship. By the time the vessel was alight, the Fallen Angels were fighting the spiders on the rocks. When the last of the spiders were killed, Iguchi saw movement behind Ramulas.

'Lord of Sanctuary, more spiders behind you.'

Ramulas turned to see a stream of spiders come out of a cave in the rocks one hundred yards from the docks. He tapped into Oriel's magic to investigate the cave, and his eyes widened in shock.

He had found the doorway where the giant spiders were coming through from their world. He remembered this when reading the spider's mind in Turtha. Ramulas knew that there were countless spiders on the other side of the doorway. He needed to find a way to close it.

'We have to stop them,' Ramulas cried as he spurred his warhorse forward.

The group stopped fifty yards from the cave to dismount to make their way over the uneven rocks. Scores of spiders had come out of the cave and made their way towards the group. Ramulas cursed, knowing that fighting these spiders would delay them getting to the cave. He cast a spell, and a strong wind came down the surrounding cliffs, blowing most of the spiders into the ocean.

Ramulas led the group to the mouth of the cave where twelve more spiders were hiding. He felt their presence and released a magical fireball that bounced around inside the cave, setting half of the spiders on fire and flushing the rest out.

The Fallen Angels fell onto these spiders, killing them instantly.

'Spiders coming in from the beach,' Miles called.

Ramulas turned to see the creatures he had blown into the ocean skipping across the rocks towards the cave.

'Iguchi, kill the spiders; Shigar, come with me.'

Ramulas led the magician deep into the cave, which was wide enough for the two of them to walk side by side. Twenty yards into the cave, they stood before a doorway of light. Several dark legs probed from within the light.

Shigar cast a spell and manifested four spinning blades. With a wave of his hand, the magician sent them through the doorway and the legs vanished.

'I need to study the doorway and ensure that nothing comes out,' Ramulas said.

Shigar opened his book and started to read. Four more blades appeared before him and turned to flame as they spun. He waved his hand, sending them into the light.

Ramulas held out his hands and chanted while trails of white energy drifted from his fingers to the doorway. He moved his hands around, shifting the strands of energy around the doorway and into it.

After several minutes of this, Ramulas cursed and dropped his hands to his side. 'Damn. This cannot be.'

'What is it, my friend?' Shigar asked.

'After I sent the undead through to Remus' world, I closed the portal without giving it any direction. I allowed my emotions to cloud my judgement and did not cast the spell properly. This is only a shard of the original portal.'

'How did it come to be in this cave?'

Ramulas shook his head. 'After the portal left Sanctuary, it somehow found itself floating on the surface of the ocean, and then the spiders dragged it here. And there is more.'

Shigar came up to Ramulas with a worried expression. 'Are the Legion going to come through?'

Ramulas shook his head. 'They cannot come through; their side of the portal has collapsed on itself. This is only open from the spider's world to ours. There are hundreds waiting in the passageway for your spell to fail, then they will come through, and the rest will follow.'

'Why don't you close the portal?'

Ramulas shrugged. 'When the other end of the passageway collapsed, it released a lot of built-up energy. If I close this doorway, it will cause a big explosion, and there is no way for me to protect everyone.'

'How big will this explosion be?' Shigar asked.

Ramulas sighed. 'It will blast the town of Shes far into the ocean.'

'There must be something you can do to stop the spiders from coming through.'

I need to seal the cave from the outside. Follow me.'

Ramulas led Shigar out of the cave in time to see Iguchi kill the last of the spiders. They stopped twenty yards from the cave, and Ramulas began casting spells while waving his hands through the air.

After a moment, a few small rocks began to rise around the duo. He moved his hands in tight patterns, and rocks of various shapes and sizes floated up from the beach. When Ramulas had enough rocks, he sent them into the mouth of the cave.

In a short time, the rocks were stacked together, sealing the cave. Then Ramulas turned to the sand and chanted while waving his hand. The sand rippled and moved, and then a giant snake of sand moved towards the mouth of the cave. It broke apart, filling the gaps in between the rocks.

He turned to Shigar. 'Will you help me, my friend?'

Ramulas held out his hands sending streams of energy at the cave entrance. The sand and rocks turned red. Shigar began chanting and throwing fireballs at the cave. The wall became white hot, sending shimmering waves into the air.

'That should do it,' Ramulas said as they both stopped and stood back.

'None shall come through,' Shigar said.

Ramulas sighed as he turned to the Fallen Angels. The portal was blocked, and the threat of the spiders was no more.

Noises from the town caused everyone to turn and see a few riders coming towards them. They were shouting and waving their arms. As they came closer, Ramulas understood what they were saying.

They had found someone alive in the town.

***

The queen of spiders watched as the Lord of Sanctuary led his group into the town. She saw her children attack them only to be killed with magic and their weapons. She waited until the Lord of Sanctuary led a small group down to the ocean. The ship was burnt and more of her children killed.

The queen almost revealed herself when they were sealing the cave doorway; however, she knew her task was important for her race. The queen needed to study the people of Sanctuary. Then she would call for the ten thousand spiders to come and feed.

When her children first consumed the people of Shes, one human had stood out. It was protected by most of the town. The queen of spiders took the form of this human before meeting the group from Sanctuary.

24

Ramulas, Shigar, Iguchi, and the Fallen Angels rushed up the hill to the town to find a young woman standing in the centre of the main street next to a small group of Sanctuary's soldiers. She had long black hair and wore a simple brown earthen dress. Her eyes were wide with fear. But what caught Ramulas' attention was the small baby wrapped in a blanket that she held tightly to her chest.

Ramulas stopped the group ten yards from the woman and asked, 'Where did you find her?'

One of the soldiers pointed to his left. 'She came out of the alleyway.'

Ramulas climbed down from his warhorse and walked over to the woman, smiling. Her eyes widened in fear, and she clutched the baby tighter and took a step back.

Ramulas stopped and held up his hands. 'No-one is going to hurt you. You are safe now. Are there any other people here?'

The woman looked at Ramulas in fear and did not respond.

Rain walked up to Ramulas. 'I do not think she will speak to you.'

Ramulas shook his head. 'I will find out what I need to know,' he said, casting a spell.

Purple mist streamed from his hands and covered the woman, causing her to scream and turn away. Ramulas stopped casting and gasped as Berenice came up to the woman, putting an arm around her and turning to Ramulas.

'She has been through much pain and suffering. Imagine surviving all this time hiding from the spiders.'

Ramulas saw the dead bodies of the spiders in the street. 'I want every building searched in case we have more people hiding.'

Everyone scattered in different directions. Ramulas, Berenice, and Iguchi stayed with the woman.

***

The search was completed, finding no other survivors, and it was decided to make their way home to Sanctuary. Bernice helped the woman and her baby onto Rygar's horse. He would ride with Rain. It was decided that Berenice would travel with the woman to comfort her. No-one else would try to make her talk.

Ramulas knew that once the woman was in Sanctuary with other families, she would tell them of what happened. He gave her a sideways glance, wondering what horrors she had endured. She was safe with the people around her, and her new life would start when she arrived in Sanctuary.

***

Over the past few days, Lucas had come to talk with Aleesha about what she needed to do to become a proper queen for the people. Each time, they drank wine in celebration. Lucas began showing effects of the poison, slurring some of his words and becoming disoriented, and certain foods he could not keep down.

Every time Aleesha expressed her concern about him, Lucas passed it off as the stress from dealing with the giant spiders.

The two agents had told Aleesha that if she placed the same amount of poison in the wine, the captain of the royal guard would be dead within eight days, then Aleesha would have her power once more.

However, Aleesha could not wait that long, she wanted everything returned to her as soon as possible. This is why she had doubled the dose in his wine that day.

Lucas smiled while raising his goblet she had given him. 'Aleesha, I am very proud of you. In a very short time, you have shown me that you want to be a true queen. The people will be happy.'

She nodded while forcing a smile. 'I was wrong in the ways that I acted. Thank you for showing me the way, but first we drink, then we can talk.'

Aleesha drank, trying to see if Lucas had drunk his wine. As she put her goblet down, Lucas dropped his and suffered a coughing fit, holding a hand over his chest. Tears rolled down his cheeks as he fought for breath. He fell to his side with a moan.

Aleesha stood over him with a cruel smile. 'I am your queen. Who are you to tell me what to do? You had no right to do these things to me. I will watch as you die a painful death.'

Aleesha walked to the door as she thought of how her father was killed and how painful it was to have everything taken from her. She stayed there until tears streamed down her face, then she pulled the door open, startling the two guardsmen at the door.

She pointed into the room. 'Help me, something has happened to your captain. I don't know what to do.'

The royal guardsmen rushed into the room, where they found Lucas sweating and softly moaning on the floor.

'We must bring him to a healer,' one of them said.

'No. Put him on my bed, and bring a healer to me.'

Both royal guardsmen hesitated, and Aleesha said, 'I am your queen. Place him on my bed.'

They picked up their captain and carried him to the bed before they raced off to find a healer.

***

The healer left Aleesha's chambers after giving her instructions on how to administer the medications to the captain. He had wanted to take Lucas to his own quarters to help him better, but Aleesha stated that she was the queen and would watch over him.

She had sent for a servant to bring her broth for the captain; however, instead of medicine, she would put the poison in the broth and feed it to Lucas. She only had enough for one more dose, and she waited for the agents to bring her more.

The two royal guards came in to check on Lucas several times, only to be shooed away by Aleesha. 'He needs rest. He will never recover if you keep coming in and disturbing him.'

After they left, Aleesha walked to the tapestry the two agents had come out of. She pulled it back and saw a blank wall. Aleesha sighed and walked away.

***

A small serving girl walked into Aleesha's chambers carrying a bowl of broth on a tray. Aleesha waved for the girl to place it on the table beside the bed.

The serving girl stepped back to the foot of the bed, watching Lucas; Aleesha ignored her. The queen walked to the bowl and took out a small blue flask from her robes and poured the contents into the broth. As Aleesha stirred the broth with a spoon, she noticed the small girl.

'Oh, my. You startled me. I thought you had gone. Off with you now.'

The young girl hurried back to the kitchen.

***

They set up camp in the forest. Iguchi and the Fallen Angels had left in search of danger. Berenice stayed with the woman and her baby; she gave the woman food, which she took away from the fire to eat alone. She was still extremely timid and would shake if anyone came too close to her, and she would not allow anyone to see the baby.

Everyone gave the woman space, and she began to make soft whimpering sounds. Ramulas had spoken to everyone, saying that she must have been through quite an ordeal and to leave her be as much as possible.

When the camp was settled, Ramulas wanted to speak with his daughters.

***

Ramulas' image arrived in the throne room to find Rachael and his girls waiting for him. Kate and Grace ran up to him excitedly. Rachael stood back and smiled in a similar way that Jacqueline used to, which caused internal conflict for him. He still mourned the loss of his wife, but a small part of him felt affection for Rachael, and for that, he felt guilty.

'Hello, my beautiful girls. We will be home by late tomorrow afternoon.'

His girls cheered while jumping around, and Rachael took a few steps forward and gave him a shy smile. 'Ramulas, I have something to tell you when you come home.'

Kate and Grace looked at each other and giggled. The butterflies in Ramulas' stomach caused the room to spin for him.

'I—um—will see you tomorrow,' he stammered before calling his image back.

***

The queen of spiders watched as the Lord of Sanctuary sat on the ground at the edge of camp and saw his astral image return to his body. She turned away from him and lay on the ground.

The form she had taken worked better than she had anticipated. The form of a female human with an infant had the group wanting to help and protect her.

The queen of spiders had communicated with the psychic spiders who accompanied the group of ten thousand. They had returned to the town of Shes. She would wait until they had arrived in Sanctuary before she called them. Then everyone in Sanctuary would be eaten.

***

Ramulas opened his eyes and tried to control his heartbeat as it raced in his chest. His mouth was dry; he did not know how to cope with his emotions every time Rachael looked at him in a certain way. He knew that she wanted something from him, but he was unsure if he was able to provide it.

'Damn,' Ramulas said as he slapped the ground. He was in so much of a hurry to get away from Rachael that he had not spoken to the mayor of Turtha.

Ramulas concentrated and sent his image across the plains, arriving in Turtha an hour before dusk. He sounded the tone before appearing before the mayor.

The mayor smiled as he stood from his chair behind his desk. 'Hello, Lord of Sanctuary. What news of the spiders?'

'All of the spiders in Shes have been killed, and there seems to be no more in the kingdom. We also found a lone survivor—a woman with a child. We are taking her to Sanctuary.'

The mayor smiled. 'We have received news from Covedon; the soldiers have returned, and the mayor would like the three of us to talk when things calm down.'

Ramulas' expression was puzzled. 'Do you know why he wished to talk?'

The mayor sighed. 'Like me, I think he is upset about the queen not sending help to deal with the spiders, and we were both led to believe that the people of Sanctuary were enemies of the kingdom. But after our fight with the spiders, things have changed.'

'Are the Khilli still with you in Turtha?'

The mayor nodded. 'They plan to return home in a few days with promises to return. They have made many friends here.'

Ramulas shook his head. 'It saddened me to know that they were kept prisoner for so long and no-one knew about it.'

Ramulas felt his magic waning. He said a quick goodbye before returning to the camp.

***

Aleesha paced her room as the sun dropped below the horizon. She had not heard from or seen her agents all day and was beginning to worry. The last of the poison was gone, and the captain only needed a couple more doses to die and leave her to rule in her own way.

The small serving girl returned to collect the tray, and Aleesha waved her out of the room. Just before reaching the door, the serving girl screamed and dropped the tray and held her ankle. Two royal guardsmen rushed into the room, and Aleesha came over to see what had happened.

'What has happened here?' one of the guardsmen asked.

The small girl looked up. 'Please, help me; I have hurt my foot.'

The small girl's face was red and contorted with pain. Aleesha did not care about the girl, she just wanted the guardsmen out of her chambers, along with the girl.

'Take her out of here. I need my rest,' Aleesha said with a dismissive wave.

The guardsmen picked up the serving girl. She winced in pain and moaned as they moved her.

Aleesha's eyes widened, thinking the noise would wake the captain, and if he woke, they might find out about the poison, and she would be in trouble.

'Make her stop,' Aleesha said.

They picked her up by her arms with her feet a few inches from the floor. The girl turned to Aleesha. 'My queen, please take my feet. I have heard stories of how kind you are.'

Aleesha froze as the two guardsmen looked at her. The young queen wanted nothing more than to have these three out of her chambers. She forced a smile and helped carry the small girl out the doors.

'Argh! Walk slower. It hurts so much,' the girl cried.

The three slowed to a gentle walking pace, and the whole time the girl glanced over Aleesha's shoulder. By the time they entered the hallway, the serving girl wore a mischievous smile. 'It doesn't hurt anymore.'

The two guardsmen, and Aleesha gently put the small girl on the marble tiles of the floor. She smiled and waved at them before running off down the hallway.

Aleesha's jaw dropped at the young girl's recovery. The astonishment on her face quickly replaced by annoyance as she turned to the guardsmen. 'Leave me be.'

Aleesha walked into her chambers, closing the door behind her. She made her way to the bedroom and held back a scream.

The captain of the royal guard was not in her bed.

He was nowhere to be seen. She dropped to her knees, searching under the bed to find it empty, and then searched the whole room. He was nowhere in sight.

Then Aleesha noticed something else.

The blue flask that held the poison was also missing. What could this mean? Did her agents return and take the captain while she was dealing with the young girl? And if someone else took the captain, who were they, and why would they do such a thing?

So many thoughts raced through the young queen's mind. She need to sit down and work out what to do next. She would wait for the agents; they always knew what to do.

25

Ramulas smiled. They had ridden most of the day, and the walls of Sanctuary would soon be in sight. The woman with the baby still cowered away when anyone came close to her. Ramulas stole a sideways glance at her and saw that Berenice still rode next to her. She was the only one who did not upset the woman.

Miles and a few Angels came riding back from Sanctuary. Iguchi had sent them ahead to tell Owain they had returned and not to run training drills that day.

They came into the clearing, and the woman climbed down from her horse and walked into the clearing while ignoring those around her. The rest of the group followed.

Ramulas saw the archers lining the top of the wall with Owain and Pip in the centre above the gate. He rode fifty yards into the clearing, and Pip started screaming. Her emerald eyes were blazing. She pointed at Ramulas. 'Run!' she yelled. 'There is a giant spider right near you!'

Ramulas took out his battle axe and war hammer and saw that everyone else had their weapons ready. Everyone scanned their surroundings, looking for potential danger. Then Pip fired one of the archer's bows. The arrow arced down, tearing at the woman's dress.

Ramulas looked up at the wall. 'Pip, what are you—'

The rest of his words were forgotten as the woman's dress tore open, the spider queen transforming into her true body. Everyone gasped and stepped back as she grew. The spider queen stood ten feet high, her dark legs and body covered in spikes. Her eight eyes seem to shine as she scuttled, turning left and right.

She rushed at Ramulas, causing his warhorse to rear back. Berenice leapt off her horse and severed one of the creature's legs with a swipe of her sword. The spider queen hissed and scuttled back towards the wall, with the Fallen Angels, Joshua, and Rain in quick pursuit.

Arrows rained down onto the creature as a blast of ice hit her in the side. The queen's left side was frozen; she could only move in small circles. Joshua roared and leapt into the air swinging his iron ball. The creature waved her legs at him. He smashed his iron ball into her face.

He was knocked back and slid across the ground as the creature moved towards him while hitting her left legs on the ground, trying to dislodge the ice from her body. Joshua pulled himself to his feet as Berenice and Iguchi rushed past him.

The father-and-daughter team danced around the giant spider, attacking from both sides in such a way that the spider queen did not know where to attack. Then the creature shuddered once before dying.

The spider queen was in communication with her ten thousand children during the battle. Her last message was for them to come and attack Sanctuary.

***

'Everybody step back,' Ramulas called as he waved his hands and moved closer to the spider queen. Then he gasped.

'This was the queen of spiders; she was with us the whole time and could have done so much damage to us on the way here. Do not worry. It is dead.'

'My friend, she had us all fooled,' Shigar said.

Ramulas shook his head while letting out a breath. 'We are lucky that Pip saw through the magic of her form. Who knows what damage this spider would have done inside Sanctuary.'

Ramulas walked closer to the spider queen with Shigar and Iguchi while the Fallen Angels formed a circle, searching for any more surprises.

'The druids would like to examine this,' Shigar said.

Ramulas turned to answer the magician when Pip came running up to them.

'How did you know?' Ramulas asked her.

Pip frowned and punched Ramulas in the shoulder. 'If you let me come with you, I would have seen her straight away. From now on, I go with you. I could see her true form as she stepped out of the trees.'

Ramulas nodded and organised for the druids to come out and examine the creature in the clearing.

Ramulas turned to Pip as they walked to the gate. 'We killed all the spiders in Shes. She is the last one.'

'That is good. Your daughters are waiting for you. Come into the castle.'

'I will take my Fallen Angels out to see if there any more creatures,' Iguchi said as the Angels melted into the trees.

***

Ramulas walked into the throne room to find Kate, Grace, and the two hell hounds waiting. Smiles broke out on his girl's faces as they ran to embrace him in a hug. The hell hounds were close behind, and Fenris jump around them, barking.

Ramulas was about to tell the hell hound to sit when something in the corner of his eye caught his attention. Rachael walked into the room, wearing one of Jacqueline's red silk dresses. Her hair had small ribbons and flowers woven into it. She smiled at Ramulas, and he felt his knees go weak.

His daughters had also noticed Rachael. As they released him, Grace ran to Rachael. 'Look, Da. I helped make her hair pretty.'

Ramulas thought it was strange that he was not angry about Rachael wearing one of his wife's dresses. He was happy that his girls had helped make Rachael 'pretty'—it told him that they liked her. This thought brought a smile to his face.

He looked at Rachael once more and found her to be beautiful.

They stood twenty feet apart, staring at each other. Kate, Grace, and Pip waited for something to happen. Then Ramulas took a step forward, followed by Rachael.

The spell was broken, and they came together as if some invisible force was pulling both of them. Rachael threw her arms around Ramulas' neck and kissed him passionately. For a moment, he was stunned, unsure what to do. Then his hands fell to her hips, and he kissed her back.

When they separated, Ramulas felt his head swim. Rachael looked up at him with tears in her eyes. 'I thought you would not return.'

'How could I not return,' Ramulas said. 'I needed to come back for my daughters.'

At the mention of his daughters, reality set in for Ramulas, and he realised they were still in the room. They had seen him kiss Rachael.

He looked at Kate and Grace and saw they wore the biggest smiles as they ran to hug Rachael and began talking excitedly. Kate reached out to take Ramulas' hand and gently pull him to Rachael. As Rachael held his hand, he did not think he would ever feel this way again.

Pip smiled at him. 'Life is short.'

***

Aleesha opened her eyes with a start. She had had a terrible nightmare where the captain of the royal guard had gone missing and her power would be taken from her when the people found out what she had done.

She had fallen asleep on her bed wearing her clothes. She turned to her side and saw that the captain was not there. Aleesha quickly sat up on the bed as her breathing became short and shallow. She turned her head left and right, searching for any sign of the captain. Then she saw the note.

A small note had been placed on a cushion at the end of the bed. Aleesha quickly crawled across the bed and picked it up to read it.

We have taken care of the captain of the royal guard.
Announce a holiday in celebration that the spiders were defeated.
The people will see you as a kind queen.
This will bring you power.

Aleesha read the note two more times and was still confused. The note did not say who took the captain. If it was her agents, why did they not come to speak with her? Did they take him away because she gave him too much poison? And why give the people a holiday that they did not deserve?

For now, Aleesha would follow the note's instructions. She was sure that her answers would come soon. Her main priority was that no-one knew that the captain had gone missing.

Then another thought came to her—what if the note was not left by her agents, but by someone else? And what did that mean for her?

Aleesha quickly brushed those thoughts away. She needed to plan a holiday.

***

In a room somewhere in Keah, Lucas woke in a panic. He struggled against the bonds that held him to a table by his hands and feet. The blindfold prevented him from seeing anything. He fought as strong hands forced his mouth open and a bitter liquid entered his mouth. The hand clamped over his mouth and nose, forcing him to swallow the liquid.

The hand was removed, and Lucas spluttered and coughed, sending waves of pain through his body. He let out a moan. 'Who are you? Where am I?'

Lucas strained his ears as he heard the person walking away a short distance before a door was closed, and he was left alone in silence. There were no noises coming from outside the room that would hint at where he might be. Lucas knew something was wrong with him; his whole body seemed to be on fire from within, and he had no energy.

Whoever held him in this room had not killed him yet.

***

Ramulas stood on the balcony of the throne room overlooking the people of Sanctuary. With him were his daughters, Rachael, Pip, Iguchi, and Shigar. He waited for the people to settle. There had been a lot of talk about the queen of spiders coming to Sanctuary and being killed.

With the upcoming celebration, Ramulas felt the weight of guilt on his shoulders. He raised his hands, and a hush fell over the crowd.

'We have much reason to celebrate. We have defeated creatures never seen before on this world.' Ramulas paused while the crowd cheered. He held his hands up once more and continued, 'The people of Sanctuary helped the people of Turtha with the help of the Khilli and Covedon. A short time ago, the people of Sanctuary were known as enemies of the kingdom. Differences have now been put aside, and we now work together with our former enemies. A greater enemy has brought us together, and for that I am happy that we found allies.'

Ramulas took a deep breath. 'It is with much sorrow that this battle came at a cost. We have lost eleven of our people. After midday, there will be a ceremony as they become part of the fallen. Then we will celebrate our victory.'

The crowd below cheered, and Ramulas felt a comforting hand on his shoulder. He turned to see Rachael smiling proudly at him.

***

A wall of fog covered the rear cliff of Sanctuary, and the crowd waited in anticipation. Ramulas stood in front of the fog and waved his arms while chanting. The white mist lifted, and a collective gasp could be heard.

Eleven new statues of the fallen stood proudly amongst the others. This made a total of one hundred and sixty-two. People came forward to pay their respects, and the celebrations began. With the people's attention on the fallen, Ramulas made his way to the courtyard.

He stood in front of Jacqueline's statue. The feelings of loss and heartache had returned. This was the main reason he avoided coming to see her; the pain was too much to bear.

Ramulas reached out and placed his hand on her shoulder. 'Hello, my love. I miss you,' he said as tears filled his eyes. 'I have met someone. Her name is Rachael. She lost her husband when the Legion came. Kate and Grace really like her and enjoy being with her. I have feelings for her, but I do not know if I am doing the right thing. I need a sign to tell me what you want me to do.'

'I come 'ere to talk wit' me boy all the time,' Rygar said, walking up to him.

Ramulas turned and smiled at the dwarf. 'I did not see you there.'

The dwarf nodded. 'Aye. I was comin' to tell me boy about the spiders we squished.'

Ramulas smiled, imagining how much the giant would have enjoyed squishing the spiders. 'I only wanted a sign that I am doing the right thing. I don't want to do the wrong thing.'

'By me thinkin', I'm sure you'll be seein' those signs,' Rygar said before turning away. 'I can hear the people having fun. I think the Lord o' Sanctuary should be joinin' them.'

Ramulas nodded and followed the dwarf out of the courtyard. As the duo left, the eyes of Jacqueline's statue glowed purple for a few seconds before fading.

***

A few hours into the celebrations, Tilly came flying into Sanctuary and hovered above Ramulas. The people were excited watching the sprite.

Ramulas smiled. 'Hello, Tilly. What brings you here?'

'You must come to the clearing. Eady has important news for you,' she said in a serious tone before flying away.

This puzzled Ramulas. He asked his girls to stay with Rachael before walking out into the clearing with Pip. Eady and four other dryads waited for them with grim faces.

'What has happened?' he asked.

'There are more spiders in the forest near Shes,' Eady said.

'What!' Ramulas and Pip said in unison.

Eady nodded, and Ramulas said, 'This is impossible. We closed the entrance to the cave.'

'We counted four thousand coming this way, and there were many more behind them.'

***

The people of Keah danced and sang in the streets in celebration. Word of the holiday had quickly spread, and so too the queen's change of heart towards her people. Aleesha stood on her balcony on the third floor of the castle, watching the people enjoy themselves. Part of the holiday included no taxes for the next seven days. Now she understood why her father did not like holidays.

A few of the people saw her on the balcony. They waved and shouted their thanks to her, and others quickly joined. Soon, hundreds were chanting her name. Aleesha stood while forcing a smile before waving and returning to her chambers.

She was still worried about the captain of the royal guard. Where could he be, and who had left her the note? She now kept the door to her bedroom closed, telling the royal guard that the captain needed rest and was not to be disturbed. She accepted food and broth from the serving girls. The strange thing was she had not seen the girl who had hurt her foot.

Aleesha wondered where she had got to.

***

'What do we do?' Pip asked.

'How fast are they coming?' Ramulas asked Eady.

Eady shook her head. 'The giant spiders are running.'

'Oh no,' Ramulas said as he looked to the sky, thinking how long the spiders would take to arrive. 'Are you sure the spiders are coming here?'

Eady nodded, and Ramulas turned to Pip. 'The earliest they can arrive is around this time tomorrow if they do not rest. We need to prepare and tell the people, but first we need to visit Journey's End. Tell Shigar, Rygar, and Iguchi to meet me at the passageway.'

Pip nodded and raced into Sanctuary.

Ramulas walked through the gate, his head swimming with thoughts. They had killed all the spiders in Shes and sealed the cave, so where had these spiders come from, and why did they not attack Ramulas' groups in Shes?

He hoped they would find the answers in the paintings and tapestries at Journey's End.

Ramulas arrived at the passageway to find everyone waiting for him on horseback. By their expressions, he could tell that Pip had told them about the spiders.

Berenice came up to the group as they were entering the passageway, announcing that she would come as well. It seemed strange to Ramulas, as the sounds of the celebrations faded, that the people of Sanctuary were so happy at the thought of defeating the spiders, yet it turned out that were a lot more coming to Sanctuary. He needed to find out where they came from.

They came out into the valley in silence as they focused on Journey's End. They were searching for answers and hoped to find them here. Ramulas used his magic to communicate with the dragons and found they were still in the far east dealing with the ancient evil magic. He knew there would be no help from them in fighting the spiders.

The people would have to face them on their own.

***

They walked into the throne room, and Pip gasped. Ramulas turned to see her eyes blazing fiercely. He followed her gaze and saw that the artwork had changed once more. Iguchi and Berenice rushed forward, with the rest following. This time, there were a lot more spiders, and several of the battle scenes had changed completely.

The situation looked dire for the people of Sanctuary.

Iguchi and his daughter closely studied each piece of artwork while having intense conversations. Rygar walked along the tapestries until one stopped him in his tracks, and his mouth fell open.

'Me boy. Oh, me boy,' the dwarf said with tears streaming down his face. 'Would ye just look at me boy.'

Ramulas, Shigar, and Pip came over to inspect the artwork, and all stepped back with wide eyes before glancing at the dwarf and each other.

'Could this really happen?' Pip asked.

Ramulas shook his head slowly. 'I don't know. '

Shigar walked along the wall and stopped at a painting a few yards away. He began to shake his head and mutter to himself. The others saw this and came over.

'We need to prepare and pray that somehow these paintings aren't accurate,' the magician said.

Ramulas shook his head, hoping that this was all wrong, because if the artwork depicted what was going to happen, the people of Sanctuary were in a lot of trouble.

'Oh no,' Pip said, looking at one of tapestries at the far end. 'Ramulas, you need to see this.'

Everyone came over to where Pip was standing, and Ramulas turned pale as a cold chill ran through him. 'Grace and Emily, what are they doing?' he whispered.

Pip moved her finger along to another section of the artwork with a grim expression. Ramulas followed her finger and flinched, feeling as if he was kicked in the stomach by his warhorse. Kate was held by Rachael, and they were surrounded by giant spiders.

Ramulas turned to Pip. 'We need to get back home.'

As the group left the throne room, the images on the artwork changed once more. If Ramulas had seen the new images, he would have raced home as fast as he could.

***

They returned with the celebrations still underway. Ramulas and his small group were the only ones not smiling.

'We need to tell them,' Pip said.

Ramulas nodded. 'I know, but not now. Let them celebrate a little longer. I want to see the group of spiders for myself.'

The group broke apart, each person knowing what they needed to do. Ramulas entered the throne room and sat on the floor. Soon, his astral image raced towards Shes.

Ramulas sighed as a sad smile grew on his face. His people were so happy with the latest victory, and they would soon learn that they needed to fight again with the spiders coming to their home. All he wanted was for them to find peace.

He passed over Sanctuary's Forest before flying over the plains. He found that the more he used his astral image, the easier it was to travel further.

He saw the army of giant spiders a few miles from the forest near Shes coming out from the trees. As he came closer, Ramulas almost lost concentration and fell to the ground from seeing the sheer number of spiders. It reminded him of a wave washing upon the shore.

From what he could see, there were at least twice as many spiders than attacked Turtha. They flowed out from the trees, running and bunched together in a way where they were running over each other. Ramulas could not see the ground beneath them.

He moved over the forest, and there were spiders jumping from tree to tree while those on the ground crawled over one another.

Ramulas needed an advantage for the upcoming battle and decided to communicate with the creatures in a different way. Instead of trying to talk to a creature, he would just listen. He moved around, probing the minds of the giant spiders below. After a few minutes, he had enough information. Then he flew back home.

When he left, the spiders were miles from the forest. He found it interesting that some of the spiders could communicate with the queen and each other. They were doing this as they came for Sanctuary.

They were coming to avenge their queen and were totally enraged that the doorway had been closed. The army of giant spiders moved with one purpose—to kill every person in Sanctuary. Ramulas needed to get back; there was so much to do.

26

Lucas woke to a world of pain. He opened his eyes to find he was in a dimly lit room, and then his stomach churned. Lucas quickly rolled on his side to dry retch. His moaned as drool flowed from his mouth. His insides felt as if they were on fire as his body convulsed. When Lucas was finished, he rolled back on his bed.

The thought of the bed shocked him. His last memory was of being tied to a table. The sound of bare feet slapping wooden floors brought him back to the present. A woman's smiling face appeared over him. She used a warm wet cloth to clean his face.

'Where am I?' he asked.

'Hush now, you need to rest.'

She walked to the other side of the room to a table and returned a moment later, placing a warm cloth over his face. It was warm, damp, and had a sweet fragrance. Within seconds, Lucas was asleep.

***

Ramulas opened his eyes and saw Pip in front of him. 'We need a council of war. Tell everyone to be here in half an hour. I will return soon.'

Ramulas closed his eyes again and sent his image to Turtha.

He flew over the walls, happy to see the Khilli were still there. He sounded the tone, entered the mayor's quarters, and saw K'ayden talking with the mayor.

'My friend, what is wrong?' K'ayden asked seeing Ramulas' expression.

'Thousands of giant spiders are coming for Sanctuary; they will arrive tomorrow.'

The mayor gasped and stepped back. 'You said that you killed all the spiders.'

Ramulas sighed. 'I thought we did.'

'How many are coming to Sanctuary?' K'ayden asked.

'More than twice the number that came to Turtha.'

'My people will come to help you.' K'ayden said.

Ramulas shook his head. 'It would take too long. I can't let your warriors ride for hours; they will be tired and may be caught out in the open with the spiders.'

'What can we do?' the mayor asked.

'Stay within the walls of Turtha in case the spiders come back.'

Ramulas left without waiting for a response, bringing his image back to Sanctuary.

Ramulas opened his eyes and rose to his feet; he was alone. He went to the balcony while tapping into Oriel's powers. He leapt off the ledge, bathed in purple flames. He flew over the wall and into the forest. Moments later, he landed in the dryad's secret grove and waited.

One by one, the dryads stepped out of the surrounding trees. Eady walked over to him and smiled.

'I have seen the spiders in the forest near Shes,' Ramulas said.

'What part do the dryads play in this?' Eady asked.

Ramulas smiled. 'I have heard of a trick where dryads can pull someone into a tree and they explode. There are a lot of spiders; are you able to harm them without being hurt yourselves?'

Eady nodded, and Ramulas continued. 'I need the dryads to wait until the spiders are a few miles from Sanctuary before attacking. If you move too soon, the spiders might go to Turtha instead.'

'We will do this.'

Ramulas nodded before leaping into the air and heading home.

***

He came into the throne room through the balcony to find Pip, Shigar, the druids, Iguchi and Berenice, the Fallen Angels, Owain, and Rygar waiting for him.

Ramulas sighed as he shook his head. 'I have seen the army of giant spiders coming for us and have read their thoughts. We face more than twice the number that attacked Turtha. They have come to avenge the death of their queen. They will not stop until every person here has been killed. We can learn from the battle at Turtha.'

'What o' the dragons?' Rygar asked.

Ramulas shook his head again. 'There is an ancient evil magic in the valley. They will not leave until they know what it is.'

'Then we must talk of battle tactics,' Iguchi said.

The group started talking until an hour after sunset. By that time, everyone knew their role in the upcoming battle, and they would be working through the night to prepare. There was one major change from the battle of Turtha—the people of Sanctuary would have an escape route if things did not go to plan.

It was also agreed that residents of Sanctuary would not be told until the following morning. Ramulas did not know when the next celebrations would be, or if they would ever have one.

***

Ramulas arrived at his quarters to find two extremely excited daughters.

'Da, close your eyes,' Grace said. He closed his eyes and felt both of his girls take a hand each and slowly lead him forward. After a few moments, they stopped. 'Open your eyes, Da.'

He did, and he saw Rachael standing at the foot of his bed. His daughters giggled and whispered to each other. Rachael wore another one of Jacqueline's dresses, a long purple silk dress, and Ramulas was lost for words.

'What are you thinking?' Rachael asked with a smile.

'Life is short,' Ramulas said as he stepped toward her.

***

Lucas opened his eyes to see the sunlight coming through the window. He attempted to sit up in his bed and moaned softly. He sighed and fell back down. Lucas had no strength. He moved his head around to find that he was in a different small room.

The sounds of gulls, dock workers calling out to each other, and waves told Lucas that he was close to the docks. He could tell that he was not on the ground floor. All he could see through the windows was clear blue sky, and the area of the docks had the highest density of buildings in the city.

The door opened, and the same woman walked in. She smiled at Lucas. 'Oh, you're awake. There is someone who wants to see you.'

She walked out of the room and closed the door before he could reply. Lucas wondered who this person was and how he had come to be here in this predicament. As hard as it was, he lay on the bed listening to the sounds coming from outside. He knew that he had no control over his situation. He would just have to wait for the answers to come to him.

Several sets of heavy footsteps sounded in the distance and came closer to his room. Lucas turned his head to the door and waited. A moment later, the door opened, and the Master of Shadows walked in, followed by two of his enforcers.

He smiled at Lucas. 'We meet again.'

'Did you bring me here?'

The Master nodded. 'Here and other places. We have been moving you around.'

'Why?'

'To save your life,' the Master replied. 'You were very close to death. The young queen was poisoning you.'

'What?' Lucas asked, trying to sit up. He regretted it instantly, falling back down after a dizzy spell.

The Master laughed. 'I make it my business to know the darker side of Keah, and I was curious to find the two missing agents that you had been searching for. They were purchasing blood of the pufferfish. Quite a dangerous poison. If taken in small doses, it will cause a slow, agonising death.'

'The two agents?' Lucas asked.

'Yes. They were purchasing the poison and giving it to your queen. One of my little spies saw the vial of poison in the queen's quarters and watched her place it in your broth when you lay sick in her bed. I believe that she had been slowly poisoning you over time. The agents were seen discussing this method with the black-market vendor.'

Lucas' mouth fell open at the news. Memories returned of how happy Aleesha was to talk about becoming a proper queen, but she had always insisted on drinking wine beforehand.

'That little bitch,' Lucas whispered.

The Master laughed in a low, sinister tone.

'How long have I been under your care?' Lucas asked.

'You have been with us for a few days. It was difficult at first, because you did not want to take the antidote, but now you are becoming stronger every day.'

'What about Aleesha and her agents?'

'The agents are in a safe place, and the young queen is now a puppet for the Shadows.'

Lucas baulked at this. 'What do you mean?'

'My young spy made quite a performance in the queen's chambers. When the queen was distracted, we took you out through a hidden passageway. We use this same passageway to leave notes on her bed, telling her what to do. She thinks the notes come from her agents.'

'I want to talk to the agents.' Lucas said.

The Master nodded. 'When you have fully recovered, I will take you to them.'

Lucas winced. 'I need to get back to the castle before Aleesha does something terrible.'

The Master smiled. 'As you know, one of your royal guardsmen works for the Shadows. He has passed word to the other royal guard that he has spoken with you, and through him, he controls the soldiers and royal guard. They all await your healthy return in a few days.'

Lucas sighed. 'Once again, I thank you. How will I ever repay you?'

The Master chuckled. 'Don't worry, my friend. When you are well, I will ask for payment.'

***

Ramulas, Pip, Rygar, Shigar, and Owain stood on Sanctuary's wall. The dryads had told them that the giant spiders were at the edge of the forest and would arrive by midday.

Ramulas looked along the wall and saw that the archers were ready, each one with a hundred arrows at their feet. The people of Sanctuary were ready and knew their roles in the battle. He was surprised at how ready and eager his people were for this battle; as soon as they were told, their faces hardened, and they raced off to prepare.

Kate, Grace, and Emily were safe with Jenna in the castle. He told the girls it would be safer for them there. Now everyone waited for the giant spiders to come closer.

Shigar's eyes were bloodshot, and he shuffled along, holding a large leather-bound book to his chest. He had studied all through the night. He had several spells that he could activate with a single word, and the process had weakened him.

Iguchi and Berenice stood in the courtyard with the Fallen Angels. This group would charge out of the gate when the spiders came. Joshua and Rain would follow with the half-giants. Ramulas wanted to utilise the crystal sword from the wall, but Rain argued that his place would be beside his friend on the battlefield.

The twelve druids appeared behind Ramulas; they too had been working on spells that would be more effective on the spiders. Ramulas communicated with the hell hounds to ensure his girls had not left the castle. Valkyrie was with Kate in the castle, but then Fenris told him that he was with Grace in the forest.

Ramulas looked over the trees while communicating with his youngest daughter. *Grace, where are you?*

Hello, Da. I am having a tea party with Emily.

Ramulas' eyes widened as his heart began to beat faster. *Where are you having this tea party?*

We are in the forest.

The communication was cut off, and Tilly flew out of the trees and up to the top of the wall to hover in front of Ramulas. 'The spiders are very close. They will be here soon.'

'Grace and Emily are in the forest. Tell the dryads to help them,' Ramulas said to the sprite.

Tilly's eyes widened as she raced off into the trees. Ramulas gripped the wall as he searched the forest. The dryads were Grace and Emily's best chance of coming home safely. He was upset that Grace had not stayed in the castle like he asked her to.

Ramulas' fingers grew cold and numb. He saw that the front of the wall had been covered in an inch of smooth ice. Rain had spent half an hour covering the front of the wall; the giant spiders would find it difficult to climb the ice.

His thoughts were shattered when an explosion in the forest shook the trees, sending chunks of earth and trees into the air a mile away.

'What was that?' Pip asked as her eyes blazed fiercely.

Ramulas just shook his head, not knowing what to say. Pip scanned the area where the explosion was, and after a moment, she said, 'Oh no,' and ran from the wall as fast as she could.

***

'Emily, does your doll want some tea?' Grace asked.

Emily nodded and held her doll in front of her. Grace made the motions of pouring tea into the doll's hand.

As the girls played, Fenris lay on the ground. He could sense something coming towards them.

Grace smiled at Emily. 'I'm talking with my da.'

The girls continued to play while Grace spoke with Ramulas. Then Grace felt movement in the trees around her. For a fraction of a second, her eyes turned dark before returning to normal. The dryads were trying to come out of the trees near them, and she stopped them. Grace did not want any interruptions for her tea party.

This magic cut the communication between her and her father.

Then Fenris stood and growled, its spikes coming out as his ears flattened. Something was coming their way very fast.

Emily squealed and dropped her doll as giant spiders crept out from behind trees and bushes that surrounded them.

Grace's eyes darkened as magical energies crackled around her. 'We are having a tea party. Leave us alone.'

The small clearing they were in was now encircled by forty giant spiders that slowly closed the gap, coming closer to the two girls and Fenris.

Grace stood, her whole body shaking as the dark energies flowed from her eyes. 'You're making me mad.'

The air around Grace vibrated, and her hair danced on end as the magical energies grew. Emily sat at her feet with tears streaming down her cheeks. The giant spiders paused, and Emily thought that the creatures would leave them alone.

A gladiator spider had climbed the trees above the girls. It slowly dropped towards them as it readied its net.

'Fenris, go home now,' Grace said without turning away from the spiders.

Fenris attacked one of the closest spiders, leaping on a hunter before it could react. Biting down on the creature's head, the hell hound shook violently and tore half of the head away. Then Fenris sprinted home.

The other spiders still did not move. They waited for the gladiator to strike. It was ten feet above Grace when she thrust her hands out wide.

Her little fingers opened like flower petals, small arcs of blue energy dancing in between her fingers.

With a primal scream, Grace brought her hands down.

A shockwave of energy exploded from her body. Everything within a twenty-yard radius died instantly, from the tallest tree to the smallest shrub, from the small bugs and insects to the giant spiders.

The earth beneath them rumbled softly. Then everything around the two girls exploded into the air. The area around Grace and Emily was the only place untouched.

Graces eyes glowed as she turned towards Shes and saw thousands and thousands of giant spiders coming their way. The creatures had stopped after the explosion, but she knew that they would come.

Grace took Emily's hand, and both girls raced to Sanctuary.

Thirty seconds later, the horde of giant spiders gave chase.

Pip raced down the stairs, taking three at a time, and she ran into Iguchi. 'I need you and your Fallen Angels; Grace and Emily are in the forest running from the spiders.'

Iguchi, Berenice, and the Angels raced down the passageway while Pip raced for a nearby horse and chased after them. She passed Rain and Joshua, calling out what had happened, and they followed her out into the clearing.

Ramulas called down to Pip. 'Where are you going?'

Pip waved to him before racing into the trees with the Angels, Joshua, and Rain. She did not want to tell Ramulas that his youngest daughter was being chased by thousands of spiders. Pip knew that he would waste most of his magic killing the spiders chasing Grace, and they needed everything to protect Sanctuary.

Pip's emerald eyes glowed fiercely, and what she saw made her smile.

***

Grace and Emily raced as fast as their little legs could carry them. Every few seconds, Grace would release a shower of multi-coloured sparks behind them, keeping the spiders back.

Then Emily stumbled and fell, bringing both girls sprawling to the ground. Three hunters took advantage and rushed the girls. Emily threw her hands out in front of her as a hunter leapt through the air. She turned away, not wanting to see the end.

Two strong hands came out of a nearby oak tree, grabbing the hunter's rear legs and pulling it halfway into a tree before releasing it. The creature screamed before exploding, sending a shower of blood and gore over nearby spiders.

Then other dryads stepped out of the surrounding trees. More than a score of spiders froze in surprise and were pulled into the trees before they could recover. By this time, both girls were covered in gore.

Grace pulled Emily up from the ground, and they ran for home with thousands of spiders giving chase. The creatures had flanked the girls in a few moments. As they closed in, dryads came out of the trees. The first lot of dryads sent streams of darts at the spiders. The closest creatures scurried away from the stinging darts only to be pulled into trees by other dryads.

'Grace, Emily!' Pip called she rode towards them.

She slowed the horse and leant down to pick up Grace up and place her behind her on the horse. A blast of ice shot past Pip as Joshua, Rain, Iguchi, Berenice, and the Fallen Angels raced into the small clearing. Joshua scooped up his daughter as he swung his iron ball in his other hand, sending the broken bodies of two hunters back into the trees.

'Back to Sanctuary,' Pip shouted.

The group raced off with blasts of ice shooting into the trees. Carnage surrounded the group as they ran. Dryads shot their darts and pulled spiders into the trees. Any creature that avoided the dryads were cut down by the Fallen Angels.

A few hundred yards from the clearing, Pip saw mist out of the corner of her eye. She turned to see Rain running behind the Angels with his crystal sword in the air. Thick streams of mist flowed from the blade.

Pip's eyes glowed as she saw through the mist; the spiders were running into each other and the trees.

27

Ramulas watched from the top of the wall as Pip came racing out of the forest with Grace holding on for dear life behind her. Everyone on the wall cheered as the rest of the group followed. Ramulas fought the almost overwhelming urge to go to his daughter. The spiders would be there soon, and the people of Sanctuary needed him on the wall.

'Take her to the castle,' he called down to Pip as she rode through the gate.

Ramulas smiled when he saw Joshua race into the clearing holding Emily. Then a dark shape shot out of the trees as the Fallen Angels came through the gate.

It was Fenris.

The hell hound was closely followed by a large group of spiders. Archers shot at the creatures closest to Fenris as the gate slammed shut behind him. Ramulas looked up to see a wave of darkness spill onto the clearing as the spiders came out of the trees.

***

Pip had slowed her horse by the time they reached the courtyard. She helped Grace down before hoping off herself and turning to Grace. 'What were you doing in the forest?'

'I was playing with Emily.'

'But you knew that the giant spiders were coming, and your da told you not to go.' Then Pip tilted her head. 'When did you go out into the forest?'

'Not long ago,' Grace replied.

'But your da and me were on the wall; we would have seen you.'

A mischievous smile spread on Grace's face. 'We did not want anyone to see us.'

Pip's eyes widened. 'You used magic to sneak by us?'

Grace nodded with a proud smile. At that moment, the Fallen Angels arrived with Joshua and Rain.

Pip took Emily out of Joshua's arms and knelt in front of the girls. 'I am going to make sure you two stay in the castle and not get into any more trouble.'

***

Pip arrived at the throne room with the girls and Fenris. Rachael, Jenna, Makayla, and Tao were waiting for them.

'I want you two to promise me that you will not walk out of the door unless Rachael takes you.'

Both girls nodded, and Kate walked into the room, and Pip turned to her. 'You all need to stay in this room until the fighting has stopped, and Fenris, you stay with Grace,' she said to the hell hound.

Rachael walked over to Pip. 'Ramulas will stop the spiders, won't he?'

Pip forced a smile. 'Of course. You have nothing to worry about.'

Pip raced back up to the wall, knowing this was going to be a hard fight.

***

'Rygar!' Ramulas called.

The dwarf held his head high, his face a mask of concentration. He had a role to play, but it was too early for it just yet. The dwarf waited until the wave of spiders had passed the halfway mark of the clearing before raising his arm and dropping it. 'Now!' he shouted.

Several clay pots filled with molten iron ore were thrown over by mini catapults. The molten missiles landed amongst the horde of creatures, the pots breaking and showering the creatures in sticky, hot ore. The spiders hissed and screamed while others quickly backed away.

'Owain!' Ramulas shouted.

The blind archer stopped clicking his tongue and whistled. The first wave of arrows hit the front line of spiders. As these creatures died, the ones behind quickly jumped over them.

Wave after wave of arrows rained down on the giant spiders. This only seemed to anger the creatures. The giant spiders crawled and jumped over the dead as fast as they could. In a few moments, they had reached the base of the wall.

The spiders attempted to climb the ice-covered wall. Ramulas watched with a mix of horror and curiosity. The spiders were becoming agitated trying to climb over each other to reach the top of the wall.

Pip walked up to Ramulas. 'They look really upset; I think we need to cool them down.'

Ramulas smiled, lifting his war hammer. 'Let's help them.'

He inhaled while holding his weapon in two hands above his head. A warm sensation exploded in the pit of his stomach, and he was covered in purple flames. Pip stepped back as Ramulas came forward, swinging his weapon down with a scream.

A loud crack echoed across the clearing. Everyone on the wall stepped back. After a moment of silence, the ice on the wall groaned. Then, in slow motion, the layer of ice peeled away from the wall. It moved a few inches, and everyone on the wall stepped closer to watch it.

The sheet of ice began to crack and break apart as it fell into the clearing. The spiders at the base of the wall seemed unaware of the danger as the ice fell.

The sheet split into three separate vertical pieces with a resounding crack. It was then that the creatures saw the danger coming from above; however, it was too late for them.

The sheets of ice hit the clearing, squashing hundreds of giant spiders. When the sheets hit the ground, they shattered, sending shards of ice in a shockwave, killing scores more nearby.

Ramulas nodded and smiled in satisfaction. This was the first blow by Sanctuary, but now the spiders could climb the wall.

'Iguchi!' he called out.

Iguchi, Berenice, the Fallen Angels, and the half-giants raced out into the clearing before the gate closed behind them. Ramulas heard stone grinding against stone. He knew the maze was now active.

Iguchi, Berenice, and the Fallen Angels stopped fifty yards from the gate. Most of the clearing was covered in shards of ice of varying sizes and broken spider bodies. Hundreds of giant spiders waited at the edge of the clearing as if waiting for a signal. Iguchi scanned the forest for any hidden dangers.

Then a primal scream shattered the silence as Joshua and Rain raced to the left, with Joshua swinging his iron ball above his head and Rain shooting a blast of ice into the trees, and the spell was broken.

The spiders rushed into the clearing from all sides just as the two half-giants caught up with Joshua and Rain.

***

The druids on the wall waved their hands while they chanted. A score of giant stone wasps flew over the wall and into the clearing, Ramulas saw something out of the corner of his eye and turned. These were almost the same, but there was one major difference.

These wasps were covered in long spikes.

The wasps dropped down randomly onto pockets of spiders as they rushed into the clearing. Ramulas watched in fascination as a wasp picked up a spider. The wasp held the creature in its spike-covered legs and attacked other spiders.

The creatures waited for this opportunity and jumped onto the stone wasp, and almost instantly, they fell to the ground with severe cuts or severed limbs. The wasp would shake and vibrate its body when attacked, causing the spikes to cut into the spiders.

The druids dropped their arms and pulled out their wands. They shot streams of green and black bubbles into the clearing. These bubbles were a lot smaller, making them easier to control; for every ten green bubbles there would be one black.

The smaller bubbles flew much faster. The green bubbles would hit a target and explode into webs of sticky green goo, trapping nearby spiders and others that walked into the affected area. The black bubbles would explode on contact and eat through the outer shell of the spider, causing it to scream in pain as it struggled in the sticky web.

***

Shigar stepped forward, holding his large leather-bound book to his chest. He raised his free hand, uttered a single word, and dropped his hand. People on the wall stopped what they were doing and watched the clearing with wide eyes and opened mouths. Small pockets of spiders began to attack other spiders close by.

'By the gods,' Ramulas whispered. 'What is happening?'

The magician smiled. 'I just gave the spiders the illusion that we were amongst them. They think the spiders next to them are really people.'

A smile grew on Ramulas' face. 'That's a good trick.'

The magician waved his hand. 'This trick will be even better.'

Shigar uttered another word, and six balls of light appeared before him, each the size of a small apple. There were two green, two blue, and two red balls. He touched the blue spheres, and they shot towards the mass of spiders. Ramulas' eyes widened as the balls hit two spiders and they froze instantly while others close by scuttled away with parts of their bodies frozen.

Next, Shigar touched the red balls, and they raced towards the creatures. The balls hit, setting several spiders on fire and sending others flying.

Finally, Shigar touched the green balls, and they headed for the giant spiders. This time, Ramulas noticed something different—one of the balls changed its path as a giant spider raced away, following the creature as it climbed over others in its way. The green balls hit two spiders, sending out sticky goo covering the spiders and slowly restricting, cutting through their bodies.

'What happened? That ball just moved,' Ramulas said.

Shigar smiled. 'I choose which spider will receive which ball before I touch them. It does not matter where that spider goes; the ball will find it.'

'This is wonderful,' Ramulas said.

The magician nodded as he sent more balls into the clearing. This time, they raced towards where the Fallen Angels were.

***

As Pip and the Fallen Angels raced through the forest with Grace and Emily, the dryads followed close behind. They jumped in and out of trees, forming a protective barrier around the group. Any spiders that came too close were pulled into trees.

The few spiders that avoided the dryads were quickly cut down by the flashing blades of the Fallen Angels. The dryads continued to follow until the clearing, where they stopped and watched the group take the girls into Sanctuary. Then hundreds of the creatures rushed past them into the clearing.

The ice layer in front of the wall had just been dropped, and many of the giant spiders died, but hundreds more poured into the clearing to attack the Fallen Angels, who had come back from the gate. The spiders raced to kill the Fallen Angels; the dryads pulled as many of them as they could into the trees.

Then the spiders would jump away from the trees a moment before the dryads came out. Sometimes, they would pull a dryad out of the tree to attack it. When this happened, other dryads would come out of the trees, shooting streams of darts at the creatures.

Most of the dryads escaped, but an unfortunate few were dragged away. The rest of the dryads moved away from the clearing. It had become far too dangerous for them, having lost the advantage of surprise. They could no longer attack without fear of being taken.

For now, they would wait for a better opportunity.

***

Grace, Emily, Kate, and Rachael stood on the balcony of the throne room listening to the sounds of battle. They watched people move along the wall and saw flashes of light as Shigar cast his spells.

Garce's eyes became dark. 'I want to help Da.'

Dark energies crackled around Grace as she lifted an inch off the floor.

'No,' Rachael and Kate said in unison.

Rachael walked over and placed her hands on Grace's shoulders. 'Grace, your father wants you here with us.'

The dark energy subsided as Grace lowered to the floor. 'But I have magic, and I can help.'

Rachael shook her head. 'Your father says that you need to learn how to control your magic or people will be hurt.'

Rachael led the three girls away from the balcony and into the throne room. She did not want them to see the giant spiders if they climbed over the wall.

As they walked, Emily reached out to touch Grace's hand. Grace turned and gasped as Emily's eyes flashed with dark energies.

***

Joshua screamed in rage as he swung his iron ball around his body. Broken bodies of spiders were thrown in all directions. He was in his element. He did not have to worry about hurting anyone, and his near-invulnerable skin kept him from being harmed.

A blast of ice hit a nearby spider, turning it into a frozen statue. Joshua turned to see Rain standing on a mound of frozen spiders. He was surrounded by hundreds of spiders attempting to attack him. Rain would alternate between shooting creatures near him and targeting those out in the clearing.

Rain waved to Joshua before shooting a few blasts where the half-giants were fighting. He was rewarded with yells of protests from the giant-kin. The half-giants took offence to Rain's interference and fought their way towards his frozen mound of spiders.

When they were twenty yards away, the giant-kin yelled to Rain, voicing their displeasure.

Rain waved them away. He did not have time for their foolish games. He raised his sword and created a wall of thick mist in between himself and the half-giants.

This was the height of disrespect for the giant-kin to be ignored. They continued to shout and focus on Rain's position. This was the perfect opportunity for several nearby hunters to pounce on one of the half-giants and bring him to the ground.

The other half-giant roared in outrage and swung his sword, cutting one of the creatures in half and knocking his companion into the mass of spiders. The half-giant jumped to the aid of his brother, who was covered in spiders, pulling off as many as he could. This left him open to attack, and he was also covered.

Soon, both giants disappeared under the sea of giant spiders.

***

Ramulas watched the spiders converge on Iguchi, Berenice and the Fallen Angels, Joshua, Rain, and the giant-kin. The Fallen Angels had taken the form of a star that slowly turned. After a few seconds, the star broke into small circles comprised of five Angels each.

Iguchi and Berenice stood back-to-back as the creatures rushed in to attack the pair. The father-and-daughter team slowly turned as their blades spun in patterns. Any spiders that came close were soon cut to pieces.

The small groups of Fallen Angels moved through the mass of spiders, cutting down as many as they could. Ramulas turned to Joshua and Rain, who seemed to be holding their ground. Rain shot a blast of ice at the half-giants. This angered the giant-kin, and they moved towards Rain and Joshua while yelling at them.

'What are they doing?' Pip asked.

Ramulas shrugged. 'I don't know.'

'They should be paying attention to the spiders and not worrying about Rain.'

They watched as one of the half-giants went down under the weight of the nearby creatures that jumped on him, and he was quickly followed by the other. It was like a magic trick; one moment both giant-kin were there, and the next they had gone.

A warm sensation exploded in the pit of Ramulas' stomach and spread through his body. His arm shot out, sending streams of white energy at the mound of spiders on the giant-kin, sending a dozen into the air in flames.

Ramulas turned to Pip. 'You're in charge of the wall.'

The Lord of Sanctuary dived off the wall into the clearing. Halfway down, he was bathed in purple flame, and he slowed himself down by the time he reached the clearing.

Groups of giant spiders charged this new target.

Ramulas waited until they were ten feet away before outstretching his arms and bringing his hands together. A thunderclap rolled across the clearing, followed by a wall of purple flame. The creatures closest to Ramulas burst into flame and were tossed into the air.

The spiders that survived this rushed the Lord of Sanctuary. Ramulas concentrated and brought forth his full magical ability, causing his purple flame to flare, making him invulnerable for a short period of time.

He charged into the mass of spiders while swinging his weapons. He felt free knowing that all he needed to concentrate on was attacking and not worry about defending himself. Creatures were cut to pieces and knocked aside as Ramulas walked through. He smiled each time a spider attacked and was repelled by his flames.

However, Ramulas knew this would not last long and would make every second count.

28

Pip watched Ramulas wade through the giant spiders in the clearing while wave after wave of arrows rained down on the creatures. The druids had stopped their bubbles and placed their wands inside their robes. There were large patches of green webbing in the clearing that held scores of spiders. The druids turned to Pip, who nodded.

Their hands dropped to pouches, and each took out a handful of stones and tossed them into the clearing. They transformed into stone wasps. These wasps would land on a trapped spider's head and burrow into its brain. The spiders that were being attacked like this struggled against the web but could not move.

The druids began to chant while waving their hands above their heads. Movement could be seen at the edges of the clearing as thick vines pushed their way through the earth, reaching out blindly until they touched a spider. The vines would lift the creatures in the air, crush them, and search for another.

After a few seconds, the spiders quickly learned their lesson and moved away from the vines.

Then, as one, the giant spiders rushed the wall and started to climb.

Pip turned to Shigar. 'Hurry; they're climbing the wall.'

The magician, still clutching his leather-bound book, looked over the wall. He waved his hand and uttered a phrase.

The clouds above the clearing darkened and the rumbling of thunder could be heard. Three forks of lightning came down from the clouds to strike at the spiders climbing the wall. The lightning would hit a spider then reach out to others close by.

More than half of the spiders climbing the wall fell dead; however, the rest continued to climb.

Shigar waved his hand again, uttering a different word, and the dark clouds above moved in a slow circle, which slowly picked up speed until it transformed into a mini-tornado. The tornado dropped to the base of the wall, bouncing back and forth for a few seconds before disappearing.

Pip watched in fascination as the giant spiders were sucked into the funnel and spat out against the wall with devastating effects. The main body of spiders had moved away, but forty had chosen to climb the wall. The archers stopped shooting into the clearing and focused on the spiders climbing the wall.

'Git yer arrows away from the wall,' Rygar cried.

Pip watched as the dwarf dived off the top of the wall, holding his axe and shield, with a rope tied to his waist. The rope grew taut, and he swung back and forth against the wall, striking out at any of the spiders that were close enough.

After Rygar had killed ten spiders, his momentum slowed, and two hunters jumped onto him. The three fought fiercely at the end of the jerking rope.

Pip yelled. 'Owain, help him.'

Two archers shot at the spiders as the dwarf chopped off one of their legs. This leg had been right near the rope holding Rygar, and his axe sliced through the rope as well.

With the rope severed, the three fell to the ground. Pip saw a group of Fallen Angels twenty yards from the wall watching Rygar fall. Miles led his group to the dwarf just as the giant spiders surged towards the wall one last time.

Archers concentrated their arrows on any spiders that came near Rygar.

Pip's eyes blazed as she looked at Rygar. He lay on the ground unconscious and could not defend himself.

***

Ramulas heard Pip call out and turned to see the dwarf fall from the rope. He used his magical ability to communicate with the giant spiders and found they were all talking to each other. He finally understood why they moved as one and not as individuals. Some of the different species of spiders were psychic.

Then he heard the call for the spiders to rush the wall and get into Sanctuary.

Ramulas knew that it was time for him to return to Sanctuary. This was what Rygar and Iguchi called a tactical retreat. Ramulas focused his magical energy into his weapons and brought them together. A beam of white light shot out from the head of the battle axe. This light hit the wall, sending arcs of energy along the wall's surface. Spiders on the wall popped and sizzled before falling.

Pip called out a command, and everyone on the wall except for her and Shigar ran a few steps and jumped off the back of the wall, falling into the maze sixty yards below.

***

Iguchi and his daughter looked up to see the beam of light and knew it was time to return to the gate. The Fallen Angels would rush to the gate and wait until all the survivors had made it back safely before entering.

***

Ramulas was not far from where the half-giants fell. He saw Joshua wildly swinging his ball while screaming. Rain stood on a mound of frozen spiders. They had not seen the signal, and he needed to warn them.

Ramulas put his weapons away, clapped his hands, and released a spell. The giant spiders surrounding Ramulas were thrown into the air, and a pathway was cleared from him to Rain.

He sprinted to the frozen mound.

'The half-giants?' he asked Rain.

Rain shook his head and nodded to a nearby mound of spiders. One of the giant-kin's arms showed; it was covered in bite marks.

Ramulas swore. 'Time to go.'

Joshua and Rain ran to his side. They turned to see the wall one hundred yards away. Every inch was covered with spiders.

Ramulas sighed. 'We will have a hard time getting back inside.'

'Looks like fun,' Rain said.

Joshua roared, swung his ball, and raced ahead.

Shigar stood on the wall watching the carnage unfold, helping where he could. Iguchi, Berenice, the Fallen Angels, and Rygar waited by the gate. Only Ramulas, Joshua, and Rain were left, and they were halfway across the clearing.

The magician had a difficult choice to make.

If he concentrated on the spiders around Ramulas, the ones on the wall would be able to climb over. Shigar made his choice. Several coloured balls appeared in front of the magician; he chose the spiders near Ramulas.

***

Ramulas jumped when a giant spider near him burst into flames. He turned to see Shigar sending his magical balls into the clearing. He smiled, knowing that the magician was trying to help. However, it would take a lot more to get through the sea of giant spiders.

Ramulas held out both of his hands, sending purple arcs of energy into the surrounding creatures. As their dark bodies flew into the air, Ramulas saw a gap in front of them. A warm sensation exploded in the pit of his stomach and spread through him. Covered in purple flames, Ramulas gripped his battle axe in two hands, turned in a tight circle, and released his weapon.

The battle axe spun through the air, cutting through countless spiders. He focused on his magic and brought his weapon back to him before sending it back out again. In and out, the weapon flew, opening a path to the gate as they ran forward. Joshua and Rain ran on either side of Ramulas, protecting him from any spiders trying to attack them.

Twenty yards from the gate, Ramulas caught his weapon and stumbled. His magical power had almost gone. Iguchi and the Fallen Angels rushed to his side, using their swords to keep the creatures at bay until everyone was through the gate.

As the gate closed, Ramulas placed his hand on the inside of the wall and sent one last powerful surge of energy into the wall. The giant spiders climbing the wall were thrown off by arcs of energy.

***

Shigar looked down from the top of the wall, watching the group come in through the gate and Ramulas send his magic into the wall. Scores of spiders fell from the wall, but there were thousands more in the clearing. The last thing the magician saw before jumping off the wall was hundreds of spiders climbing the cliffs on either side of the wall.

Shigar jumped off the wall and fell twenty metres before he slowed, drifted over the maze, and slowly descended until he landed in the courtyard. The people cheered, and Shigar saw the people of Sanctuary ready in battle formations.

'The spiders are coming and will be here shortly,' he said before dashing into the castle.

The spiders had become wary of the wall. Too many times, they had suffered losses trying to climb it. Now they scaled the cliffs on either side of the wall. A score of spiders climbed each cliff until reaching the top of the wall.

The other spiders saw this and swarmed up the cliffs. When they were halfway up the face, Royce and Shayn stepped out from the rocky face. The elementals lashed out at any nearby spiders, each blow killing a creature instantly. The creatures acted instantly, attacking the new threat, but they soon found that their fangs had no effect on the elementals' stone skin.

The creatures changed tactics and tried jumping on the duo to knock them from the cliff face. Royce and Shayn smiled as they sank back into the rocks up to their knees so they could not be moved. They spoke to the mountain, and large slabs of rock slid down the mountain.

The sound of stone grinding against stone was almost deafening as clouds of dust rose in the air. When the dust settled, most of the giant spiders had been knocked off the cliffs, but hundreds more raced up the cliffs, jumping over each other.

The elementals threw chunks of rocks at the masses racing up the mountain, but many got past them. There were far too many for the elementals to stop.

***

Ramulas, Iguchi, Berenice, and the Angels raced through the maze. The stone octopuses became active and swam along the walls. Ramulas thanked the gods that the octopuses were on their side and not fighting against them. The walls of the maze opened and closed around them, giving the group the quickest way to the courtyard.

They came into the courtyard, and Ramulas turned. His eyes widened as he said, 'Oh no.'

Hundreds of spiders swarmed over the wall and the mountains. They would be in Sanctuary soon, and his people would fight for their home.

Pip ran up to him with a mischievous smile. 'Let's have some fun.'

***

The wave of giant spiders swarmed down the wall and into the maze. As the first group of forty entered, the maze burst into life. Over one hundred octopuses had been watching the creatures come down. They swam through the maze and waited for their prey.

The spiders entered the maze, running along the floors and walls. Stone tentacles reached out to crush the enemies of Sanctuary. The giant spiders had no chance of fighting back. A large group of spiders saw this and rushed in as one to attack. Four hundred flowed down to challenge this new enemy.

Within moments, they discovered their mistake. Over half of the group were torn apart before they realised the stone octopuses could not be harmed.

Spiders jumped away from the area only to have octopuses jump out of the walls to pull them back down, where they were literally torn limb from limb. The message was sent for the spiders to avoid the maze, and they ran along the cliffs on either side of Sanctuary.

****

Ramulas watched the creatures flow down the mountain sides into Sanctuary as his people called out in alarm. He closed his eyes and focused. *Hello, little one. Are you and your sister in the throne room?*

Yes, Da. Are the spiders here yet? she replied excitedly.

No, but they will be soon.

I can do magic; I want to help.

Ramulas smiled at her eagerness, but it was far too dangerous for her. *I do not need your help. Who is in the throne room with you?*

Emily, Kate, Makayla, Tao, and Rachael.

I want you to look after them and promise me that you will not walk out of the throne room until I come for you.

I promise.

The communication ceased, and he was happy that he did not have to worry about his daughters. He opened his eyes to see Pip smiling at him. 'This is going to be messy,' she said.

Ramulas saw that Pip held two slightly curved swords. 'Why are you holding swords? Will you not use your throwing knives?'

The former thief shook her head. 'Too many spiders, not enough throwing knives.'

Flashes of bright light brought their attention to the castle wall, where the magician was sending his colourful balls to the spiders climbing down. This spurred the creatures to move faster as spiders on the cliffs burst into flames.

'Let us bring the fight to them,' Ramulas said, running to the mountain with Pip following.

As the pair ran to the tunnel, they saw that the people of Sanctuary were ready in their tight formations. The giant spiders would be met with barriers of swords and shields. Shigar, the druids, and the archers would help from the walls of the castle where they could.

There were two possible ways for this battle to end—either the people of Sanctuary would kill all the spiders, or a signal would be given and everyone would retreat through the passageway into the valley.

They saw Edwin talking to a group as they came up to the tunnel. The dwarf waved his pickaxe and smiled at them.

Then the giant spiders came down into Sanctuary.

Ramulas shouted, 'Weapons ready!'

Many of the giant spiders jumped from the walls onto the people below. A lot of these were cut down before doing any damage while others were successful in knocking people down. The reaction of the people of Sanctuary was instantaneous. When a creature knocked someone down, blades would come in from every direction, cutting the spider to pieces, and the person was lifted to their feet.

***

Ramulas and Pip stood back to back, spinning their weapons in front of them. The stream of giant spiders coming down the mountains seemed endless. In a few moments, both were covered in blood and gore.

Through using his weapons, Ramulas' magical ability had been restored, and he saw something along the cliff face. Several gladiator spiders were perched on the cliffs, stretching nets. One jumped off and entangled a nearby soldier.

Ramulas shot his hand out, sending streams of energy into a few of the spiders, knocking several from the wall. Others were hit with blasts of ice, and he heard Joshua screaming as several spider's broken bodies flew into the air.

Rain and Joshua were only ten yards away. Ramulas and Pip moved towards them.

Ramulas turned to Pip. 'Stay with them.'

Purple flames covered Ramulas as he leapt into the air.

***

Shigar watched the battle rage from his balcony on the fifth floor. The giant spiders had come into Sanctuary from both sides and fought the people as they came in. Giant stone hands came out of the mountains to slap away and squash the spiders as they came down; this seemed to spur the creatures to move faster.

The archers fired at the waves of spiders as they fought with the people. The druids rejoined the fight, spraying their bubbles towards the spiders.

Shigar sent a few dozen coloured balls into the cliffs on both sides before sighing. Sooner than he would have liked, his magical tricks were almost finished; he only had two more tricks up his sleeve.

The magician laid several small red crystals in front of him. He would save them for later. Shigar uttered a phrase; a wooden staff appeared before him, and he grabbed it. The staff was made of dark, polished oak with a shining emerald embedded in its tip.

Shigar held out the staff before him, and an arc of green energy shot out at the spiders, blasting several from the cliffs. After a few more shots, he saw Ramulas float into the air. Shigar waved his staff, trying to get Ramulas' attention.

***

Rachael paced the floor of the throne room, worried about the sound of battle outside. It had brought back memories of the last battle, when she lost her husband.

She saw that Kate and Jenna were scared, and she needed to put on a brave face for them. Makayla and Tao played at Jenna's feet, while Emily and Grace sat under the stone oak tree whispering to each other. Every time Rachael asked what they were talking about, they would just giggle.

29

Ramulas floated twenty feet in the air, facing the mountain. The spiders swarming down reminded him of a waterfall. He brought his hands together, and a shockwave of purple energy exploded from his body.

One hundred giant spiders fell from the cliff face; however, there were many more. He turned in the air to see Shigar waving at him.

He flew over to land next to the magician. 'What's happening?'

Shigar shook his head. 'There are too many giant spiders coming in from both sides. We are overwhelmed.'

Ramulas saw that, below them, small groups of people were attempting to hold back the flood of spiders. These groups were supposed to stop the spiders, but he could see some creatures already getting through.

'Damn,' Ramulas swore. 'We were supposed to hold them longer than this.'

'What can we do? the magician asked.

Ramulas looked down at the scene below. Iguchi and Berenice led the Fallen Angels to the spiders that avoided the groups. He would not be able to use his magic soon for fear of hurting his people.

Ramulas turned to Shigar. 'How much magic is left in your staff?'

The magician shrugged. 'Quite a bit. Why do you ask?'

'You take the left, and I'll go right.'

Ramulas turned to his right, holding both hands out. Arcs of white energy leapt to the spiders on the mountainside, sending chunks of rock and spiders flying into the air. Ramulas adjusted his power along the cliff, killing scores of creatures.

On the left, Shigar sent streams of energy from his staff, and even more giant spiders fell. Ramulas turned and cast a spell on the Fallen Angels; they were each covered in a light aura, making them invulnerable for a short period of time.

The first of the defensive groups broke apart, leaving the individuals vulnerable. He knew they were in danger and needed to do something.

'Time to go,' Ramulas said to Shigar.

The magician nodded as Ramulas leapt into the air.

Ramulas flew to the top of the castle and looked down at the town of Sanctuary. The Fallen Angels had cut a path through the spiders and were headed towards the rear of the town. Iguchi and his daughter had joined Pip, Joshua, and Rain near the tunnel, surrounded by dozens of dead spiders.

Hundreds more still streamed into Sanctuary, and the tide was slowly turning in their favour. Ramulas cast a spell before bringing his arms out wide. A clap of thunder rolled over Sanctuary, and the sky grew dark.

A moment later, forked lighting shot down into Sanctuary. The sudden brightness caused the creatures to run back for the cliffs, only to be cut down by the people of Sanctuary.

The signal had been seen and heard.

The people of Sanctuary knew the battle was lost and they needed to head for the passageway. The archers on the wall fired one last volley of arrows before leaving. The druids shot out bursts of green bubbles towards the groups of defenders who were fighting giant spiders.

The bubbles hit one group and exploded. Sticky green web shot out covering both man and spider. Then something extraordinary happened; the giant spiders struggled in the web and the soldiers walked away unaffected. This was their chance to run to the passageway.

Shigar watched as events unfolded before him. Once the soldiers were free of the web, Shigar picked up the red crystals and threw three on either side of the castle. The crystals transformed into fireballs before hitting the masses of spiders trapped in the webs.

Shigar ran from the balcony; he was needed in the passageway.

***

Ramulas saw the people of Sanctuary moving towards the passageway. They knew it was time to leave. Then his shoulders slumped as he saw hundreds of giant spiders climbing along the cliff faces following the people of Sanctuary. He did not have enough magic to deal with the creatures on both sides. He quickly flew to the rear cliffs.

***

'That's the signal,' Rachael said. 'We need to leave.'

Kate, Jenna, Makayla, and Tao ran to her. Grace and Emily still sat whispering and giggling under the stone tree.

'Grace and Emily, we need to leave now,' Rachael said sternly.

Both girls turned, and Rachael froze. The girl's eye were dark and dark energies crackled around them.

Rachael shook her head. 'Girls, what are you doing?'

Grace and Emily stood holding hands. Their hair danced with crackling energies that surrounded them. Without saying a word, they ran to the balcony and jumped off, still holding hands.

***

Women and children ran out of the rear of the castle. They had been told to stay in a group for safety. They streamed into the streets and ran for the passageway only to be stopped one hundred yards away by hundreds of spiders that came down the cliff face to block their path. They turned to run back and found another group of creatures had blocked their path.

The women and children huddled together as the spiders slowly closed in. Children began to cry as the women held them close.

A primal scream cut through the air nearby as two broken spiders went sailing through the air. This was followed by blasts of ice hitting several spiders, and Pip was seen dancing in and out of the spiders with her spinning swords.

Joshua and Rain had arrived. The women and children looked around, knowing that they would need more than this trio to help them out of this situation.

***

A young boy, his eyes wide with fear, broke away from the group and ran as fast as he could while the women screamed for him to come back. One of the hunters gave chase, with Pip calling out a warning as the creature closed in on the boy.

Rain turned and cursed. 'Can't shoot at the spider without the risk of hurting the boy.'

With arms and legs pumping, the young boy increased his speed, but the hunter jumped through the air and pushed the young boy sprawling to the ground. The young boy curled into a ball and covered his head with his hands.

The hunter dashed forward as one of the statues of the fallen stepped down and impaled the creature with its sword. The boy raised his head to see the statues of the fallen all with blazing purple eyes stepping forward holding up their swords.

The first statue flicked the dead giant spider from its weapon. The rest of the statues formed a circle around the boy.

***

Ramulas flew to the rear of Sanctuary, where scores of spiders were jumping off the wall, blocking the peoples' retreat. The Lord of Sanctuary dropped into the midst of the creatures and released his magical energy.

A wave of purple energy rolled out from Ramulas, sending spiders into the air where arcs of white lightning cooked them. Those creatures unaffected scattered, which made a path for the people to run for the passageway.

Ramulas saw Rain, Joshua, and Pip fighting the spiders. He raced towards them, pulling out his weapons. His people needed as much time as they could to get to safety.

Ramulas smiled, knowing that Rachael and his daughters were safe and in good hands.

***

Rachael and Kate screamed as the two girls jumped from the balcony. A few moments later, Garce and Emily shot by the window, bathed in crackling dark energy.

Kate turned to Rachael. 'What do we do?'

Rachael grabbed Kate's hand. 'We will find your father. He will know what to do.'

They turned to see everyone had left the throne room with the hell hounds. Rachael grabbed Kate's hand, and they raced out into the hallway. They went down the stairs to the ground floor and found the castle was empty; then Rachael gasped and froze. Kate saw Rachael's eyes widen as she backed away. Kate followed Rachael's gaze to see a hunter crawling off one of the marble columns. The skin of the creature was the same tone as the marble, making it almost invisible. Then it darkened as it moved towards the two.

Kate's demeanour changed as she stepped in front of Rachael, pulling out her sword. The creatures slowly moved forward as Kate's body became as still as a statue. Kate seemed to stare into space as the giant spider came to within ten feet of her. Then Rachael gasped as other creatures came into the area.

Rachael screamed as the hunter jumped at Kate. Kate rushed forward, slashing out with her swords, taking off three of the creature's legs. It scrambled away hissing, leaving a trail of ichor behind it. Three other hunters rushed at Kate, who twisted and dodged the spiders as they attempted to attack her.

Kate's sword spun in tight circles, scoring minor hits on the creatures, and they backed away before changing tactics. They took turns rushing in at Kate, rearing up and flailing their front legs and forcing her to focus on one spider at a time. As Kate was fending off one hunter, another rushed in behind her.

Kate spun and thrust her sword behind her, impaling the spider, then quickly returned to her original position to find the other spider flying towards her. Kate rolled forward and came up leading with her weapon, opening the creature's abdomen and covering Kate in sticky gore. She coughed and spat the fluids from her mouth while shaking the gore from her hair as the last spider closed in.

'Kate, be careful!' Rachael called out.

Kate turned and saw a gladiator spider lowering itself from the ceiling above Rachael, preparing its net. Kate screamed and rushed the last spider, cutting it open with a slash-thrust-slash attack. As it scurried away, Kate spun and threw her sword like a spear and impaled the gladiator spider.

The creature jerked once then hung in the air twenty feet above Rachael with Kate's sword in its body. Rachael looked up and screamed for Ramulas to help them. Kate looked around for another weapon, but all she saw were giant spiders crawling out of every space coming into the hallway.

Then Kate looked at Rachael wearing one of her mother's dresses and crying. This brought back memories of her mother being killed. Kate lost her fighter stance as she ran to Rachael and hugged her.

Everywhere they looked, all they could see were spiders, and there seemed to be nowhere to go. Then the long, spiky leg of a hunter brushed Rachael's arm. She saw it, screamed, and ran down the hallway, dragging Kate behind her.

As they ran down the hallway, hunters could be seen all around them as the creatures darkened their skin. They crawled out from behind statues, columns, the walls, and the ceiling. The sight of more than two dozen giant spiders spurred them on, and soon Rachael and Kate found themselves in the courtyard, closely followed by the spiders.

Halfway across the courtyard, they stopped when they saw a score of giant spiders run across and block the entrance of the courtyard. They had been herded by the giant spiders, and the creatures slowly started to close in around them. Fighting could be heard at the rear of Sanctuary, but all they could see were the giant spiders.

There would be no-one coming to help them.

Kate released Rachael's hand and ran ten yards to the statues of Jacqueline and Lodi. Rachael rushed to join her as the spiders rushed in.

'Mother, help us!' Kate screamed as she touched Jacqueline's statue.

Nothing happened.

Kate cried as Rachael pulled her in close, placing Ramulas' daughter's head against her shoulder. She did not want the young girl to see the creatures coming closer.

The spiders were ten feet away when Rachael closed her eyes and hugged Kate fiercely.

The statues of Jacqueline and Lodi opened their eyes.

***

Hand in hand, Grace and Emily flew over the wall and into the clearing. Amongst the bodies of the dead spiders, they found what they were looking for. Dark magical energies shot out of the girls' hands into the clearing, and the pieces of the twenty giant stone wasps rose into the air and reassembled into wasps once more.

Grace and Emily covered the wasps in dark energy and sent them over the wall into Sanctuary. The reanimated creatures dropped down near the people and began tearing apart the spiders. The people cheered seeing the wasps join the battle, and they fought with more enthusiasm.

Another wave of giant spiders flowed down the cliff face to attack the people. A blast of dark energy hit the mountain, sending arcs of power that killed the surrounding spiders. The flow of spiders scattered along the mountain.

***

'Help them,' the boy said to the statues of the fallen as he pointed to the people fighting the spiders. Despite the efforts of Pip, Rain, and Joshua, the spiders were overwhelming the people of Sanctuary.

The statues made their way to the women and children, slow jerking movements quickly turning into smooth, running strides. The people cheered again as the statues of the fallen surrounded the women and children. Any giant spider that attempted to break through the barrier was cut down, and some of the statues launched themselves into the air to catch spiders that attempted to jump over them.

The statues of the fallen slowly fought their way towards to the passageway while protecting the women and children. Pip, Rain, and Joshua saw what was happening and jumped into help. They fought for a minute; then Pip looked up into the sky and laughed. 'Would you look at that.'

***

Ramulas helped the first lot of people into the passageway. Everyone was told not to wait in the valley but to head straight for Journey's End.

Iguchi and the Fallen Angels raced up to him. 'Hello to you, Lord of Sanctuary,' the small man said with a bow. 'There are too many spiders. We need to make the people move quicker into the passageway.'

Ramulas nodded. 'I know. Have your Angels stay here to protect those coming through.'

'What of those people?' Iguchi said, pointing behind Ramulas.

Ramulas turned to see the statues of the fallen with Pip, Rain, and Joshua leading a large group of women and children to them. 'Help bring them here.'

Ramulas sent arcs of energy at the spiders as Iguchi and Berenice led the Fallen Angels towards the women and children. In a few moments, they were running into the entrance of the passageway with Miles and nine other Angels escorting them through. Iguchi ordered his Fallen Angels to stand guard as he and Berenice rushed off to help another group of people.

Ramulas smiled, seeing that the statues of the fallen had stayed nearby to help people as they came closer to the passageway. He turned to the Angels close to him. 'We need to stay here until the last of the people have made it through.'

Then his mouth opened as Jenna ran towards him with tears in her eyes. With her were Makayla, Tao, and the hell hounds. She stopped in front of him, crying.

'Where are Kate, Grace, and Rachael? '

'Grace and Emily jumped off the balcony, and I do not know where the others are.'

Ramulas looked over the sea of people running and wondered where his daughters were.

***

A large shadow fell over Rachael and Kate. Rachael looked up to see the statue of Lodi standing over them. The giant's eye glowed a bright purple, and he wore a menacing scowl. He swung his club, sending the broken bodies of five spiders through the air.

The other giant spiders moved away as Lodi moved towards them swinging his club. He turned once towards Kate and Rachael before charging at the spiders, sending them scattering out of the courtyard. Every few steps, spiders would be sent flying through the air.

As the giant disappeared around the corner, they saw two hunters slowly make their way to them. They looked to where Lodi had gone, and Kate said, 'He won't make it back in time.'

They huddled together as the hunters came to within six feet of them. Then the statue of Jacqueline came to life.

With her eyes blazing purple, the statue dashed forward, knocking away one of the hunters with a backhand and slamming against a wall. Jacqueline picked up the other spider and tore its head from its body.

For a moment, Kate and Rachael stood in silence.

Then Kate ran over to hug Jacqueline's statue. 'Mother, everyone is leaving Sanctuary to go to the valley.'

Jacqueline took Kate's hand and ran into the castle with Rachael close behind.

***

More and more people flowed into the passageway as Ramulas, Pip, the Angels, Joshua, and Rain kept the giant spiders at bay. The statues of the fallen had broken into two groups, helping people come to the passageway.

Ramulas constantly searched for his daughters amongst the sea of people. Then Iguchi came up to him and pointed to the sky. Ramulas followed the small man's finger, and his eyes widened when he saw Grace and Emily flying above them.

He communicated with Grace. *Little one, come back down here right now.*

Grace released Emily's hand in surprise and, with a popping sound, the magical energies around the girls vanished, and they fell screaming to the ground.

Ramulas shot both hands out and caught the girls in a white aura and lowered them to the ground in front of him. He dropped to one knee and hugged them both tightly, then he released them. 'I do not want you scaring me like that again. Where is Kate?'

Emily and Grace smiled as they looked over his shoulder.

'She is coming with her mother,' Emily said.

'What do you mean?' he asked.

Without saying a word, Grace ran past Ramulas, and he turned to follow her. Then he gasped and held his chest. Jacqueline's statue had come to life, and she was holding both of her daughters.

Ramulas took a few hesitant steps towards Jacqueline, not knowing whether it was real or he had gone mad with the pain of losing his wife.

Kate and Grace's faces were beaming as they held their mother. Then Jacqueline reached for his hand. As Ramulas placed his hand in hers, the pain of losing her intensified. Jacqueline's other hand reached out for

Rachael's. When she held both hands, Jacqueline placed Ramulas' and Rachael's hands together.

Ramulas' jaw dropped, and Rachael gasped. Jacqueline released their hands and ran off to join the other statues of the fallen fight the giant spiders.

'No, wait,' Ramulas called out.

A strong hand gripped his arm, and he saw a very determined Pip.

'We need to go. Now.'

Ramulas pointed to the statues of the fallen. 'But Jacqueline is there.'

Pip shook her head. 'The last of the people have made it through the passageway. We need to go.'

Ramulas glanced around and saw that Pip was right. His people had all gone, and the Fallen Angels and statues fought back hundreds of giant spiders. Ramulas nodded, and they ran into the passageway with Iguchi and the Fallen Angels close behind.

Once they were inside, Ramulas stood ten feet away from the entrance, facing Sanctuary with Pip, Berenice, and Iguchi. They watched as the spiders crawled over the entrance of the passageway. It was like watching things crawl on the outside of a window.

'They cannot get through,' Pip said.

Ramulas waved his hands and cast a spell. Purple mist flowed from his hands to the entrance. Then his eyes widened. 'They can't see the entrance.'

Pip raised her eyebrows. 'What do we do now?

'Go to Journey's End for some rest. After that, I don't know.'

30

Lucas sat at a small table waiting. He was in a small house by the docks, and he woke with the biggest appetite. The remains of his fourth meal had been taken from his room. His strength had almost fully returned. He told the woman who was looking after him that he ready to leave.

Now, he waited.

Over the last few days, Lucas had mastered patience. He watched the clouds move across the sky as he listened to the sounds of the docks. Heavy footsteps came down the hall when his door opened. The Master of Shadows walked in with two of his enforcers; one of them handed Lucas his uniform.

The Master smiled. 'You look better.'

'I am,' Lucas said, putting on his uniform. 'When do I speak with the agents you have been holding for me?'

'Once you are ready, we will leave.'

After Lucas was dressed, the Master handed him some long brown priest's robes. Lucas threw the robes on and was led out into the streets. After a few minutes, they stood outside one of the derelict buildings of the poor section.

The Master made a few quick hand signals, and a door opened. Lucas walked inside and saw both agents chained to the far wall. Both agent's eyes widened as Lucas removed his brown robes and walked forward.

He walked twenty paces and noticed that there were only a few crates along the wall and two other enforcers inside. Both agents were chained by a bolt above their heads and their ankles had been shackled.

'Why were you trying to poison me?' Lucas asked in a low voice.

One of the agents sneered. 'It was for the queen.'

A fist shot out as Lucas hit the agent in the nose. The agent's head hit the wall, and then blood streamed from his nose. The two agents looked at Lucas in shock. The four enforcers glanced at the Master, and he waved them back.

Lucas sighed as he pulled out his short sword. 'Since the death of King Zachary, you and your fellow agents have caused nothing but trouble, using Queen Aleesha as your puppet. The people of the kingdom have died. They needed our help, and because of your selfish actions, they died.'

Lucas paced back and forth in front of the agents while tapping the flat of the blade onto his open palm. Everyone held their breath, waiting to see what would happen next.

Lucas stopped suddenly and pointed the sword at the agents, his face an emotionless mask. 'I will give you both a choice. I can have the Shadows beat you to death or send you both to Gullytown with the others.'

'What? You cannot do that; there are laws,' one of the agents protested.

Lucas shrugged. 'You have a choice. Make it, or I will make it for you. But if I choose, it will be painful.'

The uninjured agent shook his head. 'You wouldn't dare.'

Lucas smiled as he turned to two of the enforcers. 'You may start with this one.'

The Master of Shadows nodded, and the two hulking brutes walked towards the agent with glee in their eyes.

'No, wait!' the agent screamed. 'I want to go to Gullytown.'

Lucas held up his hand, stopping the enforcers. 'Are you telling me that you are both willing to go to Gullytown?'

The uninjured agent nodded quickly. Lucas walked over to him with a smile and plunged his short sword into the agent's stomach. The agent's mouth fell open as he jerked on his chains.

The other agent glanced at Lucas, terrified. 'Wait. What are you doing? You said that you were sending us to Gullytown with the others.'

Lucas ripped out his blade and turned to the agent with emotionless eyes. 'None of the other agents made it to Gullytown,' Lucas said, watching the blood drip from the blade of his sword.

'This sword is your Gullytown; you will meet the rest of the agents at the bottom of the harbour.'

He rushed in and pierced the agent's throat; the tip of the sword became stuck in the wall behind him.

'Now, that is a sight I never thought to see,' the Master of Shadows said as Lucas pulled out his sword.

Lucas shrugged. 'I found that following the law restricted me in certain areas. A friend taught me you need to think like a thief to catch one.'

The Master smiled. 'What are your plans now?'

'I think I will pay a visit to the queen; it has been some time since we sat and drank wine together.'

'I have just the right bottle for you. We can leave soon,' the Master said.

Lucas smiled; it felt good to be bad.

***

Ramulas and Pip walked through the valley towards the passageway. Rest had been hard to come by for the Lord of Sanctuary. All of the previous afternoon and into the night he had healed the wounded with the help of Shigar and the druids. A quick count at Journey's End told him that just over one hundred people were missing.

One hundred people he was responsible for.

Well into the night, Ramulas lay awake with Rachael asleep in his arms. He could not get the image of Jacqueline's statue out of his mind.

Kate and Grace talked excitedly for hours about their mother and asked Ramulas if she would come back to them.

He could not give them an answer.

Through the night and into the morning, Iguchi, Berenice, and the Fallen Angels watched over the passageway to ensure that the giant spiders did not come through.

'What do we do now?' Pip asked, breaking the silence.

'I will call the dragons and ask for their help once more.'

Pip shook her head. 'They have not returned since coming to the valley. Why would they come now?'

'This time, I will tell them of the danger if the giant spiders come into the valley,' Ramulas said, closing his eyes.

***

Ramulas' eyes snapped open to see Pip staring intently at him.

'What happened?' Pip asked.

Ramulas smiled. 'The dragons are coming. The threat of dark magic has passed.'

Pip jumped up, punching the air with joy. She could not wait to see the dragons again. A few moments later, the dragons could be seen on the distant horizon. Pip's eyes glowed fiercely as she watched the mythical creatures come closer. A score of mighty green dragons landed in the valley in front of them. Two of the dragons came forward and lowered their heads to the ground.

Ramulas smiled at Pip. 'Climb on. We have work to do.'

Pip raced to the nearest dragon and climbed on.

***

Once the Fallen Angels had left the passageway, Ramulas and Pip led the dragons into Sanctuary, with the mythical creatures knowing that they needed to kill a lot of spiders. They saw the entrance still covered with the bodies of crawling spiders.

Ramulas' dragon opened its maw and shot a stream of flame, clearing the way.

A score of green dragons took to the air as they came into Sanctuary. Ramulas saw that there were at least one thousand spiders crawling around below. He also saw thousands of dead spiders and scores of cocoons hanging along walls and buildings.

'Pip, check the cocoons,' Ramulas shouted.

Her eyes blazed once before shaking her head.

Ramulas communicated with the dragons to burn everything. They dropped from the sky, unleashing streams of fire into the town. Hundreds of spiders were cooked instantly while others scattered into houses and crevices.

The dragons gave chase.

'Wooohoooo!' Pip cried as her dragon dived down.

The dragons tore through the houses to kill the last remaining spiders. When the last of the creatures had been killed, the dragons took to the air and circled above Sanctuary. Ramulas looked down to see burnt spiders and broken buildings. The dragons had damaged half of the houses to kill the spiders.

'Look!' Pip shouted, pointing to the rear of the castle.

Ramulas almost fell off his dragon when he saw what she was pointing at; a dozen of Sanctuary's dead had been picked up by the statues of the fallen. These bodies had not been burnt. The dead were instead laid in front of the magical flame of the altar.

Then Ramulas felt a presence in his mind he had almost forgotten about.

He turned to Pip. 'Wait for me here,' he said before jumping off his dragon. Purple flames engulfed Ramulas when he was ten feet from the ground, and he flew into Oriel's tunnel.

He stopped when he reached the cavern filled with gems and gold. It was here that the mountain spoke to him.

****

Ramulas walked out of the tunnel to find Pip waiting for him. 'What was in there?' she asked.

'Answers.'

Ramulas explained what the mountain had told him: Sanctuary's ancient magic would repair the town, but this would take a few weeks. Then the people could return. The statues of the fallen had been affected by the magic as well. They now had the power to transform any of the dead into statues.

Ramulas finished and Pip asked, 'What now?'

'I will contact the mayor of Turtha and K'ayden to tell them what has happened, then you and I will bring the dragons to Keah. I want to personally thank the young queen for her help.'

'Why did the dragons not help us with the battle of Turtha?'

'They will show us when we return to the valley, but for now, I have unfinished business in the kingdom.'

***

The young serving girl who hurt her leg in front of Aleesha walked into the queen's chambers carrying a tray. She placed the tray onto a table, pulled a small bell from her dress and rang it. A moment later, Aleesha walked out of her bedroom wearing a confused expression.

'What are you doing here? I did not call for anyone to disturb me.'

'I have brought something for the captain of the royal guard.'

Aleesha jumped when she saw two goblets of wine sitting on the tray. In between the goblets was the blue crystal vial that held the poison.

Aleesha rushed for the tray, but the girl snatched the crystal vial and hid it behind her back.

Aleesha grabbed her by the shoulders. 'Give that to me now.'

The small girl twisted and struggled. 'No. The captain asked me to bring it.'

'You lying little—'

'Hello, Aleesha,' Lucas said, walking out of her room.

Aleesha screamed as she released the young girl and fell to the floor.

The door burst open, and two royal guards rushed in. One of them was the agent for the Shadows.

Lucas smiled. 'Everything is fine. I am well again and wish some time with our queen.'

The young girl handed Lucas the vial before rushing out of the chambers. The two guards gave slight nods before leaving and closing the door behind them.

Aleesha sat on the floor, watching Lucas as if he were a ghost.

Lucas walked over to her. 'Are you surprised to see me, Aleesha?'

She nodded weakly, and Lucas helped the queen to her feet and led her to a chair. He sat opposite her, and on the table between was the tray with the wine. He picked up a goblet and handed it to her.

'I do miss our talks over wine,' he said, playing with the crystal vial in his hand. 'Your wine is a special wine; please drink it.'

Aleesha's eyes widened as she slowly shook her head.

'The agents who gave you this poison are now dead. I killed them myself, and there is no-one to help you.'

Aleesha dropped her goblet, and its contents spilled across the table. She frantically turned her head, searching for a way out.

'I tried to teach you how to be a proper queen, and you repaid me by trying to kill me. I need to work out what to do with you.'

Aleesha looked over Lucas' shoulder. Something had caught her eye. Then she began to scream. The Shadows had arrived and were coming out of her bedroom. Two enforcers walked over and took Aleesha by her shoulders, which made her scream louder.

Lucas smiled at her with emotionless eyes. 'No-one can hear you; the guards have been sent away. Come, I will show you.'

Lucas cupped his hands around his mouth and shouted, 'Help, help! The queen is in danger!' He dropped his hands and laughed bitterly. 'Take her.'

Aleesha was led into her room where, for the first time, she saw the entrance to the hidden passageway. Her screams stopped as she was led inside.

***

Ramulas sat on the ground and sent his astral image to Turtha. He entered the mayor's quarters to find the mayor and K'ayden studying maps on the table. He sounded the tone and appeared before them.

K'ayden sighed with relief. 'My friend, we feared the worst when we heard no word.'

Ramulas smiled. 'The spiders have all been killed, but Sanctuary is damaged.'

'What happened?' the mayor asked.

Ramulas told of how the giant spiders attacked Sanctuary, forcing the people to flee into the valley, and how the dragons then came to kill off the remaining spiders, destroying Sanctuary in the process.

'What will you do now?' the mayor asked.

'I will bring the dragons to Keah and speak with the queen; I want to understand why she did not help her people. I will speak to you after my visit with the queen.'

The image faded, and Ramulas opened his eyes in Sanctuary. He stood smiling at Pip. 'Let us take the dragons to Keah.'

'Let's go,' she replied.

Pip held on for dear life as they flew across the sky a mile in the air, her hair and cloak flapping wildly in the wind. The forests of Sanctuary fell behind them. Next came the towns of Turtha and Covedon. From this height, everything seemed so small; to her, people and livestock appeared like ants.

Every now and then, Pip would release one hand to shake the feeling back into it. Ramulas wore a mask of determination as he rode his dragon. Pip kept turning her head in wonder at flying with twenty dragons.

Pip gasped as they flew over the ocean. She could not take her eyes off the water. Then the Symiak mountains came into view and, a moment later, the city of Keah. They started to drop from the sky as they came closer to the city.

They came inland to fly over the King's Highway, following one of the main roads to the city from one hundred feet in the air. Travellers and merchants fled from their horses, carts, and wagons, screaming out warnings and pointing to the sky.

Then Ramulas brought the dragons to fly over the city of Keah. Soldiers on the wall pointed to the sky while orders were called out. A few arrows were fired at them but missed by twenty feet.

People within the city started to scream in panic as they raced through the streets, trying to get away from the dragons. After a few moments, when it was clear the dragons weren't attacking, people came back out into the streets. A few brave people ventured out at first, followed by others when they saw nothing had happened.

The dragons circled the city a few times, and Ramulas cast a spell that amplified his voice. 'I am the Lord of Sanctuary, and these dragons will not harm you. I have only come to speak with the queen.'

The dragons carrying Ramulas and Pip dropped down and landed in the docks. People scattered while vendors pulled their carts away as the dragons came down.

Ramulas called out again. 'People, hear my words. The dragons above are loyal to me and will obey my commands. If anyone attempts to harm me or my companion, the dragons will attack the city.'

Pip led Ramulas towards the castle, and soon they came across old John and a few other Shadows. She winked at them while giving them hand signals before the Shadows disappeared into the crowd. The people lined the sides of the street as they walked talking excitedly amongst themselves. Other people hung out of first story windows and sat on roofs, reminding Ramulas of parades he had seen.

Then something strange began to happen.

A few of the people on either side of the road bowed their heads and fell to one knee as the duo passed. Soon others followed, and before long, people on both sides of the street were all on one knee bowing their heads.

Ramulas turned to Pip. 'What's happening?'

Pip shrugged and smiled. 'I think word has spread of the man who escaped from the tombs and has returned to free this city.'

'How do you know this?'

'I may have spread a small rumour.'

They reached the gates of the castle to find a score of soldiers waiting for them. They stood to attention holding spears upright and blocking their way in.

Ramulas clicked his fingers and was instantly covered in purple flames. 'We have come to see the queen.'

A sergeant stepped forward. 'Someone is coming to see you. Please wait here.'

Pip poked Ramulas in his side, and he turned to her. She raised her eyebrow and tilted her head to the castle and shrugged.

Ramulas shook his head. 'We will wait one minute before entering the castle.'

The soldiers stiffened at this, and one ran into the castle. A few moments later, a dozen royal guards walked out to greet Ramulas and Pip. The soldiers parted, allowing Ramulas and Pip to walk through.

One of the royal guards spoke. 'We will escort you to the queen's quarters.'

With a thought, the purple flames surrounding Ramulas vanished as they walked into the castle. No-one spoke as they walked through the hallways. Ramulas was lost in his own thoughts; from being trapped in the tombs to the last time they were here freeing the Khilli families, so much had changed in his life since then.

They stopped at the doors of Aleesha's chambers.

Ramulas gestured to the doors. 'The queen is in here?'

The royal guards glanced at each other for a fraction of a second, a moment of hesitation that spoke volumes for Ramulas and Pip. They both reacted without thought.

Two throwing knives appeared in Pip's hands, and the two guards were pushed up against the wall, each with a knife at their throat. Ramulas used his magic and sent the rest flying ten feet down the hall to land in a heap.

Pip dug the tips of her knives in the guards' throats. 'Where is the queen?'

'She is in the dungeon. The captain of the royal guard now has the power. He waits for you both inside.'

The two knives vanished as Pip stepped away from the wall. Ramulas and Pip looked at each other stunned before walking in through the doors.

'Welcome, Lord of Sanctuary,' Lucas said as he sat on the throne.

31

Ramulas stepped forward. 'We have come to speak with the queen, but we have been told she is in the dungeon.'

Lucas nodded. 'What business could the people of Sanctuary have with Queen Aleesha?'

'I asked for help for the people of Turtha and sent warning of giant spiders that killed people in Shes. The queen did not want to help her people. I wish to thank her.'

Lucas sighed as he stood and walked away from the throne. 'Giant spiders attacked this city.'

Ramulas nodded. 'I read the message.'

'Did you go to Shes and kill all of the spiders?'

Ramulas shook his head. 'It is a long story, but yes, all of the giant spiders are now dead.'

Out of the corner of his eye, Ramulas saw Pip's eyes glowing fiercely. Then her arms blurred as she threw several knives at the curtains behind the throne. Muffled protests could be heard as two Shadow enforcers stepped out from behind the curtains.

Lucas jumped away from the throne. 'What are you doing?'

'There were enforcers hiding behind you.'

'Pip, we need to talk,' the Master of Shadows said as he walked out from Aleesha's bedroom, followed by a dozen enforcers.

Ramulas stepped back and held up both hands; they were covered in arcing energy. 'What is happening?'

'What?' Pip said in shock, looking from the Master to Lucas and back again.

Lucas held up his hands. 'I know this seems very strange. We have a lot to discuss. After the death of King Zachary, Aleesha became queen. Her advisers were the king's old agents and spies; they used her as a pawn. She has done inexcusable things against her own people, and her last mistake was trying to have me poisoned.'

Ramulas and Pip looked at each other before turning back to Lucas.

Pip asked, 'Why is she in the dungeon? Attempted murder is punishable by hanging or life in Gullytown.'

Lucas sighed. 'Zachary's death was not that long ago, and I was told that it was a young former thief with purple hair who killed him. You wouldn't know anyone fitting that description, would you?'

Pip crossed her arms and tilted her head, letting her purple hair flow over her right shoulder.

The Master of Shadows laughed. 'I know that look very well.'

'The king deserved to die,' Pip whispered.

Lucas fought back a smile before responding. 'Queen Aleesha now rules over the kingdom. Removing her so soon after the death of her father would bring chaos the kingdom, and there would be riots in the city. We have been making the decisions and letting the people think it is the queen's doing.'

'Who is *we*? Who else is helping you run the kingdom?' Ramulas asked.

Pip gasped when the captain of the royal guard pointed to the Master of Shadows.

Ramulas stepped up to Lucas. 'I need to see something.' He waved his hands in front of the captain of the royal guard, who jumped when he was covered in a purple mist.

Pip laughed. 'It won't hurt you; he is just seeing what kind of person you are.'

Ramulas clicked his fingers; the mist vanished and he turned to the Master of Shadows. 'You're next.'

The enforcers grew tense as the Master was covered in mist, but he remained calm and smiled. After a few seconds, the mist was gone.

'Did you find what you were looking for?' the Master asked.

Ramulas nodded. 'I came to Keah for a reason, and now the two of you have made things easier for me.'

Lucas stepped forward. 'What was that reason?'

'After the actions of King Zachary and his daughter Aleesha, I have come to claim my role as ruler of the kingdom. Are there any who wish to oppose me?'

'I have a question for you,' the Master said. 'How loyal are your dragons to you?'

'They are very loyal to me and the people of Sanctuary.'

'How do you speak with them?'

Ramulas smiled tapping the side of his head while communicating with the juvenile dragon. People screaming and shouting could be heard moments before the young green dragon crawled through the window of the balcony and into the room. Lucas and the enforcers jumped in shock.

The Master smiled as he walked towards the mythical creature. He got to within ten feet before it took off out of the window. He turned to Ramulas. 'They are truly beautiful.'

Lucas recomposed himself. 'You cannot stake your claim as ruler of the kingdom. The people would rebel in the streets.'

Ramulas turned to Pip and winked before speaking. 'Someone told me that by escaping the tombs, I had become some sort of hero to the common man of the city. By winning the two battles of Sanctuary, I became even more of a hero, and now that I have come with dragons, who would not want me as their ruler?'

The Master of Shadows laughed as Lucas stood in stunned silence.

Ramulas held up two fingers. 'There are two conditions of my ruling. First, I will ask for the people's approval of me as the kingdom's new leader, and secondly, I will explain that I will not leave Sanctuary. I will need to leave someone to rule in my name.'

Both Lucas and the Master of Shadows looked at the former thief.

Ramulas nodded to Lucas. 'I will have you rule in my place, and the Master of Shadows will give you advice in private.'

Everyone except for Pip stepped back with mouths open and eyes wide in shock.

Lucas pointed to himself. 'You want me to run the kingdom and the Master of Shadows to help me?'

Ramulas smiled. 'That is what you two have been doing already, and I know that you want what is best for the city and kingdom.'

Ramulas paused for a few seconds while looking out of the window.

'What is it?' Pip asked.

'I have an idea,' he said, turning to Lucas. 'Ask all of the soldiers to come down from the wall.'

'Why?'

'Once they are down, I will have the dragons sit on the walls. I think Pip and I will stay here for a while. There is much to discuss, and I think the people will enjoy watching the dragons.'

Lucas appeared worried. 'The soldiers do not have good memories of the dragons.'

Ramulas waved his hand. 'Do not worry. The dragons will harm no-one, but I will need to ask for something.'

'What is that?' Lucas asked.

Ramulas smiled. 'An audience with the queen.'

***

Ramulas and Pip stood on the balcony, watching the people's excitement grow below as the dragons landed on the walls. The buzz of the people talking drifted up to the balcony.

Ramulas sighed. 'Time to go.'

He leapt off the balcony and released his magical energy, covering himself in flames and flying to the top of the castle.

'People of Keah, the dragons will not harm you. They will stay on the wall until tomorrow,' he said in an amplified voice.

He dropped back to the balcony. 'Let us go visit the queen, Pip.'

***

Lucas walked into the dungeon and the two guards jumped to attention. Looking around the dungeon, Ramulas' and Pip saw that Aleesha was the only person there. She sat on her cot, staring at the floor.

'Hello, Aleesha,' Lucas said softly.

Her head snapped up, and Aleesha sneered at him.

Lucas sighed. 'I have someone who has wanted to talk to you for a long time.'

Aleesha's sneer melted away and was replaced by a confused expression.

'May I introduce the Lord of Sanctuary and his companion Pip, the one who killed your father.'

Aleesha stood as they walked into the dungeon. The young queen's face was a mask of rage. She stood perfectly still; only her head moved as she followed the pair as they walked into the dungeon.

Pip smiled and waved. 'You're dressed a bit too fancy for a place like this.'

A primal growl escaped Aleesha's mouth as she threw herself against the bars, reaching out with her hand trying to grab Ramulas and Pip. When this did not work, she spat at them.

Queen Aleesha had transformed into a feral animal. 'I will have you both tortured and killed,' she screamed while holding the bars. 'All the people of Sanctuary will die as well.'

Ramulas sighed. 'Hundreds of people died throughout the kingdom because of your selfish actions.'

Aleesha stamped her foot. 'I am their queen. They will do as I say, and the spiders were sent to punish those who supported Sanctuary.'

Pip's mouth fell open, and Ramulas slowly shook his head. 'I came here to talk about the people suffering under your rule. After our talk, I was going to work out what to do with you, but now you have made things easier.'

Ramulas turned to Lucas. 'Give the queen her favourite wine and food. Tomorrow she will face judgment.'

Aleesha screamed. 'You cannot kill me. I am your queen.'

Ramulas smiled. 'You will soon discover there are things far worse than death. You are no longer queen. I will tell the people that I now rule the kingdom.'

She laughed bitterly. 'Why would they accept you as their leader?'

'I brought twenty green dragons with me; they are sitting on the walls of the city.'

Ramulas turned and walked away without another word. He was followed by Pip and Lucas. They could hear Aleesha's screams as they walked up the stairs.

***

As the sun set, Ramulas, Pip, Lucas, and the Master of Shadows stood on the balcony watching the people of Keah as they gathered around the dragons. Ramulas had told them that there would be a show.

As one, the dragons raised their heads and roared into the night sky. People gasped and spoke excitedly to each other; then the dragons opened their maws and streams of flame shot into the air. They repeated this three more times before their heads lowered.

Pip sighed. 'I miss being a Shadow at times like this.'

Ramulas tilted his head. 'Why?'

'With everyone looking at the sky, a lot of things could go missing.'

Ramulas smiled. 'Then let's give the Shadows a reason to smile.'

Ramulas took a deep breath, and he cast a spell before raising both arms. A ball of white light shot two hundred feet into the sky and exploded into smaller lights, which drifted down. He repeated this for two minutes with the people below cheering and clapping.

Ramulas amplified his voice. 'People of Keah, I am the Lord of Sanctuary. The actions of your queen have caused great suffering, and hundreds have died with the giant spider attacks. The people of Sanctuary and these dragons have killed all the spiders.' The crowd cheered. 'I have removed the queen from her throne and made myself ruler of the kingdom. Will you accept me as your new ruler?'

The people below erupted into even louder cheering, waving their hands up to the balcony and working themselves into a frenzy. Ramulas smiled at Pip until things calmed down.

Ramulas held his hands high. 'People of Keah, my home is Sanctuary, and I will not leave there, but in my place, I will leave the captain of the royal guard. He is a just and fair man. He will speak and act in my stead. Do you accept him to stand for me?'

Once again, the crowd cheered.

Ramulas smiled and sent a few more fireballs into the sky before leading the others inside.

He turned to Lucas. 'I would be happy for you to show Pip and me to our quarters. Then we will discuss how this city will be ruled.'

***

Ramulas sent his astral image racing across the plains towards Sanctuary as the sun was setting. He flew over the wall of Sanctuary, into the passageway, and across the valley to Journey's End, where he found his daughters waiting for him in the throne room.

The first thing he noticed was that the paintings and tapestries were no longer there. He made himself visible as Rachael entered the room. Kate and Grace ran up to him, excitedly asking him questions. Rachael slowly walked up to his image and smiled.

'All of the spiders have been killed.' The girls jumped around and cheered while Rachael's smile grew. 'But the dragons caused a lot of damage when they killed the spiders. It will take a couple of weeks for Sanctuary to repair itself; until then, we will stay here.'

'Where are you, Da?' Grace asked.

'Pip and I are in Keah. We are staying overnight and come home in the morning.' He turned to Rachael. 'Can you please pass the word of the spiders being killed to the people, and I will talk with them tomorrow.'

Rachael nodded, and Ramulas moved his astral image back to Keah.

***

Ramulas opened his eyes to find Pip smiling at him. 'What happened?'

'I spoke to my daughters and Rachael of what happened. Rachael will pass word to the people, but we have a long night ahead of us. There are things within this city I want to change, and I am not sure if the captain of royal guard will be happy.'

Pip smiled. 'You have magic and dragons; you can do whatever you want.'

Ramulas shook his head. 'A leader must learn to listen and compromise instead of talking through power. He needs to earn respect and trust of the people. I would rather be a ruler who is loved rather than hated and feared.'

'Why is that?'

'I want to be the kind of person that I would be happy to serve under.'

32

Discussions went until early into the morning, with Lucas, the Master of Shadows, and Pip each having a say on how things were going to be in the city of Keah. The private partnership between Lucas and the Master would remain.

Ramulas sighed as he brought up the subject of Gullytown and how he wanted it closed and all the people set free. Lucas disagreed, saying that the place deterred people from committing crimes. Pip exploded, saying that her parents had been unjustly sent there to die. The pair argued for a couple of minutes until Ramulas intervened.

'Captain, when was the last time you visited Gullytown?'

'My duties are in Keah; I have not travelled that far.'

'Then I have a solution for this problem,' Ramulas said.

Ramulas waved his hands through the air while chanting. In a few seconds, all four of them were speeding past the Symiak mountains. Lucas and the Master looked down at the passing landscape in wonderment. In a few minutes, they came to a low mountain range that housed Gullytown.

As they touched the ground, Ramulas spoke. 'No-one can see or hear us.'

The valley itself had fallen into darkness, with the only light coming from several torches that illuminated a few areas. They walked past the entrance, where six guards talked quietly amongst themselves. Ramulas led them to the tunnels where the prisoners were kept.

Two guards stood outside the steel door of the tunnel. The group stopped at this entrance and stepped back in shock, covering their mouths when they saw the state of the prisoners inside. A dozen people who were no more than skin and bone huddled near the bars, some stretching their hands out and pleading for food.

Their eyes were dark and vacant, their cheeks hollow, their skins covered in dust, scabs, and sores. The moaning from the tunnel cut Ramulas to the core as the people begged for more food. The guards would answer that food would come when they found gems. Every now and then, one of the guards would lift the lid from a boiling pot near the entrance and wave the smell into the tunnel, making the moans more desperate.

Pip shook with rage as Ramulas led them to the other tunnels where similar scenes played out.

Lucas shook his head. 'I am sorry. I did not know it was like this.'

Pip glared at Lucas. 'My parents died in this hell, and they did nothing.'

Ramulas knew they had seen enough and brought the four astral images back to Keah. As they passed over the Symiak mountains, they saw scores of camp fires, which meant there were still thousands in the mountains.

The four opened their eyes and found themselves back in Keah. Lucas' face was pale, and he looked at the others in disbelief. 'That place was terrible. I had no idea that people were treated that way.'

'My parents were sent there for questioning the raising of taxes,' Pip said with her fists clenched by her sides.

Ramulas coughed, and they turned to him. 'I have a suggestion for you. I want several wagons sent to Gullytown tomorrow with food for the prisoners. When they are well enough to travel, they will be brought back to the city and allowed to return to their old lives.'

Lucas nodded. 'It's the least I can do.'

'The guards at Gullytown are to be stripped of weapons and armour and told they need to walk to the town of Boer,' Ramulas said.

Pip gasped. 'That's almost sixty miles.'

Ramulas nodded. 'They will have plenty of time to think about how they treated the prisoners during their walk.'

Lucas nodded.

Ramulas took a deep breath and let it out slowly. 'Did you see how many camp fires were in the Symiak mountains?'

Lucas shook his head. 'There was more than I would have liked. Are you going to move them away from the city?'

'Yes and no,' Ramulas replied.

'What are you saying?' the Master of Shadows asked.

'I want the Symiaks and the people of the kingdom to come to a truce. I want the Symiaks to be able to come down from the mountains and roam the plains outside of the city.'

Pip, Lucas, and the Master all flinched as if they had been slapped.

Lucas shook his head slowly. 'You cannot be serious. The people of Keah have been fighting with the Symiaks for generations. It is the main reason for the wall around our city.'

Ramulas smiled. 'Think of what could happen if the Symiaks could trade with you and saw Keah as part of their home. They would join you in defending your city.'

Lucas shook his head. 'Why would the Symiaks want to trade with us? At the first chance, they would start killing the people.'

'I will talk to them tomorrow and bring the dragons so they understand there will be no more fighting. Once I have spoken to them, I will return and hear your decision.'

'I am not happy about the Symiaks,' Lucas said.

'And yet you marched alongside them the last time Sanctuary was attacked,' Ramulas said with a cold smile. 'I lost my wife in that battle. If I am not mistaken, you marched on Sanctuary twice, and we lost people both times. I could see you as an enemy, but I come as a friend.'

'I was just following orders.'

'I need you to start thinking for yourself. There is one more thing I will do tomorrow: when Pip and I leave, we will be taking the young queen with us.'

Lucas and the Master of Shadows glanced at each other before Lucas asked, 'Where will you take her?'

'Somewhere she will not be able to cause trouble.'

***

Ramulas and Pip woke at dawn and prepared to leave. They were escorted to the royal chambers, where Lucas waited for them.

'Are you going to talk to the Symiaks and then take Aleesha?'

Ramulas nodded. 'I will tell you what they say when I return.'

'I will walk you downstairs,' Lucas offered.

Ramulas shook his head. 'We will leave by the balcony.'

'But we are three storeys high,' Lucas said.

'I know,' Pip said as she raced for the balcony.

Lucas could hear shouting and cheers from outside and saw that the dragons were flying around the city. Pip's hair flowed behind her like a purple flame dancing in the wind. The former thief dived off the ledge just as a dragon flew by; she landed on its back and held on tight.

Ramulas' body was covered in flame as he flew out with the dragons. He led the dragons towards the Symiak mountains.

***

Ramulas flew the dragons low over the mountain range. He wanted the Symiaks to know that he was coming. The score of green dragons circled the top of the mountains for a minute. The Symiaks ran when they first saw the creatures, but after a while, they came out to investigate and gained confidence.

'There he is,' Pip shouted, pointing to a clearing on a plateau below them.

Slesht stepped out his large tent of animal skins and stared at the dragons while holding his stone sword. Hundreds of other Symiaks gathered around him. Ramulas communicated with the two dragons, and they dropped he and Pip off two hundred yards from the edge of the encampment.

They walked towards the Symiaks, and Ramulas tapped into his magical ability. Pip jumped when they were both covered in purple flames.

'Stay close,' Ramulas whispered. 'I don't think they will attack.'

They passed the first row of tents, and the Symiaks began to hoot and stomp. Ramulas and Pip stopped twenty feet from the frenzied group of Symiaks.

Slesht walked towards them, swinging his swords with every step. 'Why you is come here? Symiaks not attack humans.'

'I have to talk about peace between Symiaks and humans,' Ramulas said.

Slesht growled and smashed his swords together. 'Symiaks will not have peace. If see men from Keah, we will crush.'

'Um, hello,' Pip said waving her hand. 'Did you forget that we brought dragons with us?'

Slesht flinched while Ramulas shook his head at her, and Pip shrugged.

'I have spoken with new king, and he agrees to trade with you if there is peace.'

'What Symiaks trade?' Slesht said.

Ramulas removed a large pouch from within his robes and handed it to the Symiak. Slesht's eyes widened as he opened the pouch and looked inside before pouring out diamonds and gems onto his hand.

'This is for all the tribes to trade with Keah and make peace,' Ramulas said.

Slesht turned and shouted something, and several Symiaks ran off away from Slesht's tent.

'You stay. More is coming,' Slesht said with an evil smile.

'How many?' Pip asked.

'Hundred.'

Ramulas and Pip waited by the dragons, watching as several clans poured into the plateau. Pip counted thirteen different clans and almost two thousand Symiaks had joined them. Slesht came to the edge of the camp and waved them over.

Ramulas sighed. 'Here we go.'

Pip elbowed him in the side. 'This will be fun.'

All the chieftains waited outside the large tent. 'We talk inside,' Slesht said before leading the other chieftains inside.

Ramulas and Pip walked in to find no-one was smiling. Some of the Symiaks spoke to each other in their guttural tongue while pointing to Pip. Then she sent a stream of guttural words at them that silenced the tent, and Ramulas looked at her in shock.

Pip shrugged. 'They were saying that I was a weak human who did not belong in this tent, so I told them that I could kill any one of them in combat and put their head on a spike.'

Ramulas shook his head; this was not the start he wanted. He explained in the simplest terms how they could benefit from trading with the people from Keah. They could hunt the deer on the plains and fish in the ocean; all they needed to do was make peace with Keah.

One of the newer chieftains spoke. 'Other human looks like you said we get shiny gifts.'

The others nodded and murmured in agreement.

Ramulas waved a hand through the air and chanted. A pouch of gems dropped in front of each Symiak, they quickly opened them to inspect the contents.

'I have heard that once a Symiak gives their word they will not break that bond.'

They looked up from their gems and Slesht said, 'Have honour; not break. Fight with honour.'

Ramulas smiled. 'I have the word of new king in Keah. He wants trade; no more fighting with Symiaks.'

Slesht quickly spoke with the other Symiaks and turned to Ramulas. 'Have Symiaks word; no fighting.'

'I will tell the new king, and you will be able to trade from tomorrow.'

The Symiak chieftains ignored Ramulas and Pip as they left the tent. They walked to the dragons as the thousands of Symiaks outside watched them. Every Symiak was silent until the dragons took flight, and then the hooting and stomping began.

***

Arriving back in Keah, they were greeted by cheering crowds as they landed in the docks and walked to the castle. Once at the gates, a score of soldiers escorted them to Lucas, who waited for them in Aleesha's quarters.

'What happened with the Symiaks?' Lucas said as they walked in.

Ramulas smiled. 'It went well. Thirteen Symiak tribes have given their word of truce and wish to trade.'

Lucas raised an eyebrow. 'You would trust the word of a Symiak?'

Ramulas nodded. 'They might be big and stupid, but they have a sense of loyalty and honour. They have given their word, and they will keep it.'

'What would the Symiaks have that we could want to trade with?'

'I have given them crystals and gems. They will come down at dawn tomorrow. I suggest you have some of the market vendors waiting for them.'

'This cannot happen,' Lucas said. 'The people will panic.'

'Just think of the giant spiders for a moment. If something like that attacked again and you had Symiaks as allies, they would be good to have on your side. I have told them they can hunt on the plains and fish in the ocean. This will keep them close but occupied.'

Lucas thought for a minute before he sighed and nodded. 'You are right. This will be hard, but it can be done.'

'The only thing left is for us to take Aleesha and leave.'

Lucas smiled at the mention of the former queen. 'I will take you to her now.'

He led them down to the dungeon. As they walked down the stairs, Aleesha's screams could be heard. When Ramulas and Pip walked in she became an animal, snarling and spitting at them. Ramulas clicked his fingers, and Aleesha collapsed to the floor into a deep sleep.

'It's safe to open her cell. She will be sleeping for a while.'

Lucas opened the cell door. Ramulas cast a spell; Aleesha was covered in a white nimbus and floated towards him.

'We will take her out of your hair to a place where she will cause no more trouble.'

***

'Look at that,' Pip said in awe.

Ramulas smiled seeing the giant trees in Shangri-La in the distance. The forest of Shangri-La was ten miles away, but with the dragons, they would arrive soon. Aleesha still slept lying in front of Ramulas.

Soon the dragons flew over the tops of the giant trees, carrying Ramulas and Pip to a clearing in the middle of the forest. They landed near the village, where a few hundred people came out of the trees and houses to gather around them.

Pip's mouth dropped when she saw the strange clothing worn by these people; colours of greens and earthen browns mixed in together, making the people very much a part of their surroundings.

'Our dragons have returned,' a man shouted.

The people cheered and began to dance and sing. Ramulas remembered this man as the one from the council who had wanted to kill him as an outsider the last time he was there.

Then the people noticed the sleeping form of Aleesha. There were curious murmurs throughout the crowd.

'Months ago, I came here to warn you of an evil army coming to this world and asked for help,' Ramulas said in a loud voice. 'I showed your council what this army would do if the army came. The council ordered my death, and I am thankful for Owain saving my life.'

The man from the council stepped forward, thrusting a finger at Ramulas. 'Where is Owain?'

Ramulas glared at him before continuing. 'The dragons now talk to me. They call me "spirit of the dragon", and I am the Lord of Sanctuary. Dragons have protected this place for many years; it would not be fair to leave you with none.'

'What do you mean?' the council man asked.

'The dragons have found their true home and will not be returning here.' Ramulas waited for the people to stop talking before he continued. 'But I am a fair person, and I wish to show thanks to the people of Shangri-La for how I was treated. I leave you one dragon.'

People started to protest that all the dragons should stay. 'Do not worry. The dragon I will leave you is very fierce and will scare all away from Shangri-La.'

Ramulas clicked his fingers and Aleesha floated towards him. When she was ten feet away, he waved his hand; the nimbus disappeared, and Aleesha fell to the ground. In the blink of an eye, she jumped to her feet and grabbed the nearest man by his vest.

She pointed to Ramulas and Pip and screamed, 'I want those two arrested! They killed my father.'

When no-one moved, Aleesha threw a temper tantrum, stamping her feet and shaking her fists in the air.

Ramulas smiled while climbing on his dragon. 'The dragon I give you is the former queen Aleesha.'

As they flew towards Sanctuary, Ramulas turned to Pip. 'The dragons want to show us what the dark magic was in the valley.'

***

After coming out into the valley, the dragons flew east over the mountains. Pip was awestruck at the scenery below. There were a few small valleys in between the mountains, and then gradually, the mountains faded away to reveal larger valleys and pockets of forests that stretched for miles.

Farms with livestock could be seen on the outskirts of towns visible from two hundred yards in the air. Pip became excited to see people on this new world. Farmers and villagers ran in fear when they saw the dragons flying above.

On the horizon, they saw a large city, and Ramulas brought the dragons a mile into the sky. He could see Pip becoming excited, and Ramulas had mixed feelings about this situation. He had brought his people into this world and did not need conflict of any kind.

Ramulas judged this city to be one hundred miles from Journey's End.

Then the dragons told him that the dark magic had come from this city. As they came closer, Ramulas and Pip could see that this city was ten times the size of Keah. Then came the outskirts that went as far as the eye could see.

Pip's eyes blazed fiercely, and Ramulas used his magical ability as they both inspected the city below. The main buildings in the middle of the city were made of dark onyx and marble. Most of the larger structures were covered with polished domes. Then they saw the palace itself, which was the size of Keah and twenty storeys high.

'Look at that,' Pip said, pointing down the main road.

Ramulas' heart skipped a beat, and his shoulders slumped when he saw what she was talking about. Soldiers dressed in red and black were marching down the main street past the palace.

They were Legion soldiers.

'Where are we?' she asked.

Ramulas waved his hands through the air, casting a spell before turning to Pip. 'This city is called Waticali. This is the place where Remus and I were born and raised.'

Pip's body jolted. 'How did we come here?'

Ramulas shrugged and slowly shook his head. 'I don't know.'

'We beat the Legion once; we can do it again,' Pip said.

Ramulas shook his head and smiled sadly. 'Each of the Legions has ten thousand soldiers, and this city alone has ten Legions.'

'What about the dark magic?'

Ramulas waved his hands through the air in patterns while chanting with his eyes closed. His eyes snapped open. 'Remus has found a way to become a magic user once more, only this time, he has more power.' Then Ramulas gasped.

'What happened?' Pip asked.

'Remus knows we are here and that we are staying in Journey's End.'

***

Remus walked into the First Legion's training grounds. Their numbers had been replenished from other Legions, and they were under the command of a new captain. Remus smiled to himself as the Legion soldiers went through training drills that were strange to them but also very familiar.

This new style of training had been used by the only enemy that had been victorious against the Legion. This enemy had very few soldiers but still outmatched the Legion, and Remus would take full advantage of this opportunity.

He stood next to the captain of the First Legion as the soldiers stood on one leg while holding rocks above their heads. 'How does my favourite Legion take to your training methods?'

Benji turned to him, his face a mask of hatred. 'My warlord, they have picked up Iguchi's training quite quickly. They will be ready to face those I once saw as family and destroy them.'

Dark energies flowed from Remus' eyes as he smiled. One of the first things he had done when he received his new magical ability was to wipe most of Benji's memory and alter the one memory that continuously played in his mind. Benji was taken and tortured, the Fallen Angels could have saved him, but chose to run away.

Betrayal fuelled Benji's hatred for Iguchi and the Fallen Angels. With this Legion, he would make them pay.

www.ingramcontent.com/pod-product-compliance
Lightning Source LLC
Chambersburg PA
CBHW030528190726
48283CB00006B/1815